The Emerald Twins

BOOKS BY HELEN FRIPP

The French House
The Painter's Girl
The Girl from Provence

The Emerald Twins

HELEN FRIPP

Bookouture

Published by Bookouture in 2025

An imprint of Storyfire Ltd.
Carmelite House
50 Victoria Embankment
London EC4Y 0DZ

www.bookouture.com

The authorised representative in the EEA is Hachette Ireland
8 Castlecourt Centre
Dublin 15 D15 XTP3
Ireland
(email: info@hbgi.ie)

ISBN: 978-1-83525-955-9
eBook ISBN: 978-1-83525-954-2

To Nicholas with all my love

'The most beautiful things in the world cannot be seen or even touched. They must be felt with the heart.'

— HELEN KELLER

BOOK ONE

CHAPTER 1

INTO THE DARKNESS THEY GO, THE WISE AND LOVELY

Coco says our hair is like spun gold and strawberries and she ties it in tight plaits. I ask for the red ribbon, but Odette wants it, so I pull her hair. She doesn't cry and I know she won't because that's giving in. But I asked first and it's not fair.

Coco says two such pretty little chicks shouldn't fight. Me and Odette just look at each other – it's like looking in a mirror every single time – then we burst out laughing at the idea we are pretty little chicks.

We hug and tumble onto the rug, which is smooth and warm, and we press our cheeks to it and pull faces.

'Nina and Odette Lefevre, stand up and behave,' Maman says, so we stop because when she says our second name we are in trouble.

'Oh let them, mischievous little fairies,' says Coco, giving us a wink.

I like seeing Maman's face go smooth instead of scared. She thinks we don't know she's frightened, but we do because we've heard her talk to Coco about the bad people, the Nazis.

They want twins, so we have to be a secret. The secret is like a monster. We have to sit in the dark every night, and we can't play outdoors together, which is boring. Even if we could play outside it would be sad because all our friends have gone away.

Coco has lots of pretty things here. She says it's the Best Suite in the Ritz. Everyone else calls her Mademoiselle Chanel but we can call her Coco. Sometimes she lets me and Odette play with her travel case. Inside there are different spaces and each one has a precious thing in it. There are bottles with black ribbons and lipsticks and make-up like jewels and there's a special lid that hides gold like a pirate's treasure chest. That's where she keeps her most precious thing.

Coco isn't looking so I put on the ring with the big green jewel that looks like the glass in the window at church when the sun is out. It's heavy.

'Let me try it,' Odette whispers, reaching out.

'No!' I say, because the green stone is like magic, and anyway it's my turn.

'Ma chérie.' Coco sees us. 'This is too valuable for little people to play with, even careful ones like you.' I put it back, even though the stone is glittering and glimmering and I want to keep wearing it.

A man with golden buttons and a tray comes in and Coco gives him a coin and he puts the tray on the table. Odette is first to the cakes and she picks the strawberry one but that's all right because I like raspberries. I take a big bite and squeeze the cream between my teeth and cross my eyes to make Odette laugh before Maman can stop me. She pretends to be angry but I know she's not, because she's trying not to smile and her eyes are all shiny.

Instead of telling us off, Coco pours us a hot chocolate out of the silver jug and me and Odette sit on the golden chairs next to each other with Maman and Coco opposite us, and we have a tea party. We are very proper, much more grown up than nearly five, and we speak with posh voices and say la di da and how do you do. It's quite hard to eat the cakes *and* be posh because they're so squashy and cream gets on our pretty dresses and that makes us laugh.

The big windows are open because it's a sunny day and me and Odette run to get the sunshine on our faces and look at the people in the square.

'Get away from the windows right now! I've told you a million times!' Maman's voice is all dark and angry and scared and she's never angry. I don't like it and I know Odette doesn't either. We don't even have to talk about it, because we are the same.

The day is so nice, and Coco spoils us with good things and this room has pretty wallpaper in colours like the sky and the sun. There are five sofas and there are only four of us, I counted, so Maman should know that nothing bad can happen to us here. We hug her tight. 'It's all right, we are always safe on a sunny day, because God is sending us sunbeams.'

She holds us tight and she's sad even though she says she's not, and I don't understand why she doesn't believe me because what they say at Sunday school is never wrong. We cuddle her even more to make her feel happy.

Someone knocks on the door and it's a very loud knock so I run to answer it, but Maman grabs my arm so hard it hurts.

'Don't answer. Just stay very quiet,' says Maman and her voice is all shaky.

They push so hard that it breaks the wood and cracks the gold paint. Two men stand like ghosts in the doorway and stare like they are looking for something.

When they see me and Odette, it's like they've found it.

They are wearing smart soldiers' clothes and buttons like the hot chocolate man, but their faces are not kind. I feel sick.

'What is the meaning of this?' says Coco. She stands up in

front of us, and she's angry with them. They should be scared because when she's angry she can get anyone to do what she likes and they have to say sorry, but they look at her like she's in the way. Maman holds us so tight we can't breathe.

The bad men sit on the chairs where me and Odette were, and finish our hot chocolate.

'That's mine!' says Odette. She is braver than me and she stamps her foot and I wish she wouldn't because the man looks at Maman like she's dirty.

'Hush, Odette, the gentleman is very welcome,' says Maman. Her smile is like begging.

Coco's pretty room feels like a cage now and we are all trapped and I want to run away but I can't in case the men do something mean. Odette feels it too, and we cling as tight as we can to Maman who is all trembly and doesn't feel safe.

One man is tall and looks like a wolf with big teeth. The other one looks like he's his pet. Every time the wolf says something the pet goes small and does what he says.

'Bring the girls to me, Major Fischer,' the wolf says to the pet. I think I'm going to wet myself.

'Don't be ridiculous,' Coco says. 'Can't you see they're terrified? What do you want here?'

'There are penalties for absconding from Lebensborn homes. Those children are the daughters of a once-fine SS officer, so if I were you I'd keep quiet,' the wolf says.

'We don't have a daddy!' says Odette. Good. She doesn't fidget like I do when I lie.

The wolf turns to Odette. I get ready to hit him if he hurts her.

'Your maman has been lying to you. You won't remember, because you left us before you were born. But you are perfect Aryan twins, a miracle, and thanks to your father you are children of the Reich – part of our Lebensborn programme, and therefore our property.'

I don't understand Lebensborn or Aryan but it doesn't sound good.

'You wouldn't,' says Coco. 'They're my god-daughters. I have friends in places you wouldn't want me to go.'

'Everyone has friends in high places nowadays. As do I. Now. You and the twins' ungrateful mother here know as well as I do that she signed a contract, a pledge to the Lebensborn programme to assure the future of the master race. Camille found a worthy SS officer as a consort, a man far superior to anyone an admittedly pretty young seamstress could ever have hoped for otherwise. She was unmarried, but due to her racial value, we took her in. The resulting young children are the property of the Reich. When she absconded from the mother and baby home we provided, and fled back to France pregnant with *our* babies, she forfeited all rights to these children.'

'I had no choice. You threatened to take them from me and they're mine, I'm their mother!' Maman shouts. The man holds his hand up to make her be quiet.

'Their father deserted so you have both acted against your agreements. He has been court-martialled and executed and now we are here to deal with the consequences of your behaviour. We are here to take what is rightfully ours, that is all.'

'But they're just little children, they're innocent, and they need me! I was forced into it, I didn't understand what I was agreeing to. Please, let them stay.' Maman is sobbing. and I want to, but I don't because there's a stone in my throat.

'Impossible, mademoiselle. Twins are useful, and these two are pretty as Aryan pictures and remarkable-looking. Bring them to me,' he says to his pet.

I wish Coco hadn't plaited our hair and put us in matching sailor dresses. That makes us look even more like twins.

Maman doesn't let go of us, even when the pet holds out his hand with a stupid, dribbly smile. The adults argue. I watch their faces. The men are winning, Coco is angrier than I've ever seen her, and Maman looks like she's going to faint.

Me and Odette stay very still, stiller than we've ever been. Maybe if we don't move or make a sound, they'll forget about us.

The man puts a piece of paper on the table, with writing on it from a typewriter. Maman looks like he's taken his gun out of its holder and shot her with it.

'You can't!'

Coco is holding Maman, and we hide behind them.

'Orders from Heinrich Himmler himself. It's all official, so don't worry, madame, it will be documented, and they will be well looked after. The Reich will do a far better job of bringing them up than a single French mother ever could. We won't even prosecute you for the mother's absconding, or your misguided protection of the mother and children. On my personal recommendation, the girls will be processed through the Lebensborn home at Lamorlaye, where they'll want for nothing. It they're lucky and meet all the correct criteria, they'll be adopted by a fine SS family. They'll have lots of pure little friends who have all been bred through the same glorious programme. I'm sure you understand.'

I want to say I don't understand and I don't like him, but I don't because even though he has a piece of paper and a pen and he is trying to look like everything is normal, the air around him is thick and choking.

He waits for an answer, but not even Coco speaks, so he carries on.

'Lebensborn...' The wolf says the word like he's sucking a sweet. 'Fountain of youth, in your language. It has a certain poetry to it, don't you think? Madame, you should be proud to have bred with an SS man. Twins are invaluable for medical studies, so, in the unlikely event that their colouring and features don't measure up for our Lebensborn scheme, they will be useful in other ways. No harm will come to them. And you'll be free to pursue a new life.'

Maman gets on her knees and she's crying so hard that her whole body is moving.

'Please, don't do this.'

We hate Maman crying and we are so scared, we don't understand what's happening, but we know we need to get as close as we can to her and cry with her. Then the wolf man says, 'I can't stand this women's stuff.'

He makes Maman let go of his jacket and says to his pet, 'Major Fischer, clear up behind me and have them taken to the secure location where they can be properly processed. Make sure you tell them it was me who rescued these two remarkable pieces of Aryan treasure from the dirt of Paris.'

He slams the door when he leaves, which is very rude, but I am glad when he is gone.

The pet looks smaller when the wolf is gone, and Coco looks bigger. She starts talking to him like she talks to people who work for her in her shop. Maman whispers to us, 'Run with me, now!'

We run for the broken door, but the man points his gun at us.

'*Halt!*' he yells, jumping up from his chair.

'Don't hurt Maman!' shouts Odette.

'Sit down,' the pet says, moving his gun to show us where to go. Maman sits on the golden chair next to him and we sit on her lap even though she says we're both too big for that. I don't want to leave Maman.

'Now, I don't want to make this any more difficult than it needs to be, so let's make this quick. You may pack them a change of clothes and then we'll be on our way,' he says to Maman. 'I'll be watching, so don't try anything stupid.'

'Wait,' says Coco. 'Let me make this worth your while.

There is a lot of money involved if you just let me show you something? It's just here in this leather case in front of me.'

He looks greedy and nods.

Coco leans forward very slowly so she doesn't scare him, and gets the ring with the green stone out of the travel case. I wanted to play with it so much before and she wouldn't let me, so now I don't understand why she wants to dress up.

'If you let them go, I'll give you the real companion to this travelling ring. The real one will make you rich for the rest of your life. The stone is the famous Emerald Lake gem, twenty carats. You can see how big that is from this replica. The Emerald Lake is rumoured to have been owned by an Inca princess. These children are worth more to me. You can say they escaped. I'll vouch for you.'

The pet looks like a greedy-guts at my favourite piece of jewellery.

'I have my orders, mademoiselle.'

'You know everyone's on the make in this war. You'll sell it easily. The auction houses are looking the other way at the moment, and I can put you in touch with a dealer who can help you sell, no questions asked. In fact, I know there's an auction this afternoon. I'll make the call for you right away, then you can go straight there, and have the money in your pocket today before anyone notices you're gone.'

The man points his gun at her, and we hold our breath, but Coco narrows her eyes like a cat thinking.

'Go on, pull the trigger. And that would make a big, unauthorised mess, wouldn't it? I'd rather die than tell you where it is, and you'd never get your hands on the real ring, so the whole exercise will be entirely pointless for you.'

Coco is winning. The man puts his gun away.

'I can see you're that rare thing. A woman who can do a deal. I'm not without feelings, and I know that as twins these two don't stand a chance. But, I'll also be court-martialled if I don't fulfil orders. I'll take one child, and the jewel. Then everyone's happy. Let the mother choose. Either that, or it's both and no deal.'

'How do I know you won't take both anyway once you've got the jewel?' Coco asks.

'I'm not going to kill you, we all know you have friends in high places as you say. Any other risks to me are compensated by the pay-out. The mother and one child stay. You have my word as an officer.'

'Why should I believe you?'

They stare at each other. 'It's all you have at this moment,' he says. 'My deal, or both the children.'

Maman is crying so much that she's trying to speak but she can't and she's kissing our heads and squeezing us close, and I wish I could close my eyes and make a wish and be drinking hot chocolate and laughing again instead of feeling like it's night and there are monsters when it's still daytime.

Coco goes to a big painting of flowers and takes it off the wall. I squeeze Odette's hand. There's a secret door behind it that she opens with a key on her necklace. We watch, trembling, as she takes out a leather box and opens it. It's a ring, exactly like my favourite, except even greener and deeper, like velvet.

She gives it to the pet. He shakes Coco's hand and she looks like she could bite him.

'Which one?' says the man.

'Not me!' I say, expecting Odette to say it too, like with the red ribbon, but she doesn't. She's quiet as a mouse.

'I can't... please.' Maman is kissing our heads over and over again. Her tears are making our hair wet and I wish I could make her happy. Odette clings to me. 'We are one,' she whispers, 'they can't split us up.'

The pet looks at the clock on his wrist. 'I'll count to ten. Best to get these things over with. One, two...'

I can count to ten and I wish I couldn't because then I wouldn't know when it would end.

'Nine, ten.'

He tugs Odette away from us. I won't let go. Odette is screaming and kicking. The man unlaces our fingers and I'm screaming and kicking too and the pet says, 'Any more of this and I'll take both, let her go.'

Maman grabs Odette, 'I love you, I love you, I'll find you with the ring, be brave, never give up, we'll find you, I love you.'

'I don't want to go, please, Maman, I don't... Nina, dream to me,' but she's gone and half of me is gone and Maman is on the floor and can't wake up.

Coco is shaking as much as me and she puts Maman in her bed. Then she cradles me and gets the other ring, the one that isn't real, and says, 'While you have this, you can find your sister. The green jewel, the Emerald Lake, brings people together and you will find her.'

She puts me into bed next to Maman and I cry myself to sleep. The ring is like my teddy bear. I wish I had given Odette the red ribbon this morning. I dream of Odette screaming. I will find her.

CHAPTER 2

ONE DOOR CLOSES

A shaft of light found Judas's green cloak in the stained glass and threw emerald shadows on the flagstones. Nina would have loved that – Judas caught in the act, creeping away from the Last Supper with a bag of money, captured forever in the window of the little church on the hill in Somerset. Nina had always hated greed and injustice. Except she wasn't here, and never would be again. It was her funeral.

Fleur sat on the unforgiving pew, bones brittle with grief, ready to shatter. *Don't cry little one, life is for living, every moment.* Her Grandma Nina's spirit warmed her a little, nothing could ever take that away. But, at twenty-six, Fleur was now an orphan, without one living relative. A fierce light had gone out in her life. Nina had been grandmother, mother, father, brother, sister and everything to her. *Stop*, she told herself. *Don't think about it*, but the damp fog of loneliness made her shiver in the cold church.

The entire congregation was wearing green, Nina's favourite colour. Fleur tried to be happy for her – Nina had insisted that this would be a celebration of her life. It was typical of her joie de vivre right to the end. Now the congregation was full of Fleur's friends from childhood, and the eccentric gaggle of her new London friends who'd made her house their weekend retreat. They all adored Nina almost as much as Fleur did.

Jake squeezed her hand. Her fiancé. His marriage proposal had come as a complete surprise, in the wake of the news that Nina had only days to live. She'd said yes. He was kind, older, and a stable influence, and he didn't ask too much of her, that was important. But grief did funny things to you, ripped out your insides, gave you a laser focus on what mattered, and now she wasn't so sure.

Nina had pressed a speech into her hand on her last day in this world. 'No tears, no mawkish memories, little flower, just be happy and read this out for me.'

She unfolded the note ready. The vicar gave her a kindly nod, and she climbed the steps to the pulpit, dizzy with homesickness for Nina.

'Deep breath, head up, you've got this with diamonds and pearls on,' she imagined Nina whispering through Chanel-red lips, navy eyes full of warmth and wisdom, from wherever she was.

Fleur took a deep breath and started reading out loud.

'*Treasure your family, that golden mess of affinities, affection, ties, similarities, irritations, connections and repeat motifs that make up the tapestry of you. Time is immaterial, and love is the golden thread that will trace the pattern of your life. Know that your loved ones are with you on borrowed time. Never take them for granted. That's the serious bit, short and sweet, but then isn't life? All that remains to be said is, look after my Fleur, and follow your heart – it's always right. I'll be watching!*'

Fleur felt for the ring in her pocket, ran her fingers over the familiar shapes. It was just green glass, not worth anything much, but so *Nina*. It was baguette-cut, an enormous showy dress ring that Nina had worn every day of her life. On the inside of the band, two little stars were scratched into it. Nina had done it as a child, she'd told her. Fleur had often wondered why Nina was so attached to a ring that was worthless, but something had stopped her from asking. Just before she died, Nina had asked her to keep it and wear it every day, but Fleur had planned to place it on her coffin to be cremated with her. It was against her wishes, but she was sure that the ring belonged with Nina. At the last minute, though, she just couldn't do it and it stayed in her pocket.

Fleur nodded to the choir, who burst into song. 'Things Can Only Get Better'. Jude and the London gang danced in the aisles, trying to stick to Nina's orders by crying and laughing at the same time. Nina was there, but gone forever all at the same time. Fleur used the moment to slip out into the graveyard and blink back tears under the bruised sky.

Damn. Nina had asked for cheerfulness. 'Sorry, Grandma,' she murmured.

Jake was by her side immediately with his arms round her.

'She certainly had a good innings,' he said brightly.

He had a way of putting his foot in it, but he meant well. She fished in her bag and found her camera, her refuge. She took a picture of the sky, focused on the scudding clouds.

'I can't bear to see you like this. At least *we* won't leave any grieving children behind.'

They were agreed on that, no children. Better to slip away, a light footprint, no ties. She never wanted to feel like this again and she'd never inflict it on a child.

She stuffed her camera back in its case. 'Let's go back in,' she said.

They went back to the cottage, her childhood home, for the wake. Theirs was always the place her friends had gravitated to in the village, a house full of love and fun and a certain glamour.

Nina always made everything right, but now it seemed so empty. The heart was gone, faded with the old furniture, even filled with people. It was spring, and all the vases were stuffed with apple blossom, sweet narcissi and hyacinths from the garden, like it always was at this time of year. Next to the cherry blossom vase was the only photo of Fleur as a little girl, in her least favourite dress. It was a sailor dress, and her strawberry-blonde hair was in tight plaits, tied with red ribbons she remembered hating.

Where were the repeat motifs, the threads of family resemblances that Nina had written into her funeral speech? What were the features and foibles Fleur shared with extended family? Fleur's own mother had died when she was a baby and she had never met her father. Now her grandma Nina was gone, Fleur would never know, and it was better that way. She could be anyone she wanted, she told herself, with no baggage. But maybe she wanted baggage.

'There just never seemed to be enough time for pictures,' Nina had always said breezily whenever Fleur asked. She had her own photographs now, a version of her own world that she'd been creating since she could first hold a camera.

There had never been any pictures of Fleur's mother and she and Nina never talked about her. She realised now, as an adult, that as a child you learn to be silent about a subject that adults find painful, without ever questioning it. Now it was too late.

Her best friend Jude was busy serving champagne and choux buns (another insistence of Nina's) and she handed Fleur a glass.

'Here, get that down you, it'll do you good. You know you don't always need to look brave when you don't feel it?'

'Don't be ridiculous, I'm big and tough.'

Jude hugged her tight.

'She was much loved. We're here for you, my friend. Now,

you asked us all to write down a memory in three words, do you want me to kick it off?'

'I'd love that,' said Fleur.

Jude chinked her glass with a spoon and Jake turned down the music.

'Stylish, inspirational, French,' were Jude's words. 'In all the best senses!' she added.

'Dreams, possibilities, journeys,' said one of her old school-friends. Perfectly said. In Nina's world, everything was possible, and no child's day trip was ever too far to go.

'Pleats, ribbons, sunshine,' shouted another. It was true; Nina had made all Fleur's clothes when she was little, and many a fancy-dress costume for summer fêtes. Her collection of ribbons was legendary and unrivalled.

'Picnics, orchards, red lipstick, sorry that's four!'

Nina had done everything to make her friends feel welcome with delightful events and parties, always worried that Fleur would feel like an only child.

'Wonderful weekend retreats,' said her London friends in unison. After uni, Fleur had moved to London and started working in the bank where Jake was her boss. Before she'd moved in with him, her flatmates were her family, and naturally Nina had made their cottage a home-from-home, and they all flocked there for Nina-style respite from the big city.

Evening fell, and with it a dread that that would be the last of Nina, the final goodbye, a whole forever without her. It didn't seem possible.

People began to drift off, and Jake said the farewells on her behalf before coming to join her in the conservatory where she was willing the sun not to go down on Nina's last party.

'Bed?' said Jake.

'Not yet,' said Fleur. 'I've been dreading this moment, when all the people who loved her have said goodbye and are thinking about tomorrow, their jobs, their normal lives. For me it's only the beginning.'

'Fleur, that's the first time you've admitted it. The world won't fall apart if you cry. Come here.'

He hugged her, but Nina didn't want her tears.

'I'd like to spend the night here on my own, do you mind? It'll be just me and her, like the old days, one last time. Don't look at me like that, I'll be all right, I promise, and I have to see the lawyer in the morning, then I'll close up the house and be back in London tomorrow evening. Then I'm yours, a hundred per cent. I'm lucky to have you, but you know what a sad loner I am sometimes. Only-child syndrome.'

Jake protested, but not much. She knew him; he'd be itching to get back to the office, to London and civilisation, and have her back in his flat on his own terms, on familiar territory. There was also another reason she needed time to think, something she hardly dared admit, even to herself. But she'd deal with that another time.

She put Nina's ring under her pillow. 'You were a force of nature, and I'll never forget you,' she whispered, and she hummed herself to sleep with the old French lullaby Nina always sang. She drifted off, dreaming to Nina and wishing her back. Something Nina would never have approved of... *don't dwell, always look forward.*

She woke early, stiff and drained, packed hastily and put on Nina's ring to take a little bit of her with her. As she double-locked the old French-blue door, she tried to think of new beginnings, as Nina had wanted.

But who was she kidding? The low cloud was as flat as her heart, and the last thing she wanted was to deal with soulless paperwork at the solicitor's.

'I'm sorry for your loss,' he said, handing her a sheaf of documents as he must have done a thousand times before. 'I'm here to help you interpret any of the jargon. I'm afraid this is the first time many people encounter the likes of us lawyers.'

She can't be reduced to a few legal documents and a professional handshake, Fleur wanted to scream, but instead she opened the envelope addressed to her in Nina's handwriting, still all French-style loops and slants after all these years in England.

My darling, beautiful, clever Fleur, how can I ever bear to leave you? But if you're reading this, I've already left. I am lucky to have loved you and you have given me everything that's important in life, my little flower.

With these deeds, I'm gifting you a part of my life I shut away. You'll wonder why I never told you about it. There were too many memories I wanted to protect you from. Now I'm gone, you can use the house however you like, and give it a new and much-needed lease of life. I hope I've taught you to be happy, and that is my sole wish for your future. You must do whatever it takes! Don't you dare grieve for me, but honour our life together by squeezing every last ounce of joy and happiness out of life. Forward – don't waste your life away looking back, my sweet angel.

Fleur bit her lip, forced back the tears, opened the documents in a blur.

'Do you need a cup of tea?'

She shook her head. Tea made her feel sick nowadays. 'No, thank you. It's just...'

'A shock?' he said kindly.

'Yes.'

She was holding the deeds to a house that Nina had owned. But not the cottage. A house she had never heard of or visited, in the South of France.

CHAPTER 3

BEGINNINGS

April sunshine found its way into Fleur's heart as she stepped out onto the tarmac at Marseille airport. Joyful reunions played out in front of her, taxi drivers held up signs, families chatted excitedly about their plans and she felt utterly alone. How could someone you loved so deeply, such a huge presence in your life, just slip away as quietly and finally as an apple falling off a tree? How could someone who filled a room just not be there any more?

Jake had been pleased with himself at how magnanimously he had given her the week off and sent her with his personal blessing.

'Find the house, enjoy your week away and grieve all you need to. Don't forget we have a wedding to plan, that'll help you put it all behind you, I'm your family now,' he'd said. How was she going to tell him about the other thing? The nagging feeling she couldn't name? Was she running away?

She turned off the main road, and the countryside stretched out in vineyards, olive groves and fields of spring flowers which as she neared the coast became thickets of umbrella pines and swathes of gorse, a pretty village in the distance. Further along the winding coast road, Fleur realised that the precipitous track she'd seen snaking down the hill between the pines on the edge of the village was actually a driveway. The lawyer had told her she'd need a four-wheel drive, and now she could see why. She jerked the jeep into first and took the steep track, but, once she'd cleared the trees, the reward for her efforts was classic Nina – unexpected and wonderful.

A glorious expanse of sparkling Mediterranean was the breathtaking backdrop to a belle-epoque villa, a picture-perfect tableau of French windows and galleried balconies, with budding orange and lemon trees next to ancient olives, all soaking up the spring sunshine in the gardens.

Fleur parked up and got out. It was paradise.

'Well, Nina,' she said to the ether, 'this is the other you. The one I never knew.'

Why hadn't Nina ever brought her here, or told her about this perfect place?

The couple the solicitor had told her were the housekeepers, the Souliers, were waiting at the front door, which was the same French-blue colour as Nina's cottage door in Somerset. Fleur gave them a wave, pretended to take a few snaps of the view while she pulled herself together. This was going to be a rollercoaster.

Madame Soulier kissed her on both cheeks.

Monsieur nodded, and muttered, 'The same eyes, so unusual.'

'You *are* like her, bless you.'

They both looked like they'd seen a ghost.

'Everyone says that about me and my grandma. It's the red hair, I suppose.'

Monsieur went to say something, but Madame elbowed him.

'Leave off our weary traveller. We'll show you round the villa and get you settled, you must be exhausted.'

'I'm fine,' lied Fleur.

'Are you sure? It's not long since…'

'Yes, really. I just can't believe I never came here with her and now it's too late.' Speaking French, the language Nina had taught her, was like coming home. 'How well did you know her?' asked Fleur, curious.

'Not that well. She rented this place out, so we managed it for her. She was always very generous, but she rarely visited. She and her maman were friends of my family, more my parents' generation. Come on, we'll show you around, then leave you to it.'

This place was like balm, like Nina. The house adored the sea and the sky, and every aspect of it was designed to invite them in. On the ground floor, three floor-to-ceiling French doors opened onto a veranda with a stone balustrade. The doors were flung open, framing the shimmering sea and intense blue sky, punctuated by the tips of the cypress trees that edged the gardens. The scent of orange blossom drifted in, and oblongs of light drew architectural shapes on the parquet floors.

'We live next door. Promise you'll give us a shout if you need anything?'

'Of course, and thank you.'

Madame looked sceptical, and she was right. Fleur hated asking for help.

The couple left, and Fleur explored the house and grounds. It was so Nina's style. She always loved a flea market, and it was the mix of old and new she did so well – well-chosen elaborate gilt chairs next to a comfy corner sofa in the living room, old oil paintings and Picasso favourites on the wall. The kitchen was practical and chic at the same time, and, upstairs in the main bedroom, vintage Chanel perfume bottles, a compact engraved with interlocking Cs and a gold lipstick case on the dressing table stopped her in her tracks. Nina only ever wore Chanel make-up, and these vintage treasures were beautiful, mellowed with time. Had young Nina sat here and done her make-up in this dressing table mirror? Fleur looked at her reflection, watched the tears well and fall.

'I miss you so much, Nina,' she said to the girl staring back at her.

Fleur imagined all the times they might have had together here, the school summer holidays, times with Nina where they could have sat on the veranda and Nina could have told her everything about this place. Had she ever lived here? What was she hiding? Why on earth keep it a secret? It made Fleur nostalgic for a life she might have had, or the conversations she should have had with Nina, all too late and final now. Maybe this place would reveal itself if she stayed a while. Was Nina trying to tell Fleur something in death that she couldn't in life?

It was dark now, the sea whispering through the open windows. Fleur turned on the light and an enormous iridescent green butterfly barged in and circled her hair before settling on the wall. Nina? It was just wishful thinking, but this place did things to you, made you look for signs.

Fleur crept closer. It was beautiful, a deep, velvety green, with huge gossamer wings. It fluttered away, skirted the ceiling as Fleur tried to usher it back out of the window. It was then that she saw that the hatch in the ceiling was open.

The butterfly swooped out into the evening, and Fleur went to fetch a ladder she'd seen in the kitchen cupboard so she could shine her phone light into the attic space.

It was tricky to see anything, so she climbed in and shone the torch around her, illuminating clouds of dust. There was nothing much to see – a broken chair, a roll of insulation, and what looked like an old tin of paint with a dried-up brush. She put one foot back on the ladder and found the hatch door to close it up. Just beyond it was a leather vanity case of some sort.

Another of Nina's vintage finds? She reached across to pull it towards her, and blew away some of the dust. A gold Chanel logo was embossed on the lid. Fleur was intrigued.

Balancing it on the ladder, she closed the hatch, and gingerly climbed back down with her treasure.

She put the box on the dressing table, dusted off her hands on her jeans and opened it up.

Inside were three compartments, one containing two faded red ribbons, another with a Chanel business card, the third containing a carefully folded newspaper clipping.

Jewellery with Nazi links expected to fetch over €20 million at auction in Switzerland the headline read. The article went on to say that the sale of a hundred lots, referred to as the Magnificent Rare Jewels auction, included jewels of impeccable provenance and flawless quality. However, all the lots were undisclosed and it was to be a private auction, so it was impossible to tell exactly what was up for sale. There was some question over Nazi links that Bullinger's Auctioneers were refuting. Nina had circled the date and venue in red: 20 June 2024 – just a few months away.

Fleur caught her breath. The article was from about six months ago, just before Nina had got ill. Could she have visited here in secret and left this newspaper article here? Was this something to do with the memories Nina had said she'd wanted to protect Fleur from in her final letter? Why was the hatch open? Did Nina want her to find it? If so, why didn't she explicitly say something?

Fleur placed the clipping carefully back and picked up the business card, which had the details of a Chanel archivist in Paris printed on it, then realised the whole tray lifted up. Underneath, there was a package wrapped in tissue. It was a tiny A-line dress, embroidered with a petal motif, and a pair of booties. They were beautiful, fragile things. Who had they belonged to? She wrapped them back up in their tissue paper, then put everything back.

Fleur swallowed a lump in her throat. This was not a good moment to find treasured baby clothes, but she couldn't delay any longer. She'd return to the business card and the auction later, but now it was time to find out about the other thing. The thing she hardly dared name that had been nagging her since the funeral. She'd have to face up to it now, whatever the result.

She rummaged in her handbag, found the chemist's bag and took it to the bathroom. She could barely breathe for the few minutes she had to wait. She checked the results, searching for what her body already knew. The test confirmed it. She was pregnant, and she was pretty sure it was the last thing she wanted in the world.

To distract herself, she decided to contact the archivist on the business card she'd found, and began by introducing herself as next of kin. She began to write, then immediately regretted it when she tried to think of ways to announce that Nina, her grandma, was dead. No one told you about these things, these little banalities that almost killed you after someone has gone forever. Nevertheless, she pressed send, and exhausted, longed for sleep. She crawled into the unfamiliar bed and tried to settle, but the night was dark, slow, anxious, and filled with confused regrets. Sleep came late, but the sun had a way of slipping past every barrier here. Fleur looked at the clock, 6 a.m., and shards of light were slicing through the old shutters, the sea breathing in and out, birds celebrating the dawn in a cacophony of life.

She put her hands on her stomach. She'd missed her period two weeks ago, but she couldn't be more than a few weeks. Time to think, no need to say anything to Jake quite yet. Light flooded the room when she threw open the shutters, and she stepped out onto the balcony. God, this place was so beautiful she could cry. The early morning air was so fresh, tipped with salty ozone from the sea, the orange blossom hung heady on the breeze, and huge languid bees were already busy collecting pollen from the tangle of wildflowers. It was so ridiculously perfect it made her sob for Nina, for the baby she might never have.

Cooling her swollen feet as she descended the marble stairs, she went out into the garden and found the sandy path to a faded gate that led to a track to a cove on one side and, on the other, a landing stage with stone steps straight into the sea. She sat on them and let the water foam over her toes, surprisingly icy, the glassy depths mesmerising in undulating blues and greens.

What the hell was she going to do?

CHAPTER 4

TWO ETCHED STARS

PARIS, 29 APRIL 1944

Odette, aged four

The pet pulls me along so fast I can't keep up and I can still hear Maman crying and the hotel corridor is dark and long like a bad dream. I see the hot chocolate waiter with the buttons.

'He's stealing me!' I yell.

He turns his head and walks away faster.

'You come with me and keep quiet or I will have to hurt your sister,' says the pet.

I keep going, Nina, because you're the quiet one, and I look after you and I want you to be safe.

The pet puts me in the back seat of a car that is waiting outside the Ritz and no one stops him and I am trembling and I feel like jelly.

'For God's sake, stop snivelling. You're the lucky one, you'll be better off with us. You should know that your maman is a French slut.'

'What's a slut?' I whisper. It doesn't sound nice.

'You'll learn,' he says and switches on the engine and starts driving.

I don't like it when I can't see the Ritz any more. I ask again and again when I am going home, and he doesn't answer, so I shout it in case he didn't hear and he says *shut up* and *never*.

He's so mean that I can't be brave. I cry until there are no tears left. Without tears, my whole body cries and it makes my throat sore and my head so full of hurt it will blow up and kill me and I think, it's worth it, because this feeling is so bad, it will kill the pet, too.

I look out of the window and try to remember all the streets and buildings, but I can't because my eyes are all blurry and I see my reflection and my face is all melted. The car is going so fast and further and further away. I hate this man and I am hot with hate, and cold and aching and I am so far away from you, Nina, and we have never been apart and we are one.

We get to a big building and go inside. There are people on rows of benches and someone on a stage. Everywhere I look there is a skull badge.

The pet's hand is so big it can close tight round my arm. He squeezes very hard and whispers in my ear.

'If you keep your mouth shut and don't cry, I won't hurt you. Do you understand?'

He's hurting me already, but I nod and I sit on the bench next to him. I miss Maman and Nina so much it is hard to sit up.

The man on the stage starts speaking and everyone goes quiet.

'OK, here we go, the jewel of the day, the Emerald Lake twenty-carat solitaire ring, of rare value, known for its clarity and depth of colour, and from the best mine in Colombia. The Inca believed emeralds were the tears of the moon goddess, but this one is rumoured to bring people together, and who can resist that in these times? Starting bid, a steal at ten thousand francs. Ten thousand to the man in uniform, eleven thousand, thank you sir; twelve, heil Hitler, madame; thirteen thousand to the handsome officer; who will bid me fourteen...'

I keep my eyes on the ring. If I do, Maman will know where I am. I remember what she said. *I'll find you with the ring.* It was a promise.

I want to shout, 'No, that's mine, and Coco's, and Maman will kill you and you're a LIAR and liars are not safe!' but I don't because the pet says he will hurt me.

'Twenty thousand francs!' the man on stage says.

'Isn't this exciting, see how much money you're worth to me? You'll soon forget and be happy in a bright new future.'

I know he's lying because his eyes stay unfriendly and his lips look all stretched.

I cross my arms and try not to cry, close my eyes to remember before, when me and Nina were tumbled together on Coco's sofa and everything was golden and warm and right but then I have to stop because tears squeeze out and I don't want him to see.

The man shouting about the Emerald Lake cracks a hammer down, which makes me jump because I think it's a gun, but it's not.

'Sold to the dashing Officer Gustav Raschmann for a song. Heil Hitler!'

'Not enough,' says the pet and he's angry with me but I don't know why because it's me who should be angry with *him*.

The pet pulls me with him to the man with the hammer and says, 'I don't want to sell, it's worth three times that.'

The hammer man says, 'Major Fischer, please, these are difficult times. Mademoiselle Chanel kindly referred you to me at the last minute, and it's as much as you can expect, especially from a high-ranking SS general. Speak to him if you have a dispute.' He looks at me and says, 'What a perfect little specimen,' and the pet looks scared.

They start to argue, and the ring is still there next to his hammer, and I climb the steps to look at it. It's so beautiful, like the day that me and Maman and Nina went to the country with a picnic and jumped in the water, which was green like a fairy tale.

I look at the pet and the hammer man. They are very angry, and everyone is leaving, and they go to the side of the hall to argue more, so I find the compass in the pencil case I keep in my pocket and scratch two tiny stars made of lines on the metal, one for me and one for Nina. I whisper, 'I am here' to the stone, to God, to Nina and Maman. When the hammer man comes back, he doesn't even look at the ring before he snaps it into the case and takes it away.

The pet drags me so hard out of the room that my wrist hurts but I don't say because even though he was a pet when the wolf was with him at Coco's, he is like a spitting cat with mean claws with me.

He puts me back in the car and I am scared, but I am angry too, which makes me feel strong.

'You can wipe that look off your face, and learn to behave like a decent German *Mädchen*.'

He drives and drives and I try to stay awake to see where I am, but I'm so tired that I fall asleep and when I wake up it's dark and there are trees everywhere and no buildings. We drive more and we get to a place with pointy roofs and big gates, like a bad place in a fairy tale.

Inside, it's very quiet and cold and it echoes and there's a lady in a brown dress who writes things down that the pet tells her and she looks at me like I'm bad.

'I'd like her to be called Odelia from now on,' says the pet. 'If she passes the tests, and is properly processed back to Berlin, my wife and I may well be interested in adoption.'

'We have better ones than this.'

'Nevertheless, she looks the part, and my wife sets looks

above any other consideration. The rest can be achieved by discipline and re-education. I'd like her German name to be Odelia.'

I am not called Odelia I am called Odette. I say it to myself in my head over and over again, Odette Lefevre, Odette Lefevre.

The lady in the brown dress takes me up a big staircase, and, when I see there are lots of other children tucked up in rows of beds, I am glad. It's not nice, though, Nina, because none of them look at me. They are all staring up at the ceiling and I can tell that some of them are trying not to cry. They must be missing their mamans and sisters, like me.

I am a long way away, somewhere wrong and dark. How will Maman and Nina find me, especially if the ring is gone and I don't have a name any more?

CHAPTER 5

THE HIDDEN CHÂTEAU

LAMORLAYE, FRANCE, 1 MAY 1944

Nina, aged five

Missing someone is everywhere. In the mirror I pretend I'm Odette and I give her the red ribbons and say sorry and show her the ring that connects us, but she doesn't smile. She looks lonely, and scared that the wolf soldier will hurt her.

Me and Maman are on the train and there are so many people wearing lots of clothes even though it's hot. They are dragging suitcases they don't have enough arms to carry and some even have pots and pans and things from their kitchen tied to them and everything looks wrong. We are leaving Paris. Odette will never find us and, as we leave each station, I am sure I see her running after us with her plaits flying in the sailor dress we were wearing that day, but it's too late because the train is too fast. Maman asks what I can see out of the window but I can't tell her because she has been in bed for two whole days and I daren't say Odette's name in case she gets ill again.

After ten stations, the man shouts, 'Lamorlaye' and we get

off and go to a café. It's the first one we've been to since Odette was taken and the hot chocolate tastes sour without her and Maman is twisting her glove again and again and when she smiles it's like she's pretending.

'Drink up, little chick,' she says, 'we're going on an adventure.'

It's very quiet in here, not like the big cafés in Paris. There is only one other lady on her own at a table, but she says bonjour.

Maman asks the waiter the way to the Lebensborn nursery, and his face goes mean.

'We're closing now,' he says and takes away our cups.

'But that lady's got a whole cake and a drink to finish,' I say in case she gets locked in.

'Hush,' says Maman pulling me out of the door. 'Ouch!' I shout because she's squeezing my arm so tight.

The lady with the drink says, 'Thank you for noticing,' and leaves with us. She is angry with the waiter because she could have got locked in all night. She gives me a lily-of-the-valley in a little vase that she stole from the café table. 'Happy May Day, to a sweet little girl and her beautiful maman.'

'That's so kind,' says Maman, but her voice is sad. 'Can you tell me the way to the Lebensborn nursery?'

The lady smiles, but she's sad when she looks at me and Maman.

'I can show you to the path through the trees if you like. It's not far, but it's totally cut off from the village, so no one will see you,' says the lady, and Maman hugs her even though she doesn't know her.

When we get to some trees, the lady points and says she'll wait with our suitcase, and we can already see the château through the leaves.

I don't want to leave our suitcase because it has the ring in there, but Maman says we might find Odette if I come with her, and I'm not to tell a soul and do exactly as she says.

I'm so excited, and the château has pointy rooves and big high gates and it's like a fairy tale. But fairy tales have monsters and when we see a soldier I hide behind Maman. She tells me to keep my head up and walk tall.

This soldier says hello. He has a nice face, and he doesn't have a skull and crossbones badge like the soldiers who took Odette, but he sounds German, which is bad. I stay quiet and small.

'I'm afraid this is out of bounds. I suggest you go back the way you came before anyone sees you.'

I tug Maman. We need to run as far away as we can.

'Wait a minute, chérie, let me speak to this man.'

I squeeze Maman's hand because it is shaking and cold.

'I understand there is what you call a Lebensborn nursery behind those gates, and I believe that my daughter is in there.'

The soldier goes kind of stiff, but his face is still soft.

'You are mistaken, madame. The building is classified and heavily guarded. You should take your little girl and stay away from here.'

'Let me pass. If my daughter is in there, we want to be with her, and we are happy to join her in whatever fate is assigned to her.'

Maman is talking loudly to the soldier and she is wearing her best suit so he listens. Odette is in there, I know because I can feel it in the tips of my hair. I let go of Maman's hand and she doesn't notice because she and the soldier are arguing and the bars are wide enough for me to squish through. I run fast. There is a drum in my ears trying to stop me but the hedges are high and I am small and I can hide. There must be a hundred windows and I look for Odette but all the shutters are pulled tight and it looks like the château has its eyes closed. I stop to breathe and look back. The soldier is trying different keys on a big ring and Maman is screaming, rattling the gates.

I run to the front door but the handle is too high, and I can hear voices, so I follow them to the back of the house. There are children playing in the garden. Their eyes are like ghosts' and there are nurses in brown dresses and aprons watching them and stopping them doing anything fun like climbing trees or running. A nurse with a scared face tells me to slow down in case I fall, and I walk away into the orchard and hope they can't see me any more and I find a girl on a swing that is tied to a blossom tree. She asks me to come and play like we are friends and I know she thinks I'm Odette, and so do the nurses, because this was our best twin game. I say hello, but before she says anything back the soldier has caught me and picked me up. I am kicking and screaming Odette's name but he squashes his hand over my mouth and it smells of sausages and I can't breathe.

Maman is crying when the man takes me back through the gates and she holds me tighter than the soldier did and whispers, 'I'm sorry, I'm sorry, I can't lose you, too. Thank you,' she says to the soldier.

'She's here, Odette is here,' I try to say but my voice is so tight it won't come out.

'Listen, madame. You have to believe me, there is no one who looks like her here today, I promise. There are only ten children, I know them all and she's not one of them. You say you think your daughter was brought here yesterday? We did have a consignment arrive, but they were assessed, changed, given documentation and sent straight on.'

'Where to?'

'We don't know. But madame, please take comfort from the fact that she will be well looked after, especially if she looks like her little sister here. She will have passed all the tests.'

'What tests?' I say.

'Racial assessments,' says the soldier quietly.

I don't know what he means, but I think about the skull and crossbones on the pet's jacket and imagine it has come alive with red eyes and he's got Odette in hell.

A feeling like sick and hurt turns into tears and I shout that she will be afraid and lonely but the skull makes my words melt.

'Please, madame. The guard will change soon and I can't protect you if they find you. Take your beautiful little girl as far away as you can from here and try and forget.'

I don't know what Maman says to him, because I am sending my dreams to Odette. *I love you over the sky, I'm here.*

We walk away and Maman looks like one of the ghost children and I am scared she is made of glass that will break.

When we get through the trees, the kind lady is waiting with our suitcase. *We still have the ring, Odette,* I dream, and she's swimming in a green lake where we can both meet. Maman falls into the lady's arms, and the lady whispers, 'You poor things.' She strokes my plaits and says, 'It's all right, chickadee, you can both stay with us tonight and your maman will be better in the morning.'

But I know she won't be, not until Odette comes home.

CHAPTER 6

LOST CHILDREN

Fleur

Fleur had an immediate response from the Chanel archivist.

I'm sorry for your loss. Your grandmother was a remarkable woman, and very dear to Mademoiselle Chanel herself. She has bequeathed us an extensive archive, which will not be accessible to the public. However, she did add a codicil. Should any family member make enquiries, the full archive is to be made available to them. The archive consists of a large collection of original documents, annotated photographs and letters, dating from WWII to 1962. We are in the process of digitising the first batch, covering the period of 1944 to 1947. Once digitised, under the terms of the bequest, any immediate family member has the right to request the original documents for study if required.

I'd be happy to arrange a call to update you further…

Fleur arranged to speak to the archivist the next day, and sat open-mouthed as she explained the circumstances under which Coco Chanel and Nina were linked.

A lost twin sister, a ring set with a stone so rare it had its own name – the Emerald Lake – and so valuable that a replica was made for travelling with. A word, *Lebensborn*, she'd never heard of...

'Mademoiselle Lefevre?'

'Yes, I'm still here. It's just – such a shock. Did Nina ever find Odette?'

'I'm afraid we don't know. The whole story is only just coming to light for us. It's a fascinating set of documents... I'm sorry, it's easy to forget that these things can be difficult for living relatives, with far-reaching links and revelations they may not have known about.'

'Would you send everything you have so far?' said Fleur, her mind racing. So that meant she had a great-aunt she never knew about. What if she was still alive? Would the collection include information or photos about her mother?

'I can't understand why she never told me any of this,' said Fleur.

The archivist hesitated, a world of questions swirled in the silence between them.

'Very often people who were involved in atrocities in the war are so traumatised that they didn't want to talk about it, or they don't want to pass their sadness on to future generations. Perhaps...'

She didn't hear the rest. There *was* always something unspoken. She could never ask about her mother without Nina changing the subject. Nina never wanted to answer any questions about relatives or ancestors, grandparents or great-grandparents; there'd always been a kind of prickly haze around the subject and Fleur had accepted it as just the way things were. How is it that children sometimes know not to ask, become watchful for the flicker of hurt, unwilling to inflict unnecessary pain, and, in doing so, take a little of the pain on themselves without being able to name it?

'It's just you and me, little Fleur, and that's just fine with me. Forward!' Nina would say.

Any further questions made it seem like Nina wasn't enough, and Fleur was made to feel that she was poking at a kind of wasps' nest that shouldn't be disturbed.

While she was waiting for the files from the archivist to come through, Fleur searched feverishly for the Emerald Lake online.

The ring had been gifted to Coco Chanel by an aristocratic admirer – a lover's gift, and ever-practical, she had a replica made because it was too valuable to travel with. The Emerald Lake was five hundred years old, and was rumoured to have brought people together as it changed hands down the centuries. Collectors eulogised about it, talked about the velvety viridian green, typical of the Colombian mine it originated from. It was very rare. It was huge – twenty carats, set in twenty-four-carat gold – and Fleur enlarged the picture she found of it, studied it from every angle in disbelief.

She'd recognise it anywhere. She had the exact replica. She'd known it since she could remember, Nina's favourite dress ring, that was just *her* somehow. And the archivist told her that Nina had spent decades looking for the real thing, and for her twin sister. Before Fleur had ever been born.

The first batch of documents from the Chanel archive arrived two days later in a box file. Given her status as the only living relative, the archivist had agreed to send the original documents once they'd been digitised so that Fleur could benefit from every nuance the ageing pieces of paper brought with them.

What she found was utterly heartbreaking. Correspondence between Nina's mother, Camille, and various refugee agencies. The letters were all addressed to this house. So Nina must have lived here with Camille. No wonder she never brought Fleur to this beautiful place; it must have held so many sad memories for her.

Why did Nina send all these letters and documents to Chanel and not keep them for her? She wondered again, had she meant Fleur to see all of this, and, if so, why not just tell her? She'd left so much to chance. Perhaps it was easier for her like that, leave it to fate. Whatever Nina had intended, there was no going back. Fleur was burning with curiosity and sympathy for what her grandma and great-grandma must have gone through in those dark days.

Fleur read on. Each of them mentioned that chilling word, *Lebensborn*, again. Camille's desperate pleas for help went unanswered for several months at a time; it was all a tragic puzzle, fragments of information never leading to anything, destroyed documents, with the Emerald Lake and its replica a central part of it.

Fleur hugged the replica ring that Nina had worn every day of her life. Poor Nina, those children, their mother... her great-grandmother, Camille, a name she'd never heard uttered until now. It was so much to take in, so far away, but part of her, too.

The setting sun blazed a trail over the darkening sea as Fleur tried to make sense of the files. Nina and her mother had returned again and again to a place just outside Paris called Lamorlaye. The place had haunted them. One letter was so desperate and tragic, she could hardly read the whole thing. Camille had written, suggested that her little daughter Nina was absolutely positive that her twin sister was being kept at Lamorlaye on their first visit there, that her twins had a sixth sense for their siblings, that it should be followed up. She had gone on to hound each subsequent owner after the war with her entreaties for information. Some of them were kind, others dismissive, many didn't even reply.

A faded copy of a Red Cross poster from 1945 knocked the breath out of her. A picture of a little girl, hair in plaits tied with red ribbons, and a sailor dress.

Who knows me? Who can tell me where I'm from?

Another photo of a child underneath. It must have been Nina, two years older than the sailor-dress picture. She was holding a slate, chalked with a message:

Do you know my twin sister, original name Odette?

Fleur read up as much as she could about what happened to Lebensborn children. After the war, the Nazis made bonfires of their meticulous records. The Lebensborn buildings were returned to their original use as châteaux, asylums, hospitals and schools, and the doctors, nurses, SS officers and *Oberführers* melted into the community once the war was over and they were back in Germany. Made up of the Nazi elite, many of them were now lawyers, judges, university professors, and keen to distance themselves from the evil. Any Lebensborn cases of stolen children that did go to court were thrown out by the very people who'd sanctioned the scheme, so trails were lost, children rejected.

Of the hundreds of thousands of children who were born as Lebensborns, or taken because of their looks, only 20 per cent were reunited with their families. It would be like finding a needle in a haystack.

Stories about the Lebensborn floated in Fleur's mind, lost children, displaced and lonely. They only took the most 'beautiful' children, the ones that fitted their Aryan ideal. The programme started before the war, but as more and more Germans died in the war, Himmler became even more obsessed with creating a pool of future Aryans through the Lebensborn homes. Young girls were persuaded to 'voluntarily' sleep with SS officers and then were forced to give up their babies. Later in the war, as so many German soldiers were lost, they resorted to raiding nurseries, schools and parks in occupied territories, arbitrarily tearing children from their mothers, sending them to be measured, processed and categorised. Rather than send children back to their families if they didn't make the grade, they put them on trains to be 'liquidated'. Rounded shoulders, sticking-out ears or a filled tooth could get a child sterilised. Requests were made by elite childless couples to be able to adopt a racially perfect child, created by a pre-vetted 'racially valuable' couple. The whole thing was a real-life *Handmaid's Tale*. If the child turned out to have the 'wrong' features or colouring, they were sent back to God knew what fate.

The stories were endless... In Czechoslovakia, mothers who lay on the tracks in front of a Lebensborn transportation train were beaten with rifles and dragged away, forced to watch the train pull away. Adopted children lay awake at night crying for their real mothers. The same children were often rejected after the war, a shameful reminder of their new families' Nazi pasts, shunned by the local community as they grew, displaced and lonely.

What happened to Odette? Fleur picked up a fragile document. It was battered and yellowed, but the information it gave her was priceless. Odette's name was listed.

```
Date of admittance: 1 May 1944
Age: Four years old.
Parentage: Father, anonymous, racially
approved SS officer, deserter. Executed.
Mother: Camille Lefevre. Approved racial
characteristics.
Racial value: Approved for adoption.
Notes: Despite her Aryan features, she
is a difficult child. Refuses to speak
German, sleeping patterns disturbed.
```

Isolation measures taken to prevent
disturbing other children. Crying,
rebellion, and constant references to
previous unsavoury life. Corrective
education in place, prior to transportation and adoption.

Chills prickled Fleur's neck. Whatever thread connected the twins on that first visit to Lamorlaye had brought them to the same place, but Nina had left without seeing her. Fleur could weep at the cruel near-miss.

Who was the SS officer, her great-grandfather? He was executed for desertion. Fleur tried to take it all in. As an SS officer he must have at least been witness to atrocities, even if he hadn't taken part in them. Did he desert as a protest, to be with Camille and his twin babies? She hoped that he did the right thing. Or had Camille left him, too, realising what he stood for? It was all so confusing, and there were things she'd never know. Nina and Odette's mother was on her own, trying to protect her little ones, having lost their father, Fleur's great-grandfather, in the most brutal way.

She looked in the mirror and Odette stared back, a furious, heartbroken little girl from the Red Cross poster, with the same almond-shaped bright blue eyes, wide-set, almost alien-like, the same half-smile that characterised pictures of Fleur and Nina.

By the time Fleur came up for air after being buried in the documents for the whole day, the sun was already low over the sea.

She hugged Nina's ring, mourned the old hands that had worn this every day of her life till her death. Was Odette still out there somewhere?

If you are, I'll find you, said Fleur to the mirror.

Was this why Fleur had vowed never to have children?

Some inherited sadness, fear of motherhood, of the horror of losing the most precious thing in the world to you?

Her mobile buzzed from another world and made her jump. Jake.

'How's my French refugee?' he said. It was like surfacing from under water. She put a protective hand on her stomach.

'In a whole new world. It's so weird being here, like being someone else.'

The line clicked, Jake missed a beat. Fleur could hear his distracted typing at his laptop.

'That's good, I miss you,' he said without conviction.

She couldn't bring herself to say the same back. 'How are things there?'

'Busy. The Swiss are giving me grief and the exchange rate is playing havoc with profit margins. I'm definitely going to need you back next week, I can't manage it all without you and, apart from that, the bed's too big without you and I worry about you all alone out there.'

Fleur looked out at the sea melting into the hazy horizon, the piles of papers arranged over the coffee table with fragments of her broken family somewhere in the pages.

'I'm fine, really. It's actually lovely to get some time away to think. There's a whole other life that Nina led, one that she never told me about. It's almost like she's here with me.'

Fleur outlined what she'd found, but Jake was barely listening.

'Sounds like it was all a very long time ago. Nothing you can do about it now, and Nina clearly didn't want you to know about any of it, or she'd have told you. You have to let her go, get on with your own life now.'

'I know, I just need time.'

'Well, you've got until next week, then it'll be good for you to get back into a routine. I checked your work emails, already three hundred and counting, can you believe it? Everyone loves a cc to the whole world, half of them are probably totally irrelevant...'

She wasn't going back, not until she'd followed every lead, exhausted all possibilities.

'Fleur?'

'Sorry, the reception's bad here. I've already made some progress with finding out more about Nina's family. I still can't believe what happened.'

'I've already said you shouldn't dwell on it. Leave it in the past, where it belongs. You've lost someone precious in your life, and I know it's difficult, but you can't bring her back, or her twin, or whoever it was. Why don't you wait until a bit of time has passed, when you're feeling stronger?'

'I can't, there's an auction—'

'Grief's misting your vision, Fleur. I can see how this would make you feel Nina's still here, but you have to accept it and try and move on. You've got me now. Don't shut me out. Listen, why don't I come out, soak up a bit of sun, try out the local rosé, then bring you home? I could bring my laptop, do a bit of work from there...'

She knew it was partly true, she was good at shutting out the world.

'Don't worry about me, really, and thanks for offering to come but you'd be bored and when I come back next week you can wrap me up in cotton wool and save me from myself.'

'That sounds more like the Fleur I know and love. And I do love you very much. You know that, don't you? I'm not very good at all the soppy stuff, but... I'm here for you, whatever you need.'

Fleur felt a pang of guilt, for not needing him.

'I know. I love you too.'

All she could think about were the details swirling around in her head about Lamorlaye, the Red Cross poster, the listing in the log about her lost great-aunt. It was everything to her, and while she was absorbed in it she didn't need to think about her and Jake's child, the one that might never be.

There was no way she was missing the Magnificent Rare Jewels auction in Geneva that Nina had circled. How did you even begin to pick up this trail, and unravel it, when Nina had apparently spent so many years searching? Judging by the discoveries in the box in the attic, and the newspaper clipping from only six months before she died, Nina had never stopped looking. Fleur had to try. It was like a golden thread joined them all through time, Great-grandmother, grandmother and twin sister, her own mother. It was almost as if a second child was planting itself in her in this place where the land met the sea.

That night, as Fleur hovered above sleep, shimmering ghosts of people who weren't yet quite in focus floated around in Nina's secret house, haunting her dreams, unknowable, yet part of her, as if she always knew. Is that how genes worked? Was there a kind of memory that was passed down?

The next morning, she got straight to work. Bullinger's Auctioneers in Geneva were cagey about the upcoming auction. The previews were private, they said, but in terms of provenance they'd been assured that the collection had been in the family for centuries. So this was how it had been for Nina. Hunches, dead-ends, faceless corporations, rejections, even suspicion.

She had the ridiculous idea to check on the Bullinger's website for a friendly face. There was Nicolas, an intern and gemmologist. Broad smile, a bit scruffy, a self-professed love of the stones for their mineralogy, and an interest in ethical sourcing and mining.

She wrote to him on a whim, asking for his help in giving more information about the auction and wondering about how a gem might be traced, or recognised, after so many years in hiding. She got an email straight back. He was interning at Geneva, but he lived in Antibes and was back at his flat for the week. If she could get herself there, he would be happy to meet and help if he could. He had a free day from the auction house and would be in his workshop tomorrow.

Bingo! If Nina really had left things to fate, surely this was a sign that Fleur should keep going?

Fleur set off early, left the car in the main car park in Antibes and found her way into the old town, a jumble of alleys, terracotta rooves and pavement cafés, all adorned with little vases of lily-of-the-valley to celebrate May Day.

Following his instructions, she found the shopfront with antique display cases filled with stones and fossils, exactly as Nicolas had described in his email. Inside, at a desk, with a loupe held up to his eye, turning a stone in the light, was the man from the Bullinger's Auction website. He must have been about the same age as her, floppy hair, Jesus beard and moustache, faded jeans, espadrilles and a hoodie, totally absorbed in whatever it was he was studying.

She waited a moment and he jumped.

'Shit, sorry, I didn't hear you come in. This little number is a beauty.'

He held up the stone, and she politely went over to look. It was a lump of dull resin.

'You're right,' he said, seeing her apparently unimpressed expression and brushing his fringe out of his eyes. 'Nothing much to look at in this state, chemically a lump of calcium with titanium and oxygen.'

He smiled, expecting her to understand.

'You've lost me already. I'm Fleur, by the way.'

'Sorry, I'm a complete nerd, and I should have said hello instead of launching straight in. It's just that these things really get me.'

He looked at the lump of resin with a kind of loving awe.

'It's a sphene. Rubbish name for a thing of such talent.'

Fleur put her head to one side, trying to love it for his sake.

'Wait, I'll show you a cut one,' said Nicolas, pulling out a sample drawer full of gems. He picked one out and beckoned her over to the window, where the sun was streaming in, and held it up to the light.

Little pixels of colours in amber, sage and quartz showed themselves through the earthy hues like sparkles on a seabed.

'See? They have to speak to you for you to love them.'

'It's mesmerising, the way it catches the light and splits it into prisms.'

'Technically sphenes have a high refractive index, which means they have strong dispersion. Diamonds split the light into rainbows, but these little gems do it on steroids. The only thing against them is that they're soft, so they're not an ideal ring stone—' He stopped and held out his hand. 'Nicolas, by the way. And this isn't why you're here, sorry.'

She laughed for the first time, she realised, since Nina. They shook hands, which seemed pointless at this stage in proceedings. His hand was warm and dry, reassuring. He grinned, and lovingly put the gem back in its place.

'Well, you're just the person for the task I bring,' she said. 'I need someone who knows about gems, and I'm really hoping you can help.'

'I hope I can, too. From what you said, it's an interesting story – a gem with a history attached. I like those.'

'It even has its own name. I suppose that's a good start?'

'Without question. If it's rare and beautiful enough for that, it's a gemmologist's dream.'

Fleur told Nicolas everything she knew so far. He listened without a word. No interruptions, no platitudes, no entreaties to leave off a hopeless hunt for lost family.

'It's an almost impossible task, but a gem like the Emerald Lake can't just completely disappear, surely? Something worth that much has to have surfaced or changed hands for money over the decades?'

He frowned. His expressions had a way of filling the room.

'I'm not sure why your grandma was so interested in the auction, because this particular gem isn't in it. There are rumours about Nazi connections though, so maybe there's some link? From what I've seen so far, the kind of money a gem like that would fetch brings with it a whole world of corruption. If the dodgy provenance can be whitewashed, there are plenty of people prepared to use their so-called expertise to clean it up. I'm warning you now, there's a whole underground, bigger and more sophisticated than the legit world of gem-dealing.'

'Would you recognise that sphene you just showed me if it turned up in fifty years' time?' said Fleur.

'I'd know it anywhere. It has an inclusion – a tiny defect – unique to it. It would be the same for the high refractive index, the colour, and everything else I love about it.'

'That's what I'm hoping for, if we find it. That there's some kind of proof.'

She took Nina's ring off and showed it to him.

'This is an exact replica of the ring, a travelling companion. When the twins were split, this was their last connection.'

He took the ring, rolled it around in his palm.

'It wouldn't be the first gem that's surfaced after decades. From what you've told me, Nina never gave up hope, and neither should we.'

Fleur studied one of the display cases, hard. She should have brought her camera, which was always useful when she wanted to deflect attention from herself.

'At this stage, hope is all I have,' she managed. Everything was heightened; it was difficult to keep control of her emotions. In fact, in a lovely kind of way, she just felt everything more deeply, happy or sad. Was it the baby, or this encounter with Nick, or Nina, or all of them at once?

Nicolas looked at the ring through his loupe. 'I have to admit to a little enlightened self-interest,' he said. 'If there's really an emerald out there this big, I want to know about it. Fifty-fifty? I'd say at least two million each, more if we can prove the provenance.'

'It's not about the money, I just want to find Odette – my great-aunt – and restore it to her if she's still alive. But that much, really?' Fleur asked.

'It's possible. The Rockefeller Emerald sold for over five million dollars, that was six years ago, and it was eighteen carats, whereas I understand the Emerald Lake is twenty.'

'For a collection of minerals?'

'For the story, for the energy they pick up from whoever's wearing them, for the way the stones catch the light, the tales they can tell from the depths and the centuries. They choose you, rather than the other way round, you know that, don't you?'

'I don't, and that's a step too far for me,' said Fleur. 'I can see the attraction, all those drawers of loveliness you have here. But they're just things.'

'You'll learn.'

'I can't help thinking that wherever it is it will give me a clue to Odette, so I suppose you're right in that way. I've been reading up about Nazi loot, too. Every restoration of a stolen piece of art, furniture or jewellery to the rightful owner is a victory against the Nazis and what they did to those children. If Odette's still out there, it should be hers, or her children's. Plus, Coco gave whoever stole Odette that ring specifically to lay a trail that could be followed. I just know it's up to me to take up the baton. I'm the only one left who can find her now.'

'The Emerald Lake was taken around 1944, you say?' Nick said, his eyes lighting up. Before she could answer, he was at his laptop, bashing the keys feverishly.

'1944 to 2024. Eighty years. The statute of limitations! If it was going to be sold, now would be the time.'

He looked at her expectantly.

'I'm not sure what any of that means,' said Fleur hopelessly. 'You might need to rewind a little.'

'So, as far as I know from working at Bullinger's, the law says that if a piece is stolen, or taken as a result of Nazi looting, it still belongs to the original owner. It doesn't matter if it's been bought and sold in good faith down the decades, the piece would still revert. If the original owner were dead, then it would belong to the heirs.'

'Would that apply to Odette's case?' asked Fleur.

Nick nodded. 'The statute of limitations is a time limit that varies by country. In Geneva, it's eighty years, which brings us to 2024. There have been cases where pieces of looted art have emerged from the woodwork, even this long after the war. I've never heard of it happening with jewellery though.'

'God, I wouldn't know where to start. Poor Nina. Maybe there *is* something about this auction then?'

Nick picked up his sphene and held it up to the light again, as if it would help spark something.

'The fact that it's famous will really help. You need proof, and if there are any identifiable attributes to it like an inclusion, or engraving on the metal, that will work in our favour. The other thing would be a photograph of one of your family wearing it, or best of all an official letter or document of owner-ship. But that's assuming we even trace it. I do have access to certain databases, auction catalogues and things like that. I can have a root around for you if you like.'

'So you're in, just like that? Really, I only came for advice,' said Fleur.

'Like I say, a gem finds you rather than the other way round,' he said, smiling. They looked at each other a moment longer than they should.

'This ring was given to a child in an attempt to keep track of her in the theatre of war,' Nick continued. 'I can't walk away now. A famous gem, steeped in that much hope, just has to leave a trail. We might as well believe that until we find otherwise.'

It was so nice to have someone on her side. He'd immediately understood, without her having to spell it out.

She put the ring back on, and realised her hands were shaking. Nicolas noticed, with a blink of sympathy.

'You must have driven over an hour to get here in this heat. Do you want to get a tea or coffee, or something to eat? There's a place just round the corner and I can grab a notebook so you can tell me everything you know so far.'

'I'm buying. It's the least I can do,' said Fleur.

Nick took her to a bistro in a little side street. It didn't look like much, a row of rickety tables and chairs outside, a red awning and mismatched tablecloths, but the place was buzzing.

The maître d' kissed Nick on both cheeks and gave them a shady table with a view of the cobbled street and a little vase of lily-of-the-valley on the table to celebrate May Day.

'Sitting here in Antibes in 2024, the sun shining, families having their May Day picnics on the beach, friends at café tables, blissfully oblivious, peace. It's unbelievable to think that it actually happened, isn't it?' said Nicolas.

Fleur put her hand on her heart. 'I feel it here, like a stone, and I didn't even know this twin existed until a few days ago. It's as wrong today as it was then, and my grandma died never knowing what happened to her. Maybe my great-aunt is still out there, with a whole family I never knew.'

Nicolas whistled sympathetically. 'That's big.'

The waiter brought over the menus and Fleur was glad to have a diversion. It *was* big. There was so much to process, more questions to ask than had been answered. She'd only just lost the Nina she knew, but what about the one she didn't? Death was so horribly final; she'd never be able to ask. She hoped that Nina, in raising her, had found some comfort, having lost her mother, a twin, her daughter. Anyone who met Nina would have no clue about the tragedies she'd experienced. She chose life, and Fleur, instead. Now, here Fleur was in a new country, having lunch with someone she'd never met before, but feeling like a different person, full of new possibilities.

Fleur ordered fish soup and sparkling water. Nick decided on urchins and a glass of Picpoul. Even in the shade the sun was blissfully warm, Nick was easy company and time slowed in their little Mediterranean alleyway.

She found herself telling Nick everything. About growing up with Nina in Somerset, her unquestioning, happy childhood in their country cottage. The fact that her mother died soon after she was born, that she never knew her father.

'I never dared to ask. It was just one of those questions... somehow I knew I couldn't go there.'

'Seams of gold are always buried deep, but that doesn't mean they're not there, or that one day they won't be discovered.'

'Part of me doesn't want to know. Nina must have wanted to shield me, and maybe herself, from what happened. Funny, my great-grandma, and my grandma, and my mother, were all single mothers. Must run in the family.'

This was straying into dangerous territory. What about her and the pregnancy she was trying to forget just for today. And Jake? She hadn't mentioned him yet, she thought guiltily.

She'd love to stay here, linger all afternoon, bask in Nicolas's easy warmth. But that was impossible, and this life wasn't hers. She was engaged, with a life to unravel, and a lost child to find, and she didn't know if it was her own, or Nina's twin, or both. Everything was so messed up.

The church bell struck three and she asked for the bill a bit too abruptly.

'Of course, we should go,' said Nick, picking up his coffee.

'Sorry, I just didn't realise the time.'

'Is there something you need to get back for?' asked Nick.

'Yes,' said Fleur, desperately trying to think of something. 'I've got a delivery arriving. They said after five.'

'On a bank holiday?'

'I'll go and pay inside. Don't rush. You stay here and finish your coffee and I'd better run.'

He stood up. 'Let's go halves.'

'No really, you've listened to me rambling on all afternoon.'

'I've enjoyed it. And I want to help.'

'Exactly. Let me pay.'

He kissed her on both cheeks to say goodbye.

'My turn next time.' He hesitated, pulled his jacket around him even though the heat was baking the cobbles. 'Drive carefully, and let me know if there are any developments.'

Driving back to Sanary, Fleur went back over the afternoon. There was no appropriate moment to mention Jake, and it was all so complicated with the baby and everything. It was just easier not to say. She thought about Nicolas's analogy of the seam of gold buried deep underground.

What else was she going to uncover in this new place?

CHAPTER 7

ECHOES

Fleur

Lights from a lone boat in the bay blinked as evening fell. Fleur shivered. Nina hated flashing lights and this one was so bright it momentarily flooded the room. The green butterfly that had settled in the villa the day she'd arrived fled into the shadows. An echo of something flashed across Fleur's vision, so fleeting it wasn't really there.

Now she was seeing ghosts? She was being ridiculous. It wasn't a baby, just a collection of random cells. The first thing was to see the doctor, make a decision from there. She could fly back to London under the radar without telling Jake, give herself a little time to make up her mind. She picked up her mobile, found the surgery number and hesitated. Why was she doing this alone? The phone lit up with a call and she let herself answer.

'I've found two things.'

'Is this Nicolas?'

'Yes,' he said distractedly. 'You saved my number, didn't you?'

'Yes, but normally people say hello or something.'

'First, the Emerald Lake is known to have a very recognisable inclusion, in the shape of a heart. That will at least double its value, and the trouble it attracts.'

'Why's that?'

Good, the more trouble, the less time to think.

'An identifiable, heart-shaped inclusion in one of the largest and most pristine emeralds ever to emerge from the greatest emerald mine in Colombia? It's obvious, isn't it?'

'It's a lovely coincidence, but, no, not to me.'

'I told you, it's about the story, the provenance. A highly prized emerald with a naturally formed heart marking, that's rumoured to bring people together? Surely you don't need to be a gemmologist to understand that?'

'I can see that would be very beguiling if you had a few million at your disposal.'

'Exactly! It also means it's very traceable and, with the replica ring you have, proven provenance to Coco Chanel herself, and by association to her lover, who was a well-known aristocrat and collector whose family go way back. Rumours are that it can be traced all the way to the Inca before it fell into his hands. The point is, the recognisable inclusion gives us a better chance to recover it for you, if we can find it.'

Damn, the doctor's surgery was closing in five minutes, but this was too important. Tomorrow wouldn't make much difference.

'This is absolutely bloody brilliant. How did you find all this out so quickly?'

She'd only left his workshop yesterday.

'I'm dogged when I get the bit between my teeth, and you looked so des...'

'Desperate?'

'Sorry,' he said. 'But completely understandably. It's such a sad story and it's rightfully yours if there are no other living relations.'

'I don't care about the value, I just want to find Odette for Nina.'

'And a family for yourself.'

Nicolas just got it. But rather than think about that, or reply, she flicked the camera on her phone and snapped a carefree little gecko scuttling up the wall.

He responded to her silence. 'You're not going to cry, are you? God, sorry, I have no filter. Listen, it's May, and emeralds are the Gemini birth stone – the twins. All the stars are perfectly aligned if you believe in all that, which I don't, but I'm clutching at straws in a clumsy attempt to stop you from crashing and burning. And seriously, these big famous gems don't just disappear. People can never resist cashing them in at some point, and that brings me to my second point, which might cheer you up.'

Fleur swallowed the lump in her throat, tried to keep it light. 'You have all those bits of shiny minerals to keep safe, you don't need to worry about me as well. It's just more than I'd hoped... and there's more to tell?'

'So.' His voice had turned from caring back to excitable again. 'The Emerald Lake turned up at an auction in Paris in 1944, three months after the date you said Odette was taken. It was sold to an SS commander called Gustav Raschmann for a fraction of its worth. He was a Nazi war criminal and, on further investigation, one who escaped to Colombia through the ratlines. Can you believe it? That little piece of green perfection with a heart somehow returned right back to where it came from. The Nazi hid out in Muzo. That's where the mother of all emerald mines is based, a place that produces the most perfect, most coveted gems. There've been some stonking emeralds come out of that mine, and... sorry. All you need to know is that the ring likely landed there with a desperate war criminal keen to sell. My suspicion is that he wanted to get somewhere that the dealers would understand the real value in those chaotic times. I haven't had time to search any records there yet.'

Fleur's head was spinning, but her heart was racing. Nicolas was all over the place, speeding through leads and concepts that were like a multi-connected vein of his beloved gems.

'You've already gone way beyond the call of duty. What can I do? Can you pass any of the research to me? If I could find the name of the person who put the Emerald Lake up for auction, that would feel like a step towards finding Odette.'

'You don't have the access to the auction records and provenance verification certificates that I do through Bullinger's. Plus, I'm in now, and I'm not letting the Emerald Lake out of my sight. If we find it, it would be the discovery of the century. If you'd wanted to keep it for yourself, you should never have tempted me with it. These things can corrupt the saintliest of hearts, you know.'

'And you're being kind and I'm never going to be able to pay you back for what you've done so far. What on earth is a ratline, by the way?'

'I'm only just finding all this stuff out myself. It's appropriately named. Apparently, there were certain factions of the Catholic Church who helped Nazi war criminals escape to South America via Spain or Italy, where they were welcomed with open arms. Pretty chilling stuff.'

Coco had been clever. She could see how something as valuable as the Emerald Lake would be hard to hide. Nicolas was right. If the gem was taken in return for a child, and was a risk to the officer, he was going to want to profit from it immediately. As was the next person along. And that was the biggest hope of a trail she'd get from the echoes down the decades.

Fleur fell asleep with her laptop propped up in bed,

following trails online to try to trace Gustav Raschmann, firing emails off to the Red Cross and the International Tracing Service. Most of the people Nina had once been in touch with were long gone, so it was like starting from scratch. Drowning in bureaucracy and dead-ends, she drifted off.

CHAPTER 8

THE COUNTRY ORCHESTRA

Nina, aged five

Maman is wearing the same clothes as yesterday, and they are crumpled because she slept in them, the jacket and everything. The lily-of-the-valley flower that the café lady gave me is in my pocket, all dried up, but I have to keep it because I got it the day of the château and I know that Odette was there.

We are on another train and I am hungry and Maman hasn't said anything since we got on and I daren't speak because there are so many people. One kind man let us sit in his seat but some of the people who were squashed in the corridor got angry and said it was all right for some and a woman shouldn't travel alone when she looked like that, a face like that is asking for it. Maman is pretty, is that what they mean?

The café lady let us stay at her house last night before the train and she gave me a sandwich for the journey. That made Maman cry instead of saying thank you. I ask for it and she says, 'Hush, wait until we are on our own somewhere because lots of people are hungry.' Being hungry makes me cross and I say I want it loudly and the other people in the carriage tut and look mean, and one man asks where the sandwich is, so Maman gives it to him.

'We are tired, please take this and leave us in peace.'

I want to take it out of his greedy mouth but I don't want to get stolen, so I keep quiet and I am sitting on Maman's knee and it's not comfy because she has gone so stiff.

The train takes a long time, but I can't sleep in case I see Odette. There are so many people squashed everywhere that it takes me until it's dark to make sure that I have looked at every face and checked in every dark corner, and sometimes I think I can see her sticking out her tongue at me or calling me over with her finger on her lips like she does when she's got something exciting and secret to show me that she'll know I like, but then it's not her and I know she's not there because I would feel it if she was, and I feel like I'm drowning.

I let my eyes close, but Odette needs me and she's in the château screaming my name, but no noise is coming out and the train is taking us further and further away and I want to sleep. The train stops all of a sudden and I slide off Maman's lap and everyone is falling forward and someone steps on my hand and I scream, and Maman picks me up and squashes through the people until we get to the door and we have to jump even though the train is still moving slowly.

'Keep quiet, and stay with me.'

Her voice is strong again, not all husky from crying. She pulls me away from the train where there is a big hedge. I look behind me and we are near a station where there are men with guns and they are shouting and people from the train are taking papers out of their bags and they look like they are begging.

We walk across fields and stay in the shadows and my shoes hurt, but Maman finds us a place where the tree god is looking after us and Maman wraps herself round me and makes herself a blanket for me and I wish Odette could see because we always fought for Maman's cuddles but now I would sleep without her forever so Odette could have Maman and not be alone and afraid.

My tummy is rumbling and I can't sleep because I'm so hungry, but then I wake up, and Maman is looking at me and humming our favourite song and the birds are joining in.

It's not cold here like in Paris and I can hear something loud and swishy.

'We can walk from here, little chick. We'll be safe then, and there'll be things to eat. Do you think you can walk the furthest you've ever walked?' says Maman.

'Will Odette be there?'

Maman sneezes but I know she's crying. I wish I hadn't said her name, but she said we'd be safe.

'No, it will be just you and me,' she says, pretending nothing has happened, but her voice is tight.

When we see a man in a flat cap and a big hay fork, I am afraid. I don't like strangers any more but Maman waves to him and he puts his hand over his eyes to shut out the sun, which is very bright, and then he throws down his big fork and comes running over.

We don't have a suitcase because we had to leave it on the train but Maman is still walking like she is carrying something heavy. When the man gets to her she falls on the ground and he sits her up and gives her some water and says what happened to you and Maman is sobbing and he can't understand so I say, 'They took Odette and she has been gone for four whole days and she'll never find us here we have to go back.'

Odette would have loved the ride on the hay cart. I lie on my back and watch the clouds and the hay floats away from the bales in strands like Odette's hair and I wish it would swish together and be her.

There's a buzzing noise, and the hay fork man who's

Monsieur Soulier says, 'That's the cicadas and they're our country orchestra and they're here to chorus you into the South of France. There are no soldiers to hurt you here, and we'll look after you so you don't have to worry any more, little one.'

He sounds so kind and Maman is smiling again and I'm so tired that I let myself fall asleep. When I wake up, Monsieur Soulier says he can't understand how anyone could sleep when the roads are so rutted. Some of the hay bales are sliding backwards and I sit up and see what the swishy noise was because it's very loud now, it's the sea and it has a hundred million sparkles on it and we are going down a steep track.

He helps me down into the grass, which is as tall as me and insects are crawling on every flower and there are so many colours. There are trees covered in blossom that smell like sweets and Maman laughs and says they are orange trees and I could cry to see her laugh, so I do a roly-poly in the grass and tell her I love it here but I don't say Odette would, too, not this time because I don't want her to break again. There is something buzzing inside my tummy like one of these insects that won't let me be happy because the more lovely something is, the more I miss my sister because she would have loved it here. There is even a swing on the tree like the one at the scary château and it's swinging in the breeze.

There is food here to eat, but not like in Paris. There are no patisseries or hot chocolate, but we have honey and brown bread and vegetables from a thing called a kitchen garden that is at the back of the house. There are jars of lentils and preserves but we can't eat them all at once.

I wish I could show Odette the cove down the track and the steps that go right into the water from our garden, and Maman is going to teach me to swim. We get up early, then in the afternoon we close the shutters and cuddle up and go to sleep because it's so hot, and there is always one person missing and that's you, Odette, but I talk to you in my daytime dreams and you talk back, but when you speak now it is in a language I don't understand.

At night Maman thinks I don't see, but I do. I count to twelve on the church bells in Sanary-sur-Mer because I can't sleep because if I do I dream about Odette and that makes me sad. On Wednesdays there is a boat outside our house, you can't see it until it's close, then the man stops rowing at our steps and he flashes a torch and Maman goes to the gate in the middle of the night and he passes her something then he rows away.

One night I wait by the gate to see. There is no moon and the night is so dark but I am not afraid because worse things have already happened. I hide until Maman comes, and he gives her something long and heavy and he says, 'Be careful, those guns have hair triggers.' I jump up from my hiding place and say, 'Maman don't take those, they kill people and the men who took Odette had them!'

The boat man is cross and says, 'I knew we shouldn't have women working in the Resistance, they have too many hangers-on, and big mouths.'

'And men take people and use guns and are rude monsters and that is too heavy for my maman, she's made of glass.'

I know he's not bad, just scared. I have seen a lot of scared people now so I can tell.

He thinks it's funny so I tell him to go away.

'A chip off the old block, I see,' says the man and Maman tells him to take care when he rows away, even though he's been rude.

'Off to bed, my little angel,' says Maman. 'And never, ever breathe a word to anyone about this. It's very important, do you understand?'

I don't understand anything, but I nod, and everything's so strange that I want to cry. Maman puts down the long bag and sits on the beach and wraps me up in her arms and the stars are so much bigger than in Paris and the air is warm and she shows me how the sea turns to golden sparkles when you run your hand through it.

'You mustn't breathe a word because I'm doing this to help Odette, and all the other children who are away from home in this war. We have to believe that most people are good, or they've won.'

'I'm only half when she's not here,' I whisper.

'Me too,' says Maman, and we cry together and even though it should be sad and it is, I am glad we have each other and I am glad that Maman says she misses Odette and isn't pretending any more.

She thinks I don't know but I've heard her whispering with my new friend Jacques' maman in the parlour. We are still in danger. They say we're going to win the war, and then we'll get Odette back. Does that mean that soldiers with skull badges will come to our house here by the sea where Monsieur Soulier says we are safe? Why did the man give Maman a gun? What if Odette gets shot if they are angry when we win?

CHAPTER 9

FOUNTAIN OF YOUTH

Odette/Odelia

I am Category One. I am getting a gold medal because I look right. The Brown Sisters say that is good, but I don't want it. I hate it. Rosie and Klaus are Category Four, *Untermensch*, so they will split us up. They don't have the right blood and Rosie has brown eyes that are the wrong shape, and Klaus has a limp and that is Category Four even though he has blond hair and blue eyes. It's stupid because inside I am the same as them.

Rosie is my best friend. She is the only one who knows I'm a twin because she has met Nina. She met her when she was playing on the swing in Lamorlaye and she thought she was a ghost at first because she knew I was told off and they had locked me up. She drew a picture of sunshine and a rainbow and posted it underneath the door and it made me smile and then she went outside. She said the me at the swing was differ-ent, with a different kind of look in her eye, softer, and not afraid, and she'd never seen me with red ribbons. That's how I knew it was Nina.

Every night I dream to her to tell her where I am. I tell her about the Brown Sisters who are our nurses. They wear brown dresses and white aprons but they are not real nurses. I try to remember the road names and I have a book where I draw pictures of everything I see. The train that took us, the different kind of houses I see with wood on the outside and pointy rooves, the place we are in now that has big streets and buildings like Paris but even more flags with the bendy cross on that means Nazi. I draw the face of the person who took me so you can see him, Nina, if I think hard enough. Do you remember him?

We called him the pet, but everyone else calls him Major Fischer. Now he says he will be my new daddy. He has small eyes and big lips that are too red and every time he says he's my daddy I miss you and Maman from my toes to the top of my head and it makes everything hurt.

I've also drawn a picture of the ring that was sold, the writing on the sign at the train station they took us to – B-E-R-L-I-N. That's the first bit, then at the back I draw what I have to remember. You, Nina, which I draw by looking at my own face in the mirror, but with the scar on your eyebrow from when you fell off the swing. I draw Maman with kind eyes and a big smile and her hair in a ponytail, and all of us are holding hands, but then I can't do it any more because it is too sad.

Rosie and me share a room and at night we hug each other even though we are meant to stay in our own beds, and we whisper stories about our mamans and try and make each other laugh when we feel like crying and Rosie tells me my favourite story again and again. The one about Nina, when they played on the swing at Lamorlaye, and Nina shouted so loud that her and Maman will look for me forever, before the soldier put his fat, stupid hand over her mouth.

Me and Rosie and Klaus are playing a game with a hammer

to bang the right shape in the right hole. Then the Brown Sisters come with the pet who I have to call Daddy and I carry on banging, but with the star in the square to show them that I can't win because I don't fit into their stupid family. There is a lady with him who has a mean face and stiff hair.

'This is my wife, and she will be your new mummy,' he says, smiling like I should be happy. I don't even look at him, I just keep banging very hard.

'Say hello nicely, Odelia. We will look after you and you should be proud. When you grow up, you will give birth for the Third Reich,' he says.

I feel all hot inside because it sounds wrong. I want to run away from them but I can't say anything because I am afraid of her and I am not allowed to look sad. I want my own mummy and my sister but here they are called bad, and I have a volcano inside me that would burn everything if I let it explode.

They take me away from my friends and make me go inside with them. My new mummy has brown eyes and her hair is high on top of her head in a big wave and it doesn't move and it is dark. Dark hair is wrong in the Lebensborn home, so I don't understand how all the soldiers and the Brown Sisters salute her and get out the best coffee cups and give her a cake with white flour and jam and a dish of strawberries that look like heaven.

She doesn't even eat the cake, just half a strawberry, like it's poison.

'You should eat more because food is precious,' I say.

Maman says it is polite to eat when food is put in front of you.

'Goodness me, she looks correct, but I hope you're not bringing a peasant into the house, Dieter dear.'

'She's the prettiest one in the home, and has passed every test. Not even an eyelash out of place,' says the Brown Sister. She doesn't usually smile, but now she's being kind and it's a lie.

They normally speak French like dogs barking, and they say I must learn German and forget French.

I rub my eyes, hoping my eyelashes will fall out or go bendy.

'Don't do that, you'll get wrinkles. Come here and kiss your mother on the cheek.'

She leans forward and shows me her cheek, which has a line of red make-up on it. I kiss it but I want to wipe the red powder off my mouth but I don't dare so I stand very still in case I do anything wrong.

'She *is* very pretty, and with the right clothes and instruction I'm sure we can make something of her. I would be happy to give this little orphan a home,' she says and she is so pleased with herself and thinks she is being so kind when she's not that I can't help it.

'I'm not an orphan,' I whisper.

'What did you say?'

'I'm NOT an orphan. I have a maman and a...' I don't want to say twin, because I remember what the wolf said at the Ritz, that twins are valuable, and I don't want them to find Nina and give her the wrong measurements and tell her she has the wrong blood.

'Now, now, dear. We have told you that unfortunately your maman is... no longer with us.'

I can't help it, the volcano spills over. 'I hate you!' I shout and I run out of the room and into the courtyard before they can get me. I am fast and I see my friends, the Category Three and Four children, all being pushed into a van with no windows and there are so many of them that they can't even sit down and the sun is so hot it hurts. My friend Rosie blows me a kiss out of the back of the van door and she is glad because she is going on an adventure, but then more and more of my friends are pushed in and they are all squashed and it doesn't look safe and Rosie falls on the floor.

I rush towards the van and I try to get in to help her. But a

Brown Sister catches me and tells me to stop being a rebellious little minx and I must learn to be more polite and I will be on my own with no food until I can learn to understand that my maman is dead and to be grateful that I will have a new maman. I stamp on her foot.

The soldier with the skull badge closes the van door and Klaus screams and shouts to me to help because they've trapped his finger in the door, but they don't open it again and I will never forget their faces all squashed together and hot and cuddling each other because their mamans aren't there.

CHAPTER 10

A DANDELION SEED

Nina, aged six

'Smile!' says the man, but I don't because I am holding a slate that Maman has written on, saying *Do you know my twin sister, original name Odette?*

Lightning strikes my eyes and I blink and there is Odette in a green field, just her alone, trying to tell me where she is. I see her lips moving but I can't hear the words then I blink and she's gone and I shout, 'I can't see you!' and Maman says, hush little chick, it's just the flash.

It's our birthday, mine and Odette's, but I don't want to be six because that means I will have a birthday on my own, even though God made us be born in May and that's the perfect time for twins because it's Gemini and the stars know about us and our birth stone is an emerald and that was meant to keep us together.

Coco is a liar because she said that the emerald would help us.

The war is nearly over, and two weeks ago we went to a fête called Jour de La Victoire en Europe, European Victory Day, and all the church bells rang and everyone danced in the streets, and even Madame Soulier did a spin in the village square with the priest and the shop girls kissed the soldiers in front of every-body and nobody minded.

I searched and searched for Odette, and I had the ribbons ready to give her, so that she could look pretty for the party, but she didn't come back, and I didn't want to stay, and I went to sleep hearing everyone laughing and shouting, which spoiled my dreams to Odette.

Maman says I have to go to school in September. There are lots of new people in our village who look tired and old even though they are young, and Maman is one of them. Hitler did it to them and I hate him.

Maman says that now the war is finished, there's a good chance that Odette will come home, and this photo is going to be sent to Germany and they will glue it to walls and lamp-posts and trees and even outside schools and because I look so much like her I will be helping to find her. Maybe she is starting school, too.

Odette will like it here. I can climb right to the top of the orange tree and wave to Maman on the balcony and she is too far away to stop me and from there I am closer to the sun, which feels warm and kind, and the tree sends me perfume in clouds and I can sing to the sea and the sea whispers back, *Odette, Odette, Odette.*

I have new friends. We meet in the village square and sit on the edge of the fountain with our toes in the water and giggle and play games. I tell them I have a twin.

'No you haven't, she's an imaginary friend because you are stupid,' Jacques says.

I punch him because it's him who's stupid and he doesn't know and then he looks like he wants to cry and runs away.

Good. But Maman sees and makes me go to his house and say sorry but I won't and Monsieur Soulier, the one who found us in the hay cart, says it's OK I don't need to and Jacques says sorry to me because I DO have a twin and she's there in every game I play, my shadow in the bright southern sunshine.

Maman doesn't go out any more for the Resistance like the time I saw her getting the guns from the boat. But instead I can hear her crying at night, and it makes me sad because at the end of every day Odette is not here, and I want to cry too.

In the day, when I am with my friends, and we are tumbling in the meadows, or watching the ants take crumbs bigger than them back to their nest, or making daisy chains, or playing hopscotch, or using hazel to divine for water (no luck yet), or running races with the boys, Maman is sewing clothes for ladies in Paris.

Even though she uses a thimble, her hands look sore. Sometimes we don't have enough oil for the lamps and she can't work in the evenings and I tell her she should play games in the day with me instead but she says you're sweet, little chick, but Coco pays me better than most and when I'm working I'm occupied and don't have too much time to think and better that my silly brain doesn't have time to make up stories that won't let me sleep. I don't understand, because it doesn't work, because I know she doesn't sleep very much and she always looks tired.

I tell the priest at Sunday school that Maman is not happy, that I have lost my twin, but he says the lord works in mysterious ways, and many people have lost someone in the war, and it doesn't pay to dwell, and that I must look forward.

He's wrong, Odette, I will never forget you. Maman says we will never stop looking, but sometimes I think I will go to hell because when the Red Cross send a letter and Maman gets so excited and she is like she was before, I wish we didn't get them. That's because afterwards there's always another letter, which makes Maman's hands shake, and she won't even let me see it, and she throws it on the fire and is even sadder than before.

I ask her if the photograph helped. 'Yes, little chick, everyone is doing what they can so don't you worry,' she says, but I can see in her eyes that she thinks it's a lie.

I feel so small in this place by the sea, like a dandelion seed that's caught on the wind with no strength and no way of deciding which way to go even though I try so hard to find Odette in my dreams.

CHAPTER 11

THE DARLING IS A LIE

BERLIN, MAY 1945

Odette/Odelia, aged six

I live in a house now, with the pet who is actually called Dieter Fischer and his wife. I have to call them Mummy and Daddy. We have a housekeeper who is called Frau Müller. It's my birthday today and Frau Müller says my birthday cake is wasted on me because I'm a little Nazi and now the war is over the whole family will be sorry for what they have done.

She is leaving because she won't work for Nazis a day longer and anyway my mummy and daddy will lose their jobs and get punished so they won't be able to pay her the pittance she got for looking after a little Nazi brat and cleaning up after everyone.

I look at the cake. It's an *Apfelkuchen*, an apple cake, and if Nina was here, we would fight to get to it first but now I have it all to myself and I'm not hungry.

'What is a little Nazi brat?' I ask her.

'You,' she says, and slams the door.

I hear her arguing with Mummy, then another door slams, and I hear Mummy crying, and I know my birthday will be sad, because when Mummy cries we all have to be sad.

I leave the cake even though it's not polite and creep out into the hallway to see what's happening. Frau Müller's coat isn't on the hook, which means she's gone out, and I hear snuffling sounds coming from Mummy's bedroom, so I creep up the stairs and peep through the crack in the door.

'What do you want?'

I hide in a shadow.

'I know you're there, you little sneak. It's like having a bloody ghost in the house, always creeping around, always spying.'

I swallow a lump in my throat. This isn't safe.

'Come in here, now!'

I tiptoe in, trying to make myself small. Mummy sits up on her bed.

'See? This is what you've done to me, Odelia.' That's my new name now.

She points at the tears rolling down her face and I don't know what to do. I've tried to love her but I can't because of the volcano in my tummy. It burns me every day, hisses out *Odette, Odette, Odette.* There was another surname, a second one instead of Fischer, a French one, but I can't remember it anymore and I'm not even sure what I remember. A green ring, you Nina, Maman in a sunny place, in heaven. It's safe in my drawing book.

'Can't you speak for once?'

'I'm sorry.' But I'm not.

'You should be. We're going to lose everything. Your father's going to lose his job for being nothing more than a good soldier and following orders, and every time I walk down the street with you people say we stole you, when all we wanted to do was help.'

The word help makes her cry again and I put my hand on hers, like she's told me to, like a real daughter. She throws me off so hard I fall backwards but I jump up again, she doesn't like me to show weakness.

She narrows her eyes at me. 'You're not to mention the word Lebensborn, *ever*. Do you understand?'

I don't understand because everyone told me again and again that it was good, but I nod anyway.

'If anyone ever asks you about another time, in France, where you think you had another mother, a sister, you are never to mention it. You are mad, you were dreaming it anyway, but I've had enough of your nonsense. Do you understand?'

I can't let her. She's wrong. *Odette, Odette, Odette. And Nina.* Next time in the street with Mummy, if I hear someone whispering they stole me I will shout that it's true, if I dare.

I fold my arms and shake my head and she leaps from her bed and shakes me like a rag doll.

'Promise! Now!'

And I can't help it, I start to cry. She slaps me and it stings so hard and it's so unfair that it stops me crying. The volcano inside is bubbling like a witch's cauldron and I hit her back and scream to let it all out before it kills me.

I have counted seven night-times when I haven't been allowed out and my food was so small that I was hungry a lot. Mummy found my drawing book and the drawing of her, and she said it was ugly and it was all nonsense and she took it away. Even though I didn't cry about being locked up or hit, I sobbed about the drawings. How will I remember what came before? Mummy says I'm not allowed to draw any more even though at first, before she saw the drawing of her as a witch, she said they were good.

Today she is dressing me up in a stupid dress like a doll and we are going to the Webers' house where I have to be polite and not like a French peasant or I'll feel the back of her hand.

She goes into a *Konditorei* to buy a cake and she tells me to wait outside, she doesn't want me pressing my grubby hands all over the glass and drooling.

Then I see, on the lamp post, a picture of me.

It's a poster with a red cross on it and I am holding a slate saying something I can't read. Then I look properly. Soft eyes, a scar on her eyebrow. I haven't got a scar on my eyebrow. I check, and Mummy is still in the shop, so I scream, 'I am stolen, she stole me!' as many times as I can and Mummy comes rushing out and smiles like she loves me and says, 'Silly girl, what's upset you, come on I've got you a cake,' and she tears the picture and squeezes my arm so hard and pulls me down the street and I look at the people who heard me, but they are turning the other way, or looking kindly at Mummy like it's me who has done something wrong.

'You will pay for this behaviour,' she whispers and she sounds so mean, but she is smiling for the people in the street. I don't have any money so I can't pay her for my behaviour and I don't want to be locked up again in the dark.

Mummy makes me sleep in the cupboard under the stairs and the next day she doesn't speak to me for a whole day.

MAY 1946

It's my birthday again, but this year there is no cake. Mummy has had a baby boy called Wolfgang. I am not allowed to speak to her when she is with him, which is most of the time. I don't have my own room any more because he needs it, and Mummy and Daddy painted it blue, which is for boys, and put lots of toys in there. He has lots of teddy bears and he can't even hold them yet, so one day I picked up the biggest one to cuddle. I'm seven now, and I am too old for teddies, but I couldn't resist it because I miss cuddles and it was so nice and soft and its eyes were made of marbles and I pretended they were kind like Maman's. Mummy saw me and after that she said I am A Liability Who Can't Follow The Simplest Rules and I will be the death of her.

The cupboard under the stairs is not a punishment any more, it's my bedroom, and Daddy put a light in it, and I should be grateful. At night I wonder if they are right and I *am* bad, because I think so many bad thoughts about them.

My best times are when I sleep and I meet you in my dreams, Nina. We're squeezing cream through our teeth and laughing and everything is golden. When I can't remember what it was like to feel warm and safe with you and Maman, I imagine us swimming in a velvety green lake, our fingertips touching and I repeat, *Odette, Odette, Odette* and then I can sleep.

It's Very Important that I keep out of the way. I've learned how to be very quiet so that I can find out what is happening in the house and make sure I'm safe. After Wolfgang has gone to bed, Mummy and Daddy light a fire and drink schnapps and that is when they talk. It's dangerous to creep out of my room but sometimes I do, and tonight I listen at the door. They are talking about me in a mean way.

'I can't stand it. She's always *there*, like a dark shadow.'

'She's just a kid, I think you're overreacting.'

'Am I? Have you seen the way people look at me in the street? She's the only link to your SS past, and she's living proof, no matter how hard we've tried to cover it up. What if she blabs?'

'She doesn't remember anything; she was so little. Kids move on and forget. It's called survival.'

The volcano bubbles inside me. I remember everything. I remember you, Nina, and Coco, and Maman and the ring. They stole me.

Mummy's voice gets louder. 'We need you to get this job with the Soviets. It's the future, and I don't want Wolfgang to suffer for our past. She gives me the creeps with those staring blue eyes that look like they're on the verge of tears all the time. It's depressing. I've tried my hardest, darling, but I think we'd all be happier if she went.'

The *darling* sounds like a lie. She never calls him that. I should go, but I peep through the crack instead. He's kissing her. He's got his eyes closed, but hers are open. It's disgusting.

They pull apart. 'Will you think about it? Or maybe we can just sell the ring and get the hell out of here,' says Mummy.

'The ring's too recognisable, but since it's landed back with us we can't let it go again. Now the war's over we could sell it again for what it's really worth, but to get enough funds to live off for the rest of our lives we'd have to give it provenance, and that risks exposing us. We'll keep it and bide our time. I'll think of something.'

I am still peeking through the crack and trying very hard not to breathe too loudly. The ring. We sold a ring, the day he stole me. But did he get it back?

'In the meantime, God knows we need to move on if we're going to make it in East Berlin. She's a pretty little thing, a perfect-looking specimen, and I still dream of the master race, but you're right. Times have changed. I've managed to alter all my records, and downgrade my involvement in the war. There's nothing anywhere to suggest I was a fully signed-up member of the Nazi party and an SS officer, so you shouldn't worry. But I do take your point that she's living proof and she's the only thing left that I can't totally control in that respect. Maybe she's not worth the risk. I'll talk to the principal at Unter den Linden. She'll help. She was a Brown Sister and I helped cover that up for her, so she owes me.'

I don't like the Brown Sisters who ruled the Lebensborn homes, and I want to find out more, but I daren't stay any longer. I creep back to my room, avoiding all the creaky bits. I've learned. Maybe Mummy is right. I *am* a ghost, floating around this house trying not to be heard or seen and I don't belong anywhere. Nina, when are you and Maman coming?

The next day, Mummy wakes me up early and says some Very Important People are coming and I'd better not show her up. It's best if I keep my mouth shut and just smile when people talk to me, she says, and if I'm good I can have a doll and have her in my bedroom.

I want to say my own bed is in France but I don't dare, so I just think it and try and smile although my mouth feels all twisty. She puts my hair in rags to make ringlets and makes me wear a dress that I hate, with a sash that she pulls too tight but I don't dare tell her. I hear Daddy talking downstairs in his whiny pet voice, trying to sound like he is nice when he isn't.

'Go in, and smile at the gentlemen and try not to look like a peasant,' says Mummy.

I like peasants, I want to say. Rosie from the Lebensborn home says she was a peasant, so I'd rather be like one than any of my false family.

'Go on,' Mummy says, pushing me towards the stairs with her sharp fingernails. 'Make sure you kiss your daddy on the cheek when you see him.'

I go down. Daddy is in a brown suit. He never wears his uniform any more, and I'm not to speak about the skull badge I hated so much. The other men are also in brown suits and they are all saying things like comrade and socialism and talking about someone called Stalin but I don't know him and I don't understand any of the words.

'Guten Abend, Papa,' I say, then my tummy swirls because I still have a French accent and Daddy gets angry when I sound French.

He doesn't get angry though, he smiles with his big red lips but not his eyes, and he sticks his pink sausage cheek in my face, and I remember to kiss it, even though it tastes of sweat.

The men say *what a sweet little girl, so kind of you to take her in*, and I think about telling them that I'm not sweet, inside I'm bad and angry all the time. But I don't, I just sit in the corner and swing my legs while they talk and I try not to hum because only French peasants do that.

Then Mummy comes in and she has stiff hair and her face is caked in powder and her red lipstick makes her look mean. The men all stand up and she smiles at them trying to please them like she wants something, and they're all looking at her hand and looking kind of surprised. Then I see it. The ring that Coco gave to Daddy, and she said it would stay near me like a promise, and he sold it and he got lots of money and he stole me. Now *she's* wearing it and I miss my real maman and my sister so much that I can't pretend any more and I feel the volcano making me so hot that I explode.

'That's mine!' I shout. I charge Mummy and kick her. It feels good.

'What on earth?' she says and I start crying and turn to the men and say, 'That ring is mine, and...' I start to tremble, and everything is going wrong and I'm so scared that I nearly wet myself but I cross my legs.

My wrong family don't get angry though. Mummy hugs me and she smells of hairspray and perfume.

'Dear thing. Her mother gave this to me for safe-keeping. These little refugees need time and love, that's all. There, there,' she says, squeezing my arm so hard I almost fall over.

'Yes,' says Daddy. 'In fact, that's partly why I asked you here today. Sadly, her family were bourgeois collaborators, and I'm not sure how this valuable piece came into their hands, but I intend to gift it to the glorious new republic, to the Littenstrasse Museum, so everyone can enjoy it. I understand it's a magnificent jewel, with a long history, valued by the Colombians for its size and flawlessness down the generations, and with many a story to tell, if the myths surrounding it are to be believed. Of course, I could have kept it, and profited from it, but as a symbol of my dedication to the future of the Union of Socialist Soviet Republics, and a revocation of all worldly goods in favour of the equal distribution of wealth, I'm gifting it to the state.'

The men look sideways at each other and nod like he's done something good.

Daddy is pleased and he carries on. 'It's not entirely mine to give, however. She's right, this little girl's mother wanted her to have it, so I suggest we put it in trust for her until her twenty-fifth birthday, at which point her re-education will be complete.'

I'm so relieved that they don't put me in the cupboard that I calm down, and let Mummy cuddle me. It feels nice to be cuddled and my body is still shaking from big sobs.

When they leave, Mummy slaps me and shuts me in the dark straight away. I shout and shout to be let go until it hurts and nothing comes out. I lie on the hard floor humming the song Maman sang us to sleep with, but it just makes me miss her even more so I stop and close my eyes and try and pretend I'm at home again.

The next day, Mummy says, 'I told you that this little devil will be the death of us. She's cleverer than you think, and she did it on purpose. You can't be a Stasi commander while you've got a Lebensborn brat in the house. The new regime has ways of finding things out, and if they do, we're finished. She'll have to go to the orphanage. We've done our best.'

If there's a Brown Sister in charge, it won't be good.

BOOK TWO

CHAPTER 12

MELTING STARS

Nina, aged sixteen

And she is there, just beyond my reach, as she has always been for the last eleven years.

I look at myself in the mirror. My eyebrows are tweezed, which makes my scar more prominent, but I'm still happy with the results.

'Happy birthday, Odette, sixteen today,' I whisper. My reflection smiles back. My cropped haircut, lopped fresh and new to say goodbye to the war years, ironically reminds me of the two of us that fateful day at the Ritz, two little things with soft, cropped curls, stuffing ourselves with cream cakes and arguing like any other children. I still wince when I think about the red ribbons.

I hope you've cropped your hair, too, Odette, so we still look identical. Have your lips grown full and hungry, hoping to be kissed? Do your pale-blue eyes have the same tinge of sadness, too old and knowing for a teenager? I hope they're defiant, too.

I'll never forget, never stop looking. I know you're looking too, Odette. Don't ask me how, I just do.

Are you dressing up? Will you go to a party? I won't look like the other girls at the fête tonight. They're all planning nipped waists, pretty flower prints and full skirts, but Coco has given me a dress, which I love, Odette. Do you remember Coco? She still helps us, gives Maman a little work in return for having an excuse to pay her.

I wish you were here to help me with Maman. She's sad more than happy nowadays, and I try not to think about it too much, or I'd never smile. She talks about you every single day. The Red Cross are looking for you, and every year they take a picture of me, make up posters and flyers, update the files and pass it to all their contacts in Germany. I worked hard on German at school so when we find you we can talk.

I twirl in the mirror and the black chiffon floats out elegantly, the thin cream ribbon cinches the waist, the same colour as my seed pearl necklace. It's simple, a classic Chanel Little Black Dress with a square neck and spaghetti straps, and everything fits perfectly.

I hold up my hand to the mirror. See? I'm wearing our ring, the fake Emerald Lake. Imagine you standing next to me, wearing the real one! It's yours, worth a million red ribbons. I'd happily stay poor for you to be rich. I'm blowing you a kiss, Odette. Please don't forget us. Have a lovely evening, I hope, wherever you are.

But I don't want to leave the mirror, to leave my sister. Just... please come home, tell us you were happy and safe. Tell us he didn't hurt you.

I often think about the twin life that might have been. The one where you were here over the years, playing in the garden with me, giggling at the dinner table, playing twin 'swap' jokes on people, sitting next to me at the school desk, siding with me in playground fights, making Maman laugh like when we did roly-polys and jumped up at exactly the same time with our eyes crossed. Now we'd be sharing secrets about boys and you'd be standing beside me, looking in the mirror. Your dress would be the opposite, cream with a black bow at the waist, black seed pearls instead of my white ones, and we'd be the most stylish May Queens at the fête. There'd be four of us with the two in the mirror, happy and carefree, the light side of the mirror instead of the dark.

'Jacques is here, Nina.'

I have to go, he's taking me to the fête tonight. I think you'd like him, he's got dark skin like carob, and the bluest eyes, and he makes me laugh. I hope you have someone, too.

I blow a kiss to the mirror, a Brigitte Bardot pout, less for Odette, more to see how it looks for Jacques.

I'll tell all later, Odette.

Maman looks at me strangely, like she's lost something.

'You look absolutely beautiful, chérie.'

I give her a distracted smile, but Jacques is waiting in the hall, wearing a suit and a white shirt, and I've never seen anyone so handsome in my whole life. I let my wrap fall a little from my shoulders and his blue eyes melt, and...

'Nina?'

'Yes, Maman?'

'Home by ten, promise?'

'I'm sixteen, that's so early. Everyone else is allowed until eleven, it's not fair.'

'Life isn't fair,' says Maman wearily.

'Mine isn't, that's true.'

I know that look from Maman, the shadow of Odette, standing next to me. I immediately regret lashing out, because she seems tiny and thin all of a sudden and I want to escape this horrible feeling of guilt, so I kiss her on both cheeks and she waves me off with tears in her eyes. Happy ones, I hope, because oh it's a glorious evening, the sky is translucent, flushed pink, the sea inky, the rising moon filled with possibilities and Jacques' arm is warm around me.

It's another year since the war, another year without my twin. Just tonight, I want to forget. I dance all night with Jacques in the village square, sip champagne with my friends, watch the stars blur as I spin and laugh for being here on this night in my pretty dress, feeling beautiful. Sixteen is fear and lust and mischief and heaven and I drink enough champagne to obliterate Odette's shadow and lose myself in Jacques' blue eyes.

The boats in the harbour are strung with lights and flags, the stars have melted, and the moon traces us in silver as we kiss on the beach, Jacques' urgent weight on top of me, my Chanel dress pulled up to my thighs. I vaguely hear the church bells strike ten, but I don't care.

'Stop,' I whisper when Jacques' hand slips under my dress.

He rolls onto his back, we hold hands, the sea fills the silence, breathing in and out, rolling the pebbles.

'Remember when you punched me, and I had to apologise to you?'

Odette again, the day he said I didn't have a twin when we were playing in the village. I am never free. 'You deserved it.'

'Do you ever think of her?'

'Every day... every minute.'

'I'm sorry.'

I touch the replica Emerald Lake instinctively. 'It's like we're still connected. Maybe it's wishful thinking.'

'To think there's two of you. Devastating,' he says with an affectionate grin.

I run to the shore, feel the foam on my feet, scoop up the water, phosphorescent sparkles trailing like shooting stars in the sea, and throw it at him. He kicks up the water and it splashes my dress, so I run, every part of me sparking like an electric wire for him, and we kiss and walk back to the party, fingertips touching, charged with the night.

The church strikes eleven, the half-hour, then twelve. Maman is going to kill me, but I don't care, I feel as light as a feather, revelling as I float on the wind, no longer the helpless dandelion seed taken against its will.

Jacques walks me home along the firefly lane.

'You were different tonight.'

'It must be the dress.'

I twirl and he catches me for another aching kiss. He was right, tonight I was just Nina. Not Nina without Odette, and the sadness that follows me is gone. I resent the guilt at its return, make myself hope that Odette has had the same blissful sixteenth birthday. Odette falls into step with me in the moon's shadow and the spell with Jacques is broken. I'll never be whole without her.

'Now you're doing it again.'

'What?'

'Like you're only half here,' says Jacques.

'That's because I can't let you have the whole of me, not yet.'

I look at him through my lashes, revel in the hope in his eyes.

'Come on, I'll dance you home.'

And he spins me in a kind of old-fashioned waltz down the lane, the fireflies making circles in my eyes. The air turns colder when he leaves me at the front door.

He turns and waves. 'Can I see you tomorrow?'

I wave and blow him a kiss. His tall figure disappears back down the sandy lane, and I send a little bit of my heart with him, shocked at how lonely I feel without his eyes on me, but desperate to tell Odette every detail of the night.

I don't hear a word from Maman, so I slip my shoes off, creep up the stairs and find Odette in the mirror.

A girl with dreaming eyes, a dishevelled strawberry-blonde crop and a chic black dress, slightly skew-whiff, stares back, bewitched and breezy from the sea air, champagne and kisses.

'Let me tell you about Jacques...'

Odette listens, but I drift off, and I can't find her in my dreams. It doesn't matter. I'm sixteen now, time to put all those babyish notions behind me.

I wake up, the sun creeping through the shutters in shards, and I've found her again, in the hours just before dawn. We're two stick figures with triangle dresses, a line flicked at the shoulders for our hair, floating through the green stone in parallel, hands not quite touching, the sound of the pebbles rolling on the beach drowning out our voices. I hoped my dreams would stop because, although Odette needs me, it makes me so sad. Now I know that they'll never stop, not until we've found her and I feel guilty that I ever wanted them to.

I jump out of my bed, hop over my little black dress pooled carelessly on the floor, and go to find Maman. Time for another photo, another Red Cross poster. There's always hope.

Maman is still asleep, the church bells ring nine times. It's so late. I thought she might be up last night, ready to scold me.

I knock on her door. No reply. I push it a little, peep round the door.

'Maman,' I whisper, creeping closer. Something isn't right. Marble skin, red hair flecked with grey, worry lines smoothed out, a stillness in the air, a void. Rising panic... no, no, no. I force myself closer to her face. No breath. I touch her hand, it's freezing cold. *Maman. Maman, you can't leave me.*

CHAPTER 13

GREEN VELVET

Odette/Odelia, aged sixteen

I knock on the door of the principal's office and visualise my drawing of her in my notebook. Head of a kitten, body of a Rottweiler. Obviously she doesn't answer straight away. Power's her schtick and she does it well, but Odelia Fischer, über-rebel of the Unter den Linden Children's Home, has got her ways, too, and we both know it.

'Enter,' rasps the voice forged by a forty-cigarette-a-day habit and decades of shouting at small children.

I sit down before she can offer me a chair. She looks down her nose at my brown knees and tight pencil skirt, taken in expertly from the frump-fest it was.

'Shorter than regulation.'

She just can't help herself, even though she can't tell me what to do now.

'It's my leaving outfit and I like it.'

Code for, however hard you tried, you never broke me.

She takes a drag on her fag, shuffles some paperwork on her desk, peels the top page off and hands it to me.

'Just sign it, and we can get this over with,' she says.

Nice, coming from my surrogate mother for the last eleven years. I read the words I've dreamed of since the tender age of four.

```
Unter den Linden Children's Home

Notice of release: Odelia Fischer
Age: Sixteen
Onward accommodation: Schönhauser
Women's Hostel
Profession: Seamstress
```

I point to the rest of the paperwork on her desk, slowly getting contaminated with her smoke fug.

'Let me see the rest before I sign,' I say.

'We clearly didn't succeed in teaching you any manners during your time here.'

'I learned everything I know from you.'

How to protect myself, how to shut down any human feelings. Life's easier that way.

'You are a rude, rebellious, nasty little madam and you will NOT be missed.'

Yesss, riled. I don't bother answering. Partly to show her I couldn't care less, but also because I don't want her to know how much I want to see the documents. Klaus told me that when you leave, they give you your history, everything, including all the information they have about your birth parents.

My hands are like jelly as I scan through the papers.

```
Parents: Dieter Fischer, Commander of
```

```
Intelligence, STASI. Spouse: Elke
Fischer, housewife.
Reasons for placement of adopted daugh-
ter, Odelia Fischer: Rejection by
parents of Nazi ideology, request for
correction of child, born to deceased SS
officer and unknown female Nazi
sympathiser.
```

I'm floored. That evil Nazi who stole me is now a top brass in the Stasi, the feared Ministry for State Security who have spies in practically every building in East Berlin. But his Nazi past has been kept secret all these years: it's the only way he could have made it in this brave new world. I've kept quiet about it all this time because he told me to, and – I have to admit – I am still a bit afraid of him. But now me, branded with his poison?

He won and I lost. He visited me occasionally in this home. Mainly to remind me of the dire consequences of naming any false memories I might have about my earliest years as part of his family. If you could call it that.

I was young, and the details are hazy. One thing I do know, never mind whether they insist otherwise, is that he was a Nazi. He stole me. I have a twin sister out there, and a mother, and a different name, Odette, though I don't remember a surname. And there's a ring, a beautiful emerald ring, supposedly in trust for me. I've never forgotten that, though everyone else seems to have.

None of it's any use to me now anyway.

I wish that Wolfgang would be friendlier. He's the kid who essentially supplanted me in that house, but he was only a baby, and you could say he's a half-brother. They brought him here a couple of times, but he looked at me like I was a wild animal, which in a way I suppose I was. Even though they were so horrible to me, I still felt a pang of envy when I saw the genuine love in my ex-parents' eyes when they looked at him, the pride when he spouted some lame fact he'd learned at his posh school. That's the problem with orphanage kids. Real families, however messed up, just *get* you.

I look the principal in the eye and see the look of spite, of victory, can't control the welling tear that she's relishing as it slips down my cheek. I'm not sure if it's rage, or heartbreak. It's both.

'I thought the Nazis kept immaculate records,' I manage. 'Where's the rest?'

'Sorry, I'm afraid that's all we know. So many records were lost in the chaos of war. I think you have enough to understand that you are irreconcilably born of bad blood and that gives me very little hope for your future, though we have done our best. Now, I think our responsibilities for you are finally disposed of. I don't expect any thanks from an ungrateful little Nazi. However, I do wish you the best for your future.'

She stands and offers me her hand.

The molten mess inside me rears up and I slap her fat cheek. It's heavenly to feel the flesh yield, hear the snap of the blow, see the red shape of my hand before she can even shuffle round the desk.

I'm out of there, clutching my papers and a small bag of belongings, before her little Rottweiler legs have reacted to the shock. A gaggle of kids, my gang, aged from five to fifteen, disperse into the shadows like frightened starlings. They were listening at the door. I can't allow myself a goodbye, show the regret I feel at leaving them to this hellhole. They salute me fleetingly, the two-fingered victory secret sign we have, and I send all my strength to each of them before the warder unlocks the door and I'm out, out, out onto the big wide boulevard.

It's raining in rods and I don't have an umbrella and I'm terrified, it all looks so big and looming, but I'm free, half of me feeling like a dandelion seed taken by the wind with nowhere to go, the other half as light as an angel's feather.

I dash to Littenstrasse and there's Klaus, like he promised. His sky-blue eyes are bright in the rain and his skin is brown as coffee. He never lets me down. From our earliest, terrifying first days at the Unter den Linden Children's Home to this moment, terrifying in a different way now that we are free, he's always been there.

We kiss, our first, away from the strict eyes of the children's home. He puts his hand on the small of my back to pull me closer and it's like the rest of the world has disappeared. The rain pelts us, mixes with my tears. He's the only one who's ever seen them.

'I still don't know,' I whisper.

'They didn't give you your papers?'

'Just about my ex-adoptive parents, nothing about the real ones. She's won, that witch had the last laugh.'

He tries to dry my tears with his hands, impossible in this rain, and I laugh and cry all at once.

'You never have to see her again. Don't let her win. You're out here, free, and she's still there, loathing her life and everyone around her. Just picture her, trapped at her desk, her arse getting wider, full of hate.'

The sound of marching feet makes us jump apart. Littenstrasse is filled with the FDJ, *Freie Deutsche Jugend*; the Free German Youth, marching to Alexanderplatz to mark the end of the war ten years ago. Soviet Liberation Day, my birthday. It makes me happy to see all those young people, excited about the future, in their blue shirts, waving rising sun banners.

'Equality! Freedom! Humanism! Democracy! Peace! Friendship amongst nations,' they yell. Yes please, to all of those. I am *not* a Nazi, I am one of them, and someone else, too.

We wave to them, 'Bravo!' and I wipe away the tears. *Forward*, I command myself. It's over.

No more corporal punishment for wetting the bed because of night terrors, no more force-feeding an ungrateful, 'deluded little madam' who can't eat when she dreams of her dead mother and sister, of being somewhere sunny near the sea, who cries like a baby when the principal tells her she was given away, that poor Frau Fischer couldn't wait to get rid of her, and who could blame her with such a difficult child?

I thought I was safer in the children's home at first, away from my adopted mum and dad. They just gave me back, like a broken toy. In those days I still had hope and faith, but I soon learned those things were just weakness.

I took care of myself. That's why I sew with my right hand, but the thing I really love, drawing, I do with my left. Left-handers were not permitted at the Unter den Linden home, but it's my secret. One day, I want to sketch my own designs and make jewellery with the most beautiful stones, like the one in the ring I'll never forget.

It's not the kind of ambition you tell anyone in a children's home about, but I have known it since I was ten years old. There was a day Klaus and I escaped. We made it all the way into West Berlin, just strolled right through the Brandenburg Gate like we owned the place. We saw the flower stalls and the shops packed with beautiful things and the women dressed in fashions we could only dream of in the East, pressed our noses on the windows of the jewellery shops. I had my notebook with me, sketched the clothes, picked a flower from the Tiergarten and pressed it in the pages, drew all the jewellery I remembered and filled a whole precious notebook. We were just children, but partners in crime, always running away and exploring. No one was ever the wiser and I knew there was a big wide world out there.

Now, I've escaped again: for good. I'm going to ace my life, prove everyone wrong, use the burning feeling that's always there as rocket fuel, so watch out, world... *I think.*

And part of me knows there's something else, too, something or someone I can't reach or see. Another me, but not me. It's hard to know what's truth and what isn't any more. Did my maman let me go, or did she fight to save me? Did I really speak French, did I really once see a poster with my face on it, but not my face? Did Rosie see my sister from the swing that day at the Lebensborn home in Lamorlaye, or was she just being kind?

Wild stories of family members sighted, desperately wished for, are rife in a children's home. Best not to think about it too much.

'Come on.' Klaus pulls me by the hand. 'What do you want to do to celebrate your freedom? Where shall we go to show off my beautiful girlfriend?'

He looks appreciatively at my pencil skirt and fitted blouse. I've cut my hair off too, and with it my last ties with childhood and that place. I cropped it like Audrey Hepburn in *Sabrina* (another escape with Klaus, to the cinema – free seats when we slipped in the trade entrance. Easy). It's a bit uneven at the back, because I let Frida do it and we were laughing so much her hand wobbled. But I like it, and so does Klaus.

We fall into step with the FDJ, then peel off into the place I've always wanted to go to. The Littenstrasse Museum.

We get a ticket from the desk, where the woman looks disapprovingly at the dripping mess we are, breathless from the rain and freedom, and start with the Romans. It's really old stuff, even jewellery that the Romans wore. Weird to think that people were obsessed with it, walking around in loincloths or whatever they wore.

There are gold bracelets, and necklaces that look like they were made yesterday, ones I would happily wear, and there are vicious Roman curses written on pewter, wishing illness and dark happenings to people who've wronged them.

'The principal's ancestors must go back a long way,' I whisper to Klaus and we giggle like kids.

Each room covers a century of styles, and by the nineteenth century, while I'm marvelling at gypsy rings made to fool highwaymen and lockets hiding old photos of lovers caught in silver, Klaus has had enough. That's all right. I haven't told anyone about my ring. Not even him.

We arrange to meet at the café back on Littenstrasse in an hour. He has got a job as a mechanic and he can afford to buy us a hot chocolate *and* dinner now. Poor Klaus looks so relieved to be leaving, but I just *have* to see everything.

The twentieth-century room is full of art deco linear shapes, fringed bags, jewelled insects, and designs inspired by the Romans and Egyptians, and I'm mesmerised to see how everything goes in circles. Then I'm stopped dead, because it's there, just as Fischer said it would be the day before they put me in the orphanage.

In a display case out on its own is a huge, oblong emerald, the size of a pat of butter, set in a gold ring.

I edge closer like it's on fire, try to keep a hold of myself like I've taught myself, but my insides are melting again. All the dream meetings, the passing like death from light to dark the moment that door closed behind me at the Ritz. The jumbled sequence of events, the auction where I felt the life drain away from me when I lost the last connection with my sister, my maman. It all floods back like a train about to smash into my tiny brain. Dangerous, real, terrifying, full of hope.

It's soft like green velvet, a pure, deep hue, set in gold, huge and beautiful and inaccessible. It belongs to me.

I can usually talk my way into, or out of, anything, but I'm incoherent when I speak to the bored-looking woman on reception.

'I need to speak to the museum director, or the person who

acquires stuff for this place, or anyone who knows about that emerald ring in the glass case.'

She finishes filing something, muttering to herself under her breath as she finds the exact spot for the paper, a study in contempt. I could learn a lot from her.

'Please, it might be the only way I can find my mother, and I may even have a twin sister!'

I sound like a mad thing. She slams the filing drawer shut and turns round, eyes hooded with disdain.

'You're going to have to be more specific.'

What do I tell her? I was taken, I shouldn't be here. I should be in another, better life with a double I'm not sure even exists. She looks me up and down.

'I'm busy, spit it out.'

I do the top button up on my threadbare re-fashioned blouse, untwist my skirt and lift my chin.

'I'm a student at the Humboldt University, studying jewellery design. My father, Dieter Fischer, the Stasi Intelligence Commander, sent me here to study the magnificent emerald you have on display as part of my research. It's very short notice, but would I be able to speak to someone who knows a little more of the history of the piece?'

My ex-dad's name gets her ruffled; a high-ranking Stasi official opens doors, it seems. No one needs to know we haven't spoken for years. All that training; years of white lies to avoid punishment for imagined misdemeanours at the Unter den Linden home had to pay off somehow. Apart from sewing, it was the only education I got.

She half closes her eyes, expressionless doesn't nearly cover it, and holds out her hand.

'ID.'

I hand it over. Odelia Fischer, fully signed up member of the FDJ, all-round good little soldier and ex-daughter of one of the most feared officials in East Berlin.

She hands it back with the silent treatment. I keep my face from showing the dark tide of homesickness that is threatening to knock me off my feet.

'Wait,' she says abruptly.

I have to sit down while she's buzzing through to whoever.

I can't hear what she says on the intercom, but when she's done she looks at me over her glasses and flicks her head in the direction of a dingy-looking corridor.

'Second on the left. He has five minutes.'

'Thank you,' I say, and I mean it. She almost cracks a smile.

Herr Abel, Curatorial Director is etched on a brass plaque on the door. I knock.

'Come,' says a thin voice.

Herr Abel is all angles, bony shoulders, pointy nose, triangular beard, a leather satchel slung over the back of his chair.

He looks up from a big old book with parchment pages like he's surfacing from under water.

'You're interested in the splendid emerald we have on display, I hear, young lady. What do you need to know?'

'How it got here,' I say. I know I should say more, but my jaw is trembling.

He cocks his head to one side. 'How so?'

I don't think I need to lie to this man.

'I mean I think I recognise it, from my childhood. I know this is going to sound completely ridiculous, but I think it could be the link to my real parents. I was taken under the Lebensborn scheme during the war and I've always wanted to find out more.'

Cards, and my heart, on the table. He looks cynical.

'The receptionist says you believe the ring is yours?'

'In a way, yes...'

He presses his little wire-rimmed glasses further up his nose.

'It would certainly make you rich,' he says wryly.

'It's not that I care about, it's the links...'

Even I don't know what I'm talking about.

'All I can say is that it was loaned to us by a generous donor, for a fee. A Herr Fischer, who I believe is your father. He told me that he'd acquired it from a Nazi who'd escaped through the ratlines, aided by the Catholic Church, to Colombia... and it's now back with its rightful owner. It's a splendid example of a near-flawless twenty-carat emerald, the best I've seen in my entire career, set in twenty-four-carat gold. That's all I know, and I don't really want to get involved in any family feuds,' he says.

I feel sick. He sold it, the day he stole me. Now he's got it back and he's making money out of it.

'He's not my father. He took me. I was a twin and he was a Nazi. I'm Odette, not Odelia, and, please, I need someone to help me. There's a link through that ring to my roots, I just don't know what it is.'

The man looks like he's seen a ghost. 'Listen, if I were you I'd just get on with your life. There were many displaced in the war, things we all want to forget. Your father's a powerful man and I'm busy. I'm very sorry.'

He stands.

'I can prove it,' I say. 'There's a mark on that ring that I made myself.'

He sits down again, leans forward and looks me straight in the eye. I return his stare. He exhales like he's been holding his breath all this time.

'What mark is that?' he says.

'Two stars, made from four lines each. I scratched them in desperation with the compass I always carried with me. They were to represent me and my twin sister,' I stutter, choking on the words. I'm drowning in a green lake, swirling, our hair mingles like seaweed and we giggle, then I'm ripped away by a fierce current, drifting in nothing.

'That was you? I wondered what vandal scratched that crude piece of graffiti onto something so precious,' he says gently. 'You were lucky it was twenty-four karat gold, it's soft enough for a child to make marks in. Are you all right? You're white as a sheet.'

'Can I hold it? I just want to see what it feels like on my finger. I've dreamed of it all my life.'

He shakes his head, then stops and looks up at me, and he looks like a different man. Softer, less like a curator with the Stasi for a boss and more like a person.

'You have to promise never to tell a soul.'

'My life is packed with secrets, that's easy.'

He takes some keys out of a safe. We walk in silence to the emerald room, and he locks the door behind him and lifts off the glass case.

The colour's even deeper than I thought, the hue of my dreams since I can remember. I look closer. It's crystal clear, but with just one tiny flaw, in the shape of a heart. That almost kills me.

'May I?' I say.

He nods encouragingly. I pick it up and it's like it's charged with an electrical current, with memories. I turn it over, and, there on the gold behind the stone, are my two stars: me and my sister. So I wasn't imagining it. This drawing is proof of everything they wanted me to forget. It makes me feel so utterly lonely, but at the same time, connected. If the Romans could believe in those pewter curses, I can believe in this.

I put it on. 'I'm here,' I say silently to the stone. 'Come and find me.'

CHAPTER 14

WINDS OF CHANGE

Fleur

Fleur woke up later than usual from a deep sleep. Everything felt tender, and she was weirdly tired. Then it hit her, the rising tide of new reality, like it had every morning this last week in France. Her beloved Nina was dead, taking with her a thousand secrets and Fleur's heart, and a new life was growing inside her. No, a collection of cells she didn't want needed to be dealt with like a grown-up.

She padded over to the balcony and opened the shutters. The wind took them, slammed them wildly against the wall as she flailed to secure them. The sea was racing with the wind, sending white horses speeding to the shore to crash in white spume against the rocks. Everything here was so *alive*.

The mistral wind blew her hair across her eyes, dashed past her and caught the pile of papers on the table, whooshing them in an exuberant swirl.

Fleur snatched them out of the air. 'Hands off!' she yelled as the wind flung her words to the skies. 'This is precious new information from the Red Cross and it's mine.'

She gathered it all to her chest and the wind abated. Even the mistral was stunned into silence; reams and reams of information about stolen children, little lives recorded in Nazi files like a quality-control inventory.

Fleur made herself a coffee and got straight down to work. Nina had never been great with anything online, and that was where Fleur was beginning to have new hope. Since Nina's secret searches over the years, new records had come to light, connections were made as digitised records were made available to linked agencies. Now, here, amongst the lists of departures, like a desperate, determined cry from the past, was Odette's name, circled by the new contact she'd made at the Red Cross.

```
Odette Lefevre, cleared for transfer to
Berlin through the Lebensborn programme.
10 May 1944, dispatched with B Group,
train departing Lamorlaye Lebensborn
Clinic for 09:00 Chantilly Gouvieux
train station, arriving Berlin Haupt-
bahnhof 12 May 1944 at 15:00 hours.
```

She put down the papers and hugged herself against the shiver that passed down the years. Taken from France, transported on connecting trains to a strange country where everyone spoke a different language. How did she feel as the kilometres rushed by, speeding her away from hope and home, from her mother and sister, a mite of five years old?

A photocopied black-and-white picture was next, a primary-school style picture, with rows of children arranged in height order, flanked by two nurses in dark uniform who wore aprons. They were the only ones smiling.

Fleur scanned the rows, and there at the front, amongst the

smallest children, was Odette, sitting cross-legged, scowling, her head on the shoulder of another little girl who was holding her hand.

The wind howled as Fleur wished she could reach out across the years. 'She's here,' she'd say to Odette's maman. 'Right here, alive.'

Who was the girl she was holding hands with? Fleur cross-referenced the names against the neat handwriting, so diligently done, for such horrible ends.

Rosie Beaumont Category 4. Lisp, narrower than regulation hips, flat nose, brachycephalic skull.

Racial value: Nil.

Pathway: Transportation to Auschwitz.

It is recommended that no further precious resources are allocated. Disinfection approved.

Disinfection? Fleur rushed to the toilet, vomited the coffee, wished for a moment that she could purge herself of this knowledge. But the reality of history was one she had to face.

'I'll be back,' she whispered to the photo.

Twenty minutes later she had taken the lane to the village, rushed past the little port with its old-fashioned painted *pointu* fishing boats bobbing to the dance of the mistral, past the mariners' chapel, the pharmacy, the cheery yellow boulangerie with a chattering queue, and into the morning market.

Huge yellow beef tomatoes, fragrant bunches of basil for a euro, glossy cherries, rotisserie chickens, fish stalls with red tuna and juicy prawns... it all looked tempting but made her retch.

She bought herself a plain baguette and picked at it, knowing she ought to eat something.

Delighted crowds made a hubbub, the stall-holders enticed the punters with cubes of cheese and the best saucisson in Provence while the mistral flapped the canopies and stole straw hats as seagulls wheeled on thermals and swooped for scraps behind the stalls.

It was all so precious and peaceful; like coming up for air, and she wanted to scream above the wind for everyone to treasure it, to hope for this for everyone. *Rosie Beaumont, Category 4.* How many more like her? The Lebensborns were the least of it. Many of them at least survived, but those Jewish children and others who were deemed worthless, millions of families, who died at the hands of the Nazis, were cruelly deprived of the sweetness of just living, with all the possibilities, the ups and downs, the simple pleasure of food on the table and a roof over your head. All those mothers and children torn apart.

Could she have a baby in this new place? In Nina's childhood home? She understood now that she was lucky to have the choice, and she felt different here. This little piece of France got into your bones, and it was a part of her she hadn't known till now.

She promised herself she'd think about it, make that appointment she'd neglected to make with the doctor, but now she'd chased away the nausea she had to get back to the papers, to Odette.

The mistral helped her back up the path with a chilly push. The locals at the market told stories of how this wind could drive you crazy, chip away at you until you wanted to scream, then chip away at you some more. It could cause you to drive erratically, make pets misbehave, it was said even murders could be forgiven during the mistral. For Fleur it was a wind of change; she just wasn't sure what that was yet.

Back at the villa she got back to work. The Red Cross

papers were secured with a paperweight, but the mistral was still grabbing at the edges. She closed all the windows and resumed her line-by-line analysis as a vine took up an incessant tapping at the window.

Hours passed while the wind howled, but it was worth it. There, the name again, so familiar now. Odette Lefevre. In 1944 she was adopted by Dieter and Elke Fischer, so the name to look out for would be Odette Fischer? After that, the trail went dead. No evidence of schools, medical records, none of the trails the Red Cross would expect to find. The only other information available about the adoptive family was that they had a son, Wolfgang Fischer a few years after adopting Odette.

She sent an email to her contact at the Red Cross outlining her findings, asking if there were any other trails that could be pursued, any other paths she could take to trace her great-aunt.

It was slow, painstaking work, but she still had Nicolas, and the Magnificent Rare Jewels auction in June. Nebulous, but there had to be a reason that Nina had held on to the replica ring all those years; a connection, like a fuzzy picture that hadn't come into focus yet.

The church bell rang two strikes. Where had the day gone? Jake would be on his lunch break. His workdays ran like clockwork, and if she didn't call now she'd need to wait another six hours – he never answered a personal call, not even to his fiancée, during work hours. It was time.

She superstitiously slipped on Nina's replica emerald ring to keep a part of her with her for the call. *What would you have done, Nina?*

'*Forward,*' Nina replied firmly.

Her thumb hovered over his name on her phone. Jake Parker. Fleur Parker. Mr and Mrs Parker. Fleur Lefevre. Who was she? She pressed his name. He picked up straight away.

'Fleur, you've been away too long, come home now,' he said.

She imagined him, swivelling on his chair to look out of the plate glass at the executive City view to stop himself being distracted by the emails pouring into his inbox, tugging at him like the mistral.

'I need more time, there's so much more to do, and...' said Fleur.

She heard the tap of the keyboard. The emails had won.

'Jake?'

'Sorry, just the bloody Canadians.'

'What's happening with them?'

'Without you here, they're hassling me with every tiny detail. I can't really give you any more time away. I've been more than fair.'

'Is this Jake my boss speaking, or Jake my fiancé? A bomb has exploded in my life, scattering relations I didn't know I had everywhere and—'

'Sorry, sorry, your mind must be all over the place, but life has to go on.'

The tapping stopped. He was trying.

'Jake, I've got something to tell you.'

'Shit, the deal's off! Bugger it, they're going to have my balls served up on a plate at the next board meeting. Sorry Fleur, what was that?'

'Jake, please, just step away from your computer for one minute. You haven't asked me how I am, so I'll just go ahead and tell you. I'm pregnant.'

'Jesus Christ, the Canadian deal's off, and now this! At least we can solve one of the problems quickly.'

The vine rattling on the window was driving her mad. 'Which one?'

'Being pregnant, of course. Thank God for modern medicine. It's quick, it's clean, and no one needs to be any the wiser. God, sorry Fleur, I'm so distracted, you know how I am at work. I can't think about this now, it's just a complete curveball. Can we talk about it later? Get yourself on the next flight and we'll talk and... we'll sort this out together. Don't worry about a thing.'

The wind burst open the French doors, inviting her out, out, out, of everything that had gone before.

She put the papers back in the file and pushed the doors shut against the mistral. No, he was right, she had to go back. She'd had weeks to think about this, to get used to the idea. It was a shock to Jake, and he hated surprises and change. He'd think about it tonight. He'd be sorry, and they'd face it together. It wasn't her decision alone. Everything else could wait. It was eighty years on from Odette's disappearance, and, though her story had gripped her like a fever, a few more days weren't going to make any difference.

She checked her phone. There was a flight back to Stansted tomorrow and she'd be on it.

'I'll be back soon, I promise,' she whispered to Odette, or was she speaking to her baby, or both?

It was like someone had turned out the lights when Fleur touched down in London. The train trundled past tower blocks and grey streets into Canary Wharf. At the tube station, thousands of city workers in corporate wear were plugged into earbuds, crowding the urban landscape of escalators, warrens of lit corridors, shoe repair booths, takeaway coffee shops and beeping ticket barriers, flowing everywhere like android ants. Here, in the epicentre of the City, you could smell the money, and it was a million miles away from her villa in France.

Until the last couple of weeks, this sight had filled Fleur with excitement after her Somerset countryside upbringing. This was a place with everything to play for, everyone young, ambitious and trying to make it.

She took the lift to Jake's penthouse apartment, wishing herself back by the sea, the orange trees waving in the mistral.

Stupid, just a dream she'd tire of if she actually lived there permanently, miles away from anywhere.

Jake opened the door and pulled her in, kissed her deeply, began to unbutton her blouse.

'God, I've missed you.'

'I've missed you too,' she said into his kiss, gently pushing him away. 'We need to talk first.'

He backed off, looking regretful. He *was* irresistible. Tailored trousers, white shirt with that expensive sheen only the finest cotton gives, sailing and skiing suntan, sweep of glossy hair with a carefully dishevelled lock over his brow, five o'clock shadow. She loved the confident brag in his eyes, full of desire for her. How had she forgotten so quickly? She was almost relieved to feel the same about him.

After the villa, the apartment was another world. Clean lines, tasteful lighting, a fortune's worth of *objets d'art* they'd collected together from London antique shop strolls, a view to die for over the Thames and beyond. Clinical, privileged, but breathtaking and glamorous, a bit like Jake.

'I'm such an idiot.' He smiled charmingly. 'But you're looking so beautiful, kind of wild from faraway shores. Dump your bags and I'll grab us a drink and we can talk. Sorry about earlier, I was so distracted. I'll tell you about that later, after we've talked about you. Just tell me everything,' he said, pleased with himself for being so considerate. Knowing him, he might have even practised in front of the mirror first. But with good intentions; he just didn't deal with emotions that well.

He pulled out a bottle of chilled white from the wine fridge and held it up.

'Pouilly-Fumé. Your favourite.'

'Thanks, but that makes me feel a bit sick at the moment.'

'God, sorry again. The sooner we get you sorted, the better. Perrier instead?'

Fleur couldn't help but feel annoyed at the 'sorted'

comment, but they'd talk, and to be fair he looked a bit nervous, which was not like him.

'Fine, anything.'

He sat next to her on the sofa. 'I was so worried about you, all alone out there. Nina was everything to you... and now this.'

'I don't know what to do.' Fleur hadn't expected herself to cry, but the tears were unstoppable, great heaving sobs. Jake held her tight, but she wanted Nina back. She'd know what to do.

'Hey, it's all right, we'll go to the doctor's together. I'll be with you every step of the way. I've googled it. If you're less than ten weeks, it can all happen here, in the comfort of the flat. You'll be up and running again the next day. I could even book a table at the Dorchester. Something to look forward to.'

'But... I think I might want the baby.'

He jumped back, like she was on fire.

'But we agreed! Listen, it's just the hormones going nuts. We've talked about this. Holidays, careers, travel, freedom to do anything we want. Babies are for other people, who like coloured plastic and dirty nappies and dinner party conversations about *schools*.' He shivered.

She looked out of the window across the City, darkness and a million lights, sanitised and still from up here, but the mistral was raging in her head.

He was right. They'd agreed they didn't ever want children. Fleur had been so sure. She loved her life with handsome Jake, the world at their feet, London with its theatres and restaurants and blend of cultures; never boring, always changing. Plus, with everything she was learning, how could it bring anything but heartbreak? Her own parents had died when she was tiny, Nina lost her twin sister and Fleur lost her beloved Nina too young. Who would want to bring children into the world with all that heartbreak, never mind climate change and war?

A light footprint, no ties, her clever, glamorous Jake at her side, no worries. A simple life. He counted in this too, and he was right, hormones and grief were clouding her vision. A quick trip to the doctor's and she could get on with her life.

She snuggled into him. 'You're right, I'm just so emotional at the moment, everything's happening at once. I need some sleep, and I need you. I'll make an appointment with the doctor tomorrow, see how far along I am, and I'd love you to come with me and hold my hand.'

'I'm here for you,' he said, gulping down an entire glass of wine in one go. 'Now, let me tell you about those bastard Canadians...'

He was on comfortable ground now, and his arm was warm around her, the sofa was Minotti, the softest cotton velvet and ergonomically designed to give its owner the experience of lying on a cloud. She drifted off, content, far away from all the heartache and mess waiting for her in France. She'd take a break, get back to it. Not giving up, just giving herself space to breathe, to grieve for Nina, and get over this blip.

The doctor beamed at them. Fleur had seen that look so many times when she was together with Jake – appreciative, a little wistful. It was ironic, sitting here, that they always looked like the perfect couple to other people.

'The blood tests have come back positive, and from what you've told me, it's likely you're around four to six weeks pregnant.'

Jake checked his phone. Fleur put her hand instinctively on her stomach.

'OK,' said Jake. 'Half of me was hoping it was a false alarm. But only four to six weeks gone? I believe we're well within the legal limits for an abortion at home?'

Jake had done his research.

'Yes, is that what both of you want?'

The doctor's voice was neutral, but he was focusing on Fleur's eyes. Did he know? Maybe he knew better than her?

Jake grabbed Fleur's hand. 'Yes,' he said, always so sure of everything.

'Fleur?' said the doctor.

'Yes, I mean I'm not sure, it's kind of hard to say the words,' stuttered Fleur.

'I thought we were agreed?' said Jake, an edge to his voice.

'We were,' said Fleur, trying to smile, but failing. God, this was so embarrassing in front of the doctor.

'Well,' said the doctor. 'You don't need to make any hasty decisions. It's entirely your decision. If you'd like me to refer you to counselling...'

'God, no,' said Jake. 'No need for that, is there Fleur? We're agreed.'

Fleur nodded. 'I just need a little time to get used to it all. My grandma – who was my mother really – has just died and... there's so much going on. Can you take us through the procedure?'

The doctor started to explain, but Jake was already distracted. He cut him short.

'I'm so sorry, there's a situation. I'm just going to have to step outside. You can catch me up on this later, Fleur.'

He gave her a peck and rushed out.

'Is everything all right?' the doctor asked.

'Yes, thank you, we'll work it all out.'

'Please come back if you have any more questions, and take your time,' the doctor advised. 'Rest assured, any decision you make will be the right one.'

Jake was waiting outside. He put his arms round her.

'It's all kicking off. I think the sooner we get this over with, the better, for both of us. I'll be with you every step of the way.'

'I'm still not sure, it just all feels so final. I need to talk to you.'

Jake checked his phone again, agitated. 'Listen, Fleur, I'm just not dad material. I'm too selfish, I like a tidy apartment, freedom, nice things, a beautiful grown-up like you I can play with. Let's face it, I'd probably drop the baby on its head, or the Canadians would pull a deal and I'd forget to feed it or whatever you have to do. What about your career and our plans? I think you'll feel a lot better when it's all over with. We've never wanted children, we were careless for once in our lives, that's all.'

'I've just got this feeling,' she said to his chest.

He stood back, hands on her shoulders, studying her with a strange look on his face, like he didn't know her. 'Pure chemicals, nature's clever like that. Listen, I've got to get back to the office. Let's talk later.'

His eyes were glassy and hard. She'd seen that look before, when an employee was asking for a promotion he wasn't going to give.

He hailed a black cab, gave the driver the address, told him to put it on account and bundled her in. 'Here, get yourself some rest. We'll talk, I promise.'

If he managed the Canadians as efficiently, the deal would be back on in no time.

The taxi driver caught her eye in the mirror.

'Lovely day for it,' he said conversationally.

'What, for an abortion?' she wanted to shout.

But she passed the time of day with him, pretended everything was all right while she was dying inside. Not dying, while something, *someone* was alive inside her. She couldn't shake the feeling. Was it because Nina had just died that the little life seemed so precious?

'Here OK?' the cabbie was shouting. They were outside the apartment block.

'Oh sorry, I was dreaming,' she said.

'No worries. Everyone should every now and then. Go steady,' he said brightly as she got out.

Fleur curled up on the sofa. What the hell was she going to do? It was impossible to separate all of this from Nina dying, and poor Odette, all these heightened emotions. Somehow the doctor visit had made it so real. It was one thing doing a pregnancy test on your own in a villa you didn't know you owned, amidst finding out about a dramatic new family history that set you alight. It was another sitting in a doctor's surgery on a rainy day in London with a fiancé desperate to get the whole thing over with.

She hadn't even spoken to her best friend, Jude, about it. She never said, but it was obvious she wasn't keen on Jake, so she'd be biased. On the other hand, she had to talk to someone about it, and the one person who would have known what to do was Nina, and she was gone forever.

Fleur picked up the phone and found Jude's number, but before she could press it Nicolas's number flashed up.

'You couldn't make this up. Well, maybe *I* could, but...'

'I'm assuming this is Nicolas?' said Fleur.

'Of course,' he said. 'The irony is going to kill you. That Nazi was swallowed up by the place that created it. It's like a film or something. Divine justice.'

'What are you talking about?'

'It's too complicated over the phone and I'm at work.' He lowered his voice. 'I've accessed some files I shouldn't have. I can come over tomorrow at midday. Send the address of your villa. Got to go.'

He clicked off. Fleur checked her phone. There was a flight out to Marseille that evening. It was crazy to fly there and back so soon, and she was exhausted. But the villa was the only place she could think straight at the moment, another world, different from this one, with other possibilities, a different Fleur.

From what the doctor had said, they wouldn't be able to

arrange an abortion until next week anyway, and she could talk to Jake on the phone. His physical presence was too distracting. He could just melt her with one look, and she didn't need that at the moment. Was the problem hormones for the baby, or her love for Jake? Or both?

Plus, she had to get through to him how much she needed him to talk about this. While she was there, available, in his apartment, he wouldn't take her seriously enough. He'd be shocked she'd left, but then maybe he'd understand what was at stake. Maybe even she would.

Besides, Odette was still waiting for her somewhere, either in the past or in the present, and she had to find her.

CHAPTER 15

DARKNESS AND LIGHT

Fleur

The mistral had subsided when Nicolas came bouncing down the track in a reconditioned 2CV convertible. Of course. What other car would he have? She smiled to herself as he slammed the door and strode up to the house muttering to himself in his dusty espadrilles and frayed Breton top, eyes bright blue against dark skin.

They kissed on both cheeks, then he whistled with a sweep of his arm towards the garden stretching down to the sea.

'Not a bad place,' he said.

'I didn't know I had it till a few weeks ago.' *When I also found out I was pregnant*, she wanted to add. Why did she want to talk to him about it – something about him being neutral, entirely separate from everything?

'Well I've seen worse surprises,' he said.

'Coffee?'

They sat under an orange tree sultry with blossom, heady

perfume mixing with the fragrant resin of the umbrella pines coaxed out by the hot sun, the sea shimmering in the distance. Perfect, in contrast to everything churning around in Fleur's head, and all the more beautiful for it.

Nicolas took a distracted sip of coffee.

'I'm not really sure where to start.'

'You always seem to start just past go – how about there?'

He scratched his head and laughed. 'You've got me. OK. The Nazi ended up dead at the bottom of the mineshaft where they'd originally discovered the Emerald Lake.'

'Bloody hell, what? Now rewind a little.'

Nicolas took another slurp and a large bite of the pissaladière he'd bought for them both to eat, and swirled his finger next to his head to indicate he was ordering his thoughts while he chewed.

'Right, from the start. SS officer Gustav Raschmann bought the ring at auction for next to nothing in 1944. Then he fled to Colombia at the end of the war. All I did was google his name, and Colombia. The information was pretty easy to find because he'd fallen down it and was killed and it was big news at the time. The irony was that he fell down the very mineshaft that yielded the raw gem that became the Emerald Lake. Locals refused to go down and get him, and also refused to work on that particular seam after the accident – something about the tears of the moon goddess. There's documentary evidence in their storytelling tradition which tells us what we already knew – they believe that the heart-shaped inclusion gives the emerald powers, but with an extra twist. As well as believing it brings people together, there's a kind of curse attached to it, that— Hold on a sec, I've written it on my phone.' He fished it out of his pocket and unlocked it.

'Smites down evil and rewards togetherness.'

He took another enthusiastic bite with wide eyes and open hands, waiting for her conclusion.

'I'm not quite with you,' said Fleur, struggling to keep up.

'Raschmann was an evil bastard, so he was finished off in the emerald's birthplace, and the now the emerald wants to reunite your grandmother and great-aunt. It's obvious!'

'If you believe in that stuff, which I don't,' said Fleur, laughing.

'I'm not sure I do either, but why not suspend disbelief for a moment, give divine retribution a chance? It's sublime when you think about it. I've told you this before, precious gems kind of attract things. Whether it's because they're ridiculously valuable, and therefore things happen around them, or it's the stories people imbue them with, it's perfect, and circular. You can't deny that. I'll email you the article.'

He polished off the pissaladière, and slumped into the chair, exhausted from the perfection of the tale.

'I'm glad that bastard got his comeuppance, but does it get us any closer to Odette?'

'I've already told you it does!'

'No, you didn't, I think that's still in your head,' said Fleur.

'I managed to hack the records. They were password-protected for some reason, but auctioneers are dull and predictable creatures. A bit of messing around with variations on *diamond* and *carat*, some rudimentary knowledge of coding and... voila, the Emerald Lake comes hurtling back to Europe.'

Fleur's heart skipped a beat. 'You mean you've traced it beyond Raschmann? Where to?'

'A little museum in East Berlin, donated in 1954 by a local civil servant, Dieter Fischer.'

Fleur hugged herself against echoes of the past. 'That's the name of the person who adopted Odette. You win. Now I *am* prepared to believe anything. It found its way back to her!'

Nicolas nodded enthusiastically. 'Yep. We're getting somewhere.'

'It's a breakthrough! There's something about this place that makes anything seem possible.'

'It suits you,' said Nicolas. 'Even with red hair and pale skin, you look like you belong here in this shade under the trees, the sea beckoning.'

'I kind of do,' said Fleur, 'as much as anyone belongs anywhere. Sort of half here and half back in London.'

She didn't mention Jake. Too difficult with the baby thing.

'Come on, let's go,' said Nicolas, jumping up.

'Where?'

'For a swim of course. Look at it, blue and smooth as a cabochon sapphire, just waiting for us. It's not often the mistral leaves the sea so unruffled. Can't be missed.'

The day was hotting up, and it did look very inviting.

'Why not?' she said.

They strolled down the sandy track, with its tangles of juniper, thyme and oleander lining their way to the little cove. Nina would have passed this way a thousand times with her maman, and now here Fleur was with her own baby, rejoicing in the wildness, the salty air curling her red hair.

Her own baby. Is that how she thought of it now?

Nicolas stripped off and ran in as soon as they got to the sea, diving straight under. He shook his curly mop when he surfaced.

'It's lovely! Come on.'

She stripped down to her underwear, but couldn't get in as quickly as Nick did, and trod gingerly, wobbling on the pebbles, but it was glorious, a million different colours of blue, crystal clear, with colours dotting the rocks below, the water silky on her skin.

They swam out a little way, and Nick sculled on his back to appreciate the cliffs, squinting against the sun.

'It's incredible and unique here. Limestone, sandstone and *poudinge*, from your English "pudding" – a pebble conglomerate. Eighty million years ago it created the perfect environment for fossils, and they're still in there, waiting to be discovered. So many stories, lives lived and lost. Sort of humbling, isn't it?'

The sky was pristine, the cicadas buzzed on the shore and the cliffs towered up like ancient witnesses to the madness, the beauty, all the cruelty they must have seen.

'It's like being on the edge of the world,' Fleur murmured.

She floated on her back next to Nick and sculled, body undulating with the ebb and flow as the sun played on the waves. She closed her eyes and listened to her heart swishing in her ears, surrendering to the warmth of the sun and the green-blue depths enfolding its secrets of pearlescence and bioluminescence. She'd read somewhere that sea urchins were blind, but responded to light by changing colour, and that was how she felt, suspended in this wild place.

They drifted side by side for a while, but then the peace was shattered by a speedboat rushing straight into their bay, the hull raised so high the driver was invisible. *Shit.* Their frenzied waving was useless, the roar was deafening as it cut a wide loop in a furious wake of foam, engine screaming as the propeller sawed a path straight at them.

Too late. Fleur froze in disbelief, time slowed. She swam, but not fast enough. Two arms dragged her down, she thrashed wildly, lungs burning. Nick. He was kicking hard while the motor above churned the surface in muffled booms. She fought to join the downward trajectory, drawing on every last scorching bit of air in her lungs as Nicolas pulled them closer to rocks where the speedboat couldn't follow.

They surfaced, panting, shocked and shivering violently. Fleur watched through stinging eyes as the speedboat headed back into the expanse beyond the bay.

'It's all right, we're OK, just keep floating, don't panic. Jesus, that arsehole nearly killed us.'

Fleur was shaking so hard she couldn't speak. He gripped her arm.

'Breathe, relax. Look at the sky. Can you swim now? You can't let yourself go into shock. We have to move.'

Fleur couldn't stop shaking, the sea was freezing. She shook her head.

'You have to. I'll be right next to you. Just a few centimetres at a time. Come on. Two strokes, breathe. Two strokes, breathe.'

Nick dragged and coaxed and they made it back to shore, where she collapsed onto the warm pebbles. What the hell had just happened?

Nick fetched their clothes and gave her his shirt to wear. She wrapped herself tight in it, hugged her knees.

'I'm usually a good swimmer. That was horrible.'

'You're still in shock. Come on, we'll get you back to the house and get some hot tea inside you.'

'I'm just going to sit here for a second and gather my strength,' said Fleur, hugging her knees to her chest.

Funny how life can turn on a sixpence, Nina had always said. Now she knew why. Things must have turned from light to dark in a heartbeat when Odette was taken. How different things could have been for her if Nick hadn't dragged her under, away from that whirring propeller. They leaned on each other in silence side by side as the sun brought them both back to life, bedraggled and relieved. Nick had a steady energy, like the rocks he loved so much.

'Are you OK?' he asked, and his eyes looked like home and somewhere strange at the same time and, in that moment, she let herself kiss him; a salty, charged, affirmation that they were alive.

They broke apart. He looked surprised.

Fleur jumped up, embarrassed. 'Sorry, I didn't mean that.'

She hastily shrugged off his shirt, threw it at him and wrapped herself tight in her towel, started gathering her things.

Nick picked up a glittering pebble and studied it. 'Hematite,' he mumbled before chucking it in a high arc. It landed with a sparkling splash and the moment passed. Out in the bay the speedboat was still visible, docking with a yacht in the distance, and whatever idiot was driving it was back on board the yacht. They walked to the house in silence, the low sun vivid with regrets for the end of the day.

As she opened the door to the house, a pain grabbed her whole midriff and gripped her back in a vice. She bent double, crouched on the floor.

Nicolas rushed over, stopped short of touching her.

'Are you OK?' he said awkwardly.

She curled into a ball of agony. 'I don't know.'

All she could do was concentrate on the pain. *Don't leave, I want you to stay, whoever you are*, she whispered silently to her baby. She focused on her breathing, managed to stagger to the sofa.

'I'll call an ambulance,' said Nicolas.

'No, I get this, it's... my period. Looks worse than it is.'

'I'm ignoring you,' said Nicolas, unlocking his phone.

'No, really, this is normal,' she lied. Not an ambulance. She was scared, but she'd never heard of anyone dying from a miscarriage. Better to wait it out in Nina's house. Whatever would be, would be.

'It looks pretty bad from where I'm standing. Are you sure?'

'Yes, I just need to get into bed and lie down.'

'Here,' said Nicolas. 'Link my arm, I'll help you up.'

She leaned on him, and he tucked her in when she got into bed, waited silently until the pain subsided a little.

'I'm not leaving you on your own. You look wobbly, like a gem that's about to fall out of its setting. I'll stay till the morning, and if you don't feel any better I'm taking you to the doctor first thing.'

Fleur felt lonely as hell, she wanted him to stay more than anything. She nodded her thanks.

He hesitated, not wanting to leave her. 'Do you need paracetamol or anything?'

Through her pain she vaguely tried to remember if any of her pregnant friends had taken it. Better not to risk it. 'No, I'm fine, really,' she managed.

'Shout if you need anything at all,' he said.

She closed her eyes. *Stay, little one. I'll take care of you if you do, I promise. We'll work it out together.*

Funny how life can turn on a sixpence, Nina repeated from somewhere as Fleur hovered on the edge of fitful sleep, dreaming of twins and golden threads, seams of emeralds, the cruelty of separations. Please, no more slipping from light to dark tonight.

Fleur woke to the sound of eight chimes in the village. She'd slept through, and the pain had disappeared. She checked between her legs. No blood. Oh, thank God. 'Are you staying?' she whispered to her stomach.

The iridescent green butterfly that had settled on the wall since her arrival left its hiding place and fluttered against the shutter. She opened the windows and it soared out into the morning sun. Fleur watched till it disappeared.

'Is that a sign of life, or death?' she asked the air.

The smell of coffee drifted up from downstairs. In the time between sleeping and waking she'd forgotten that Nicolas had stayed. She pulled on a robe and went downstairs, and laid out on the kitchen table was a feast. Croissants, fresh bread, raspberries, Charentais melon, orange juice, a moka pot bubbling on the hob.

Nicolas looked a bit embarrassed at the effort he'd made.

'I've been to the market and back. I was worried you hadn't eaten.'

'Thank you,' said Fleur, leaving all the other unspoken things to hang between them. She hadn't even worked it out herself yet. It was just too much to tell.

'I came in to check you were breathing last night and you were crying in your sleep. You know sometimes it helps to tell secrets to a stranger?'

'I'm flattered you think I have hidden depths, but it's just me, myself and I,' she said with a brittle smile.

'Call it gemmologist's intuition. I just know if a client has something valuable to show me as soon as they walk in the door.'

'Nothing to see here.' She hid her face in her coffee cup as best she could. Nicolas pushed a croissant across his plate.

'I stayed up last night to do a bit more research,' he said, on more familiar territory, 'but I didn't get very far because the password stopped working. It's weird because I could tell the files on the Emerald Lake hadn't been accessed for years before I found them, so there's no reason anyone should have noticed, or bothered to change the password. If I can find the person who archived everything, they might be able to point us in the right direction. So that's next on the list...'

The doorbell rang and she checked the clock. She'd redirected all her post to the house in France in case she missed anything about probate, and the postman was always on time.

She opened the door in her dressing gown, coffee in hand, and Jake was standing there in freshly pressed chinos and designer sunglasses. He pulled her to him, then saw the scene over her shoulder. Nicolas was sitting at the breakfast table, sipping coffee.

Jake's face fell. 'This looks cosy,' he said.

CHAPTER 16

PERMISSION TO LEAVE

Nina

Coco presses my hand tight. I turn away when she throws a handful of earth and a bunch of camelias for Maman's name, Camille, into the freshly dug trench. My beautiful maman's body is in the lead-lined coffin, dark and cold, the grave deep and final.

The priest mumbles some words I can't hear through the swirling grief that muffles my senses like fog, turns me in on myself. My body won't last me through this tide of longing for my maman. I just want to lie down and die and be with her again.

She knew she was going to die one day, but she waited till my sixteenth birthday, when I was old enough to be on my own, Coco told me. But she was wrong. I have never felt more like a lost, frightened little girl than today. She shouldn't have left me, but she had no choice. She died never having found my sister, knowing she was going to leave me alone.

I wish you were with me, Odette. Losing you was a long, slow death for her and if we had found you she would still be with us, I'm sure of it.

I touch the replica ring like a talisman, and the spring sun throws green shadows through the stained glass of the chapel window out into the graveyard, onto the coffin – it's Judas' cloak that casts the colour. Who was it that gave our presence in the Ritz away that fateful day a lifetime ago? So this is how it ends, in another tragedy, a blighted life, one of a million sad stories forgotten-not-forgotten behind forced smiles and glassy eyes, now that everyone wants to put the war behind them.

A hundred sympathetic gazes are on me; everyone who knew Maman in the village loved her. The priest collected stories; her bravery in the Resistance, which saved countless lives, the pride she had in me, the search she never gave up on for her lost daughter – yes, you were mentioned, Odette – the open house she kept, always full of sunshine and welcome, the exquisite creations she made for Mademoiselle Chanel herself, her love of music and poetry. It was Monsieur Soulier, the kind man who found us in the meadow the day we jumped from the train, who contributed that to the priest, and I hadn't realised how well he knew Maman.

The priest scatters holy water like teardrops onto the coffin and gives the gravedigger the nod to cover it up. Coco hastens me away with a firm arm.

'A young girl doesn't need to see that. You need to live, not grieve. You're coming with me,' she asserts.

'But what about the wake, and all the relations?' I stutter.

'You've been through enough. I've arranged the whole thing; I'll tell them you need to rest. They'll understand. Your mother has left you the house and everything she ever owned, so it'll be there for you when you're ready to return.'

She bundles me into her chauffeur-driven car and I don't protest. She came and took charge from the moment she heard about Maman. Banished the neighbours from the house, arranged the funeral, made sure I ate. She knew not to try to force cheerfulness from me with platitudes, rather watched with angry sympathy at my searing, roaring grief. Even she realised she couldn't fix that. Instead, we stayed up late into the night telling stories about Maman.

She told me how Maman started as a seamstress, but became her couture house's fieriest, most petite model, desired by aristocrats, artists and bon viveurs, much like Coco herself. She was so full of *joie de vivre*, a free spirit who did things her own way, the best dancer at the Café de Paris, the wittiest raconteur with the sharpest tongue at La Coupole. That was until me and Odette came along, and then she was a tigress with her little twins, and we were her russet-topped treasures, tumbling strawberry cream cakes sweet enough to eat, and we were her whole world. The charm, wit and vigour she had previously invested in her life as society sweetheart, she invested in us.

No mention of our father. I know not to ask. I don't think Coco even knows.

Coco had taken her under her wing, admiring her charm and core of steel, a kindred spirit, a girl who'd come from nothing, but transcended such crass concepts as class and breeding – which only exist to raise dullards above their station, Coco says – through sheer brilliance. Cream always rises, and so will you, Coco told me.

I curl up in the back seat of the car and weep until the black kohl she made me up with smudges the starched white collar of the suit she had made for me and I'm crumpled and spent as a husk. I just want my maman.

I hear Coco making arrangements, directing people, the priest thanking her for her immaculate presence in her white mourning clothes like a medieval queen, the neighbours anxiously asking her to take care of me, to keep in touch with my whereabouts and welfare. She deals with them all efficiently and I surrender to my sobs, relieved to give them permission, not to be a grown-up.

My golden maman with burnished hair, swinging me in a sunlit garden, always there. Holding my hand on the way to school, listening to tales of algebra and best friends and playground fallouts. Telling me the names of shells on our little beach – abalone, rose murex, variegated scallop – and making up stories about the lives of starfish who light up the rocks in blazing constellations when humans aren't looking. The sunlit days when we packed a beach picnic of chocolate and bread and strawberries after failed attempts to cook a 'sensible' meal.

I run the evening before she died through my head over and over again. I was so nervous about Jacques, and she told me I was beautiful and clever, and it was he who should be nervous. She kissed my cheek and told me to go out and be carefree and young, and let her do the worrying, that's what mamans are for, she told me, placing the thin strap of my dress just so. My hurtful words to her, the last words I said to her. And... I can't think any more.

Coco sits in the back of the car with me, my head on her bony lap. Her crêpe skirt is soaked with my tears, and she holds me tight and says: courage, little Nina. It's what she said to me the night Odette was taken, and now I understand why Maman went to bed for days because when the sadness is so great your body doesn't work and you must give in to it to try to numb the pain.

The car speeds through the night, along the corniche, up into the hills. She takes me to her summer villa, guides me through the cool colonnades, gives me a room overlooking the pines and the sea beyond.

'Cry it all out,' says Coco. 'If you don't cry, you no longer believe in happiness.'

I lie staring at the ceiling, hear her giving orders to servants who bring my bag into my room. They creep in, blink sympathy at me, then retreat as an owl hoots despair to the big moon that shines careless and bright when the world is so dark. A green glass ring is all I have left of my family. I bury my head in my pillow and close my eyes, and see Maman in every shadow, shut away in her lead box, and a part of my heart stays in there with her.

Coco makes me feel safe, despite the parties that swirl around this glamorous house. Her acolytes worship at her feet; they are gods in their own right – Dalì, Picasso, Cocteau – but she walks amongst them as she pleases, a harsh goddess, toying with them; vivacious and witty, scathing and cruel in turn. She's an athletic, tennis-playing society hostess despite her seventy years, and she outshines the statuesque beauties all this talent and power attracts with her magnetic allure, her pearls and chains, her aching minimalist chic, her tough insights and *bons mots*. No one can resist.

At night I shut out the music and talking and dancing and try to conjure up Maman, keep her with me, look for signs in the shadows. By day I wander the house like it's a stage set peopled with the rich and famous, figures from another world, numb with sadness, the spectacles a momentary diversion from the realisation every morning that Maman is gone.

Coco tells me about Maman's illness. She'd had cancer for years, never wanted to tell me, desperate to see me grow and be happy. I confide in Coco about the last words I said to her, which have haunted me every night, the first words that come to me every morning. 'My life isn't fair,' I told Maman, then I never saw her alive again. All she ever did was care for me and work and make up for losing you, Odette. She asked me to come home on time, and I stayed out too late.

'Those are the words and actions that gave her permission to go,' says Coco firmly. 'Every child must rebel, or the pain of leaving would be too much for you both. She never wanted a perfect child. There is no such thing. What she wanted was a happy, independent one, and you showed her that is what you are. She needed to go, and you let her. You can honour her by living your life to the full. That is ultimately all every maman wants.'

Chanel takes my hand. Hers are strong and large for such a petite figure.

'Let her go. Come with me to Paris.'

'What about Odette?' I say. 'We've always lived in one place in case she needs to trace us.'

Chanel taps my middle finger, where I always wear the replica. 'You have my ring. You can bring her with you.'

Coco wastes no time, packing up trunks, instructing me to fold up my few belongings in a suitcase. We drive away from the south, and the landscape changes; the fields become greener, but the skies darken. The journey takes two days and with each stop I whisper another goodbye to Maman, to my childhood, but not to you, Odette.

As the car rolls through the Place Vendôme, all uncompromising angles, grandiose architecture and desolate wide-open spaces, my heart is in my mouth. We're going to stay at Chanel's suite at the Ritz, the last place we were together, Odette.

I've thought about this place so often, dreamed of it, had nightmares about it, but the reality is nothing like the memories. The awnings over the windows are crisp bright white, the doorman is friendly and salutes me and Coco, the corridors are light, the thick carpets soften our step in Chinese silk, and people are smiling and laughing and eating and drinking, the sound bubbling up cheerfully as we walk past.

In my memory it's dark, there's an alarm blaring somewhere, and monsters in grey with skull badges on their uniforms prowl the corridors looking for children to take. There's a nightmarish pall of horror and rawness in the rooms.

I'm glad Maman's not here to see it, people lounging in

luxury at the scene of our zero hour. There's a comfort in it too though, that life goes on. I hope yours does, too, Odette. I clutch our ring as I walk through to Coco's suite, as if it's a crystal ball that could show me what route you took out of here, into the world full of dark unknowns.

Chanel's suite is different from the rest of the Ritz, more like a nun's cell. She's had everything stripped out, the flourishes and curlicues are gone, the colours are muted and it's all painted white. I wish I could do the same, just feel clean and fresh and unhindered from missing you, Odette, more than ever now that Maman has gone.

Coco shows me her favourite possession, a meteorite.

'You can't buy what comes from the sky,' she says, turning the smooth black rock around admiringly. 'Everything you need is already in you, here and here.' She pats my heart and my head.

It's late, and we're tired, so Coco has a bed made up for me and retires. I can't sleep and Coco's light is still on, so I creep to her door to see if she's still awake; she always has wise words to chase away demons. But I stop short. She's pale, painted-on eyebrows removed, the crimson slash of lipstick gone, and she's sitting up in bed in her white pyjamas, childlike, vulnerable, holding a syringe. She shakes it, pierces the skin of her arm with the needle, carefully presses the plunger and sinks back, closing her eyes.

I shrink away from the door, and tiptoe back to bed. Even Chanel, the great meteorite, has her demons, needs her refuge. It's just me from now on, and you, when I find you, Odette.

I've been here in Paris two months now, and I'm sure you'll forgive me, Odette, because I haven't had time to get the annual photograph done for the Red Cross as there are always a million things to do. I'm working so hard, and, if I'm honest, that photograph always upset me, and now it reminds me of Maman and our annual trip to the photographer, and I just can't quite get to it and Mademoiselle Chanel (that's what I have to call her in her salon, like everyone else) is all-consuming.

I'm here now, in her workshop on rue Cambon, in the attic room that she keeps for her special customers – I'm already involved in the fittings of her most revered friends and clients, something most people have to work years for.

Coco is harsh, even with her favourite model, Marie-Hélène, who stands there looking impossibly modern and lovely. She's so beautiful, Odette. People say she's like Coco herself when she was young, with a dark crop, black eyes, arched eyebrows to die for and wide, generous red lips.

Coco is so impressive to watch, with her scissors hanging off a white tape measure round her neck. She never sketches or sews, but she designs clothes directly on the body, pressing the bodice with the flats of her hands, digging her nails at the waist, pinning and folding the oyster silk satin until it becomes the loveliest, most elegant cocktail dress you've ever seen. When she barks instructions she sends everyone fluttering like birds, scattering the *petites mains*, that's the seamstresses like me, to action with one precisely articulated instruction.

'Make an intelligent pleat, just here and here,' she says, pressing Marie-Hélène's svelte flanks. I understand exactly. She gives me a rare atelier smile, a million miles away from the vulnerable waif I saw injecting herself at the Ritz, and I respect her all the more for this display of strength when I've seen her in her most vulnerable state.

Coco says I'm her best seamstress, that while I can sew I will always eat. I wish she wouldn't say that in front of the other girls. We are all lined up, each of us assigned something very particular: a trimmed pocket on navy flannel, a set of shoulder pads in English tweed, a weighted hem in heavy silk. Today Coco has also trusted me with a complicated appliqué panel for

Marie-Hélène's scarlet evening gown. Black, white and blood red are Chanel's favourite colours, reminiscent of the convent where she grew up.

I love the neat slice of the needle through fabric, the rows of intricate stitches, each a satisfying piece of perfection, a contribution to a work of art, a far cry from the messy, unpredictable world. When Coco sweeps in, you can hear a pin drop. If someone *does* drop a pin, Coco is cruel.

'I'm not paying you to waste my time scrabbling around on the floor. Keep your wits about you, I only want the best. If your life doesn't please you, it's up to you to make the life you want to lead on your own time.'

Everyone nods primly, making a show of working diligently. The moment she's gone, the gossip bubbles up.

'All right for some *make the life you want to lead*. If I had a choice, it wouldn't be this one, but it's better than horizontal under some aristo. That's how *she* got...'

'She did what she needed to, but now she has all this,' one of the supervisors says. 'Talent always rises.'

'What, like teacher's pet over there?' says Blanche, pointing at me.

'My best seamstress, so like your maman... an *intelligent* pleat,' says Madeleine, hands on hips, eyes burning, nostrils flared in a Chanel parody.

The girls are fierce, but I understand. Most people are here because of poverty or loss and everyone's trying to make it somehow. I'm happy to work every hour I can so I don't have to think. I put all my anger at the world into Chanel's creations. I like to think that it gives the design an extra swing, creates impregnable armour for the women who come to the workshop. They may be the most beautiful, the richest, the cleverest, the most ruthless, but lots of them are broken in some way.

The rumours are that Brigitte Bardot never feels loved even though she's the most adored woman in France; Maria Callas is tormented by the fear of failure no matter how many rave reviews she gets at the Paris opera for her transcendent voice, and Grace Kelly has an air of melancholy despite her dazzling smile. I hope to give them wings and freedom and armour with the clothes I help make. Coco says that freedom is the most important thing for a woman, that clothes that restrict them are an abomination.

Brigitte always asks for me, she says I have the most delicate touch and the best eye. She also loves to tell me about her latest conquest.

'He's an angel, he sent his yacht with full crew all the way from Cannes to Saint-Tropez just to pick me up for the evening. The full moon, the Mediterranean, a little black Chanel dress, bare feet on a smooth warm deck and a coupe of Dom Pérignon. There's nothing like it, with all the little night fishermen and their lights in the bay like fireflies.'

I smile, but I think guiltily of my Jacques, who's one of those night fishermen creating a picturesque scene for the millionaires' yachts. He would hate this world, and my part in it. But I like it. It's a million miles away from hardship and sadness and memories, and I can lose myself in it, be a new person, and there is no one here who would ever know any different.

Odette, you'll never guess where I am! Pinch me because in the first summer of my sixteenth year I'm standing on a terrace of a château in Saint-Tropez surrounded by everyone who is anyone with a glass of champagne in my hand (with our ring on of course) and a dress fashioned by my fairy godmother, Coco Chanel. It's ivory silk-chiffon dusted with crystals at the hem, and I feel like an angel. Coco tells me I look like one.

I'm here with the whole team that Coco sent south for the press shoot, and we had so much fun on the harbour setting it all up and making a spectacle of ourselves in the little fishing port.

Marie-Hélène looked beautiful in her jersey suit and slingbacks climbing out of the E-Type Jag to shop at the flower stall, and, guess what, I persuaded her to wear our ring! The photographer was so kind and made sure it was very prominent in the pictures. I hope somehow one day you'll see the pictures in *Vogue* and find me. I'm waiting for you, Odette and if you're anything like me, which I know you are, you'll love fashion and jewellery.

Funny isn't it? There's such a big world out there, and all my life we've thrown out flares in the hope that you see them somehow. Now I'm old enough, it seems like madness to have hoped. I can hardly bear to think that you'll never see Maman again. When we meet, I'll tell you everything, how much she missed you, how she never stopped looking, the imaginary life we led growing up together.

Oops, there's another glass of champagne. It's Dom Pérignon, Odette. I'm raising my glass to you, and I hope you'll forgive me in forgetting you and Maman just for tonight. It's the only way I can have fun, and, while sometimes I feel like I'm running to you and getting nowhere, I'm sorry to say that since Maman died I find myself running in the opposite direction, away from memories and sadness, and into the future, where I wish I didn't have a well of sadness in me that's always threatening to drag me under.

Coco told me that I should live for two, and tonight that is what I'm going to do. The photographer, François, is with me. He is a complete gentleman, and his photography is more than just a record, he sells dreams. No one could really lead the lives he creates with his lens, but people like to believe in fairy tales. Are you one, Odette?

Tonight feels like one, and maybe that's all we can hope for; fleeting moments of artifice, a reason to allow ourselves to believe. François is doing his best to remind me not to get carried away tonight, but I don't want to hear it. I know that

Coco has assigned him as my protector in this big, bad world of parties and celebrity, even though he's not that much older than me. What neither of them realise is that I don't need protecting any more. It's just me and the world now and I intend to experience every little bit of it.

Let me set the scene a little for you. I'm on the terrace of a château, there's a bright moon and a scintillating path across the sea, the stars are like Maman's imagined starfish constellations, chattering and undulating. I'm leaning on the stone balustrade looking out into the bay where the people here have moored their yachts. Flaming torches line the terrace, evening jasmine is floating on the air, and the grand French windows are flung open, framing the ballroom hung with chandeliers, a jazz band is playing and beautiful people you'd recognise from the pages of *Vogue* are dancing and gossiping. Don't make me feel guilty now, Odette. I know it's not real and probably fleeting, and Maman is dead and you might be suffering somewhere, but I am doing my best to be happy.

So, I'm going to say yes to the handsome man who asks me to dance, even though François whispers that he's the most notorious playboy at the party and I should be careful. I can take care of myself.

His name is Alain and he must be at least thirty and he's so sophisticated and all the girls look on with envy as he leads me onto the dance floor. We dance the Madison and the twist and he buys me another bottle of champagne and everything's a complete whirl.

'You're fascinating,' he tells me. 'An old soul. There's a depth to you that seems older than your years.'

I'm dizzy with his words, he's so charming, and I'm having so much fun, and I can't bear it when everyone starts to drift off, I want it to last forever, so, when he asks me if I want to join the after-party on his yacht, I can't believe my luck.

François is a bore as always. 'You've had enough,' he says as

Alain goes to fetch my wrap. 'You should come back to the hotel, you know that Mademoiselle Chanel wouldn't approve.'

Luckily my beau is there to rescue me from dull old François. Alain slips my wrap round my shoulders.

'You get back. I promise to look after her, I'll see her home myself,' Alain says to François. He leaves reluctantly, and a part of me wishes I'd gone back with him, but I must admit that the cocaine Alain gave makes it impossible to stop. I couldn't sleep now in a million years!

We race across the bay on his little red speedboat with another couple and, after a few drinks on deck and some more dancing, they disappear and it's just me and Alain under a canopy of stars. I do feel foolish when I hear the others giggling below deck, saying that I'm a little young even for Alain. I'm not sure how they know, because I told everyone I was eighteen, not sixteen, and anyway he finds me refreshing; an ingénue with more life in my little finger than all the bored society hostesses put together. It sounded so wonderful, and like he could see right into my soul, but the cocaine's run out, and I'm suddenly so tired and there's a little thread of light appearing on the horizon and I realise that I'm out in the bay with a complete stranger, and coming here gives him the right to kiss me, which I don't really want to do now.

He sidles closer and grabs me in a kind of cinch that is too tight and he smells sickly sweet of alcohol and acrid tobacco and I squirm away, half laughing to keep it light.

'Oh... I'm just so tired. It would be nice to go home now.'

'Not yet, just a little kiss on this beautiful night. Haven't we had a lovely time together?'

'Yes, and I'd love to see you again, maybe tomorrow, but now I'm cold and I feel strange and I just want to go home. I saw your crew are already up, maybe they could take me back?' He looks angry, so I say, 'I'm sorry,' and suddenly feel very unsophisticated and a bit scared.

'I'm afraid you'll have to wait until daylight. You can sleep here, it's very comfortable, I promise I'll keep you warm.'

And he tries to kiss me again and I don't know why, but I think of you being taken by that man and it makes me angry, and it gives me a kind of sharp focus and I can see what I need to do. I smile at him and simper for a moment while I calculate the distance. We're close enough to the shore, the sea is flat calm, and, thanks to Maman and growing up next to the sea, I'm a strong swimmer.

I'm on the ship's ladder before he realises what's happening and I plunge in, Chanel's 1000-franc dress billowing around me. It's a shock, and the dress drags me down as I try to surface. When I do, the water is pitch black and I'm suddenly terrifyingly sober. I try not to think about what's in the water, try to remember the glowing starfish Maman told me about and I fix my sights on the harbour. *It's OK, you can see it from here*, I tell myself when I've been swimming for what seems like ages and I don't seem to be any closer. Did I misjudge the distance? I power on, just keep going forward, until eventually the lights reflected in the water from the town dissipate with my strokes and I know I'll make it. When I'm nearly there, I'm so elated to have escaped Alain and his floating double bed that I don't care about the oil in the harbour staining my dress. I swim on and grab the ladder, pull myself out of the water. Thank God.

The fishermen look up from the port café and discreetly avert their eyes as I emerge from the ladder onto the jetty and stride defiantly past, barefoot in my soaking dress, even Chanel's crystals looking tawdry in the early morning sun.

Back at the hotel, François is already up, looking frantic.

'What the hell happened to you?'

'Didn't I tell you mermaid was amongst my talents?' I say. He doesn't laugh.

'Where's your ring?' he says.

I know without looking. The familiar, comforting weight is

gone. I hold up my hand and my heart drops to my bare feet. It's not there. Maybe it's at the bottom of the sea. Last night was such a blur, I don't remember. I'm sorry Odette, sorry Maman.

Coco said I should live life for two, but from now on I only have enough strength for one and I want to forget.

CHAPTER 17

THE DEAL

Fleur

Jake kissed her hard, a kiss of possession, his eyes fixed on Nicolas. Fleur pulled away and turned round to face Nicolas, who was still sitting, coffee cup in hand, looking stunned.

'This is Jake,' she faltered as he hovered on the threshold.

'Looks like you two are previously acquainted. I should get going,' said Nick awkwardly.

'No, no need, Nick. Jake, this is a friend, from the auction house. He's been helping me with all my investigations...'

Nick stood next to Fleur at the door and held out a hand to shake.

Jake ignored him. 'Darling, we need to talk. Get rid of this scruff and we can get on with our day.'

Nicolas looked at her, waiting, but she was lost for words. He gave a slight shake of the head, then picked up his car keys.

'I'll see myself out,' he said to Fleur, then, to Jake. 'Funny she didn't mention you.'

'Ditto,' said Jake with a shrug.

Nicolas stepped past them both without a word and jumped into his 2CV. The engine took three times to catch, then he was gone, skidding on the steep gravel.

'Rude bastard, or is he just French? Don't answer. I probably don't want to know. Look, we need to talk. When my fiancée runs off without telling me, I get worried. *Should* I be worried? What the hell is happening here, Fleur? I realise I've been distracted and... insensitive...'

'You can ask as many questions as you like, there's nothing to tell.' Almost nothing.

'Can I come in then?'

Fleur realised she'd been instinctively blocking the doorway to her sanctuary. She pulled him in.

'Sorry, it's just...'

'We need to talk,' said Jake, again. He stopped in the hallway and looked around.

'Nice place,' he said, sounding unsure for the first time since she'd known him.

'I finally feel like I'm home here.'

'I can see that. Somehow you just fit,' said Jake, looking like he'd lost something.

'Want to see around my new domain?'

It was hot, and Jake, usually so freshly pressed, looked crumpled.

'Later. What's the point when it's unlikely I'll be coming here very much? Let's not sugar-coat it. Something's happened to you, and it's more than getting pregnant.'

He was right. She had to let go, and embrace the new. She wasn't the same person she was before Nina died. There was a new landscape of her past family history that made her present feel different.

'It's a whole family and an addition on the way. I feel complete for the first time in my life.'

'And I feel like only half,' said Jake wryly. 'It seems they've claimed you for themselves.'

She took him out into the shade, and they sat under the orange tree.

Forward, Nina whispered through the breeze in the boughs, or somewhere in Fleur's head.

Jake's phone buzzed and he pulled it out of his pocket to check.

'The Canadians can wait this time,' said Fleur, gently touching his arm.

'Sorry, force of habit.' He switched off the sound showily. 'Not sure I can handle this conversation without my prop,' he said with a lopsided smile she hadn't seen before. 'Listen, you know I'm rubbish at talking about these things, but you leaving, and seeing you here... I think we both know it's over.'

Her relief was unexpected and overwhelming.

'There's no need to look so delighted,' he said, tears building while he tried to smile.

The interview straight out of university and the obvious attraction between them in the office right from the start. His delight in her in the early days, the romantic proposal in the ski lodge, building their apartment together, candlelit dinners at Le Gavroche, first nights at the Royal Opera House, sailing holidays in the Caribbean; it had been a whirlwind. She'd been entranced, starry-eyed at all the glamour and trappings, glad to have a place in the world when she'd always felt so alone, so alien compared to all the other big happy families.

But it wasn't real. She knew that now, looking at Jake perspiring in the overgrown garden, trembling at the idea of fatherhood. The life they'd planned wasn't for her. Or him.

'Not delighted: scared, sorry, sure, all at once. I'm going to miss you so much, but I feel like a different person here, one that was always in there somewhere.'

'And what about the foetus, sorry, the er... I don't know what you call it at this point. Zygote?'

'I think strictly speaking it's called an embryo at this stage, but to me it's already my child. And yours.'

'You want to go through with it?'

Fleur nodded.

'Final answer?'

'We're not in a quiz game, Jake. Final answer. I'm so sure.'

'I knew it from the first time you told me, I'm just not very good at listening, but I've been thinking. The only way I can put it to you is as a kind of business deal, but it's from the heart.' He smiled and patted his chest. 'There's one in there somewhere, I just need to find it.'

Fleur laughed through tears.

'This is the deal. You go ahead and have the baby. I go and do my thing for the next, I don't know, ten years, while it goes through all the dribbly, awkward stuff. Then, if it wants to meet its flesh and blood, I'm here with knobs on. Not much of an advertisement for the male of the species I know, but it's the only way I can see it working for me. I can't force you to have an abortion, and neither would I want to. It's just I can't do being a dad. I'd mess the poor little thing up with my resentment and longing. It wouldn't be fair on anyone. Of course I'd take my punishment like a man and pay... God I'm sorry, this sounds so wrong, but cards on the table. Sorry to the sisterhood, but I'd be a great glamorous kind of uncle figure. Ten years, and you know I never renege on a deal.'

Classic Jake. Any doubts she might have had about going it alone flew out across the sea.

'A baby can't be involved in a *deal*, Jake. You can't just walk away.'

Jake's face hardened. Fleur braced herself. She knew that look. He could flip from charm offensive to anger in a heartbeat when he didn't get his way.

'It's your decision to have the baby, not mine.'

'You were involved in making it, remember? Until a moment ago, we were *engaged*. How can you abandon me so quickly and completely? It's like everything we had meant nothing.'

'Ditto,' said Jake, raising his voice. 'We agreed. No children. It was a deal, like it or not, and you're reneging. Something's happened to you. You're not the person I thought you were. I made myself very clear from the start, so don't give me this *you're the father* shit. I don't want a child, and you've got me backed up against a wall. It's not fair.'

'Life isn't fair. Not everything can be arranged in advance and happen exactly as you want it to. Things change, life happens, and you just have to go with it. I want this baby more than anything I've ever wanted in my life and I'm going ahead. It's *our* baby, Jake. It's not what we wanted, but maybe sometimes you get what you need. We won't be the first couple this has ever happened to. Surely we can work it out, give this little one a daddy, arrange contact and visits?'

Jake's phone was vibrating incessantly. He couldn't resist a look before standing to face her, the spoilt, aggrieved look on his face that she hated.

'You're not listening. I don't want the baby. I don't want contact, or to see pictures of its little booties, or hear about when it first says duck or learns to press a button on some irritating plastic toy. No doubt you'll want to extort money from me, so there'll be contact from my lawyer. Apart from that, leave me out of your baby fantasy.'

Why had she always glossed over this side of Jake to herself? He was a Jekyll and Hyde. Fine when everything was going his way; non-negotiable, spoilt and unfeeling when it wasn't. Until now, this was the man she was going to marry. What planet had she been on? Maybe she would never have gone through with it in the end, pregnant or not. When Nina was ill, she thought what she needed was a new start, stability, someone to rely on. She'd projected all of those things onto this man, persuaded herself that he was the person she wanted to spend the rest of her life with, but now Nina was gone she knew she could manage. Nina would have hated her death to have pushed her into a decision she should never have made. She lashed out.

'I never really loved you, and thank God, or this would be a lot harder than it is.'

Jake deflated immediately. 'I'm sorry, I shouldn't have said all of those things, but I just can't do it.'

'Come back to me when you grow up,' said Fleur. 'I don't need your money, by the way.'

'I didn't mean it about the lawyers,' said Jake.

'You did when you said it. Just leave. You know where to find me if you ever grow up and want to know your child,' said Fleur.

Jake strolled over to a patch of tall grass brimming with wildflowers. He stumbled on the molehills in his shiny shoes, hands in pockets, head turned so she couldn't see his expression. He turned round to face her and wiped his eyes.

'Perfect place for a swimming pool,' he said.

'I've got a beautiful cove just down the track,' said Fleur.

Fleur lay back on the examination table, the gel clinical and cold under the probe. She held her breath, not daring to look at the screen.

'Good heartbeat, all present and correct. Everything safe and sound,' said the doctor. 'Bleeding can be normal at this stage, and the cramps may have been muscle strain, considering the efforts you had to make to save yourself. I can certainly see nothing to worry about, but no more dices with death, please.' He smiled reassuringly.

Fleur sobbed. Nina's great-grandchild, missed by only a few weeks. The grainy little tadpole the result of generations of love and loss and striving, so full of hope and innocence. She'd guard her child with her life.

'Sorry, they're tears of joy, really,' she said.

'It's an emotional time,' said the doctor.

Please God or the universe or whoever's in charge that my little seed lives through peaceful times.

The rest she could handle. Her own upbringing gave her a template for a happy family outside of a conventional unit, and Nina's inheritance would give her the time and space she needed, though she'd swap it for Nina being here a million times over.

'We'll do it our way,' she whispered through her fingers, which were placed protectively on her abdomen, as she stepped out of the surgery. The sun was an optimistic yellow, the scent of oleander floated on the air, and she knew the exact room in Nina's house she'd make into a nursery, the one with the view of the orange tree and the swing and the sea singing a lullaby in the distance.

She felt closer than ever to her great-grandmother Camille, who'd lost Odette, and had gone to her grave without ever finding her. Nurturing and protecting this little thing, and finding Odette, would be her two guiding lights from now on. She didn't know how, but it felt like one couldn't thrive without the other, and no stone would be left unturned to put the wrongs of the past right and secure the future for her budding little mini-family.

Pregnancy for Fleur was a kind of beautiful madness. Nature was more miraculous; a spider's web a work of art, a butterfly wing an exquisite painting, a fox and her cubs a precious treasure, wild and maternal. She smiled at the speeding landscape as she drove home, feeling a link with every mother on the planet. Just as well Jake wasn't here, he'd be horrified at the earth mother she was already turning into. Nina would laugh and call her *chou-fleur*.

God, she missed her. Being a mother made you want your own mother more than ever. *Forward*, Nina whispered. She was cut loose from everything that had gone before. No job, no fiancé, all her friends over a thousand kilometres away, a baby to take care of on her own. So why did she feel like a bird in the sky, whirling and free, catching the sun on her wings?

On the way back she stopped at the post office to collect a package from the Chanel archives, and as soon as she got home she sat at the kitchen table to open it, steeling herself for what she might find.

The box was white, edged in black, printed with a Chanel logo. The archivist had labelled it 1955 to 1960.

Fleur peeped inside. A dress wrapped in tissue paper, and some old photographs.

'I've got so much to tell you, Nina, but so have you to me,' she whispered.

First, she unfolded the dress and held it up to the light. It was yellowed in places, and the moths had made a meal of it, but even so she could see it had been exquisite. Spaghetti straps, floor-length pale silk, flattering panels expertly sewn, and the rhinestones still catching the sun after all these years.

Fleur picked up the photographs with trembling hands. A young woman – Nina – with a gamine crop, head thrown back, laughing somewhere glamorous – a balustraded balcony lit by torches somewhere by the sea – surrounded by louche-looking men in tuxes dishevelled, end-of-the-party style, cigarettes dangling from lips, Brylcreemed hair swept in handsome waves.

One, unmistakable, dressed in a neckerchief and holding up a sea urchin on a fork, staring straight at the camera. Pablo Picasso.

Fleur double-checked and gasped, cross-referenced it with a picture on her phone. It was definitely him. Nina was luminous, a candle amongst the dark-suited men, a magnet for the lens, the epitome of Fifties glamour, also gazing straight at the camera with a look she didn't recognise. Desire?

She turned the photo over. *Cannes 1960 Moi, Pablo and the gang. Photo by François.*

Was it François, the man behind the camera, she desired?

Another photo of her in a studio of some sort. Mannequins with half-finished clothes, a slim older woman with a chiselled face and wide, determined lips; a tape measure round her neck, scrutinising them. Nina was kneeling with a pair of scissors in her mouth, sewing a hem, the mirrored room reflecting the scene from a hundred angles.

Over the page, Nina's handwriting. *At Chanel's atelier, 1955, Photo by François.*

Nina on the harbour at Saint-Tropez with Brigitte Bardot. Nina outside the Paris opera house with Maria Callas, Nina in a ruched gingham bikini on the beach, holding hands with a man, a fabulous vintage Nikon camera slung round his neck. François?

Fleur looked closer. There was something familiar about him. A reticence in his smile, the curious arch of his eyebrows, echoes of what Fleur saw when she herself looked in the mirror. She took a photo on her phone, homed in on his hands. Fingernails like spades, like Fleur's. Could this be her grandfather? A photographer, like her? Or was it just wishful thinking?

'Why did you hide everything, Nina?' she whispered to the shadows. If Fleur asked about her mum and dad, her grandma and grandma, Nina would clam up, hurt.

'It's you and me against the world, little flower. We don't need anyone else, do we?'

Fleur always felt obliged to agree. She felt guilty even saying it now. Nina had been enough. She said it aloud. 'You were everything and more, Nina, but I want to know. What were you protecting me from?'

Fleur leafed through the photographs again. They were good. The framing and depth of field were perfect. François had an eye for a candid moment, picking out a focal point – usually Nina – and making it a clever exposition of the world he was introducing to the viewer; a brilliant mix of reportage and portraiture.

The photo of François and Nina was more of a grainy snap, caught in a carefree moment by an amateur. Nina would be about Fleur's age, maybe a little younger. How many lives did her grandmother live? How did she get to move in these extraordinary circles? To her she'd been Grandma, Nina, a warm, protective presence who made legendary picnics and choux buns and never minded how many kids rampaged around her cottage garden.

Yes, she had always admired a perfectly placed seam, cared deeply about the fabrics her clothes were made from and was rarely seen without her slash of bright red lipstick, but that was just the background to their lives, the way it had always been. Just... French. Now, here she was, a carefree young girl with her handsome beau, both clearly talented and moving in glamorous circles. But she couldn't have been that carefree with the spectre of her twin always there.

On closer inspection, Nina was always looking slightly off somewhere, over the photographer's shoulder, or into the distance like she'd seen a ghost.

She wished she could reach back into the past and hug this brave young woman.

'I see you, Nina.' She blew the photo a kiss. 'I'll find her.'

Fleur lost herself in the photos, studying them endlessly for clues. Another anomaly made her heart squeeze. In the earlier photos, she was wearing the ring. In the later ones, it was nowhere to be seen.

Her buzzing phone made her jump. Nicolas. Her heart responded with an extra beat. She hesitated, swiped to answer.

'I'm not interrupting anything, am I?' Nicolas sounded uncharacteristically nervous.

'No... Jake's gone back to London.'

'Already? Oh.' He sounded more relaxed.

'I can explain.'

'Nothing *to* explain. Your life is your own and I was rude to your fiancé, and to you,' he said decisively. 'Just as well I was momentarily angry, it was the only thing that got Choux back up that gravel slope.'

'Choux?'

'Choux, my 2CV. She's a beauty, but no welly. Are you OK?'

She put her hand on her stomach. 'Really well. Thanks for looking after me.'

'He shouldn't have left you alone,' said Nicolas darkly.

'I'm fine, really.'

The phone crackled.

'There's been a development, that's the only reason I'm calling,' said Nicolas.

Fleur still had Nina's dress on her lap, a ghost from the past. 'What about?'

'It seems that Raschmann found a heart while he was in Colombia.'

'Not the inclusion in the emerald?'

'No, his own. I found a letter buried in the archives where no one else would think to look. I'm not quite sure why it's been kept so carefully through all these decades. If someone was trying to stop us, this would be damning evidence, and go towards proof of ownership for Odette. On the other hand, it does give the emerald provenance, which would help command a higher price for the many unprincipled arseholes in the auction room.'

'Can you read it out to me?'

'It was in German, so I've made a rough translation. I'd

rather send it to you, so you have time to react and absorb it. It won't make easy reading, especially as Odette clearly never received it. It could have changed the course of her life and connected her with her family. Instead, some bastard, whether the museum or someone else, profited from withholding it from her.'

'Why don't you bring it over. There's still so much to unpick.'

Fleur stared down the path to the cove. She'd known the moment they'd kissed on the beach that she wasn't going to marry Jake. The salt and the breeze, the feeling of being alive, the edge-of-the-world remoteness might have been a fantasy, but it was freedom and want at the same time and she knew she'd never go back. Jake was a gilded cage, safety, like an armchair in an old people's home. You would never fall, but you'd never live.

'I'll email it to you. Lots to do,' he said.

'Nicolas...'

But he'd already gone. And what was she going to say, anyway? I'm pregnant with that man I didn't tell you about and I'm sorry? She wasn't sorry, but she couldn't bear to think that maybe something was starting that would never grow.

She refreshed her email and there it was, with no message from Nick, just the text, cut and pasted.

8 May 1946

Gómez Abogados, Colombia. Lawyers on behalf of Gustav Raschmann, deceased.

To whom this may concern c/o Bullinger's Auctioneers, Paris. I am sending this letter to you in the hope that you still have records of the seller of the Emerald Lake, and the little girl who accompanied him. We are informed that the ring passed through your auction house on 29 April 1944. Mr Raschmann has now bequeathed the ring back to the child, its rightful owner. We are holding the ring in a vault should a legitimate contact be made.

If you are unable to trace the original seller or the little girl, the ring will be held in perpetuity for her or her heirs and all legitimate claims will be considered. A letter (enc) accompanies the appeal.

———

My dear little French girl with the sad blue eyes and the Pre-Raphaelite hair, you have haunted my dreams. You were terrified, I could see, from the way you couldn't look anyone in the eye, by the way you searched the crowded room for a familiar face but saw none. It amused me to see that you refused to call him father, that he had little control over this defiant, lost little sprite, but now it grieves me to think of that little girl.

I knew the man, Dieter Fischer, who sold me this ring was not your father, that you were stolen. I knew that the ring was not his to sell, that it was a ransom on your head and that I paid him a fraction of its worth, which may well have made your life even more difficult.

I know now that no price would have given you back what you lost, that somewhere a mother would grieve her entire life for the loss of her treasure. By all accounts, the ring was given by your mother's friend, Mademoiselle Chanel herself, in return for news of you. Perhaps if you can find Mademoiselle Chanel, she can reunite you with your family.

I am deeply sorry, and I go to my death in the knowledge that I have done one thing right in my life.

Affectionately and in hope,

Gustav Raschmann

Goosepimples crept up Fleur's neck. She searched back through Nicolas's emails to her and found a newspaper article he'd photographed from the microfiche after he'd first told her about Raschmann. Gustav Raschmann had written the letter on the eighth of May, the same day he'd fallen down the mineshaft, according to the newspaper. So perhaps it hadn't been an accident after all. The act of greed and unimaginable cruelty of tearing a child from its mother, one of countless such deeds during the war, had repercussions down the decades. This man had suffered, perhaps rightly so. Odette was just one child amongst thousands, theirs one family amongst millions that had been destroyed, and every act of defiance, of restoration, was a little flicker of hope in the darkness. She'd never give up.

Fleur put Nina's dress to her cheek, the silk cool and smooth. Nina had protected her all her life from this story, now Fleur was glad that Nina had been protected from this. That this teenage Nina in the photographs didn't know the whole story, that she could stroll along the beach, so carefree with the salt spray in her hair, even if the ghost of Odette was always somewhere there, too, gave her comfort.

Nicolas would know what to say to this thought, be amazed at these beautiful photographs she'd uncovered. She pressed his number. No reply. She texted instead.

You were right. Raschmann found his heart, but too late for him, I hope not for Odette.

And Fleur was just finding her own heart, too. She hoped it was not too late.

CHAPTER 18

MOTH TO A FLAME

Nina, aged twenty-one

We're twenty-one today, Odette! It's five years since I lost our ring, but what a five years! That night I told you about, where naive sixteen-year-old me allowed an old man to trap me on his yacht, was all my own stupid fault. But my escape and swim to freedom made me something of a local celebrity.

The whole of Saint-Tropez got to hear about the girl who emerged on the harbour ladder in a Chanel dress, can you believe it? The fishermen tried to help me while I was catching my breath at the top of the ladder, but I told them it was too late. I had valiantly saved myself from the sea monster who lurked on the yacht and I was perfectly capable of looking after myself. They thought that was hilarious and told me that there were plenty more fish in the sea, and I announced that I was earning my own keep as a couturier, I didn't need a man to finance my life, and I intended to catch my own fish from now on, rather than be the one being caught.

Since then, I've been a kind of mascot for them, and they love hearing my stories from the night before.

I'm usually finishing the night at the same time as them, just as the sun's coming up. They tell me about the creatures irresistibly drawn like moths to their lights and lures, the high seas in a storm, the rogue waves that appear from nowhere on a calm night. In return, I regale them with stories of my own stormy nights, the party candlelight that attracts unwary artists and writers to our domain, the flirtations between the ingénues and film directors, and of course about Brigitte, who they all love. There's a party at hers almost every week and she always invites me.

I'm here, now at **Café Sénéquier** on the port, wide awake, with a hot chocolate and a scattering of party stalwarts who are still standing.

Oh, Odette, last night was a dream! I was at Brigitte's house at La Madrague and she threw me a twenty-first birthday party! There was champagne, and lobster, and we all went skinny dipping at midnight. There was a full moon that poured liquid silver on the water just for us, and of course I won the swimming race to the platform, guided by the shimmering path. How could I lose on such a beautiful night?

We danced on the beach, and when people started to drift off – someone said it was 3 a.m. – a few of us went to the vineyard to see the fireflies, and we lay there looking at the stars like I used to with Maman. Then I couldn't stop thinking about her, and how much I miss her, so I had to leave, and sit on the beach alone, because I just couldn't bear another moment with the crowd. Do you ever get that, Odette?

Sebastian came to find me, but I didn't tell him what I was really thinking. He's not my boyfriend, by the way. No one is. Better not to get too attached after what happened to us, don't you think? Life's so much more fun being free. Anyway, I was lying on the beach in my Chanel creation, a little black dress, knee-length lace over silk, with the cutest tulip skirt that kicks out when you dance. I thought a million other thoughts to distract myself and next to Sebastian everything was sublime. Shooting stars flitted down the sky like sparkling cigarette ash, and we talked and talked about nothing much. Well, *I* probably talked a little *too* much, but I might have had a little help. Don't be shocked, Odette, everyone here takes cocaine – you can't really enjoy the kind of parties I go to without it. Then I heard that sound that I dread; the dawn chorus. You know it's all over when the air warms just a little, and out on the horizon the sky turns from velvet to denim, then, before you can stop it, lightens to pale translucent-blue cotton, and you know that the night that seemed so endless is spent, and you're going to feel like hell.

Funny, however much I drink, or however many drugs I take, when the sun starts to rise you and Maman are the first ones I think of, and that's the worst part of my day. It doesn't matter how fast I run, how many parties, how high my star rises at Chanel's atelier, you're always there. I could see you even before that, in the Gemini constellation amongst the shooting stars.

That's why I'm sitting here now, hugging my hot chocolate at the fishermen's café. I can't go to bed quite yet. How do you still get into my dreams, Odette?

My friends start to drift off, and I'm glad. Mixing my morning and night friends is never a comfortable thing, and the party dregs who don't know any better talk loudly over the fishermen, whose stories are far more interesting than the usual party post-mortems.

When the last tuxedoed reveller staggers off, wincing at the sun like a vampire, my old friend Michel catches my eye. His boat is called *Camille*, like Maman.

'I could hear you lot and your music a mile out in the bay. Catch any fish?'

'Several big ones.' I grin, waiting for them to ask.

'Go on then, tell us who you've been hobnobbing with,' says Jean-Marc, looking up from his card game.

'Jeanne Moreau is clever, a real petite dynamo, and Audrey Hepburn is a beautiful angel and very funny. Sophia Loren loves Scrabble, and she always cheats, and Marlon Brando's Elvis impression is uncanny. He's also a complete gentleman.'

'Like me then,' says Michel. 'Apart from he's never seen a real day's work in his life.'

'It's not that easy, staying up all night, hobnobbing,' I say.

'If it was that hard, you wouldn't do it most nights.'

'I could say the same about fishing.'

'Always got a wise answer, this one,' says Michel proudly.

A man in a beret with big round eyes is staring at me. I give him a winning smile, but he returns to his pastis. His hands are huge, a workman's. On his plate are five dangerous-looking urchins, but he handles them expertly, scoops out the flesh and pops one into his mouth.

'It tastes of here,' he says. 'You know that urchins taste of the food they eat, so they're different all over the world. Here they taste of the Mediterranean, with the metallic tang of money.'

'Or starlets and ambition,' I say.

He holds out a hand. 'Pablo,' he says. He nearly crushes my hand as he pops another urchin in at the same time. He nods. 'You're right!'

'I'm sure I'm not. You're being kind, and I just talk too much,' I say.

'At least you give us something to talk about other than the weather,' says Michel.

'Speaking of which, there's a storm blowing in tonight.'

'The mistral, that's all. A north-westerly, it'll be quiet as a millpond the other side of the bay...'

I sit back, sip my sweet hot chocolate, trying not to think of you, Odette, letting the talk wash over me like waves. I love the convivial chatter, the warmth. If it didn't look bad, I'd drift off to sleep, right here, amongst all these people with families, and children and ordinary lives. None of them know about you, Odette.

I tune back in, just to have a bit more peace. If I'm tired enough, I might not dream.

Jean-Marc pulls out a pendant from under his shirt. It's orange, in a kind of toothed clasp, on a silver chain.

'I've faced a few storms with this. I'll never forget that freak wave in the 1948 storm. Swelled up like a boil out of nowhere, quivered ten feet up like she was holding her breath, then swamped us. By rights we should have capsized – I was saying my prayers all right when she hit, and I never let go of this.'

He holds up the pendant, and the men murmur in understanding.

'I swear this is the reason I'm still sitting here today. It's been passed down generations, and I've never once sailed without it.'

It makes me yearn for my ring in one big rush. It was ours, and I lost it like it didn't matter five years ago, and I'll never get it back again, or you, or Maman. I don't even realise that I'm sobbing until I notice that Jean-Marc is looking intently at the ground, Michel is squinting at something through the window, and the card-players start dealing but they're not looking at the cards.

Jean-Marc thumps me on the shoulder. 'I'm not going to give it to you just because you're crying.' He tries to laugh, but he looks desperate, and I just can't stop.

'It's an otolith,' says the man with the plate of sea urchins gently. 'They're more powerful than you think. I've seen grown men break down at the sight of one.'

'Sorry,' I say. 'I lost something that my maman gave me, and it's only just occurred to me how valuable it was, even though it wasn't worth much.'

I can't help it, I tell them all my story and they vow to try to find the ring in the harbour. Jean-Marc says stranger things have washed up, and, the way the tide works round here, it probably won't have gone far.

They are telling me sweet, foolish lies, of course. Five years at the bottom of the bay. It could have been swept anywhere by now.

I finish my hot chocolate and leave. Thank God for sunglasses, the morning is so blindingly wholesome out here as I hotfoot it towards the hotel. I count seven chimes on the church clock. Still early. With any luck I'll sleep, then be up in time for the night train back to Paris and sanity. If I keep on the move, things aren't too bad.

François is at large, heading towards me from the harbour, no doubt full of the joys of the morning. I hastily wipe the smudged make-up from my eyes, pinch my cheeks, check my dress straps are straight.

'Are you OK?' he says.

I wish he wouldn't see me like this. Especially when he regards me with that penetrating photographer's stare that always makes me feel kind of grubby after a big night.

'I'm fine. I had the most wonderful night, but maybe I'm a little worse for wear at this ungodly hour. Now, I'm dreaming of clouds for pillows and angels to sing me to golden slumbers, so I'm not going to stop.'

'What have you done to those poor fishermen? They're beside themselves that they made you cry. Something about amulets hitting a bad note. They sent me after you... Nina, this has got to stop. What are you running away from?'

'Nothing. I'm running *towards* the light. Why do you always make me feel bad about enjoying myself?'

'Is it me that makes you feel bad, or do I just remind you how you feel?'

I carry on walking. There might be downsides, but the good

thing about being an orphan is that you have no one to answer to.

He tries again. 'You know what an otolith is? It's part of the fish head, a beautiful thing, like ivory, and prized. It's actually a sensor in the vestibular system that guides all fish and keeps them on the straight and narrow. You've never been the same since you lost your ring. It was like an anchor, a symbol of the missing part of you.'

I slow down a bit and let him catch up.

'Here, let me help you,' he says. 'You look like a breath of wind could blow you over.'

I'm so, so tired. François links my arm to prop me up and I lean on him and let him guide me back to my hotel room. He hovers as I fiddle with the key.

'Will you stay with me until I fall asleep?'

'Gladly,' says François.

He tucks me in, and I sink my head into the pillow, one eye on him as he settles into the armchair with a book.

'Promise you won't go until I'm really fast asleep.'

He salutes me and smiles. 'Scout's honour.'

He looks sad, I think, as I drift off.

The summer ends like a tawdry party we've all tired of, and I head back north. I love Paris in the autumn; that first nip in the air, the trees relinquishing green in favour of fireworks of reds, yellows and browns, the mellow sun, so different from the harsh clarity of the Mediterranean summer, bathing everything in gold.

I shrug on my Chanel jacket over a silk blouse. The pastel-blue tweed is soft as cashmere, so warm and luxurious. The skirt skims my hips and the weighted hem maintains the line beautifully. The whole suit is cut for me, and Chanel's clever touches – the high armholes and set-in sleeves that are so freeing despite the tailored look, the side zips placed just right – all make me feel I could take on the world as I step out onto the crisp blue-grey Paris streets.

It doesn't matter how many Chanel suits and cocktail dresses I have though. The tickets to see Nureyev at the Palais Garnier, the premieres, the dinners at La Coupole and Le Train Bleu. I can never feel *whole*, Odette.

Forward, keep moving, don't let it get you, I whisper to myself as I pass the gallery where I'm going to a preview tonight. There'll be Picassos and Warhols and Bridget Rileys and I've learned to say all the right words about them, but I can never *feel* them.

In the workroom, I pick up the pastel tweed for the suit we're making for Jackie Kennedy.

'Every stitch must be a work of art,' says Coco. And I make it so. The silk thread is a meditative joy to work with. In a weird kind of way, the two things I'm good at – couture and parties – are both solitary pursuits.

Marie-Hélène is waiting in the mirrored studio when I finish the trim, and she slips it on. François is taking photographs and Marie-Hélène is stunning, adopting the 'Chanel pose' for the camera, hips forward, shoulders back, hand in pocket, quizzical as a cat. François shoots her taking a silk purse out of Chanel's 2.55 quilted bag, applying red lipstick with the help of a gold compact, looking back at the camera with the jacket over her shoulder to show off the tailoring of the skirt, and a hundred other lures for the customer. When he's satisfied, that part of the shoot is a wrap.

Next, we spill out into the street, where a sleek red convertible E-Type Jaguar is waiting. Marie-Hélène has to climb in and out of the damn thing at least fifty times before he gets the care-free shot of her jumping into her little sports car, a 2.55 bag in full view.

'This soft autumn sun is better than any artificial light. Just keep doing what you're doing,' says François, and Marie-Hélène pouts, loving the camera. It loves her right back.

I hope the professional flattery doesn't extend to the real feelings of the man behind the camera. They wouldn't be right together. He's clever and funny and kind, talented and handsome in a wholesome kind of way, with freckles on his nose and sandy hair, a bit like a French JFK.

'Nina, just help Marie-Hélène with the bag again, it's creasing her blouse... I need to rely on you to keep an eye on everything.'

'Sorry, I was miles away.'

'I could see,' he says. His smile is warm as Saint-Tropez.

I help Marie-Hélène with the chain strap again and François does his thing. He looks up from the camera. 'You were radiant.'

'And I trust you implicitly to make me look beautiful,' says Marie-Hélène, expectantly.

Poor François is forced into it. 'You make it easy,' he simpers.

It's all I can do not to be sick right there.

'Drink?' I say brightly to François. 'I've found the most eccentric little bar in the Marais, and they do the best champagne cocktails.'

'On a Monday night?' says François.

'Don't be such a bore,' says Marie-Hélène.

'OK, maybe just one,' François says with a dopey look on his face.

I was hoping for François to myself for a cosy chat, but I can't exactly say, so I rally.

'I'll drive!' I say.

'Are you sure you can handle that thing? There's a lot of horsepower under the bonnet,' says François sternly.

'Don't be ridiculous. Brigitte has one just the same and I

drive it everywhere in Saint-Tropez. Jump in.' I turn the keys and get the engine ticking over.

Marie-Hélène gets in next to me in the front and François, ever the gentleman, squeezes into the tiny back seat. Every time I take a corner or jump a red light, he winces, and I can't avoid his disapproval in the rear-view mirror. I wish he'd sat next to me in the front so I don't have to look at him.

The two of them adore my new discovery in the Marais, and to hell with Monday night, we're three cocktails down before we know it.

François and Marie-Hélène are talking shop, technical things about photography – the advantages of Silvertone, the natural light at dawn, Kodak or Nikon, and I'm starting to feel like a spare part, when I remember about the preview with Picasso and the others.

'I've got to rush if I'm going to get to the preview in time,' I say, and I call the waiter over and pay for all the cocktails. It's an eye-watering bill, but Coco pays me well.

'I'll deliver the car and see you both tomorrow,' I say, standing to go.

François puts his hand on the car keys. 'Come on, Nina, you've had too much.'

I'm sick of him always being so *sensible*, and I have to get out, so I grab the keys and run. I'm fast, even in kitten heels, and I've got the advantage of surprise. I'm in the car before François is even out of the doorway.

What he doesn't understand is that I can't ever stay in one place for a whole evening. Besides, Chanel should call off her guard dog if all he can do is fawn over her favourite models.

I turn the key, rev the engine and I'm off, but I don't go straight to the preview. It's wonderful to feel the autumn chill in my hair, the sting on my cheeks as I drive through all my favourite haunts, the early golden moon lonely as Midas in the sky. I pass mothers and children hurrying home for dinner, couples caught in each other's eyes like stars, a father delighting in a child wobbling along on a bike. I press the accelerator hard along the Boulevard Saint-Germain to escape the hollow feeling in my stomach.

The next thing I know my head is wedged on the horn and it's blaring like a nightmare. I put my hand on my forehead and feel something sickeningly warm. A towering plane tree is wedged in the car bonnet, the windscreen is smashed. My legs are numb and I panic, shout for help but no sound comes. A woman turns away screaming, the maître d' dashes out of Les Deux Magots, his face like a melted candle, then everything is blank.

CHAPTER 19

SEASONS

Nina, aged twenty-one

I'm climbing a wall but it leans back precariously and I can't hold on. Below is cold nothing and Odette is at the top. She's me, but she's not me. If I can get to her, I'm saved. Stretching down as far as she can, she speaks a language I don't understand. I reach up, our fingertips almost touch, but the wall isn't safe. It crumbles and I fall, screaming. I'm about to hit oblivion, but François is somewhere, calling my name like a safety net.

I jolt awake and he's there, holding my hand with that worried look on his face I can't stand. I turn away, ashamed. It's me I don't like, not him.

The walls are white, there's an antiseptic smell, I'm tucked in so tight I can't move my legs. I can't move my legs full stop. The crash, the blaring horn. I screw my eyes shut.

'Don't be scared, you're going to be all right,' says François. 'Two broken legs, but luckily clean breaks. Time's all you need.'

I try to sit up, but he presses my shoulder gently, points to the drip. I sink back into my pillow.

'Shit,' I say. 'The car. I'm sorry...'

I'm so woozy, the tears come, and I can't stop them, and François hugs me. He feels like home.

'I'm your next of kin, apparently,' he says.

'How did they know?'

'The police said you repeated my name over and over again, even though you were barely conscious. Luckily the maître d' knew how to contact me. I've been here forty-six hours, thirty-two minutes and five seconds. The longest two days of my life.'

I sleep, and, with François there, the recurring nightmares disappear. I lose track of time between the morphine drip and fatigue. I try to sleep off all the nightmares – Odette, Maman, the crash. Most times I open my eyes, he's there, and the look of concern I always hated is now my world and comfort.

There are times in the hospital weeks when I wake to see Coco standing over me, grim-faced, practical, immaculate as the nurses. She never stays long. I get the impression that illness and incapacity make her uncomfortable. Her world is fantasy and order, not reality and unpredictability, but when it's time for me to leave, she arranges everything with absolute efficiency – I can't manage the stairs to my own apartment, so she's arranged a ground-floor one for me overlooking the Tuileries with two bedrooms. One for me, and one for François, who volunteers to watch over me while I recover.

It's beautiful, with parquet floors, huge windows and a kitchen that François loves to cook in.

He reads to me most mornings – Jean-Paul Sartre, Simone de Beauvoir, Françoise Sagan – and my head is spinning with ideas, even if my body won't serve me. I'm not sure if it's good or bad, Odette, but without my packed schedule you're ever-present. I want you so much, it's almost like you're here. On the long afternoons when François isn't here, I even think I see you disappearing behind a tree in the Tuileries, weeping by the boating pond, closing a window and slipping into the shadows in the apartment across the park.

You disappear when François returns, but you're still there somewhere inside me. On the long, lonely afternoons I understand that you always will be until I find you. Having so much time to think is almost more frightening than the crash, but I'm getting better. As my legs heal and my face turns from black and blue to pink, I feel better inside, too.

François is an angel, Odette. Every evening is a dinner party just for two with whatever he finds in the market. Last night he cooked risotto with truffles from Périgord, and tonight it's bouillabaisse to remind me of Saint-Tropez.

I'm not sure I deserve this after being so reckless. You're the one who deserves all the good things because I wouldn't be leading this life if you hadn't gone with that man. Sometimes I think I should die to make space for you to live.

I confide all of this to François and it's such a relief, but he gets that worried look again and I tell him I'm fine and not to fret, even though you're shaking your head at me, Odette. How do you always know?

After two more weeks, I'm ready to explode from being confined, but soon after that my head is healed, I'm wearing make-up again, and I can go out in a wheelchair. François takes me out into the big wide world. I'm like a blind woman who can see again. The colours of the Tuileries are so vivid, there are so many different greens and the winter sun on my face is heaven, and the world is newborn.

We start to venture further afield. Just François and me walking under the dappled planes along the Seine, choosing books from the Sunday market as sunshine streams on the Left Bank. Me and my chariot driver lunching on the Île de la Cité in the shadow of Notre-Dame, laughing at the mime artist who performs in the street, making heart shapes as we pass by.

'Just friends!' I call out to him.

He mimes tears pouring down his face to François and we laugh at what an odd couple we must make, with me dressed in full-on Chanel being pushed along by Coco's minder.

The leaves drift off the trees and the days get shorter and colder and I'm up on crutches and I can't imagine a day when François isn't coming home and we put the world to rights, talk about our days, our favourite films, the ideas from the books we're reading.

On Christmas Eve, I'm off my crutches and we take a walk past the Christmas windows of the Galeries Lafayette, where scenes from our favourite childhood book are reproduced, Odette. Through the glass I see the Little Prince on his planet in a velvet sky, crystal stars on fine threads suspended in space. He's in his rose garden in another window, clutching a flock of golden birds in another, and in the fourth he's sitting on a wall, talking to a snake, surrounded by his planets.

'He looks so alone,' I say to François, nostalgic for us, Odette, for lost innocence. 'Do you ever wish you were a child again?'

'Come on, let's get back,' he says, that furrow appearing again.

If he thinks I'm missing Odette, or getting nostalgic about Maman and everything that happened, he always changes the subject. He can't bear to see me unhappy.

'No. It's all right.' I turn to face him, pull my scarf tighter round my neck against the cold. 'I'm going to stop running and start searching again.'

He hugs me. 'I'm glad. You're only half without her, I've always known that. I'll help you.'

The first flake of snow starts to fall, and we hurry down rue Saint-Honoré. By the time we arrive at the apartment, the Tuileries are covered in snow. It's a wonderland for a girl from the South and I scrunch together a snowball and take aim.

Bullseye, right on the chest. He retaliates with a fair, soft throw at my arm, but I'm ruthless, and the next one gets him right between the eyes and he hugs me gently so I can't pick up any more snow and we're laughing so hard I barely notice that I'm burying my head in his neck and he's holding me so tenderly and our eyes meet and it's like a fire crackling in the hearth and I break away. I don't want to feel like this with anyone, like I'd die if he ever left me.

I make my excuses and get an early night. Outside my door, I can hear him pacing around the apartment. I can't sleep, there's too much to say, but I stay exactly where I am, safe in my room.

The next morning, it's Christmas Day, my worst day of the year. There's a void where you should be, Odette, Maman is gone forever, and everyone is playing happy families.

But not this year. François has made his excuses to his own family and he's spending it here with me. He's planned a feast, and games just for the two of us, and arranged everything.

I pull on my red cashmere sweater and with it the anticipation of a special day, feeling like I used to before, when Christmas was good. Outside, the snow has stopped falling, the sky is blue as ice, the world is sparkling and our little apartment is cosy and insulated by the muffling snow.

François is already up, he's fixed up a tree as high as the ceiling and there's a box nestling under it tied with ribbon.

'I'm so sorry, we said no presents,' I say, pouring myself the coffee that he's made. 'I'll make it up to you, I promise.'

'You're still with us, that's the only present I needed this year. To be honest, I wasn't sure you were going to make it, but you're different now. Despite everything, you seem happier, less frantic.'

'Thanks to you,' I say. 'You're a good friend. I wouldn't be here without you.'

He reaches under the tree for the package and holds on to it for a moment, biting his lip.

'I think you're ready,' he says. 'Merry Christmas, Nina.'

Carefully untying the ribbon, I unfold the paper. It's a ring box and I steel myself. Dear François, I felt it too, but I'll never marry anyone. I hesitate, feel his intent gaze. I keep my eyes firmly on the box, forming the words that will hurt him the least. I can barely breathe as I lift the lid with shaking hands, but when I see what's inside I nearly faint. It's our ring, Odette!

'I kept it all this time. You never wore it onto the yacht that time you thought you'd lost it. I found it on the ballroom floor where you'd been dancing with that awful old reprobate. I was going to give it back to you the next morning after your swim to freedom, but you looked so exhilarated when you said you were going to leave it all behind and live your life that I couldn't bear it. It was like it was weighing you down. You're stronger now. But you were calling her name the night of the crash. I don't think you can ever be happy till you've found her.'

The weight of the ring is far greater than its bulk, but it's mine to bear.

'Thank you,' I stutter, completely overwhelmed. This is the loveliest thing anyone has ever done for me and the tears that come feel ancient. Somewhere outside the bells of Saint-Roch peal, a car buzzes by and a choir carols in the Tuileries and I'm kissing François and we can't stop. He holds me tight like he's about to lose me and flurries of snow make a tableau, enveloping us in our own world. He carries me to the bedroom and whispers words only we understand and for the first time in my life I give myself completely to another human being.

The winter sun has already disappeared by the time we emerge, starving and exhausted and tender and newly entwined like a midwinter's dream. We light a candle and pick at coquilles Saint-Jacques and duck à l'orange and sip our burgundy and sing Christmas carols but all we really want is each other and for the snow to keep falling forever so that we can stay in our little apartment away from the rest of the world.

New Year's Eve comes and goes and we venture out for crisp walks under a sleeping sun, climb the Eiffel Tower to test my newly healed legs, take our morning coffee at Les Deux Magots under the indulgent eye of the maître d' – *I wondered when you two would realise* – spend whole days wandering the streets of Paris talking and there's still not enough time to tell each other everything.

François records every precious moment on his beloved Nikon. The spare room in our apartment is now a makeshift darkroom and I love watching him work in the gloom, pegging the photos on the line and seeing the images emerge. There's me laughing on the Eiffel Tower, trying to catch my woolly hat that's caught by the wind in January. In February sun is reflected in my face outside Sacré-Coeur as it sets over Paris. On the Boulevard Saint-Germain I'm smiling under my umbrella in black and white, the raindrops catching the light in a late-March downpour. There I am again, in April, at the summer couture show. I'm back at work, reflected in the mirrored studio again, with Coco languidly smoking a cigarette and pointing to a hat that's askew. In May I'm outside Les Deux Magots with my morning espresso, Paris *Vogue* with a cover by François placed on the table – blossom trees tremble in the spring breeze.

We've named all the ducks on the boating pond in the Tuileries, Odette, and there I am, posing next to Doris and her delightful new brood of ducklings. I'm not smiling so much there. I think I already knew.

I'm sitting in the doctor's surgery now looking at a picture of me holding up a coupe of champagne at my twenty-second birthday party a few months ago.

So, our birthdays passed us by again, Odette, and I still haven't found you. Maman didn't expect to die so young and she didn't keep good records. The few she kept have moved with me several times since I was sixteen and I'm not an organiser. I have to admit, Odette, I lost some along the way.

Going back over the evidence, I realise how hard it was for Maman. It's a minefield. The organisations do their best, but information is patchy and has passed through so many hands in the years since the war. In the chaotic immediate aftermath, the United Nations High Commission for Refugees gathered what they could, but much was already destroyed or hidden. Next, the International Refugee Organization was set up. After that, it was the International Tracing Service, and so it goes on. All the painstaking filing and archiving, the slow processing of tens of thousands of desperate requests from people like Maman, and now me. It's time-consuming, detailed work, often disappointing, with so many dead-ends. It's almost unbearable, Odette, almost easier to try to forget.

Since I got the ring back, I'm trying another tack, on François' advice. Such a valuable piece can't have just disappeared into the ether, he said, and he's right. I've already found the auction house it passed through from Paris, the name of the SS officer who bought it, his escape to Colombia. I don't know what happened next yet, but I feel like it's the closest we've ever been, and the hope almost hurts. Where are you, Odette?

There's something else I have to tell you. A change in the air, a tiredness I've never experienced before. I'm tender and emotional and the doctor's confirmed what I already knew. I'm pregnant and it's the last thing in the world that I want. I can't have a baby, Odette. I feel that somehow our family is cursed until we find each other. Or maybe I just don't believe in happy families; the world is too cruel for such innocence. François doesn't know yet. I'm just going to sit here in the doctor's waiting room for a while, Odette, and try to think straight.

CHAPTER 20

HOPE

Nina, aged twenty-two

Morning sickness is horrible, Odette. Especially when no one knows, especially when you're alone. I never thought I'd spend our twenty-second year kneeling over the toilet bowl, feeling wretched and scared, but here I am, retching as silently as I can.

I pull the flush and close the door behind me, smooth down my hair, leaning on the sink to put my work face on. Coco is there In front of the mirror, applying her blood-red lipstick. Even in the reflection, her eyes could bore granite. I smile, turn on the tap, pretending to concentrate on the soap.

'You're looking very pale. You know that nothing would shock me, don't you?' says Coco.

'I still have flashbacks to the car accident,' I reply, pinching my cheeks. 'A bit of blusher will sort me out.' In the mirror, I'm a frightened ghost. Coco's gaze doesn't falter.

'I promised your maman I would watch over you. If there's ever anything you need, you know where I am,' she says.

'Thank you,' I say, more tersely than I mean to, and escape before those shrewd eyes read my thoughts.

In the bustle of the mirrored studio, it's almost easy to forget. Two new models are gossiping about Miles Davis, and Coco has created a new style to move with the times. The hemline is daringly high, above the knee, and the models look ravishing. This look will never be for me, Odette. I'm wearing jersey slacks and a Chanel boat-necked top because the accident scarred my knees.

It's wonderful to be back working the studio filled with Coco's favourite camelias, the girls in make-up, pulling on two-tone slingbacks, piling on ropes of pearls, adjusting hats, fastening stockings, the fitters pinning and adjusting. It's not real, but who cares?

François is here too, recording everything on his beloved Nikon.

'For goodness' sake, you're not here to photograph Nina, François. All these stunning, accomplished women in the finest couture giving you their best poses, and your lens is inexplicably drawn to the scruffy redhead kneeling on the floor with a pair of scissors in her teeth.'

François gives her that lopsided smile I love. Loved. Guilt makes his devotion irritating and I pretend I haven't heard, concentrate on a pin-tuck that isn't needed.

I stay late, and when I'm finished, François is waiting in the car with a bunch of summer flowers, my favourite brambly roses spilling from it. The petals are like a newborn's eyelids. I feel sick.

'Just for no reason. Your carriage awaits, Mademoiselle. I thought dinner at Le Train Bleu then dancing at Castel.'

'You're an angel, but it's been a long day, and I just got another Red Cross letter with a dead-end...' I'm sorry to use you for a lie, Odette.

'Of course, I'll just cook you dinner and we'll watch the sun go down on the Seine from our apartment,' he says.

'We need to talk, in private,' I say.

Sitting in his car, I turn to him.

'I'm going back to my little place on rue Gozlin. I need to be alone, just for a few days. It's been such a whirlwind what with the accident, and you and me thrown into living together before we've had time to think...'

He holds up his hand. 'Take all the time you need. I've seen you like this before and I know you like to be alone sometimes. You haven't had much of a chance for that, and... don't worry, we'll keep looking.'

And we *are* looking, Odette. All the agencies are helping, sifting through records, discovering new trails and following up with everyone who was at Lamorlaye. I know you were there somewhere when I met your friend on the swing.

I hold his face with both hands. 'You're too kind to me,' I say, kissing him.

He hugs me hard. 'I've always worried you wouldn't need me once you got better,' he says, not really joking.

'I need you more than ever,' I whisper, hugging him back and squashing the flowers. I do need him, I'm just not sure I want him. I love him, I don't... who knows about love? The Nazis took that the day they took you, Odette.

'I'll take you home,' François says, turning on the ignition.

'No need. Just give me some time. I'll call you, I promise.'

'Don't shut me out,' he says.

'Never,' I reply. But I have to, until I know what I want to do.

It's strange being back alone in my little studio on the fifth floor, right up in the eaves, with sloping ceilings and a skylight for a window. I haven't been back since the day of my accident, and it's like the *Mary Celeste*.

Everything's exactly as I left it. My dressing table's overflowing with expensive Chanel make-up – powdery eyeshadows broken up from so much travel, a red lipstick worn down on one side, mascara carelessly left open to dry up, brushes, rouge, business cards, ribbons, a half-filled notebook, several pairs of shoes slung haphazardly under the chair. The wardrobe door's open with clothes spilling out – toiles, tweeds, sequins, silks – the food cupboard is empty and the drinks cabinet is full. It's everything a hedonistic girl-about-Paris would need. My previous life, Odette, where I tried not to care.

I lie on my bed with a bottle of Veuve Clicquot to anaesthetise myself, remember I'll feel queasy if I drink it, and fall asleep, exhausted in a way I'm not used to. It must be the baby, Odette.

I can't get up the next day and I make my excuses to the atelier. Apart from the accident, I never take days off, not since I was sixteen, when Coco gave me the job, so I don't feel guilty.

I'm not sure what's night and day for a while. Luckily I have a few crackers and some tins, so I don't starve. In the liminal space I have time to think. I know one thing for sure. I'm not ready for motherhood, not till I find you, Odette. The phone rings and rings, I know it'll be François. I can't bear to lie to him, so I don't answer.

When there's a gentle knock on the door and I hear his voice, I know I have to face him. That worried furrow is back, and he looks drawn and sad.

We hug. He kisses me and it's like home. He's oil on troubled waters, but that doesn't take away the trouble.

'I feel like I'm losing you,' he says.

I don't reply. He changes the subject.

'I've got something for you, a real breakthrough about Odette!'

He holds up an envelope from Bullinger's Auctioneers. We perch on the edge of the bed and I unfold the letter, his arm firmly round me because I'm shaking.

They've traced the Emerald Lake, all the way from Paris to Colombia and back to a museum in East Berlin! I close my eyes, swim in the green lake with you like we used to when we were children after I lost you. My eyes snap open and I jump up.

'She's there with it, I know she is!'

'Don't get too excited. It'll be wonderful for you to find her, but you know how many dead-ends there've been. It might not lead to her.'

'You remember I told you about Lamorlaye, when I just knew she was there. I've got the same feeling now. Don't you dare say it's wishful thinking.'

He salutes. 'OK, boss.'

I hug the letter to my heart and do a little dance around my studio singing our favourite song, Odette. François spins me around in delight.

'I'll check the train times,' he declares. 'We can book the night train and wake up to Schnitzel and Bratwurst and Apfelkuchen...'

I stop dead, try not to notice the hope in his eyes.

'I'm going to go on my own. I'll call you every night, I promise.'

CHAPTER 21

THE WALL

Nina, aged twenty-two

It's the most glorious August morning, Odette. I watched the sun rise in rosy gilded clouds from my hotel and it's just half an hour till the S-Bahn opens, where I get the train to the East and the museum that contains our ring. I promised I'd find you, didn't I?

Most of the city is still asleep, but I'm waiting in a café, feeling closer to the moment we'll finally meet than I ever have since the Ritz. There'll be so much to tell, though you might be shocked that I'm pregnant. I try not to think about it, not until I know what to do.

Will we just know each other, or feel like strangers? It seems too much to hope that I'll be looking into identical eyes, that we'll share identical gestures, laugh at the same jokes... But I'm getting ahead of myself. I'm going to start with the museum and hope for the best. Why not dare to hope? Maman always

said the ring could be the link that would bring us together and
I have to believe her.

I finish my coffee and walk to the S-Bahn, almost floating on
this summer's morning, but when I get to the ticket office they
tell me all lines to the East are closed. It's never happened
before, they tell me, and no one knows what on earth is going
on. There's confusion and shouting and people are starting to
panic. I rush back up the steps two at a time. Outside, a group of
men are huddled round a Mambo portable radio, shock on their
faces as an urgent voice reads the news. My heart thuds.

'What's happening?' I say in broken German.

'*Französin?*' One of them says. *Are you French?*

I nod.

'They've closed off East Berlin. We've all sleepwalked into
it, no one had a clue, or ever thought they'd do it, but now East
Berlin is a rat trap. No one in or out.'

I stare at him, confused. This is 1961. Cities don't get
chopped up like that. I turn cold. Has some kind of war started?

'What happened?' I venture.

'The GDR want nothing to do with the West, so they're
barricading us off.'

The words roll in my head without making sense. I'm just
metres from you, Odette, I can feel it. I look around wildly for a
way across.

'Are you all right? Have you got someone there?'

'Yes,' I say. You're there. You must be. This can't be real.
They can't separate us twice, Odette.

There are groups of people hurtling up the Strasse des 17
Juni towards the Brandenburg Gate. I join the rush. The men
with the radio swoop by on motorbikes. There are families, people
of all ages running, dragging suitcases, pushing prams. I flash back
to the scenes at the Gare de Lyon, when Maman and I left Paris
and I was so worried that you'd never find us if we didn't stay.

When I get to the Brandenburg Gate, it's a horrible, brutal sight. Rolls of barbed wire attached to makeshift concrete posts form a barrier, stretching as far to the left and right as the eye can see. Behind it is a line of soldiers and armoured trucks and, behind them, a gathering mass of desperate people waving and shouting. On the Western side, people are looking on in disbelief, and it's strangely silent, like they're waiting for someone to do something.

I dig out my camera and take a snap. The motorbike boys start throwing stones and shouting at the guards. A British army jeep turns up. The crowd cheers but they just take in the scene, make notes and drive off.

I push to the front, eye the East German guards. They look back impassively, like I'm from another world. A woman holds up a baby.

'My husband is on the other side, a Herr Bremmer. He's a baker on the Unter den Linden...' as if they'd somehow know him. 'You have to let him through!'

The baby starts to bawl. The insults from the West Berliners get louder and I'm incandescent. All those years of suffering, and here I am, standing in front of soldiers again and they're dividing families and lovers and friends. How dare they! I join in the shouting.

'Bastards! Home-wreckers, communist-fascist pigs!' I scream.

It's useless. I spot the motorbike men. I hear a ripple, a call to action, and they start up their engines and drive away from the gate.

'What's happening?' I say to the one who speaks French.

'We've had word there's a way through, on Bernauer Strasse, and we're off to help. My girlfriend's there.'

'I'm coming with you.'

His hair is down to his shoulders, he's wearing jeans and a

gold hoop earring, and he tells me his name, Andreas. He's an engineering student and he's already planning a tunnel.

'We can't let the bastards win. I tried calling my grandma in the East last night and I thought it was weird I couldn't get through to her. They must've cut all the phone wires. She'll be terrified.'

We speed through the streets. People are beginning to gather along the length of the barbed wire. Where there's no hastily erected barbed wire, there are soldiers and tanks, pointing their water cannons and guns at any protesters.

'They've literally put it up overnight, it wasn't there yesterday, it's unbelievable, we never thought they'd do this.' His voice is shaking with impotent anger.

When we get to Bernauer Strasse, it's chaos. The street is lined with tenement blocks, and every single window gives over to the West, with the back of the building to the East. An escape portal! If people are getting to our side, dare I climb in to get to *their* side? My hand drops to my stomach. Can I risk it? I take a photograph to remember the sight.

From a third-storey window, a woman in a headscarf all oblongs and block colours like a Mondrian painting is hanging by her fingertips. Underneath, firemen are holding a sheet and shouting encouragement.

'Jump!' I join in. 'You'll find your wings on the way down!'

I take a snap for posterity. She lets go and the crowd cheers. An old lady in a knitted cardigan waves a handkerchief from the window, tears pouring down her cheeks. Underneath her, a family pass down suitcases, a budgie, a basket to a teenage son before the mother, then the father, who's wearing at least three suits, jumps and dashes across the road. The grandmother blows them kisses, forces a smile of encouragement before she disappears into the shadows, broken.

I look for the girl who landed on the jump sheet, but a

crowd have gathered around her and are strapping her to a makeshift stretcher.

I hope she's safe and I send her a little prayer, but then another tragedy emerges right in front of me.

'That's my sister, help!' shouts a boy in the crowd. I find her in a red dress sprawled on the floor, her ankle painfully swollen. She must be about my age. Above her, a young girl, maybe just a teenager, is hanging out of a ground-floor window, her hands gripped by a Volkspolizei in a blue uniform trying to tug her back in.

'Please!'

I grab her by the waist, she's screaming, her sister is begging him to let her go.

'It's all right, I've got you,' I say. Her waist is tiny, her breathing shallow and terrified. I feel like she'll break at any moment.

'Let her go and nobody gets killed,' says the Volkspolizei.

I have her firmly in my grip. 'Not this time, she's coming with me.'

I bite his hand, drag her back with the strength of all the anger of the eighteen years since I saw you, Odette.

We snap back. She's free!

'Bitch!'

He reaches for his rifle. Time slows. His other hand is on the windowsill and I dart forward, wrench the sash down as hard as I can, hear his cry of pain as we dash to the other side of the street. The girl and her sister melt into the alley without a word. I don't blame them. I send a silent prayer, 'stay together'.

Down the street, a soldier throws off his rifle, jumps the barbed wire and runs down a side street to freedom. Another small triumph.

Mothers send children from high windows, hanging from towels, to the waiting arms of strangers, sweethearts are reunited. I stay to help, take a portion of the jump sheet, shout encouragement. My strength comes in surges of fury. Each dash to freedom is for you, Odette.

I scan the windows, hoping against hope that you'll be one of the escapees. It gets more and more desperate as the Volkspolizei arrive. One woman falls from a third-floor window and doesn't make it. People are laying flowers for her hours later as I leave to crawl back to my hotel.

My hands are cut, my arms are bruised, but I had a hand in reuniting people who soldiers tried to part. On the radio, I hear that people are still jumping the wire, swimming canals, darting across forgotten parts of the border, and I pray for them.

It was some kind of revenge, but I didn't find you, Odette.

I call François. 'I know,' he says quietly. 'Come home.'

It's then I know for certain that I can't bring a child into this world.

CHAPTER 22

SALT AND PEPPER DIAMONDS

BERLIN, 1961

Odette/Odelia, aged twenty-two

I escaped the prison they called a children's home, but now East Berlin is a rat trap. There's a bad joke everyone here knows. Why do Stasi make the best taxi drivers? Because they already know your name and where you live.

My apprenticeship in jewellery is the best thing that ever happened to me, but now the Stasi secret police have to put their sticky fingerprints all over it.

I scan my workbench and assess the situation. The tiny blade on my piercing saw is snapped, but that's the only physical damage they've done. The Stasi modus operandi is more about messing with your brain than your stuff.

It takes a lot to ruffle my feathers, but I've got to give them credit for this. It's subtle, and spooky as hell. My files are all placed in a cross shape, neatly, the entire length of the bench. I'm left-handed, but some bright spark has moved my pliers to the right, exactly where they should be but on the wrong side.

My tweezers and triblet have swapped places. and in the crucible some oaf has sketched a smiley face in the soot with his fat finger. Nice to see they have a sense of humour. I find a rag and wipe it clean.

I try not to notice anything else. If you're torn from your mother's arms at a tender age, rejected by your adoptive family, brutalised by the state holding pen they call a children's home and then spat out into the world with not so much as the steam off their piss, it takes more than a few displaced tools to throw you off-track. That's what I'm telling myself anyway.

I've never been afraid of being alone in the workshop, until now. When Johan, the museum curator and guardian of the Emerald Lake, took me under his wing and found me this apprenticeship, I thought I'd died and gone to heaven. The minute I saw all those jewellers at their workbenches beavering away, hammering with their little tools like elves, the smell of the soldering gun, the ding ding ding of the hammers, the newly faceted gems splitting prisms under the studio lights, I knew there was nowhere else I'd rather be.

Now I have my own workbench and the wooden peg I use to steady my hand is worn down from all my creations, unique to me. Then there's the jars of files, mini drills, polishing heads, the leather skin below lined with tissue paper to catch the valuable metal filings, all waiting for me to pick them up and make something beautiful, something that matters to people.

It's Sunday morning, usually the best time of day, the time I get the whole place to myself. Rather than let the fear, and them, get to me, I try to make myself angry at their intrusion. I turn on every single light, sing as loudly and enthusiastically as I can just in case they're watching, and search every corner. There's no one here any more. This was just a warning.

I'm lucky this time. I don't know anyone who hasn't experienced something sinister at the hands of the Stasi. They sent drugs to my boss through the post and then arrested him for possession. The old lady in the apartment next door was on the phone to her sister in the West and made a joke about the Stasi. There was a weird click, then a stern voice warning her to stop communicating with imperialist spawn. The day after she told me about it, she disappeared.

I suppose I should never have confronted my ex-dad, but I was counting on even him being bugged when I stormed his office and asked for my ring back.

I think back with relish to the face-off I had with him. It was as near as I've ever seen him ruffled since the smug bastard dumped me in that children's home.

I hadn't seen him since the day I found the Emerald Lake at the museum seven years ago. Amazing how ignorance can make you brave, but seeing it pretty much every day in my work with Johan drove me to it. I got past security by saying the great Dieter Fischer and I had a meeting, that he was my long-lost adoptive father, and I marched right in.

'I've found my ring. There's a trust you mentioned to your fellow cronies when I was a kid. I just wanted to check it's still in place – that it'll be mine when I turn twenty-five.'

He barely twitched those thick lips, but his eyes looked flustered.

'It's lovely to see you, Odelia. I assume you are enjoying your employment as a jeweller? I gave strict instructions that you were to be well set up. And of course, all the paperwork is in order surrounding the Emerald Lake. The ring is yours at the age of twenty-five, but a lot can happen in three years,' he'd said, threateningly.

I was brazen, maybe I went too far, judging by the warning signs in my workshop today, but it felt good to say.

'Funny what a child can remember. It's sixteen years since I heard you saying you'd put my ring in trust when I was living at your house. I remember everything else vividly before that, too. So many people were displaced by the war, I must be one of the few people who remembers you exactly as you were in those days.'

We both knew what I was talking about, that he was a Nazi and an enthusiastic SS officer. I was too young to understand when I was a child, but now everyone knows that he and his compatriots were responsible for the deaths of millions, a horrifying six million Jews in the Holocaust.

He sat there like the cat that got the cream and it was all I could do to stop myself from saying anything else. He'd have me killed if I went any further.

Still, it was enough for him to say, 'I would have thought that, as the proper FDJ member you were brought up as, you would understand about the redistribution of wealth. However, if you insist you still want to possess it, yes, the ring is in trust for you.'

'It's all I have left of my family,' I say. Now I'm the one that's ruffled. I can't tell him that I believe that, if I have it, they'll still find me, even after all these years.

'Nonsense,' he'd said. 'We're all watching your progress with close interest to ensure your... welfare. Now, it's been a delight to see you looking so well, but if you don't mind...'

He picked up his pen, but I could see his hand was shaking. Score, 1–1. He won, and I left terrified but it felt good, too, to know there was a chance that the ring could still be mine. At least it'll be on record that he owes me somewhere in the files this spies' nest keeps.

I try to forget him and focus on the task at hand. I fumble for the keys to the cabinet, praying that they didn't get to my most precious possession. I grope at the back panel for the secret drawer, and my fingers find it, feel the soft nap of the velvet box. Thank God, it's still there. My hands shake as I prise the box open, and there it is, my dirty diamond. After emeralds, these gems are my favourite, and more affordable. They're not the usual clean, clear crystal, but that makes them more interesting.

I love the way that they're peppered with flaws and inclusions; imperfect – still a diamond, with all the qualities and sparkle, but with a story to tell. They remind me of myself a bit.

I hold it up to the light. The trade would call this colour champagne to sell it for a higher price, but I call it salt-and-pepper for its sparky, spicy appearance, and I'd never sell. In fact, I hate selling any of my creations. Maybe it's the Emerald Lake that's turned my brain because it's my only connection with real family, but I can't help thinking that every gem, every piece of metal I heat and shape and mould, has its own character, and becomes a talisman for the wearer. Wedding and engagement rings are passed down the generations, necklaces and earrings recall heydays and high days, balls and birthdays and celebrations, death and inheritance... who knows what stories my jewels will have to tell?

I arrange everything back to where it should be. I pretend it's fun, like a game of memory. But the message is clear. *We're watching you. Stay away.*

They don't want me at the museum hanging around the Emerald Lake. It's a bit too close for comfort for my ex-adoptive father, and he's right. Because one day, when I get my ring back, I intend to expose him for the evil Nazi he was. I'm not sure how, because I'm sure he's covered his tracks, but I'll get the hell out of here, away from the Stasi, get protection, and expose him somehow. It's my word against his, but he deserves to pay for his war crimes.

What they fail to realise is how badly they've underestimated me. That ring is my only link to family and I'm not giving up on it. My hopes and fears are absorbed by it. I don't even know who I'm talking to now, not really. I'm a little old to have an imaginary friend, but I've always talked to you, Nina, and you've got me through some dark times just knowing you're there, even if only in my head. To you I'm Odette, not Odelia, and for some reason that means a lot, even though missing you and Maman is like an ache I've never got used to. However fast I run, I can never escape it.

I lock up the workshop and head towards the museum. It's the most glorious August morning, the sun is still rising and the sky's ablaze, like the fiery flecks in an opal. With every step I take, I get angrier. How dare my excuse of an ex-father? He's nothing more than a puffed-up Intelligence Commander of the Stasi using such cowardly techniques to frighten me. And with anger comes a familiar friend, rebellion. I will *not* be intimidated. Doesn't he realise how much I have on him? He was a Nazi and I'll expose him if I have to. It'd be dangerous, but I'm beyond caring.

I change direction and head straight for the museum. I hope the Stasi are watching. Screw them.

There's no one out yet, and the streets of Berlin belong to me as the sun warms the world for another beautiful day. By the time I get to the Littenstrasse, I could dance and sing along the pavements like one of those Hollywood musicals they try to stop us seeing.

The receptionist at the museum looks away but lets me through, and Johan, my fairy godfather, is sitting in his office, a loupe pressed to one eye, turning over a brooch in his bony hand. I know not to disturb him when he's so absorbed. Instead, I make my assessment of the jewel from afar, then clear my throat. He looks up, startled. The loupe clatters to the desk.

'Russian, possibly Romanov, platinum, cushion-cut diamonds. My guess is the central gem is around two carats. It's a good one, a pristine beauty,' I rattle off nonchalantly.

His serious face crumples into a proud smile, and I wonder if this warm glow is how it feels to have real parents.

'Well, this is a lovely surprise. I thought I'd lost you to boys and jewels,' he says, beaming.

'You almost did, but I've still got room in my heart for my old Svengali.'

'I like to think of us more as benefactor and ward, but I know that sounds terribly old-fashioned to such a bright young thing. Here,' he says, jutting out his sharp cheekbone, 'give the old man a kiss hello.'

I owe Johan everything, and he asks nothing of me. He's the good side of life in East Berlin. He believes in social justice, education, art, equality, and he's given them all to me.

It wasn't easy being in a workshop full of men after the female camaraderie of the tailor's shop, but I soon had them all whipped into shape, and made them realise that any unwanted approaches would be brutally shunned. That was sixteen-year-old me, a face like an angel, mouth like a foghorn, who could literally fell a man twice my age with a well-placed put-down. I'm a little more subtle nowadays, but my colleagues still know not to cross me. So, with the gift of education, someone who believed in me, and my own determination, here I am, the highest-selling creator in the workshop, and something of a curiosity in the man's world of solders, metals, precious gems and creative geniuses – or is it genii? I should have paid more attention at school.

There'll be some stories to tell when I find you, Maman. I'm still here, waiting for you! I don't remember your face, but I can never forget yours, my twin sister, because I look at you in the mirror every day.

'Talking to your twin again? I almost fear you finding her. One is difficult enough, but two...' Johan whistles and I laugh. 'I'm flattered you came, but I assume you're here to visit your talisman? I hope you were careful?'

We've long suspected the Stasi were trailing me, so I don't tell him about my workbench and the visit.

'Of course,' I say.

It's stupid, but I had a weird feeling that I had to be here today, that maybe my twin would miraculously appear. Wishful thinking does weird things to you, especially when you're an orphan. Maybe I've just always hated authority.

He hands me the keys.

'Don't waste away too much of your time in that dingy little room, it's a beautiful day out there.'

I hug him. 'I won't, don't worry.'

Unlocking the door where the ring is showcased, I'm home. To think that this was mine, ours. The fact that it was little me who etched those two stars side by side makes me ache. I wish I could reach back and hug her, tell her she'd be all right.

All the broken memories, a sister with tumbling red curls, a mother who made me feel safe and dressed us in the same outfits. A hot chocolate, soldiers, cold terror, followed by home-sickness that ripped my insides out... it's all such a jumble.

The constant ache turns to pain, but at least I feel something and it's real. I can't help believing that, while I'm close to the ring, there's a chance. Of what, I don't know. I close my eyes. *'I'm here, I'm here, I'm here. It's Odette, come and find me.'*

What is it, this change in the air, like it's charged?

The door bursts open. I spin round, thinking it's the Stasi, but it's Johan, his satchel unbuckled. His satchel's never unbuckled. He's shouting something. It's urgent. I force myself out of my reverie.

'They're closing the border!'

'What?'

'Barbed wire across the Brandenburg Gate, police and soldiers right the way along. They've done what we never imag-ined they would.'

He hands me a leaflet.

An anti-fascist protection rampart is erected today, 13 August, in order to keep you safe. The rampart will prevent spies and elements who conspire to prevent the will of the people of the German Democratic Republic infiltrating from the West.

Both from the moral standpoint, as well as in terms of the interests of the whole German nation, leaving the GDR is now an act of political and moral backwardness and depravity.

Something inside me snaps. Families will be split, liberties curtailed, lives ruined... again. I tear up the leaflet, I'd burn it in their faces if I could.

Johan picks up the pieces. 'You need to be more subtle than that, my firebrand. There's a chance you can escape, but you have to be quick. And the likelihood is, you can never come back. All the lines to the West are cut, the S-Bahn now terminates in the East and they mean business.'

I look at the Emerald Lake. I've learned a lot since then, that this is step-cut to enhance its perfect colour, that the greens change within the steps depending on the light, the fact that twenty-four-carat gold is the purest you can get, but very soft, so it's quite likely that this ring will have a travelling replica somewhere out there. Leaving would mean leaving this, my last connection, and Johan, the closest I ever had to family. The possibility that it might be mine on my twenty-fifth birthday, however remote, is worth staying for. I don't care about the money, but I can use it to search for my family.

'You have to move on,' says Johan. 'It's your future you need to think about, not the past.'

'How will my family find me?'

'If it's meant to be, they will. Plus, I'll be here.'

'You're really staying?'

'I'm old, but you weren't made for cages. And how can a jeweller thrive when no one has any money? Your place is in the West.'

'Where will I go, what will I do? I won't know a soul.'

Johan scribbles something down on a piece of paper: Andreas Abel, 24 Kurfürstendamm. This is my nephew,

Andreas. He's a good lad, and he'll help you. I've told him about my protégée over the years, so he'll already know of you.

I take it and hug him. 'How can I leave you? I've already lost one family.'

'Six years ago, when I saw this determined young woman demanding to see an East German multimillion-mark jewel she claimed was her own, I knew I was looking at someone special. You'll find a way. I hear there's still a way out for the brave, through Bernauer Strasse. Maybe Frau Klein will be able to help you.'

I unlock the cabinet, put the Emerald Lake on my finger, stare into the green depths that I've dreamed of swimming in with my sister so many lonely nights, the greens reflecting themselves within the step-cut like a hall of mirrors.

'I've got to leave you again,' I whisper.

This ring represents everything to me, a life I never got to live, but Johan is right. It's time to live my own life.

I run my finger over the crude scratched twins holding hands and put it back in the glass display case.

'I'll need to get my tools from the workshop.'

'Don't be ridiculous, the place is crawling.'

'They've already been, this morning. They did their magic trick of moving everything around to warn me. I'm sure they'll have other things on their minds, what with imprisoning the whole city against their will.'

'You should have told me!'

'I didn't want to worry you.'

'Too late for that. I've never had a moment's peace since the day you flounced in here,' he says. 'Go on then, but be quick, and meet me outside the law courts on Littenstrasse.'

At the workshop, a couple of men dressed like rockers are hanging around outside smoking. I double back, take a side street, still my breathing. What the hell is happening? Rockers don't have short back and sides, Stasi do. I'd laugh if it wasn't so terrifying.

I'm more careful now, take the long way round to meet Johan. He's not there. I look around, search the parked cars to see if he's waiting in his. Then I see him, in the back of a black Trabant. One driver up front, a man in a raincoat sitting next to him in the back. They've got him. Please God, it's not my fault. He gives me a brief flicker of recognition, then keeps his gaze firmly forward.

I pull my headscarf over my red hair and blend into the gathering crowd that's heading down the Unter den Linden to the Brandenburg Gate. Loudspeakers are blasting out propaganda, leaflets like the one Johan showed me are scattered like confetti, discarded on the roads and pavements in disgust and disbelief. We can't get to the gate because there are tanks, and files of soldiers standing in the sunshine, guns slung over their shoulders. It's eerily quiet apart from the propaganda broadcasts blasting out into the streets. I strain to see beyond them. Johan was right. Ugly, spiky barbed wire is coiled round the grand pillars of the Brandenburg Gate and stretched across the gaps. There are people on the other side, standing in silent disbelief, mirroring us in the East.

A jeep with four soldiers pulls up on the other side. They're British, I think. Surely they'll do something, say something? We hold our breath for a confrontation, but they only stop for a few moments, then leave. A group of men with motorbikes on the Western side start slinging insults, but they're about as effective as gnats bothering a giant. A gradual realisation, then panic starts to ripple through the crowd... *my daughter's on the other side, please, I beg you to let me cross to her... my fiancé was going to come tomorrow... I was just babysitting for my niece, I need to get back to my family!*

We're trapped like rats, no one in or out. Johan mentioned Bernauer Strasse and Frau Klein.

I know where that is, luckily; I've delivered there from the workshop so many times. The front of the building is West, the back East, so Johan's idea of an escape loophole makes sense. I slip away from the increasingly agitated crowd and make my way through the streets, trying not to look like I'm in a hurry. Along the border, workers with jackhammers are erecting stone posts as soldiers train guns on them. No one wants this. I keep going. It takes forever to get there, but I use the time to gather my courage. I only have the clothes I'm standing up in, but I've got me, and you, my sister, somewhere in the West, and that's enough. At least it's enough to pretend that I'll be all right.

It's still early on Sunday morning, so Bernauer Strasse looks like it would on any weekend morning; quiet, a little run-down, cats stretching by the overflowing bins, washing fluttering outside the upstairs windows in the morning breeze. Calm, but with a charge in the air, like a storm is coming. At the windows, frightened faces dodge when I look up, net curtains tremble, babies are silenced.

I slip round the side of the building. I know the concierge, and he opens the door. Drunk, even at this hour in the morning.

'Delivery,' I say. He waves me through, glad to slump back into his chair.

I head for Frau Klein's apartment. She's always been kind to me and is one of my main buyers. She had a twin sister who died, and we often talk about the golden thread that connects people born from the same egg.

I pray she'll take pity on me as I knock softly on her door, careful not to be mistaken for the hated Stasi-style rap. Her eye is magnified in the spyhole, and she slides back the bolt, opens up and pulls me in without a word. I catch a glimpse of myself in the hall mirror, pallid, beads of sweat on my forehead, haunted eyes.

She takes my arm and draws me over to the window that faces the West. 'You're here for this? Johan called me. His nephew's a good boy, at least you'll have somewhere to go at first.'

It's pandemonium. While the back of the building that faces the East, where I entered, is quiet, all hell is let loose at the front, which faces to the West. Someone from next door is crouching on the windowsill plucking up the courage to leap for a jump sheet held by firemen and well-wishers three floors below.

On the ground floor, families are pushing suitcases, babies, birdcages through the windows and making a run for it. A few windows along a man is dangling, his wrists gripped by Volks*polizei*, ankles being pulled by two West Berliners who've jumped off their motorbikes to help. Gravity wins, and he's free.

I look at Frau Klein in horror and hope.

'Wait there,' she says. She comes shuffling back with a jewellery pouch. I open it, and inside is every piece I've ever made for her.

'Take them,' she says with tears in her eyes. 'It's now or never. Do you dare?'

I look down. It's a long way. Nausea and vertigo grip me. *Forward.* I steel myself.

'I dare,' I say, 'but I can't take this.'

I hand back the jewellery pouch.

'Hush.' She folds my hand back over the pouch. 'What does an old woman want with such trinkets? Pay me back when you're rich, and you will be. Use this to start you off and I'll wear your escape with pride instead. Go, now!'

There's a hard rap and a sharp kick on the door. Stasi. I crouch on the windowsill trying to gather myself as Frau Klein shuffles slowly over to answer it.

'Wait, I'm coming! No need to knock it down. You boys never clean up your mess, just give an old lady a second to get to the door...'

I balance on the windowsill, everything trembling uncontrollably. Someone spots me from below and the jump sheet is organised.

Everyone's shouting encouragement but I can't hear their words because my heart's swishing in my ears. Behind me, there's a scuffle at the apartment door and Frau Klein threatens them with dark curses if they touch a hair on my head.

'Jump! You'll find your wings on the way down!' shouts a girl. Her voice is like a dream. It gives me the courage I need, and I launch forward, hit the jump sheet at an awkward angle. Blood trickles out between my legs and I'm strangely detached from it. I only have time to regret vaguely that I somehow knew the baby inside me would never make it into the world, before the morning sun blurs and darkens and the sky turns black.

CHAPTER 23

A MONDRIAN HEADSCARF

SANARY-SUR-MER, MAY 2024

Fleur

A whole week had gone by. She hadn't heard from Nick since he'd called her about the letter from Raschmann trying to reconnect the Emerald Lake with Odette before he died in Colombia. It was a huge breakthrough, and she'd been on a high, but now the trail had gone cold again. She imagined the number of times this must have happened to Nina and felt closer to her than ever, though somehow that also made her feel very alone. Jake was out of her life, and her budding friendship with Nick was ruined. Even the photos of Nina, so young and glamorous, hanging out in Chanel's studio, laughing in the South of France with the fishermen and all those famous people, made her feel bereft. This woman in the photographs had lost her twin in horrific circumstances, but she'd nevertheless made a life for herself.

She was even in love, if these photos were anything to go by, but Nina was yet to find out she'd lose her own daughter Stella,

Fleur's mother, who died soon after Fleur's birth. It seemed Nina was in love with a photographer, and she took pictures herself, but as yet she hadn't found one picture of Stella, however hard she looked. Maybe Nina couldn't bear to keep photos of her lost daughter.

What a mess. Fleur refreshed her email and there was a message from the Red Cross Tracing Service entitled *Littenstrasse Museum, Emerald Lake*. The attachment revealed an old cutting from a newspaper called *Berliner Zeitung*.

There was a picture of two figures standing side by side next to a museum display case, and the Red Cross Tracing Service had translated the caption for her. *Herr Johan Abel, Curator and Director of the Littenstrasse Museum, with Odelia Fischer, jewellery apprentice and prominent member of the Freie Deutsche Jugend.*

Fleur's nerve endings fizzed.

There, standing next to a studious-looking man with a pointy beard, was Nina, but not Nina. It was unmistakable! The same gamine crop, but the expression was less open, more wary, a little harder-looking perhaps, with a challenge in her eye that dared you to defy her. It was like finding treasure – Odette, alive and grown up! Her clothes were similar to Nina's chic style from the Fifties and Sixties – a tight pencil skirt, wide belt, fitted blouse – but the fabrics were lighter, cheaper, more worn and creased. She was wearing a very distinctive scarf, too, like a Mondrian painting, all squares and oblongs. Next to the two figures, in a glass case, was the Emerald Lake.

Fleur would know it anywhere, an exact replica of the ring she'd worn every day since she'd arrived in France. Proof that somehow her instinct about the Emerald Lake being the key to finding Odette was correct. She read the article, feeling a surge of hope and curiosity.

The Littenstrasse Museum has many fascinating treasures, but the star attraction is an almost flawless twenty-carat emerald believed to be hundreds of years old. The gem, characterised by one small inclusion in the shape of a heart, is a much-prized artefact recovered from Nazi looting and restored to the East German people through the generosity of a secret benefactor thought to be a senior Stasi official.

How could she even begin to unpick this? She googled the museum, but found that it had closed down just after the wall came down in 1989. Fleur had found from reading up on the subject that Lebensborn children were often given new names, but the only record she could find of Odelia Fischer was the newspaper cutting, nothing more. The Red Cross Tracing Service had already found out that Johan Abel was listed as having died on 13 August 1961, the day the wall went up.

Fleur lost track of time staring at the photo, mesmerised, willing Odette/Odelia to tell her story from this digital echo of the past.

She called Nick – he'd be thrilled at this development, and she was desperate to share the news. No reply, so she texted him again.

Please pick up, I have the most unbelievable news ever!

She hugged her phone in lieu of hugging her Great-Aunt Odette, and then replied to her Red Cross contact. She tried to keep calm. The Red Cross had already warned her that they were overwhelmed with these kinds of leads, and it could take months, years even, for them to progress this.

While she was waiting for news, two more boxes arrived from the Chanel archives that Nina had bequeathed to them, marked

1961 and 1962. Fleur set them on the kitchen table. What would these bring? She lifted the 1961 lid to reveal documents, photos and receipts, neatly ordered by the archivist. Nina would have been just twenty-two, her mother already dead six years. Fleur pulled on the cotton gloves the archivist had sent with the box and picked out the file of photographs. Three of them set her blood thumping. First, a picture of the Brandenburg Gate covered in barbed wire, second, a snap of Nina with a long-haired man, standing next to his motorbike, and finally a picture of an apartment block with desperate-looking people escaping from the windows.

She turned them over, and saw that Nina had noted the date and place: *13 August 1961. Berlin Wall.*

Fleur scrutinised the faces of the people caught up in the events of that day, lost in morbid fascination. There was a family pushing their worldly goods from a ground-floor window, caught forever in a state of panic, desperation and hope by Nina's lens. Above them was a man being held by the wrists while people on the street below pulled at his ankles. Higher up, from a third-floor window, a slight woman in a headscarf was dangling from a windowsill, watched by an old woman in the shadows.

Fleur blinked. She'd been staring so long her eyes were playing tricks on her. She retrieved the newspaper cutting from her phone, compared it to this lady hanging with her back to the camera. A Mondrian-style headscarf tight round her hair, pencil skirt, wide belt. It was the exact same outfit as the one Odette was wearing in the newspaper cutting. It had to be her! Was this a long-overdue righting of a wrong, the day the two met, caught up in another momentous happening, where once again the authorities saw fit to divide innocent people?

Fleur dug around in the tin – there were a few Berlin restaurant receipts, hole-punched return train tickets, the big old-fashioned kind, dated 11–14 August 1961, with a scrawled note on the back. *She's behind the wall, I know she is. Too late.*

They must have been so close. Fleur could weep for the two sisters, for lost chances. These tiny drops of information, of lives lived without the narrative that should go with them, was almost worse than knowing nothing at all.

She checked her phone. Nothing from Nick, though he'd read her message. Fair enough, he owed her nothing whatsoever, and he'd already done so much for her. She hadn't lied to him exactly, but was keeping the truth from him the same thing?

An overwhelming craving for avocado and sushi rice drove her down to the kitchen, where she'd ensured she had copious supplies. What did her cravings mean, boy or girl? She had no one to ask what they'd felt, no mother to advise her, no grandmother to remember her experiences. She took a picture of her breakfast bowl; avocado, chilli flakes, honey, rice and pickles. *Weird, but delicious* she wrote as a caption as she dropped the pic into her 'baby' file. This child would have all its questions answered.

'Come on, we both need to know,' she whispered to her baby.

Fleur opened the 1962 box, divided into neat sections of receipts, document folders and tins of photographs.

She flicked feverishly through them. Fewer of Nina at Chanel's atelier and, in those that there were, she looked more serious than she usually did, and she was never looking at the camera. Then, tiny and black and white, cracked, with a scalloped edge... Fleur stopped dead, her heart in her mouth.

Nina was holding a baby. Mother and child were locked in an adoring gaze, Nina's head bent protectively over the girl wearing a tiny A-line cotton dress with a petal motif, and embroidered booties. They were in a hospital bed and it was the exact dress she'd found in the box in the attic.

Hot tears stung Fleur's eyes. This must be Stella, Fleur's mother, almost the moment she'd taken her first breath in the world.

'Hello, Mum,' Fleur whispered. *We never met, but I'm here, with a new life inside me, your grandchild.*

Fleur studied the little slip of a thing in Nina's arms, so precious and new. Eyes tight shut, rosebud lips, fists clenched. The photo was over sixty years old, grainy, tiny, all she had of the elusive Stella. God, she wanted more. If baby Stella's eyes were open, maybe she'd be able to make out a resemblance in the shape of them. But it was nothing more than a blurry facsimile, impossible to tell what she really looked like, and Fleur longed to know this little angel.

On the back was a date, 4 February 1962. Stella's birthday? She put the photo on the bedside table. She'd find a photo frame and keep it there. Rummaging back through the box, she found no more clues about Odette/Odelia, just a few more papers, including an end-of-tenancy agreement from Nina's Paris flat dated the end of February, soon after Stella's birth.

At the bottom of the 1962 box was a white envelope, which Fleur opened. She gasped. A woman holding a baby, wearing the same little A-line dress with the petal motif. The same dress again! *My only picture of grown-up Stella, holding Fleur, 1997* Nina had written.

Fleur could barely breathe as she took in every detail. The picture was in colour. Stella had brown hair with a red tinge, a straight nose, full lips. She was tall and willowy, not so much like petite Nina, or Fleur, but more like someone else she recognised. The man in the photos with Nina, the photographer! So she was sure now that it had to be. Nina's boyfriend, François from the photos, who was Fleur's grandfather.

She devoured the photo. Fleur and Stella had the same spade-shaped fingernails, the same half-smile, the same way of standing slightly pigeon-toed. Fleur wanted desperately to see the same devotion between the two figures she'd seen in the picture of Nina holding Stella as a baby, but this photo was strange. Stella's eyes were lifeless, and she was holding Fleur away from her, almost as if she was a wild animal. Was there something Nina hadn't told her? This must have been taken shortly before Stella died – Nina had always told her that Stella died when she was tiny – and there was an infinite sadness to this picture she couldn't quite put her finger on.

Funny how life never quite gave you exactly what you wanted. Here, finally, was a picture of Fleur's mother, holding her, something she'd only ever dreamed of, but somehow it wasn't right. Nina had loved Fleur enough for a whole family tree of relations, but this photo didn't speak of love. Stella looked so weary.

What had happened in the time between the picture of the newborn Stella was taken, and this grown-up one? Fleur tried to distance herself. It could easily be an unguarded moment, an unlucky take in the days when you just took a few photos, and what was developed was what you got.

Fleur hadn't been expecting to find any photographs of Stella. Nina always told her there weren't any, that people spent time being with each other back then rather than bothering to pose every five minutes. Strange, coming from someone who loved taking photos before Stella came along. Poor Nina, what happened? Fleur wished she'd pushed through the silent barrier Nina had imposed upon any conversation about her parents, because it was irrevocably too late now. She even allowed herself to feel angry with Nina. Whatever had happened, what- ever her feelings about losing her daughter, how could she have kept Fleur so in the dark about Stella? Even in the depths of these archives, it was like Stella had been erased from the face of the earth, almost as if she'd never existed. Perhaps her father was never known to her, but Fleur would wonder about her parents to the end of her days, and that was harder than being protected from whatever it was that Nina wanted to hide from her.

This photo was all she had, and she'd treasure it forever. She hugged the dog-eared picture to her chest. 'You were here, we were together once, and I'll never forget it,' she whispered. She was glad it was at this point she found this picture. Without her own baby to look forward to, and consequently her own family, she wasn't sure how she'd have been able to cope with the confused, mixed-up feelings the photo engendered.

She needed to come up for air, so she dressed and took a walk into the village. It was a still, bright-blue day and Sanary was as lively as ever. The cafés spilled over into the palm-lined promenade that overlooked the harbour, buzzing with chatter, mothers with toddlers, the older crowd with their *La Provence* newspapers and thirty-year tans, shopkeepers, the odd English straggler... each one of them had a story to tell, a family history with skeletons and joys, jewellery passed down through the generations. She stopped to take a few pictures of the *pointu* sailboats, their reflections vivid on the glass-still water, then ordered a decaf coffee in the Café du Sport.

Mothers and children giggled together, a dad ruffled his son's hair and pulled a face that made him laugh. Grown-up daughters treated their mums to morning coffee and generations delighted in each other.

What the hell was she doing, trying to have a baby all on her own? What if she couldn't cope, like Stella in the photo?

She stirred the milk foam into her coffee. Ridiculous to make up stories from one stupid photograph, but she couldn't get it out of her head. Her phone buzzed in her handbag and a spark of excitement flickered with the name on the screen. Nick. Her flustered thumb grappled to swipe to accept – what would she say? She needn't have worried, he launched straight in.

'OK, I couldn't resist. What is this unbelievable news?'

'Who is this speaking please?' she teased.

'Your friendly marriage guidance counsellor.'

'Then I won't require your services as there isn't to be a marriage of any kind.'

A beat. 'My professional reputation is severely compromised in that case.' The smile was back in his voice.

Fleur sipped her coffee, and sat back in her chair. 'I'm so glad you called.'

'You lured me with the glitter of unbelievable news.'

'I found a newspaper cutting, of Odette standing next to the Emerald Lake in the Littenstrasse Museum. It was like seeing Nina, but with a different look in her eyes, it was so strange.'

'Like finding a gold nugget.'

'Better.'

'Send me the link, I might be able to investigate more for you.'

'There are other things too, in the 1961 and '62 boxes. It'd be easier to show you in person, if you have the time. There are—'

'I can be there in an hour,' Nick interrupted.

A breeze ruffled the water whipping up diamonds on the surface.

'I would love that.'

Nick's arrival was heralded by the whir of his beloved 2CV skidding down the track, and, as he pulled the handbrake tight with a mechanical rasp and opened the door, Fleur ran out and flung her arms round him before she could stop herself.

'You should uncover newspaper articles more often,' he said, head to one side, taking her in. He was wearing cut-off jeans and a white shirt with the sleeves rolled up, his floppy fringe skimming his eyes.

'I'm sorry I didn't tell you about Jake,' she said. 'I was

confused, and you came along and everything was so jumbled up...'

It was already too much of an acknowledgement of what passed between them when he kissed her on the beach.

He smiled, waved it all away.

'Let's go up to the house and talk,' he said.

They walked in heavy silence, both with more to say than they dared. Inside, Fleur showed him the newspaper cutting.

He whistled. 'I can use this to search the archives a little more. Weird that there's no more news of either of them.'

'I found these, too.' Fleur showed him the two pictures she'd found in Nina's 1962 box. Nick searched her eyes for a clue and his concern was more upsetting than indifference.

'Don't look at me like that. It's my mother as a baby, then grown up, holding me. The first time I've ever seen her, and the only two pictures that exist.'

He looked closer. 'The same pigeon-toed way of standing that you have – apart from that, you don't look much like her.'

'More like her dad than Nina or me, I think,' said Fleur, and then the tears that had been threatening all this time flooded out. What if her own baby looked more like her dad, and she never met him or even knew who he was and...

'Come here,' said Nick, hugging her tight.

'I'm pregnant,' blurted Fleur.

Nick sprang back, eyes wide.

'That's wonderful news for whoever's in there. You for a mother, and it's new hope after all the tragedy down the generations.'

It was such an unexpected response, and so surprisingly wonderful to hear, she wasn't sure whether laughing or crying was winning.

'It's a bit of a mess,' she managed. Understatement of the year.

'I can see that,' he said. 'You'll just have to power through it,' he added casually.

'It's not ideal,' she ventured.

'All you have to do is love it,' said Nick. 'The rest will work out somehow.'

If it wasn't such a stupid move, she could have kissed him again. Instead she picked up the photos, and slipped them carefully back into the envelope.

'You know my own maman died when I was young?' said Nick.

'I'm so sorry, I've never asked you anything about yourself, it's all been about me. Grief does strange things to you...'

'Yes, it does. At least you're old enough to try and make sense of it all. I was only six when she died, and the only way my father could communicate with me was through geology. That's where I get it from, and why I love it so much.'

'Do you remember your maman?'

'Only fragments. I tried to conjure her up so often when I was a kid that I don't know what's real and what isn't any more. I remember the feeling more vividly than the person.'

'I'm glad you have that. It's so frightening to think that the sound of Nina's voice, her physical presence, is already fading, but the feeling of her, of home and fun and picnics and red lipstick and sewing and birthday parties and unconditional love, stays. I'll never know anything of that from Stella, but if anything happened to me it's what I'd wish for my child.'

'It won't,' said Nick. 'Lightning doesn't strike twice, never mind three times.'

Fleur crossed her fingers superstitiously.

'I thought you didn't believe in all that stuff,' said Nick with a wry smile.

'What stuff?'

'Saluting to magpies, stroking rabbits' feet, collecting horseshoes, *that* stuff.'

'No! I don't know why I did that, I just did.'

'You're on high alert. Too many bad things down the generations. Don't start looking for things now. You owe it to them to have a good life. Come on, I want to show you somewhere me and Dad visited a million times after Maman died. It's so ancient, it kind of helped to put everything in perspective. I'll drive.'

Nick threw back the hood of the 2CV and revved up the drive, then turned onto the road towards Cassis. It was good to be speeding along in the sunshine, to forget everything for a while, the wind in their hair and life to live.

At La Ciotat, Nick took a road signposted Corniche des Crêtes, and the little 2CV began a reluctant ascent up the steep winding road, the sea stretching out to the left, dramatic, jagged cliff formations ahead and to the right. It was breathtaking.

Nick was right, the ancient landscape was still and timeless, untouched by humans because of its soaring drops and crumbling stones. An impatient four-wheel drive behind them, horn blaring, was the only thing to mar the scene.

Nick tried to speed up, but the 2CV wasn't up to it on these slopes.

'Leave Choux alone – she's old and slow, but she's got more charm than your over-inflated meat wagon could ever dream of.'

Fleur looked in the rear-view. It was an orange thing with bull-bars, and so far up their rear bumper she could see the whites of the driver's eyes. His baseball cap read *Suisse Rugby SFR*. Their eyes met, she smiled, but he didn't smile back.

Just before a tight hairpin, he roared past, narrowly missing an oncoming car.

'Asshole,' shouted Nick.

'Ugly,' yelled Fleur.

Shouting insults dissipated the hairy moment, but Fleur wasn't sure about this road after that. The sheer drops made her slightly queasy – but Nick was so deep in explanations about the layer-cake of amazing geology that she didn't have the heart to ask him to stop.

When they pulled in to a viewpoint, she was glad to be back on her own two feet, and it *was* worth it at the top. A fresh breeze took the edge off the midday sun. The sea was vast and glittering, jagged cliffs descended precipitously into the foam and wildflowers basked in the scrub and clung bravely to the crags.

'This is the feeling I get when I think of Maman,' said Nick. 'Endless possibilities across the sea. Dad always told me that every layer of rock tells a story... and that's what families are like too, across the generations. Each layer building the whole.'

Fleur sat down and took in the view. Nick did the same, and they sat there in silence.

'Are you OK?' said Nick after a while.

'Yes, I think it'll all work out,' said Fleur. 'Thank you.'

'I'm glad you feel it too,' he said. 'Come on. I'll buy you an ice-cream in Cassis, then I'll get you home. You need your rest.'

'I'm pregnant, not ill,' said Fleur.

'Well, someone's got to look after you, and you've managed to scare off your fiancé. He didn't really seem like your type.'

'He was, until I came here.'

CHAPTER 24

REFUGEE

Odette/Odelia, aged twenty-two

I'm on top of a wall, reaching down. A hand appears from somewhere dark and cold, but I can't reach. The hand disappears, taking the Emerald Lake with it.

My eyes snap open. Thank God it was a nightmare. I'm relieved until I see I'm in a hospital room. Drip, plaster cast on my left leg, a young couple at my bedside. Just an everyday scenario in the life of Odelia Fischer, refugee.

'Welcome to West Berlin,' says the man. I don't reply, scrutinise him for Stasi traits. Shaggy beard (unlikely), Free University of Berlin T-shirt (clever touch), unpolished shoes (could go either way). The gold hoop earring is the clincher. No Stasi operative would countenance that, not even for Khrushchev. His girlfriend's a beauty, with a West German gloss that's hard to imitate if you're from where I am.

'Are you all right, Odelia? You look scared, but don't worry, you're going to be OK,' says the man. 'Frau Klein got a message to me and we found you here. I'm Andreas, Johan's nephew. You took quite a tumble. Are you in pain?'

Damn. I try to look like I don't care, but that's hard when you haven't got a clue where you are and you've clearly broken your leg jumping from the third-floor window of an apartment block in a police state in the hope of a new life. I give myself a break.

'Not pain-free, exactly, but not bad,' I say. 'A little confused, though. Can you take me through the events that led me to hospital corners and these attractive elastic leg bandages?'

Andreas laughs, but his eyes are still concerned.

'I'll get the nurse,' says his girlfriend kindly. 'You've been through a lot, but we're going to look after you as long as you need.'

Long blonde hair, athletic, ski tan, and the diamonds in her eternity ring are worth a fortune.

I sink my head back onto the pillow and close my eyes, dreading what's coming next. A nurse pads in and holds my hand with professional efficiency.

'You've been in a coma, and you sustained a few injuries when you jumped, I'm afraid. Your leg is fractured, but it's clean, and you should recover well. I'm afraid however that...'

I save her the pain. 'My baby?'

She shakes her head grimly.

'There's absolutely no reason why you can't conceive again in the future.'

'I'm never going to have another child.'

'You feel like that now, but...'

She carries on, but I close my eyes and shut it all out. Klaus and I were over, and now he's behind a wall. If you have nothing left to lose, you can't really lose it.

She finishes her speech, and I thank her for everything. It's not her fault.

Johan's nephew is lovely, of course – no relation of Johan's could be otherwise – and his girlfriend, whose name is Freya, is equally kind. Andreas had rushed to Bernauer Strasse from the Brandenburg Gate on his motorbike when he heard about the wall and, later, Frau Klein had got word to him about me through the people holding the jump sheet. They found his flat and told him which hospital they'd dropped me at. The kindness of strangers feels wonderful, like hope.

Andreas and Freya say they won't leave me until visiting time is over. Andreas tells me he's studying engineering at the Free University of Berlin, and Freya is a language student at the same place, majoring in French. Like me, they were born during the Second World War, and, like me, they're sick of war and walls and politics and austerity. They have a flat in the Charlottenburg district and I can stay there until I'm on my feet.

I can't thank them enough for their generosity. The words of the girl in the crowd the moment before I took the leap come back to me. *Jump! You'll find your wings on the way down.*

'You know you have a doppelgänger, by the way?'

'You mean a pale-faced inmate with three-day-old mascara and a morphine drip?'

'Ha! No. A girl, with the same cropped red hair and wide blue eyes. I gave her a lift to Bernauer Strasse on my motorbike, and it was her who persuaded you to jump, but then she disappeared. I'd swear she was your sister if she was German, but she wasn't, she was French.'

'Did you find out anything else about her?' I say, my heart thumping so much I'm scared I'll faint.

'It was chaos, and there were so many chance encounters. I saw her help some sisters, and then she disappeared. I don't know anything else about her.'

Freya and Andreas listen while I tell them my story. I'm usually pretty guarded, but they listen with such intelligence and sympathy. Surely it's too much of a coincidence?

I resolve to get out of here as soon as possible. They say that twins can lead parallel lives, that there are strange coincidences between them. Was it her who gave me the courage to escape?

It doesn't really matter either way, because the hope helps me get better. After a few days, the doctor says I can go home, and home is at Freya and Andrea's flat on Kurfürstendamm, one of the best boulevards in Berlin.

I have my own room, pretty much the size of the cupboard they called my flat in the East. It's got big sash windows, a marble fireplace with a gilt mirror, a desk and a Persian rug so thick you could sleep on it.

The fact that it's on the fifth floor makes us giggle as we all struggle to get me up the stairs. Freya and Andreas are so much fun and this life of love and fun and laughter gets under my skin.

It's strange, but, as I recover, the physical wall is like an emotional barrier between me and my old life, the old me. It's like I've left that part of me behind, the unlucky, sad part. I don't know anyone here, and no one knows me. I kind of wish that I hadn't even told Freya and Andreas my story.

I'm free, with my whole life ahead of me, no baggage, no ballast. It should make me sad, but lying here on my big bed with nothing to weigh me down, looking down onto the hustle and bustle, the linden trees, the warmth of the *Konditorei* where friends meet to gossip, the gloss of the designer clothes shops, the world seems full of possibilities for the first time ever.

Even though I'm housebound, I can get around on crutches, and most nights there's some kind of happening at the flat. Students gather to talk politics, discuss Brecht and Nietzsche, play poker, dance, chat feverishly on cocaine, languish like the day will never end smoking weed, or all of the above at once.

Freya's beautiful and fashionable in her shift dresses and long boots, and she can recite the whole of the first page of *Bonjour Tristesse* in French for her party piece. I love the sound of the language, even though I don't understand it. Everyone, including me, is a little in love with her. Andreas is the perfect foil for her – calm, intellectual and principled, with a penchant for Beethoven and the Beatles. Their flat is party central for all the beautiful people of Berlin, and Andreas and Freya are so generous and kind to me that I have to stop myself from looking for an ulterior motive.

I'm their friend, their refugee from the East, and that's enough, they say.

I open Frau Klein's jewellery pouch. This is what will buy me my independence, start me off in my new life as a jeweller in the West. My dream, gifted to me by an old lady who believed in me, wanted to give me a fresh start. I won't disappoint her. As soon as I'm back on my feet, I'll repay them all twenty-fold, starting with what I've got in here, my only worldly goods.

With so much time on my hands, I dream of a normal life, the one I should have had, with my twin. We'd be the kind of sisters who exude a secret glamour when they're together, where two is more magical than one. She'd be my best friend and confidante who's accompanied me through all the rites of growing up, from sharing a doll's house that even has electric lights (installed by a fictional loving father), to endless summers collecting shells on the beach, to our first grown-up party, sharing lipsticks in the mirror and knowing we're both beautiful. All these little privileges would go casually unnoticed because it had always just been like that. By now, we'd be sharing our own place, a flat a bit like this, but in Paris. Nothing bad has ever happened to us, and on Sundays our maman treats us to lunch or the theatre and we share in-jokes and funny stories from our childhood.

I realise it's the first time I've ever had happy thoughts about my birth family, even if they are made up. In my garret room in Berlin, I dare to think that I might be happy, rather than just always fighting. If the person who met Andreas was really my twin, by some outrageous coincidence, it feels like I have a chance of finding her again someday. But now is for healing and friends and new beginnings.

I wouldn't even know where to begin searching. Andreas told me that there are tracing agencies, but the stark reality is that my adoptive father has a lot of contacts and, even with the wall up now, that piece of dirt will still have eyes everywhere. While I'm unofficial here, I'd rather not give him a trail to follow, so I'll lie low for now. It's safer.

Two months go by and I'm steadier on my feet, and in my head. I try not to think about the baby. Not even a baby. More a collection of cells that was never meant to be. I wouldn't be a good mother, I convince myself, I'd never let the poor little thing out of my sight.

My plaster cast is testament to my new friends, and all the parties. It's covered in silly drawings, in-jokes, good wishes and 'liberate East Germany' messages, but today it's coming off, and there's one place I want to go. The wall.

Freya comes with me to the hospital, then we take the U-Bahn as far as we can east. It's weird not to be able to take it all the way through. We emerge up onto the street and it's horrible.

We're at Bernauer Strasse. The windows and doors that were facing the West are all bricked up, and now they form part of the barrier, all the gaps between the buildings filled in by a depressing, dirty wall. It's like the buildings have their eyes closed in death.

Andreas has come to this spot faithfully every week to bring me news of Frau Klein while I was laid up in bed. He got news to her too, in the early days when I was in hospital, and the border was still just barbed wire. She knew I was alive, and recovering.

Today, Andreas shows us the tall apartment building on the Western side opposite the old Bernauer Strasse building where

I jumped. Where once these apartments looked onto life, they're now facing the dead building.

Andreas has a friend living there, and he lets us onto his roof terrace. Up at the top, we can see down into the street behind Bernauer Strasse, and there, looking bent and tiny, is Frau Klein. We're too far away from each other to speak, but we blow kisses. Then she shoos me away, smiling with a wave of her hand, as if to say, forget me, and walks off into a gloomy side street.

My revenge on behalf of Johan from the museum, Frau Klein, my ex-boyfriend Klaus and all the friends I've lost will be to make a success of my life, to make enough money to buy the Emerald Lake if I need to. And wherever that is, I'll find my sister and mother.

CHAPTER 25

AUBAZINE

PARIS, SEPTEMBER 1961

Nina, aged twenty-two

I'm back in Paris now, and it's a month since I went to Berlin, a month since I lost hope of finding my sister miraculously connected to the Emerald Lake. I see on the news that the East's separation from the West is complete. Where I saw barbed wire and last-ditch escapes across the border, there's now concrete, armed checkpoints, a no-man's-land and news pictures of split families calling to each other across the wall. The whole of the Western world is stunned and news of the Emerald Lake, and anyone attached to it, is completely unavailable.

It's almost a year to the day I broke my leg, and it's healed, but inside I feel broken. The baby bump is getting too big to hide now – four months, according to the doctor. I turn sideways and there it is, a veritable bun in the oven, a curve that means I can't do up my skirt any more. It feels alien to have another being growing inside me and I'm not ready. François will never know, it's better that way, I'll save him the pain and platitudes, and bear it all myself.

Coco has been kind and efficient as always. My suitcase is packed and I won't need much where I'm going.

A horn blares in the street below. *Forward.* I take one last look at my bachelor-girl apartment, blow it a kiss, and haul my suitcase down. Coco is waiting in her Mercedes. She gets out and hugs me, holds me away from her and smiles.

'Don't look so sad. In a few months you can get back to your life. You're doing the right thing.'

Coco has arranged everything no questions asked.

'I know,' I say, and get into the front seat beside her.

So here we are, speeding away from my old life, heading to the convent where Coco grew up as an orphan. I'll stay here for the birth of the baby, then they've arranged a kind family who are longing for a child. They live in the village, in a cottage covered in roses with a big garden. They'll give the baby a life I can't, not since the day the Nazis took my sister. You may think it's cruel not to tell François, Odette, but he doesn't know where I am, or that I'm pregnant, so he won't suffer.

My stomach turns as we drive through the arch into the courtyard. The gate swings closed behind us, cutting us off from the rest of the world. Coco shuts down the engine and we both get out.

We're enclosed in a courtyard by an abbey on one side. In front is a tall, wide dormitory building dotted with mean windows, and to the back and side the square is completed by basilicas, octagons, oriel windows, turrets, barns and old stables.

I shiver. The air is clear and deathly quiet, late bees make the most of the last nectar of the year from dying flowers, and beyond, in the hills, the first leaves are beginning to turn.

An elderly nun shuffles out. Rheumy eyes, colourless face, inscrutable countenance.

Coco gives her a warm embrace.

'We were here together,' she says. 'Can you believe it? I chose life, and Sister Constance chose God. I'm not sure which of us has been happier.'

I've never seen two more unlikely friends, apart from they're both head to toe in black and white. Other than that, they couldn't be more different. Coco is seventy-eight, but she's still slim and full of vigour, with jet-black hair and eyebrows tweezed into smart submission. A slash of crimson lipstick gives her words extra emphasis and her skirt swings expensively when she walks. Sister Constance is stiff and round, her nun's habit is shapeless and shiny from wear, but her eyes turn from neutral to engaged when she and Coco chat.

Sister Constance looks me up and down. 'Who have you brought me here?' she says. 'Five months, I'm guessing?'

I nod, overwhelmed, feeling like the original sinner. I'm choked with longing for the atelier, for Paris, my old apartment, big-city hustle, kitten heels and noise and lights, for François.

'Well, we don't judge, and it may not feel like it now but you'll be glad of the peace and quiet as things progress.'

She gives me an efficient smile and I miss Maman so much it hurts.

Inside, it's all hushed corridors, stone floors worn smooth by ancient feet and portentous light streaming through stained glass. I trail along behind Coco and Sister Constance feeling like hell as they show me to my room.

It reminds me a bit of Coco's stripped-back room at the Ritz. A whitewashed cell with an arched ceiling, a narrow bed, wooden desk and chair, a small wardrobe, a washstand, and that's about it. The bathroom is down the corridor, but the view from the window is the saving grace, looking out across the pristine hills, a bird of prey shimmering above the trees.

Sister Constance hovers in the doorway as I put my suitcase down and slump on the bed. Coco joins me and we sit in silence for what feels like forever. I love that she's not trying to make me feel better. She takes my hand and pulls me up.

'You're only here a few months, I served seven years. Come on, I'll show you around.'

The abbey bell rings and Sister Constance raises her eyes to the heavens. 'Duty calls,' she says to Coco.

'Better not keep Him waiting,' says Coco, kissing her on both cheeks. Sister Constance strides away and Coco turns to me.

'Come on, my little fallen angel, I'll show you around my childhood home, but you have to swear to keep my secrets to yourself. Depending on who I'm talking to, I was born into faded aristocracy, grew up in the circus with a runaway Russian heiress, or was adopted by a failed nun turned chorus girl. You can decide what you choose to believe,' she says, reapplying her already perfect lipstick in her compact mirror.

We go to the graveyard, and Coco shows me a modest head-stone, covered in orange Lichen. *Colette, aged five* it reads.

'Tuberculosis. She was like my little sister,' says Coco, her eyes filling with rare tears. 'You know, I used to come here and pretend that I was queen of the dead, and all these people were my subjects. I'd bring my dolls here, and talk to all the subter-ranean people. They never answered back. Maybe that's why I never did what I was told, or listened to what anyone wanted me to do. The first people I opened my heart to were the dead. You know people are never dead if you think of them?'

I think of you, Odette. I don't know where you are, but I've kept you alive all this time in my thoughts.

'You rose above it all, though,' I say to Coco. 'I'm sorry things started so badly.'

'By the time I got here at the age of eleven, my mother had died, my father had abandoned me, and I was separated from my two brothers.' She dismisses it all with a wave of her hand.

'Long ago, a different life. One I was delighted to leave.

Your little one will have a happy family and you mustn't ever forget the value of that. Now, enough of all this mawkishness. I have to get back to Paris, and you need to settle in.'

She taps my head.

'Everything you need is in there. Use this time to build your resources, and don't you dare mope.'

She'd be disappointed if she knew how I felt at this precise moment, but I give her a brave smile and cross myself.

'I commend myself to the arms of the Church,' I say.

'I wouldn't go that far. Have your baby and get yourself a new life, one that you want.'

She drives off in a cloud of perfume, and supreme confidence.

I go to my room and sink into my bed. Odette, I hope you're happier than me, wherever you are.

The first days are strange and lonely, but in time the rhythm of the abbey gets under my skin – the regular prayers, the bells, the sound of singing drifting over the rarefied air. I'm a counterpoint to the metronome of their lives. I join them for meals and, in between, I walk out into the hills, follow the old monks' canal, gaze up at the sky through the chestnut forest, read, learn poems off by heart to pass the time. As the days go by, I begin to join them in their routine, and I come to love the regularity, the spiritual valued above the earthly. Coming from a world of fashion and plenty, I see the beauty of austerity, of a life pared back to its bare bones to allow for contemplation and exploration of another reality. At least that's how I'm trying to see it, Odette.

The rising bell rings at 5.30 a.m., and it's then that we meditate for thirty minutes. You'll perhaps know I talk to you often at this time, Odette. I open the window and let the morning in. Sometimes I tell you about the soft rain, or the dawn chorus, a chill breeze. The time I first felt a movement in my stomach, the daily battle with myself about giving the little thing away to a new life. Sometimes I look for God in the shadows, or just let myself listen to the dawn awakening outside, the cool morning air washing over me, the burgeoning sun on the whitewashed walls.

I join the bubble of chatter along the cloisters to the refectory, indulge in the camaraderie after the night's Great Silence, sip sweet tea and spread thick butter and jam on the homemade bread. I join the morning Mass, dream along with the readings and prayer, enjoy the sound of my voice mingling with others, echoing off the vast vaulted ceiling, watch how the colours change in the stained glass throughout the day.

It's funny how your childhood won't leave you, Odette. Even though Coco ran very far away from this place, to many even denied its existence, its influence is everywhere in her life. I see the interlocking Chanel Cs in the pattern on the stained glass of the chapel window, and a constant reminder of you, Odette. The cobbles and tiles are peppered with the five-pointed star, which Coco loves in her jewellery.

It feels like life doesn't go in a straight line, but in circles. Here I am, growing a baby, surrounded by the symbols that have followed me throughout my life. In a superstitious kind of way, every time I see the star depicted in the old stone floors I know I'm doing the right thing. A happy family, freedom from the knowledge of all that's gone before, is what this baby deserves. That way, I win, break the legacy of that day in the Ritz.

If we can be reunited, that would be the ultimate victory, a closing of the broken circle, a completion of Chanel's interlocking Cs. It's easy to believe in the power of symbols here. Ours is the Emerald Lake. Here, I'm more convinced than ever that it will somehow bring us together. I just wish I knew how.

The routine at the convent never changes, and the days meld into each other. The trees blaze, then lose their leaves,

November is sombre and December brings hoar frosts and chestnuts and crisp skies. My feet swell, my belly gains a stripe, my baby protests if I stand up too quickly. Hush, little thing. It's all planned out, this is the hardest thing I'll ever do, but I'll carry you gently until the time comes, then I'll love you forever, even if I'm not there. I hope I'm doing the right thing, Odette.

Christmas comes and goes, a special time for the convent, but with all the images of babies and adoring mothers, families and happy endings, I'm just glad when it's over.

By February, I'm fit to burst, and a package arrives from Coco. It's the layette she sewed when she was here as an orphan. Each girl had to sew their own trousseau, their own layette, she tells me. She never had a child of her own but, when my baby comes, it's her gift to the new parents.

I unfold the tiny clothes, all made from heavy cotton, neatly embroidered with Coco's own teenage hand. There's an A-line dress with a petal motif, and the little booties make me want to weep.

I lay them out on the bed and get down on my knees and pray. *Maman, am I doing the right thing?*

She doesn't reply. But wet spreads between my legs and an excruciating pain grips my entire midriff. I grab the bell Sister Constance gave me for this moment, and get on all fours to relieve the agony, panting like an animal.

The nuns come running, help me to my feet and walk to the infirmary. Sister Constance's hands are firm on my back as she guides me resolutely forward.

'Keep breathing, nearly there. You've a tiny frame but you'll be as strong as an ox.'

I'm guided past wards with young girls holding their babies, other women in labour uttering guttural cries from somewhere deep and dark and magical.

Sister Constance stays as the midwife examines me.

'Nine centimetres dilated. It's going to be quick.'

I breathe, call on all the generations that went before, grip Sister Constance's hand as she whispers steady instructions and forces me to focus. It's agony, undignified, messy, terrifying and incredible. A slick slip of humanity appears, eyes screwed shut, and the midwife cuts the cord.

'A beautiful little girl,' she says as she pats miraculous life into her lungs and the tiny thing screams in shock and wonder at this new world.

They wrap her up and give her to me to hold. Our eyes meet and something leaps between us, a kind of electricity.

'Hello,' I whisper. The church bells ring, 7 a.m., a morning baby.

She snuggles in and she's the most beautiful rosebud I've ever seen, an immaculate new piece of hope, so free of any of the atrocities in the world. I think of you, Odette, of our maman, of the last time we saw each other. The Emerald Lake replica is on my bedside table, our family star.

'I'd like her to be called Stella,' I say to Sister Constance.

'Best not to get too close,' she says, her eyes hardening as she gently pulls Stella away from me.

'Wait,' I say. 'I want a picture to remember her by.'

Sister Constance, dresses Stella in Coco's dress with the petal motif and I give her my camera. She takes the picture and I lose myself in Stella's gaze.

Click. The picture's done, too quickly.

'Are you sure you got it?' I ask, desperate.

'Quite sure,' says Sister Constance. 'Now come along, no point in prolonging the agony for either of you.'

I close my eyes, I can't watch her leave the room. Every inch of my body aches with longing as I hug myself, convulsing and sobbing. I think of Maman that day in the Ritz, when her body couldn't support her any longer, and I feel closer to her than I've ever felt in my life.

'You've given her life, and now she'll have a wonderful

family. You've done the right thing,' the midwife says, not even looking up from tidying and sterilising her instruments. Just another day to her, another sinful single mother saved from the humiliation of a fatherless child. I can't speak through the grief. I'm sore and empty and overwhelmed with yearning for that little warm body on mine, the navy-blue eyes that are half me and half François, the perfect angel who has been wrenched from me and taken my soul with her.

CHAPTER 26

THE BRIGHTER THE SUN, THE DARKER THE SHADOW

BERLIN, FEBRUARY 1962

Odette/Odelia, aged twenty-two

It's a freezing February morning in Berlin when I'm woken by a pain I can only describe as offensive. Make that torture, like someone's pressed a boulder into my lower back, then decided that won't do, so made me swallow a cannon ball to press down on my abdomen.

I check my bedside clock: 7 a.m.

I stagger to the bathroom. Nothing untoward – and the pain disappears as quickly as it came. Strange – if my baby had survived my jump to freedom from Frau Klein's apartment, this would have been around my due date. An echo from some-where, a green lake, two little girls holding hands, a recurring chimera left over from somewhere long ago. It happens often in that moment between sleep and waking.

I take a deep breath. I'm fully awake now and living for the day. Note to self – *Forward.* I take stock of the good things. Own chi-chi apartment in the best part of Berlin. Check. Persian rug from the glitzy Kaufhaus des Westens department store. Check. Double-height windows with the sun streaming onto the parquet floors, Veuve Clicquot and Chanel lipstick in the fridge, a wardrobe fit for an up-and-coming West Berlin jewellery maker with a growing reputation amongst the beautiful people. Check.

It's wonderful to be the new me, I tell myself. To be flying. Whoever shouted *jump! You'll find your wings on the way down* was right. Those words are with me every day of my new life and they're the words that prop me up every day.

And you know what my logo is? Two line-drawn stars, side by side, the same as the ones I scratched on the back of the ring. It symbolises us, Nina, the broken memories and broken dreams, separated families brought back together.

I find my Chanel red lipstick in the fridge door, give myself a quick slick and head to my workshop, which is my very own ticket to freedom, bought with Frau Klein's jewellery.

As soon as I'm there, I close the door behind me, pick up the latest piece I'm working on and get going. I love this moment, when I'm planning the next stages, creating exactly what I please, lining up the tools, checking the quality of the gems through the loupe, gazing into their depths. It's at these moments that I can completely forget everything else.

I'm never short of ideas. I take inspiration from everything I was missing before, from a trip to the seaside where suckers and seashells influence settings for pearls and precious gems, to the mountains where the hoar frosts create filigree on leafless branches. Gilded salons hung with chandeliers inspire the extravagant counterpoints to the simplicity of the little black dress, while the bombsites revitalised by brutalism and Bauhaus are the seed for geometric shapes and bold statements.

This one's a ring, sapphires set in thirty tiny settings like something from the sea. I'm just getting lost in it when the buzzer goes. I check through my door viewer. It's Freya, one of the few people I'm happy to be interrupted by.

'I have some news, I hope you don't mind,' she says.

'I was dreaming at the bottom of the sea, but I'm happy to surface for you,' I say.

Freya spots the ring. 'Beautiful. Is it the one for my aunt?'

Freya's been incredibly generous, introducing me to her wealthy family, who have helped set me up with their purchases, as well as putting me in contact with rich, bohemian West Berliners who've made me their friend.

I smile proudly. 'The very one. Now, what's this news you're bottling up? Come in and take a pew, and a breath – you look like you're going to burst!'

Freya throws herself onto the workshop sofa, curls her legs up and hugs herself.

'I am, in a way. I'm pregnant!'

I think of the pain I woke up with this morning, the little one I lost, force a smile.

'That's wonderful! I thought you were looking radiant.'

'You're the first one to know, apart from Andreas. I haven't quite plucked up the courage to tell my parents, not being married and everything.'

'What will they say?'

'They'll come round to it. They love Andreas, but there'll have to be a shotgun wedding, of course – and you'll make the ring?'

'I'd be honoured,' I say.

She's glowing, so in love. The contrast between her and how I feel inside is a wrench. I feel a bit like Berlin, littered with Second World War bomb craters, divided by a wall, but surviving, trying to forget about the war.

I hug my friend warmly.

'Lucky baby to have you and Andreas as mummy and daddy.'

'He's over the moon,' says Freya. 'Imagine, us being sensible enough to have a little one. I'm ready though. All those parties start to feel a bit empty after a while, don't they?'

'Not for me. Don't forget I was holed up in East Berlin for most of my life. I still get mesmerised by sparkly things.'

It's true, I love the whirl of my new life. At least as much as I can love anything. The great and the good are my customers, the most avant-garde artists, writers and actors my best friends. I love the gallery previews where you feel like you're at the centre of everything, the opening nights, the anticipation of parties by the lakes in summer, taking to the mountains to ski in winter. It's a fairyland I can't get enough of. I'm like a woman who's lived all my life in the desert, only to reach palm-fringed oases stretching as far as the eye can see. I drink it all in like I'll be banished back to the wilderness at any moment. That's the downside. When I was taken, it triggered a feeling in me that can never be undone. The feeling that everything good might be snatched away from me at any moment, so I work all hours so that the more money I have the more immune I become.

'Cup of tea to celebrate?' I say brightly.

'Seriously though, you know gems make brittle babies?' Freya says. 'You won't let anyone past that sassy, no-one-can-touch-me exterior. You're running so fast, no one can keep up. Wouldn't you at least like someone to share all your success with?'

'I love my life,' I lie breezily. 'After you, diamonds are my best friends. Who knows about the future? And anyway, I can get my baby fix through you now. Come on, I'll get the tea and we can put together a few sketches for the ring.'

'I'd love you to be godparent,' says Freya.

'And I love you back for asking. Yes!'

We giggle and hug. I *am* so pleased for her, but I do envy her, too. Her capacity for love, her optimistic, firm belief that all will be perfect and good, as it always has been.

It's not so simple for me. I've been given a fresh start by the authorities, so I can't be found by my ex-father, but still that dark shadow never leaves me. When the sun shines, and everything goes right, it just makes the shadow darker by contrast. We're still finding out about what really happened in the war. It makes me shiver to think about the fact that I was taken by people who believed in Nazi ideology. For so many years, I yearned to be with them rather than at the children's home, to have a family, even one that treated me so badly. I had no idea then of the true extent of what they might have done in the name of their beliefs.

Now I have a new name, new passport. I'm untraceable from anything that went before, and I'm well rid of it all. Best of all, I got to choose my new name. Odette, of course. An echo from the past, the real, secret me who still longs to be reunited with her family.

Could it really have been my twin who shouted to me to jump, to find my wings? It seems too serendipitous for my life. I've lain awake so many nights imagining the moment, but it's too dangerous right now to leave a trail for anyone. My ex-father's a powerful man, and things are going too well for me now. I've learned there's always a flaw in a gem, but then dirty salt-and-pepper diamonds have always been my thing.

I'll choose a crystal-clear, flawless diamond for my rich, uncomplicated Freya. I sketch her a classic solitaire style for the engagement ring, baguette-cut for clean modernity, and matching wedding rings for her and Andreas.

'They're beautiful,' says Freya. 'Listen, I know I'm lucky and life's simple for me. Loving parents, pony-riding lessons, then university and parties, and now I'm marrying the love of my life. I wish I could change what happened to you in the past, chase away that haunted look in your eyes. Can't you let it go?'

'Never. I can never forgive them, never forget. I'm going to build this business so big that one day I'll march right back into the Littenstrasse Museum on the other side of the wall and buy back the Emerald Lake that's rightfully mine. Don't ask me how I'm going to do it, but that's what keeps me going. And don't worry, this makes me happy. Each new sale is proof I *am* worth something. Money gives me options, protection, wings in a way. Maybe one day I'll settle down, but not yet. I've got three years until the trust for the Emerald Lake matures on my twenty-fifth birthday. I'll have forever after that. But no babies for me. I'd be too terrified of losing it every day.'

Freya and I hug again.

'Whatever happens, I'm here for you,' says Freya.

She leaves, and I get straight back to the ring design before I can think too much, lose myself in the intricacies of each of the thirty settings, and try not to think about that baby that will never be.

I go to a gallery opening in the evening, don't even remember who I talk to or what about, then walk home for the fresh air, and to delay the moment when I turn the key in the apartment door and I'm alone with my thoughts.

When I get back, the door is ajar. I switch on the hall light. The pattern on the rug is all wrong – someone's turned it round. I creep forward, switch all the lights on. Everything is in order, nothing else is touched. I check every room before I lock the front door, then go to the fridge; and, inside, there it is. A note, on Littenstrasse Museum headed paper.

When you defected, you forfeited all rights to the Emerald Lake.
Stay away, and we'll stay away from you.

So they know where I am, *who* I am, and they've been listening.

BOOK THREE

CHAPTER 27

INVISIBLE BARRIERS

Odette, aged fifty

'Go home, it's late,' I say to the two employees who are still here. They leave, give me that look, the one that says, you should be the one leaving, we've got this. But they know as well as I do that I'm obsessed. I'll stay here until late, polish all the pieces for my new collection that have already been polished twice by my team. I have thirty of them working for me now, but I still can't let go.

I pick up the emerald necklace, my pièce de résistance for this collection, hold it up to the light. They're excellent stones – clear, good saturation, green with a bluey tinge – but in all my twenty-eight years in this business, nothing's ever come close to the deep, velvety green, the heart inclusion that has my own heart trapped inside it on the other side of the wall.

I haven't forgotten you. I used to say it out loud, before the Stasi left the note in the fridge all those years ago, but now I only talk to the Emerald Lake in my head.

I check the date on my desk calendar: 9 November 1989. Is it really that long since I last saw it? Twenty-eight years, a whole generation of yearning for it.

Rubbing the yellow gold once more on the collection pieces, I feel like a genie releasing wishes from a bottle. With each new collection, my Emerald Lake fund expands. I've earned enough money to hire a secret lawyer to try to help claim back what's rightfully mine, to covertly contact the post-war agencies set up to restore stolen property taken by the Nazis. It's a thankless task and a game of cat-and-mouse. Even though my lawyers specialise in secret dealings, have a network on the other side of the wall, the man who stole me is still out there – and dangerous. Thanks to them, and my own precautions, I've had no issues with the Stasi since the day they left a note in my fridge, but I'm still afraid of him and what he's capable of.

My twenty-fifth birthday may have come and gone over two decades ago, but I haven't given up. The only tragedy is that my real identity needs to remain unknown, thanks to the Stasi and Dieter Fischer. If you're looking for me, Maman and Nina, I'm hard to find, but if you're out there, I'll find you. I'll never stop looking until the day I die.

It's dark outside and I have at least another hour of work to do. I flick on the radio.

An announcement today by Gunter Schabowski has unleashed delight and utter chaos across Berlin.

What? I drop the necklace and polishing cloth and listen closer.

The Socialist Unity Party of Germany official has caused stampedes at the border with the following announcement.

I hold my breath.

The responsible departments of passport and registration control in the People's Police district offices in the GDR are instructed to issue visas for permanent exit without delays and without presentation of the existing requirements for permanent exit.

A journalist asks him, *When does it come into effect?*

According to my information, immediately, without delay... permanent exit can take place via all border crossings from the GDR to the FRG and West Berlin respectively.

The journalist picks up the story from a chaotic press conference in East Germany.

People are already streaming through the borders, both ways. East German police haven't been given instructions, or at least if they have they don't understand them. They're telling people to come back tomorrow, but they're being ignored. Hundreds are pushing through every one of the six checkpoints. People are crying, applauding, encouraging each other through. We've even seen the first Trabant cross over.

I listen a bit more, just to make sure. The borders are open, free travel both ways. The authorities are incapable of imposing order, an official decree is announced. No more wall.

Dear God, it's taken a generation, but it's happening. I feel like that twenty-two-year-old who jumped to freedom from Frau Klein's window, bursting with fire and possibilities. Can I finally get back to the Emerald Lake? It's still the only place I think of as home, even after all this time.

For the first time ever, the workshop can wait. I lock up my collection and run. On the way out, I check myself in the mirror. Strawberry-blonde bob, the same hairstyle I had at twenty-two, with a little help on the colour nowadays, big, bold gold hoop earrings, black cashmere jumper and capri pants, moon boots, Issey Miyake cross-body bag. The epitome of Berlin luxury chic. Someone to reckon with. A few more wrinkles than when the wall went up, but the same little girl inside, searching for a family, a birth right, reparation. It's still the reason I never married. It goes too deep, too much ice in my heart. That raging, vulnerable, sad part of me never grew up.

I call Andreas and Freya. They made it through as a couple after those heady years, and I'm godmother to both their children, who themselves aren't that much younger than me when I jumped. They'll meet me at the checkpoint at Bernauer Strasse. Full circle again.

I pull my coat around me. It's a freezing evening, the kind where your breath steams under the streetlights and you smell woodsmoke on the air.

I meet Andreas and Freya at Leopoldplatz. They're wrapped up in scarves and hats. Andreas is rarely without his beanie nowadays – he lost his hair early. Freya's hedonistic youth, when she carelessly took every experimental substance there was, shows on her face now, but to me they're still those two student angels of mercy who sat stalwartly at the bedside of a refugee from the East.

We link arms and turn the corner to Bernauer Strasse, and it's such a wonderful sight that even my cynical old heart swells. Hundreds of people are standing on the graffiti-covered wall popping champagne, hugging, singing, crying, chipping away at the hated thing. It strikes me that it's the opposite of the gravity-aided escapees from twenty-eight years ago, where Westerners were helping people down. Now they're all climbing up onto the wall, reaching for hands who pull them up to join the party.

It's like my recurring dream, except here the hands succeed in connecting, and the atmosphere is filled with love and camaraderie. Everywhere around there's disbelief and wonder that the dark regime has dissolved in the middle of the night without one life being taken.

The crowd in front of the wall is hundreds deep, TV cameras from all around the world are setting up, there's a joyful, peaceful, bubble of chatter amongst the throng and skinny, tired East Berliners are pouring through the checkpoint with stunned border guards waving them through, no longer bothering to check papers. Tearful reunions play out, old ladies meet grandchildren for the first time, brothers and sisters meet brothers and sisters, people light sparklers on top of the wall, steal caps from the border guards, who look relieved not to have to retaliate. At this moment, my shattered faith in humanity is restored as groups of teenagers and young people leap about, filled with optimism for their new future.

'Reminds me of us at their age,' says Andreas.

'Apart from the stonewashed jeans and mullets,' I say.

'Some things were definitely better when the wall went up,' says Freya, sniggering.

We stay and share cheap champagne and watch the never-ending stream of East Berliners blink at the bright lights in the shop windows, hug the strangers who greet them with open arms, join the lads who've brought ladders, picks and beer to shove it to the man. I say nothing to anyone about my plan to slip through the border tomorrow under cover of all these crowds. I barely sleep all night, feverishly thinking about going back East.

I'm up bright and early the next morning and run past the workshop. It's the first day in twenty-eight years I won't have been there at 6 a.m. sharp. I feel like a kid again, and that's not good. Hard work is my Valium, I'm the first to admit that, and I'll miss my shot today, but the real me is intent on only one thing. I'll never give up looking for my family.

At the Bernauer Strasse checkpoint, the steady exodus to the West is in full flow; families heading for a new life with only as much as they can carry in a battered suitcase, lovers reunited, youngsters with neon in their eyes and fire in their bellies.

There's a fresh piece of graffiti, sprayed in red letters, which stops me dead. *Only today is the war really over.* No one wants to talk about the war any more, but so many of us are still blighted by it.

I push against the tide, a lone figure pressing forward, back to the East. Funny, I remember the way back to Littenstrasse Museum like it was yesterday. The East is almost unchanged. The grand old buildings look more dilapidated and blackened. There's a hopeless atmosphere of oppression like a bad smell on the litter-strewn verges. But apart from that, it's not much different from when I left.

I hesitate outside the museum, then push open the old wooden door, and there, on reception, is the same woman who reluctantly let me through when I was sixteen.

She looks at me over half-moon glasses, the same look of derision and sympathy she gave me all those years ago.

'I wondered when you'd be back to haunt us,' she says, deadpan.

'I won't ask how you recognise me after all these years.' I cover a stab of fear. Of course. I haven't been as clever as I thought. They've been tracking me.

I look her in the eye. Is she friend or foe? I know of old that, even if she's not on their side, she may be forced to inform. Either way, I'm here now and it's too late to go back. She raises her eyebrows, bored. Or terrified. It doesn't matter which, she's lived with it all her life.

'You know they're already selling T-shirts on the border saying *last one out, turn off the lights*? You've done your time here.'

She shrugs. 'A girl has to earn a living. We're closed, by the way,' she says with a wink, pressing the button to let me through the turnstile. *Friend*, I think. I walk through.

'Johan?' I say, hoping against hope that I'll find my old saviour and patron, the Littenstrasse curator and director, living out his final days amongst his adored artefacts.

She shakes her head and shuffles through some paperwork. Easier to shut me down than explain. Not that I need an explanation. He probably didn't make it much further than the journey in the Trabant the day I was meant to meet him to escape through the wall.

I follow Johan's ghost down the corridor, remember his intense gaze, the academic rigour, the socialist ardour, the generosity to the orphanage waif with big ambitions that I was, then reach his old office.

Herr Wolfgang Fischer are the letters on the door. It's a lightning bolt. That boy who couldn't look me in the eye at the orphanage. The one who had everything I didn't. My step-brother has grown up and got himself gainful employment, albeit via Daddy. It takes me a minute to gather up the courage. I'm a grown woman now, but I can't believe my ex-father's precious son will be sitting in Johan's chair. I steel myself; he might be sympathetic. Last time I saw him, he was just a kid; he didn't know any better than what his parents told him. Since then, who knows? There's been a lot of soul-searching in Germany since the end of the war. Anyway, I'm here now, and I'm trying to stop my whole body from shaking.

I knock.

'Come,' says a clipped voice. Even from the other side of the door I recognise the air of self-importance in that one word.

A flicker of recognition passes over his face before he glosses over it with a professional smile. He's been briefed. Either they've been tracking me for twenty-eight years, or someone's followed me here. I suspect it's the former because in all this chaos it's unlikely they'd bother with little old me. In which case, pictures have been in circulation, but no one but the receptionist and Wolfgang know I'm here. I think I can trust the receptionist – let's see about my stepbrother.

Our eyes meet. They're the same steel grey as his father's. He's slim, clean-shaven, and holds himself dead straight, like a soldier.

'Can I help you?'

I decide to play the game, even though we both know.

'I'm an old friend of Johan Abel, we used to work together, and I just couldn't resist coming back as soon as the border was open. He was very good to me. It's been wonderful living in the West, but I've always missed this place.'

'It's the kind of place you would. Please, sit.'

I'm too agitated to sit down. I shift on my feet. 'Just a flying visit. I've been waiting twenty-eight years to see the Emerald Lake again. Is it still here?'

Just saying the words is like home.

'We've taken good care of it. I see no reason why not.'

He can't resist. God complex, like his father.

He leads me through the corridors in silence, and I'm starting to wish I hadn't come until the door is unlocked and there it is, my guiding star, the subject of a thousand separation nightmares and reunion dreams. It's exactly how I remember it. The velvety green solitaire Emerald Lake, the tiny heart inclusion, the gold claws offering it up to the viewer, inviting you to adore and revere the central gem, like acolytes round a goddess.

'Can I hold it? Johan and I did a lot of work on the provenance of this emerald.'

'So I hear,' says Wolfgang, no longer even trying to conceal his foreknowledge of me. I'm entering into the unknown now and my heart drums in my ears. Whatever happens, I'm here, Nina and Maman. Where are you? I flash back to the moment I was taken, and it's all I can do to cover my terror.

'I'll let you see it for old times' sake, and I feel sorry for you, but you know there's no way you'll ever own this? You relinquished all rights to it when you defected to the West. It's reverted to our family now, but it's obvious that you have some sort of sentimental attachment to it, so I'll let you say goodbye.'

He disables the alarm, takes the ring of display case keys out of his pocket and deftly selects the correct one.

I don't bother to answer. I hold it in my hand, turn it over to see the two stars I etched all those years ago, and I want to weep. Forty-five years since I was taken and, at moments like this, it still feels like yesterday.

'You know he stole me, don't you?' I say to Wolfgang.

'I thought I was being kind letting you see it. He rescued you from a single mother who was incapable of looking after you. He warned me you might be here on the scrounge again. The West hasn't done you any favours. Greed is the only thing that's driven you back,' says the pompous, holier-than-thou little shit.

'Dieter Fischer was a child-stealing Nazi and he profited from the spoils of war. Never mind what happened to me, he must have brought misery to countless families and he's never paid for his crimes. This is mine. I don't care about the money, but I do care about reparations. He stole me from my mother and my twin, then dumped me when he realised I'd be the only one who remembered him in an SS uniform.'

Wolfgang picks up the radio. 'Well it makes no difference now, because when he dies he'll leave the jewel to me and I'll be free to sell. I think you'll find there's no paper trail to prove it ever had anything to do with you.' He meets my eye as he presses the call button.

'Security!'

I steel myself, whip my camera out and take a picture, the kind that adds a date and time stamp, and make sure that the room is included, for context.

'No pictures!' says Wolfgang, rattled.

I snap one of him, too. It's not going to be a pretty picture. I consider taking my emerald, but if I do they'll deploy everything they've got on me and I'll never get out of here. I kiss the Emerald Lake like a talisman, place it back in the open case and quickly walk out.

As I calculated, he's more concerned with locking the gem back in the display case than pursuing me, and security don't appear. I remember them from before, lounging in their back office with their radios switched off.

The receptionist looks at me curiously as I'm panting at the exit turnstile. The display case alarm sounds, footsteps muster. She lowers her eyes back to her papers, taps the 'open' button without another word.

I push through, and she hands me a pamphlet.

'Listings for the next exhibition,' she says, dying of the tedium of it, but her hand is trembling.

There's something inside it, a thick envelope. We both know I'm not going to check what's in it here. I stuff it in my bag and walk back the way I came, counting on the chaos of the fall of the wall to protect me. They've got bigger fish to fry today, and I haven't forgotten that the Stasi MO is to spook rather than leave visible marks. Besides, if they've been tracking me, they'll know I'm a well-known figure in the West and I'd be missed. Dieter Fischer has more interest in keeping me quiet than stirring up any controversy – if they dig too far into things, his past may be uncovered. It makes me happy to think that he can never really escape what he's done, even in death, that his Nazi past could be revealed at any moment.

I put my hood up, pull my scarf up to my nose and duck down the old familiar side streets. I've waited this long, I can bide my time. The photos will be invaluable for my lawyer. At least we know that it's still there. Whatever happens, if anyone sells it it's going to be difficult to do it underground and get the amount of money it's worth. It needs provenance and a legitimate buyer for maximum value – I've informed myself over the years.

Back at Bernauer Strasse, I join the joyful throngs of people still pouring through the border back West. Thank God no one's checking, and I'm buoyed up by just touching the Emerald Lake again. That gem seems to give me strength, probably because it makes me feel closer to my family. In a way, it's provided everything I own. It's given me a love for precious gems and jewellery, it led me to meet Johan, who found me an apprenticeship in jewellery making, and that trade has made me more money than I can ever spend.

Scrap that – I can spend it in one purchase – on the Emerald Lake.

If I'm prevented from making my legal claim to it, I'll buy it, pay someone to steal it, whatever. Maman, if you're anywhere, know that the gem you sent with me has given me my life and I still believe that somehow it'll lead me to my sister. Who'd have thought a fifty-year-old sceptic would be so superstitious? But it's so much a part of me that I can't let it go.

I'm good at burying other feelings. *He rescued you from a single mother who was incapable of looking after you.* That was what Wolfgang said to me. My ex-father's words parroted through his son. But I can't explode – I've learned to harness the power of the rage that's dogged me since the day he came into my life.

The moment I turn the key to my apartment, I know something's off. For a start, I always double-lock, and the mortice is unlocked. It's freezing – both sash windows in the living room are wide open. I check the kitchen – nothing visible but, in the fridge, the milk's in the wine rack and the champagne's in the door. The old feeling of malevolent eyes on me creeps up my spine.

I change back the milk and champagne to where they should be, close the sashes in the living room, force myself to go and check in the bedroom. The bed's unmade, there are boot marks on the sheets, and in the bathroom the breath is knocked out of me.

A message in red: *We're watching.*

Bastards have used my best Chanel lipstick, I whisper to myself, trying to make light of it.

It's funny. You'd think that the older I got, the less I'd care about what happened decades ago. But you'd be wrong. The older I get, the *more* it matters. The longer they get away with what they did, the more I need to set the record straight, take what's mine. The knife of pain has been twisted and heightened as I've watched all my friends have children over the years, seen the light in their eyes as they watch them.

It's not safe to open the pamphlet here. It's 1989 and surveillance equipment is more sophisticated than it used to be.

Ten minutes later, my passport in my pocket, I'm at the local police station. If I'm being watched, they can't follow me in here. I go to the desk and ask to report a theft. They point me to a plastic chair in the waiting room to wait for an interview, and I might be paranoid, but, just in case, I'm careful to make sure I take the letter out without the pamphlet, so no one knows where it's come from.

I recognise the handwriting immediately – Johan! I tear it open, trying not to make a spectacle of myself.

It's dated 13 August 1961, the day the wall went up and I escaped to the West.

If you're reading this, they've already got me. As I write, I also take comfort in the fact that if you're reading this you've successfully escaped and managed to return to the museum unharmed. You brought meaning to my dry, academic life, and made me as proud of you as if you were my daughter. I consider you my greatest achievement, and that achievement will be diminished if I am the cause of any sadness to you. Honour me by being happy.

To business. I know you well enough to understand that you can never achieve true happiness until you find the family you were torn away from, and so, here is my final gift to you. Don't detest me for not handing it to you sooner. At the time this enclosed letter came into my hands, neither you nor I were in a position to do anything about it, and you needed to escape and lead your own life. The letter came to me with the Emerald Lake. Your adoptive father instructed me to keep it under lock and key in the archives and that he'd be watching if I showed it to anyone, which would be an end for me, either by execution or incarceration. I have made this decision happily. After you left, I knew it was the only evidence left that would prove your connection to the Emerald Lake, so, if you're reading this, my death will have been a happy one...

I glance around the room. There's an old lady taking a handkerchief out of her bag to blow her nose, a couple holding hands whispering, a man in a suit reading a newspaper. No one's taking any notice. The volcano from my orphanage days is erupting again, threatening to melt the carefully formed ice in my heart.

I open the note enclosed with Johan's letter.

8 May 1946

Gómez Abogados, Colombia. Lawyers on behalf of Gustav Raschmann, deceased.

To whom this may concern c/o Bullinger's Auctioneers, Paris. I am sending this letter to you in the hope that you still have records of the seller of the Emerald Lake, and the little girl who accompanied him. We are informed that the ring passed through the auction house on 29 April 1944. Mr Raschmann has bequeathed the ring back to the child, its rightful owner. We are holding the ring in a vault should a legitimate contact be made.

If you are unable to trace the original seller or the little girl, the ring will be held in perpetuity for her or her heirs and all legitimate claims will be considered. A letter (enc) accompanies the appeal.

———

My dear little French girl with the sad blue eyes and the Pre-Raphaelite hair, you have haunted my dreams. You were terrified, I could see, from the way you couldn't look anyone in the eye, by the way you searched the crowded room for a familiar face, but saw none. It amused me to see that you refused to call him father, that he had little control over this defiant, lost little sprite, but now it grieves me to think of that little girl.

I knew the man, Dieter Fischer, who sold me this ring was not your father, that you were stolen. I knew that the ring was not his to sell, that it was a ransom on your head and that I paid him a fraction of its worth, which may well have made your life even more difficult.

I know now that no price would have given you back what you lost, that somewhere a mother would grieve her entire life for the loss of her treasure. By all accounts, the ring was given by your mother's friend, Mademoiselle Chanel herself, in return for news of you. Perhaps if you can find Mademoiselle Chanel, she can reunite you with your family.

I am deeply sorry, and I go to my death in the knowledge that I have done one thing right in my life.

Affectionately and in hope,

Gustav Raschmann

The years fall away, a roar erupts from a five-year-old trapped inside a volcano, a molten mass of heartbreak, an identical me, with red ribbons in her hair. I have a twin, the jewel is mine, it's here in black and white.

Tears prick my eyes as I read the letter again. It's here, the proof that I need. Someone remembered me, saw my pain, tried to get the ring back to me! God, if I'd seen this when I was creeping around in that horrible house, or lying awake in those endless cold nights at the orphanage, I would have known that someone had seen me.

My mind starts to race. Coco, Maman's friend, who tried to help us. I remember her name now, it was always in there somewhere.

Coco Chanel!

I have always loved her work. I can even afford some of it now. She'd have been a brilliant lead. She died eighteen years ago, but it's a start. I didn't get the Emerald Lake, that's for the future, but I always knew that, if I was near it, I'd be closer to the truth.

I snap back to the grim waiting room. Everyone's staring. The letters are on the floor.

I gather them up, pretend I'm having a coughing fit. I've never been much of an actress, but it'll do – everyone goes back to staring at the floor, the couple get called up to the desk, the old lady blows her nose again, the man with the newspaper turns the page.

Heart racing, I consider my options. I have a choice. Take my concerns to the West German police, reveal my identity as the adopted ex-daughter of the Stasi Intelligence Commander, or go into hiding and bide my time.

If I reveal myself now, play all my cards at once, I'll play into my ex-father's hands. He's a master at the cover-up and, even in 1989, a woman's voice is less valid than any man occupying a senior position.

I opt for going into hiding. I've got enough money to buy whatever I need – anonymity, private detectives, a false passport. My lawyer has contacts, and we've planned for something like this should the time come, so I decide to go straight there. He'll find a way of smuggling me out of the country, help me set up somewhere new.

In the meantime, my ex-father's going to have to sell the

Emerald Lake at some point – surely that's the reason he wants to warn me off, especially now his star is waning in the East. I'm living proof of his Nazi activities, his greed, and now I have written proof. He'll know I'm gone, but he won't know where, and it'll be a game of cat-and-mouse that I can finally control.

CHAPTER 28

WALLS COME TUMBLING DOWN

LONDON, NOVEMBER 1989

Nina, aged fifty

The ninth of November 1989, a grey London morning, all glowering low clouds and curtains of rain, the cars throwing up spray on the Embankment. I stare out across the Thames from my penthouse apartment and think of my daughter Stella, something I've done on the ninth of every month for twenty-eight years and ten months precisely.

Not a day has gone by when I don't think of her, Odette. How can it be that this little thing you've met for minutes can be so much a part of you, twenty-seven years later, that feeling as vivid now as the day Sister Constance prised her from my arms?

I know I did the right thing, Odette. The day you were taken took my capacity to look after anyone but myself, but that still doesn't make it any easier. I love my life in London; it's been good to the broken French couturier I was when I left the convent, dazed and sore. I didn't want to go back to Paris, so

Coco arranged London for me. I didn't want François to try to find me, so I moved country and fashion house, and I work for Dior now. A change of scene, a completely new start.

Through the years since that day at the convent, every time I've sewn a stitch, arranged an outfit, approved a new design, I've thought of Stella. In a cute miniskirt in the Sixties, bell-bottomed flares embroidered with flowers in the Seventies. Did she rebel in her teens, was she a Patti Smith or Blondie fan? Does she love fashion and jewellery as much as I do? Does she know she's adopted; does she wonder who she's like, how she fits into the tapestry of inherited features and hopes and dreams?

I hope she's loved, Odette, that her childhood was ordinary and stable enough for her to blossom into whatever she wanted to be.

What a different world she was born into from the one we were, Odette. We've travelled to the moon and back, eradicated polio and smallpox from the world and invented these new mobile phone things where your boss can call you or track you whenever he likes. I say he, Odette, because Coco was unusual, a woman in charge of her own multinational company, her own destiny. But things are changing and, for Stella and her future, that glass ceiling is beginning to crack.

I let myself linger a moment, sip my coffee, watch the rain slip down the window, let myself remember that moment Stella snuggled into me, wrapped in muslin, remember the smell of her downy head, the miracle of her perfect fingernails, the electricity that leapt between our eyes when she opened hers. That was the moment she was mine forever.

Forward, I think. It's a 9 a.m. flight to Paris to oversee the Dior spring/summer campaign shoot. It's a far cry from the lost girl who sewed for Coco Chanel in the Fifties.

I put on my armour – the latest Dior, a slash of red lipstick, a cloud of No. 5 (old habits die hard), and hail a black cab. As soon as I'm being swished along the Embankment to the airport, my troubled memories recede. Work's my Valium, and I can never get enough of it. Men have come and gone, but my heart was iced over that day at the Ritz when we were five, Odette. Do you feel the same? Can you remember it? I still have the red ribbons you wanted.

You know I've never stopped looking for you? You seem to have disappeared off the face of the earth. I lost the trail in Germany, but all our efforts are concentrated there as the authorities think that's the most likely outcome. I still hear of reunions, of people who were separated in the war finding each other, even after all these years. I still dream of you, Odette, now in the abstract. A parallel life, a connection, a green lake. I'll never be whole until I've found you.

The plane touches down at Paris Orly, and a car's waiting to take me to the coast, to Deauville, where the shoot will make use of the grandest houses, the swimming pools and beaches that will all conspire to create the aspirational dream that is Dior. As I walk into the studio, I'm fully present.

I assess the girls. They are so much more in control of what happens to them, the overall look of the shoot, the assignments they choose. Today's standout is Helena Christensen. What a goddess she is! Coco would have approved. She calls all the shots, and commands unimaginable fees. The shoot is high-octane, vivid and fresh. Everything is interesting, chic and new, and these girls bring the clothes and the photographs to life.

I always think of François on a shoot like this, of his kind, concerned gaze picking me out from the bustle as I sewed a hem or adjusted a hat. I know from when Coco was alive that he got married and had children. I wish him every happiness – something I could never have given him.

Thank God the world's moved on from the dark days of the Second World War. But not all of us escaped unscathed. We live in such a different world now, and no one is interested in hearing the grim war stories any more, but many of us are still living it inside, still searching for reparation.

It's a long day and we finish late. We haven't eaten, but I flop into bed, exhausted. My recurring dream returns like an old friend – it's been years since I last had it. You're somewhere, Odette, on top of a wall, ready to pull me up, but once again I fall back into nothing. I wake with a start, make sense of the unfamiliar hotel room and sink back into my pillows. My psychiatrist has helped me pinpoint the pain in the pit of my stomach that the dream leaves me with for the rest of the day. It helps to name it – separation anxiety. The lost, scared child who never grew up. I switch on the TV to distract myself, and I can't believe what I'm seeing.

The Berlin Wall is coming down! East Berliners are pouring through Checkpoint Charlie and flocking to all the border points. I snatch up the Emerald Lake replica on the bedside table and cradle it while chasing headlines on the TV, instinctively study the delighted, excited crowds, hoping for a needle in a haystack. Of course I don't see you, Odette. Would I even recognise you now?

I know one thing for certain, that I'm going to Berlin, to the museum I tried to get to all those years ago when the wall went up. I look at the replica on the bedside table. I take it with me wherever I'm travelling and touch it before I go to sleep it like a talisman, Odette. I think of the games of hide and seek we used to play when we were little – *coming, ready or not*. For the first time since the wall went up, I remember you with joy, remember the giggles and tumbles and the way you were like looking in the mirror and we were just one and we belonged together.

Thank God it's a three-day shoot, because it takes that long for my PA to find a Berlin flight and hotel and work takes my mind off things. My PA offers to come with me – she's one of the few people who knows my story – but I promise to keep in touch and go it alone.

The Steinplatz Hotel in Berlin is beautiful, Odette. Maybe we can stay here together when I find you... but for now I dump my bags and get going.

I pause by the mirror. My hair still has a tinge of red, Odette. Does yours? I cropped it into a bob years ago, and I've never really changed the style since then. Berlin is freezing in November, so I'm wearing my black cashmere sweater, and I decide on my Issey Miyake cross-body bag for a contemporary look, plus moon boots to keep me warm.

'Is today the day I find you?' I say out loud to the mirror. I only see myself in the reflection. I carefully put my replica Emerald Lake in my bag and set out, full of optimism I can't suppress even after all the dead-ends and disappointments.

There are no city maps after the Brandenburg Gate, so I need to rely on the kindness of strangers. People are lovely, and direct me all the way. I hope you've found this same kindness in your life, Odette. It's so strange to be in the East, where the shops are run-down and empty, the streets quieter, poorer. I'm struck by the beautiful buildings, still intact, even though there's an air of defeat about them, of former glory.

I cross the River Spree and my heart is in my mouth as I rush through Innenstadt Park, past the Marx-Engels-Forum sculpture, following the river. I turn off, hoping my imperfect German is taking me in the right direction.

And there it is, the Littenstrasse Museum. Do I see an echo of you pushing through this big wooden door, Odette?

On reception there's a woman with two black eyes, her arm in a plaster cast and a sling. She visibly recoils when she sees me and I wonder why she's come into work in such a state, poor thing.

'We're closed,' she manages.

I explain that I took the first plane from Paris the moment the wall came down, that I've been waiting to see the Emerald Lake for twenty-eight years, that I can't take no for an answer. I show her the replica, but I don't tell her about you, Odette. She looks terrified, for some reason, and I'm garbling in my pidgin German, desperate.

I don't know what to do, but then a man comes and takes charge of the situation, sends the poor receptionist home and asks if he can help.

He speaks a little French, and so we manage to make ourselves understood. He tells me his name is Wolfgang, that he's the director, and he's so kind.

He understands everything when I show him my replica Emerald Lake – he kind of looks like he's seen a ghost. I've looked up *Eineiige Zwillinge*, the word for identical twins in German, and he looks at me like I'm a little mad, Odette, and maybe I am. He also tells me that the Emerald Lake was stolen from the museum, only yesterday, in all the confusion of the border debacle. They're assuming it's a thief from the West who took advantage of the momentous events at the wall. Apparently, the security guards have been sacked. He even shows me the room where it was kept, in an alarmed glass case, which is all smashed up.

The disappointment is deadening, like we've been separated all over again. Wolfgang is so kind to me, even tells me that his father can drive me back to the border as he's in the area. I give Wolfgang my card in case he hears of anything, or an identical me walks in the door by some ridiculous fluke.

It's strange, Odette, because I get that same feeling I got at Lamorlaye, when I was sure you were in the orphanage building that Maman and I came to when we were looking for you. Funny what trauma can do to you, the triggers that make you feel like you're going mad, delusional even.

I'm in a black Trabant heading back to the border. It's in much better condition than most of the other cars I've seen driving around so far, polished to within an inch of its life, and brand new. Wolfgang's father is a bit creepy, and keeps scrutinising me in the rear-view mirror like he knows me.

Just to be sure, I make it clear that several people know where I am, and that they're expecting me back in London. I meet his eye when I tell him this, and he finds it hard to hold my gaze. He has the air of a man unused to being challenged. I've dealt with plenty of them in my life, Odette.

He drops me at the Brandenburg Gate, kindly tells the guards to fast-track me back through the border.

I walk away, dead inside. I don't know what I hoped to find but it wasn't a dead-end. I thought I'd find you, Odette. How could I have been so stupid? You could be anywhere. Coco was wrong about the Emerald Lake, about it bringing us back together. All these years it's been a comfort to me, the childish idea that you would be wherever it was. I never even thought to question it until this moment. Why did I expect any of those people to have heard of you?

When I get back to the hotel, everything's off, and I wonder if I'm actually going mad. It's like my suitcase has been unpacked, and redone, really neatly, but not in the order I packed it. I'm fussy about my clothes, Odette, and I always arrange my suitcase in a certain way. I never leave the lid off my lipstick, but perhaps I did this morning in my haste, and I'm sure I put my shoes on the shoe rack in the wardrobe and not next to the bed.

What next? I sit on the bed and put my head in my hands. My whole life has been counterpointed by our separation and I have a horrible feeling that this might have been our last chance.

CHAPTER 29

STILL-LIFES

SANARY-SUR-MER, JUNE 2024

Fleur

Nick had already stayed too long in France to help Fleur with her search. He was needed at the Geneva office, he told her as they drove back from the Corniche des Crêtes.

Fleur knew this day was coming, and hadn't expected to care quite so much.

'Door-to-door service,' he said awkwardly when they pulled up the villa. Neither of them wanted to say goodbye, but neither of them had any hold over each other. Fleur sat for a moment, trying to think of something to say. He turned off the engine.

'Will you be all right?' he asked, looking straight ahead. 'I know it's not really any of my business, but are you properly signed up with a doctor?'

'I've got an appointment next week, my twelve-week scan. I'll be fine.'

'Of course you will be. You're like a gem that's been placed in a different setting, cut with new facets. Still the same person, but the light refracts in different ways, brings out fresh colours you didn't know were there.'

The sun was low in the sky, the colours turning vivid, casting an enchanting light. She knew what he meant. Everything here had a different aspect, and she was a different version of herself. One who could ask for what she wanted.

'Will you stay for a bit? I don't know what you and I are, so I'm not really sure what I'm asking, but I don't want you to go. You've got work, but...'

'How about asking me to a sunset picnic on the beach?' he said straight away.

They threw together some cheese, salami, olives, grabbed yesterday's baguette and gathered together cushions, candles, matches and blankets, then headed down the sandy path to the beach.

The June day lingered late as they ate and watched the sun slide down the sky, making a trail on the sea, which was still as lacquer tonight.

When a huge June moon rose, Nick built a fire, and they wrapped themselves in blankets, lay back on the cushions and made a pact to stay silent and listen to the Mediterranean night unfold around them, a careful distance between them. They hadn't so much as brushed hands since the kiss on the beach, but it was obvious neither of them wanted to be apart, either.

The moon smiled and breathed balmy air on their little beach, the stars like gems in their velvet boxes. Amongst the white diamonds shone amber, sapphire, ruby and citrine. Fleur remembered from somewhere that there are no green stars, no emerald up there to guide her to Odette, to the secrets from the past. But she was seeing these lights from thousands of years ago, only just reaching her, and that was the only sense she could make of what she'd discovered since Nina's death. That the stories still existed, and still mattered, and were no less real or important than her own, or her unborn child's.

The cicadas set up a chorus in the *garrigue* behind the beach and Nick put his arm round her against the cold. The flames leapt for the sky in fiery motes and the quiet space between them was worth more than words.

When the fire was reduced to the last white-hot embers, they strolled back up the sandy path, the bright moon casting silver shadows, illuminating tangles of jasmine flowers that glowed between dark, glossy leaves on the villa walls.

They didn't talk about where Nick would sleep, they didn't need to. She was pregnant and everything was skewed and strange and Fleur's world was off-kilter in every way. He slept on the sofa, and Fleur curled up in bed, wishing things were less complicated.

The next morning, there was an email from the Red Cross in Fleur's inbox. They'd had some new intelligence about the Stasi benefactor linked to the Emerald Lake, and it had opened up new lines of inquiry for them.

Nick called in sick so he could be there should any further information come to light in the next twenty-four hours. Both of them knew it was an excuse. Who knew when they'd hear more about the mysterious Stasi man, if at all? The day after might bring important news, they told themselves, or the day after that. They let the days drift, neither of them wanting to say goodbye.

Nick and Fleur, Fleur and Nick. The words started to sound good together. Everyone in the village naturally assumed a budding romance, and smiled indulgently at them when they ordered their morning coffee, bought their morning pastries or waved to the fishermen on the stalls by the harbour. No one believed them when they protested that they were just friends, that they weren't together, not in that way.

There was something unspoken between them, layered

with complications they didn't speak of. They both knew they were in a fragile, beguiling bubble that would inevitably burst under the weight of reality, but in the meantime there was never enough time to finish a conversation, endless things each wanted to share with the other.

They swam across the bay at Portissol, then sat on the jetty dangling their toes in the water as it undulated glassily over the rocks, watching how the colours diffused from grey-purple rocks to turquoise sea. Some days, swimming was forbidden because of the blooms of jellyfish that floated across the bay, but it didn't matter because they were so pretty, scattered translucent in the water like delicate alien flowers.

At the market they bought picnics of remoulade, olives and anchovies, truffle Brie and fougasse to eat by the sea. Every day they sampled a different tomato from their favourite stall, Flamme Oranges that tasted like peaches, sweet white Beautés Blanches, burnished black-red beef tomatoes heavy with juice and dark flavours. If they were in a hurry they'd eat propped up at the *panisse* stall, or feast on pissaladière, cherries and salami with herbes de Provence, watching the world go by.

Nick took Fleur to see his favourite vineyard, Domaine du Météore. Fleur gave Nick a hard time about his obsession with rocks, but she had to admit she was secretly fascinated. Nestled in a dip below the vine terraces amongst the ancient oak trees, rows of grapevines crossed a circular clearing.

Nick's explanations of tell-tale magnetic lows typical of meteor sites went over her head, but the fact that meteor impacts often created microscopic diamonds in the soil felt like magic.

On a stormy Thursday they drove to the lavender fields in Valensole, where the neat lines of flowers turned dark and brooding against steely clouds. When the rain came down, they were soaked in seconds and the lavender released its sweet herby perfume and they had the fields to themselves as they immersed themselves in dripping hazes of violet and amethyst and mauve.

Friday was a day for light and shade, when Fleur shared her photographer's eye with Nick. She showed him the soft dappled shadows along the narrow cobbled streets first thing in the morning, the plane trees casting patterns to match their mottled trunks. As the sun rose higher, the two traced the sharp feathers of deep grey the palms cast on the promenade, the angular frieze of shadow sails on the harbour wall. When evening fell, they stood on the roof terrace and watched the lights turn on in the village, the church cross illuminated against an enamel sky, the boat masts strung with lights creating reflections in the black-jet sea.

Nick showed Fleur his favourite sea urchin paintings in the Picasso museum in Antibes on a stormy Saturday, and Sunday was for lazing under the orange trees and playing endless games of Scrabble, or watching the drowsy bees collect nectar while the cicadas sang louder and louder with the sun's intensifying heat.

Fleur photographed it all, creating still-lifes of their market finds on the kitchen table, the contrast of bougainvillea against an old stone wall, the outline of an umbrella pine silhouetted like a totem on a background of endless blue sky, a cut-out of turquoise sea framed by a porthole in smooth white rock, Nick holding an urchin fossil, its radial symmetry like a star-cabochon.

Monday was the day that Fleur's twelve-week scan was booked in, and Nick insisted on driving her there.

They arrived at midday and it was searingly hot. Fleur looked at the big glass doors, the high-rise building so clinical and modern, the tarmac in the car park hot and acrid as she opened the car door. Nick wrenched up the handbrake, the rasp of it like pulling up the drawbridge on their week together.

'Wish me luck,' she tried to say brightly.

'Do you need someone to hold your hand?'

'I'll be fine, really.'

'You know you say *really* when you're pretending not to be scared? I'm coming in.'

'You really don't have to, though, I'll be fine.'

'That's two reallys. Come on.'

Fleur lay back on the couch and stared up at the white ceiling while the doctor gave Nick a seat next to the bed. She felt like a specimen, lying prostrate on the blue paper towel, shivering in the air-con with her stomach exposed and glistening with gel, the screen blinking as the probe found the sweet spot.

She gave Nick a WTF smile to try to make light of it, and he grinned encouragingly back at her and nodded wide-eyed towards the screen. A blurry picture appeared and the doctor explained how they would find the bladder first, then navigated upwards to find the baby, and... The doctor fell silent, leaning closer to the screen.

Fleur was suspended in the test tube of a room for what seemed an eternity with the machines whirring and blinking, her womb keeping its inscrutable secret in unintelligible pulsing digital streaks on the monitor. Nobody spoke. It was like the world was holding its breath while her baby refused to make itself known. *Please be there, be normal, be well, I'll do anything to keep you safe.*

'Is everything all right?' Fleur whispered.

The doctor nodded as if to confirm something to herself, then beamed at her.

'Sorry to keep you waiting, I just wanted to make sure. Congratulations, you're having beautiful twins.'

Somewhere inside, she'd known all along. Fleur watched, mesmerised, as the doctor explained.

'There's twin A, and further down twin B, each with a

perfect walnut for a brain, two eyes, two legs, two arms each... The membrane between them is very thin, which means they're possibly identical, but you won't know until they're born...'

Two tiny hearts beating furiously. Her family had come full circle. From this moment, there was double the hope in the world. *I'll be all right, Nina*, Fleur thought.

The doctor continued with the medical pathways she could take, the symptoms she may encounter, the added precautions she could take, but Fleur could only concentrate on the two little spirits floating like miracles in the warmth of her womb. They'd be hers, but they'd also be each other's forever. The sheer luck and joy were overwhelming, the idea that anyone could ever take them from her, or one another, was already unbearable.

'Mademoiselle Lefevre?' The doctor cut through her thoughts.

'I'm sorry, I just...'

'I understand. The chance of twins happening in nature is 0.5 per cent. Less if they're identical. It's a lot to take in. Is there a history in the family?'

'Yes, my grandmother was a twin and before that I'm not sure...'

A chair scraped in the corner. She'd almost forgotten Nick was there and she glanced round to find him sitting quietly watching her thoughtfully.

'Emerald babies,' he said. 'The birth stone for twins. Nice work.'

Nick strapped her into Choux like she was an egg about to crack.

'Let's get the three of you home,' he said, starting up the engine.

They drove out of the car park in a kind of awed silence, Fleur's thoughts racing over each other. Should she tell Jake? Didn't they deserve to know their father? They'd agreed that she wouldn't hide his identity when the time came. They would know him, when they were ready, but they'd also agreed that she would be their sole guardian until they were more grown up. It was a weird situation, but then everything was. She'd find a way.

'What the hell's going on?' said Nick suddenly.

'I'm sorry?'

'There's bloody two of everything. I just saw two jays. Even better luck than two magpies.'

'Two red Fiat 500s at six o'clock,' said Fleur.

'My socks,' said Nick.

'Liar! They never match.'

'OK, crystal fractals.'

'It always comes back to rocks with you.'

'You know, the truth is nature doesn't produce anything that's truly identical, apart from identical twins. Snowflakes can be remarkably alike, but never exactly the same. Even crystals are made of repeating structures, but never exact replicas. What your body's doing is incredible.'

'How do you know all this stuff?'

'Just go with it. It's called being a geek.'

'I bet there's not another one of you. Thank you, Nick. You never judge, you're always just you.'

Nick didn't answer, flicked his indicator, turned the corner and picked up the A road.

'What do you plan to do now?' he said eventually.

'Sleep on it, I suppose. It's a lot to take in. Funny how life seems to have a one in, one out policy. I wish Nina knew, and I know this is going to sound stupid, but being pregnant makes you feel kind of connected to a universal lifecycle. Does this mean that Odette's dead, too?'

Nick took his foot off the gas a little. 'What about their father?' he said quietly.

'He'd be horrified there are two. Really.'

'There's that really again. Perhaps you should let him know, especially now that you've been told there are two little beings in there. You need to be sure about Jake, especially now that you know. I've been fending it off, but I've also got to get back to Geneva for work, so I'm going to drop you back and leave you to it for a few days. It'll also give me a chance to do more digging in the auctions database to see if the Emerald Lake ever surfaced after the fall of the Berlin Wall. I'm going to be very busy catching up, so don't worry if you don't hear from me. I'll see you in Geneva for the Magnificent Rare Jewels auction. That has to bring us closer to whatever Nina knew.'

Nick needed to go back to work; no surprise there, he'd already risked taking too much time out on her behalf. But there was something in his tone that had changed; he seemed non-committal, desperate to get off.

The week they'd just spent, the talks long into the night, the way he looked at her. Had she misinterpreted it all, just taken it all for granted? What was she thinking? That someone she'd known for a few weeks, who'd just found out she was pregnant with twins, would want a relationship with her? Was this what they called baby brain? He was just being kind, that was all.

'Of course,' Fleur managed. She stopped herself from saying *really* again. What an idiot. She held on to the scan photo as tightly as she could. She hadn't realised how much she was depending on Nick, and how stupid and unfair it was to think she could.

CHAPTER 30

FIRE AGATE

Fleur

Fleur refreshed her emails for the millionth time. There were no more boxes to go through, no more clues, no more news from the Red Cross. Nothing. She couldn't bear to think she'd reached a dead-end, and with Nick gone the time dragged, and everything that had delighted her about this place seemed commonplace and dull.

Everyone she encountered – the waiters in her favourite café, the fishermen on the harbour, the lady on the *panisse* stall – all asked where Nick was, then backtracked when they saw the look on her face, looked at her sideways when, she imagined, they noticed the baby bump that was getting harder to conceal.

Days turned into a week, and every time her phone rang she jumped, hoping it would be Nick. This time, it was Jude, her best friend.

'OK, what stone have you been hiding under? You said you wanted to disappear for a month, and I've given you seven whole weeks. Where the hell are you? Why didn't you tell me about Jake? I saw him last night in Soho, snogging some woman like a teenager. I cornered the bastard and he told me you split up weeks ago. If he wasn't so wrong for you, I might have said you were letting grief colour your judgement, but in this case it seems to have clarified it. Well done for that, anyway.'

It was so lovely to hear her voice, such a reminder of her life before all this, someone who knew Nina, and Jake, and it was a relief to tell her the whole thing, from the villa, to Nick, to her newly discovered family, to the twins she was carrying.

Jude listened without interrupting, and, when Fleur had finished, she didn't miss a beat.

'This Nick character's definitely in love with you,' she said.

'Then why did he leave?'

'In too deep. If he's as nice as you say he is, he's giving you a chance to go back to evil Jake.'

'What a mess.'

'Fleur, I didn't want to say anything before, but I'm going to be honest with you now. This isn't the first girl I've found him with, and it was killing me not spilling the beans. You seemed so set on him, I didn't want to be the one to say, what with Nina and everything. If you'd ever asked me or said you'd suspected him, I would have told you straight away. I was going to tell you anyway when you'd got over Nina. He's a philanderer and a narcissist who doesn't care about anyone but himself.'

Why wasn't she surprised? What a fool she'd been. They always say you're the last to know about an affair, and this was guttingly true in her case. Even her own best friend had known – as perhaps had she, if she'd let herself see the signs.

'There, I've said it. You're better off without him. He was never going to be husband or father material – you were a trophy for him, but it's obviously got a bit too real for him now.'

'He did look at the door kind of desperately when I told him I was pregnant...'

Jude roared with laughter. 'Hello, she's back. Now, let's talk details. How the hell do you propose bringing up not one, but two snotty-nosed ankle-biters on your own?'

They talked for hours, and Fleur promised to send Jude a photo of the picture she'd found of her birth mother holding her, and to keep her updated on the Emerald Lake and her search. In fact, Jude made Fleur promise several times over that she'd keep in touch regularly, or she would be on the next plane out to check on her.

'Yes miss,' said Fleur.

Two days later, two packages arrived. The first was from Jude, containing two matching Manchester United baby grows, and a note: *You can never start them too young!* Also included was a picture of her and Jude in Nina's cottage garden, Jude in her footie kit and Fleur in a fairy outfit, Nina between them. Fleur and Jude must have been about five years old and all three were pointing off into the distance.

Like Nina always said... forward, Jude had written. *PS. Does this early intervention qualify me for godparent status?*

She was right, there was no going back to Jake. She'd neglected all her friends, her old life, but the important people would always be there for her when she needed them.

She sent her a text.

Renounce the devil and the godparent gig is yours.

The second package was a flat oblong box, bound in leather. Fleur pressed the clip to open it. Inside were rows of tiny gems, all different colours and shapes, each with a name label in Nick's neat handwriting.

A carefully folded note taped to the lid made her heart somersault.

I spent the last week missing you the only way I knew how

Inside was an annotated diagram relating to the labels, like the key to a box of chocolates.

Gold, for the sunny afternoons we spent lazing and talking, said the first.

Next to it, a two-tone gem. *Padparadscha. An incredibly rare sapphire, known for its oranges and pinks, like our sunsets over the sea,* said the label.

Fleur read on, charmed.

Silver – believed by the ancients to be associated with the moon, for our midnight picnic.

Fleur picked out a brownish faceted gem in the next row and held it up to the light. It flashed violet-blue, asparagus green, dark plum as she turned it. She read Nick's legend:

Diaspore, from the Greek word 'scattering', to honour all the separated families.

A blue polished stone dotted with turquoise-green markings was next.

Cabochon-cut blue azurite and green malachite composite, like the sea washing over the stones while we watched from the jetty.

Fleur lingered over the colours to remember, then held a cool white oval, threaded with spangles, in her palm.

Aventurine – from the Italian 'a ventura', 'by chance'. What were the chances we'd meet?

Fleur replaced the aventurine carefully, then ran her finger over a rough grey stone filled with fiery bubbles.

Fire agate for the embers on the beach.

A dense, misshapen yellowish lump was next to it, and her least favourite.

I know what you're thinking, but this is moldavite, one of the rarest minerals on Earth, from a five-million-year-old meteorite. Coco Chanel kept a piece with her wherever she went.

Iridescent labradorite with a blue lustre was labelled *oil on the water in the harbour* and the last in the box was a dark orange/red polished stone in the shape of a shield.

Carnelian, to give you courage in battle. Forward, Fleur. I will always be your friend.

Fleur went over each label again and again, held the stones up to the light, which each time highlighted a different aspect of each gem. She held the smooth ones against her cheek, remembered the moments they represented, savouring each one as afternoon turned to evening.

Every highlight he remembered from their week together was hers, too. For millennia people had imbued gems with special properties and magical powers, but it didn't matter whether the myths were true. Each one represented something special from the giver to the receiver, and that was what really mattered. There was a whole world in the box of gems, moments in time that had passed but would always be there between them.

Fleur thought over his final message, *I will always be your friend.* Whatever had passed between them was different now. She was carrying twins, and she was going to need to accept that she'd be doing it alone.

Fleur made a montage of the photos she'd been editing from their week together, her own collection of gems, and sent them to him with a message:

I understand, and I feel the same. I'll see you at the auction next week.

Nick didn't reply that day, or the next, or the next. Fleur tried to keep herself busy, stop herself from checking every time her phone buzzed. The days were long, the weather sublime this beautiful June, but she was going to be lonely here without him. She occupied herself with planning the nursery room, and preparing the house for two new lives – December babies, the doctor told her. Camille had brought up Nina here, under much more difficult circumstances. If she could do it, Fleur could, too.

After three days, an email arrived that set Fleur's heart beating. The Red Cross had traced the Stasi lead she'd found in the newspaper clipping from the Berlin museum. He was dead, but he had a surviving relative, his son – Wolfgang Fischer – whereabouts currently unknown, but they were on the trail. The Stasi official was Dieter Fischer, Odette's adopted father, and Wolfgang was her brother by adoption.

There was someone alive who may have met Odette. It was incredible.

She picked up her phone to call Nick, but there was already an incoming call from him.

'I've found it! The Emerald Lake is in the Magnificent Rare Jewels auction! It wasn't there when I looked before, so they must have kept it secret until the last minute,' he enthused.

'Don't tell me, being sold by Wolfgang Fischer? Hello, by the way.'

'How do you know? Oh yes, hello,' said Nick.

Fleur told him about the Red Cross finding Dieter Fischer, and their attempts to locate Wolfgang.

'There's no need to locate him, because Bullinger's have all his details as the beneficiary of the sale. Listen, get yourself on a train to Geneva. I've spoken to some lawyers who think you may have a case to prove ownership. There's a train first thing tomorrow morning that would get you here in time for a meeting with them late morning.'

'Will there be time to put a case together before the auction?'

'We have enough evidence. Let's meet with them and take it from there. It's meant to be,' said Nick.

'I'll book a hotel,' said Fleur.

No offer from Nick for her to stay with him.

'Great, I'll meet you off the train and we'll go from there. We're so close, Fleur.'

They said an awkward goodbye, no mention of the case of gems that Nick had sent, no mention of the photographs of the week they'd spent together.

That evening as Fleur packed, she feverishly went over the facts in her head. The letter from Raschmann bequeathing the ring to Odette, the near-misses between Nina and Odette throughout her research, first in Lamorlaye, then at the Berlin Wall. Had the two ever met? Surely not – or Nina would have told her about her great-aunt in life.

Odette seemed to have disappeared off the face of the earth after the wall went up. Now here Fleur was, speeding towards the real Emerald Lake, which was being auctioned by the son of the man who adopted her. It was over eighty years since the twins were split. Nina had known something, had been on the trail, but just didn't live long enough to be able to do anything about it.

CHAPTER 31

FOOL'S GOLD

Fleur

The shimmer of family ghosts crowded around Fleur as she stood in front of the law firm's glossy door. All that human tragedy, all the torn bonds, the cruelty and the hope reduced to legalese, institutions, efficient records kept, sterile arguments made.

'Ready?' asked Nick.

'As carnelian,' said Fleur.

Nick smiled at her reference to the courage stone.

'Forward,' she whispered.

Nick pressed the buzzer and kept his finger there until the door clicked open. The receptionist handed them visitor passes, and at the top of the stairs they were greeted by a woman in a sleek suit, crisp shirt and highly polished court shoes, her dark hair slicked back in a tight ponytail.

She was in her early thirties, Fleur guessed. Every inch the lawyer, but with an honesty in her brown eyes that Fleur liked.

'Fleur Lefevre,' she said, holding out her hand.

The woman gave her a firm handshake.

'Joelle Dechaine. I'm really close to my sister, so your story got me right here.'

She thumped her heart.

'Mine too,' said Nicolas, avoiding Fleur's eye. 'I'm Nicolas Beaufoy. Good to meet you, and thanks for seeing us so quickly.'

'No problem. Time is of the essence, and we don't have many options open to us. Please, sit down.'

Joelle joined them at the sofa in her vast office.

'Nicolas has outlined the case to me, but Fleur, if you can tell me the story in your own words, I'll do my best to explain the possible courses of action we can take.'

How could she communicate the dead-ends, her deep love for her grandmother, the black hole where her parents should be, the golden family threads she was so bound by? She was only just getting her head around what it was like to be an orphan who's discovered a whole new family, never mind the fact that there was also a new family growing inside her. What a tangle of tragedy and hope. How did she explain the burning injustice of what happened, the instinct that, wherever the Emerald Lake was, it would lead her to the twin lost eighty years ago?

Fleur did her best, Nick interjecting every now and then to add the leads he'd uncovered. Joelle listened sympathetically, taking notes.

'I'm sorry for everything that happened to your family, and that you're the only one left. It's a big burden to carry.

'In one way, you're massively ahead of the game. As far as I can tell, the jewel has never turned up on the open market before, so this moment is your best chance at making reparations. If it's bought and sold privately, it could end up in a vault for another eighty years, by which time, it's unlikely any of us will still be around.'

Apart from these two, Fleur thought, protective hands on her stomach.

'Morally, that ring should belong to Odette or her heirs, and no one else should be benefiting from the sale. However, as I'm sure you can imagine, things aren't that simple. Nicolas is right about the statute of limitations. Technically, you're out of time. On top of that, we're potentially dealing with several different jurisdictions. As I understand it, the piece was originally sold in France, went on to Colombia and subsequently resided for decades in Berlin, before finally landing up here in Switzerland.'

Fleur nodded for Joelle to go on. *Please don't be another dead-end.*

'Add to that a vast service industry who are ready to fence, obfuscate and do anything to shelter goods of dubious provenance from the police, and you have a rather tricky set of obstacles stacked against you.

'In Switzerland, the law tends to favour the seller rather than the buyer, but even in other more sympathetic jurisdictions police forces are very stretched, and theft from the Second World War rarely comes top of their list.'

'So you're telling us that, even though the law may be on our side, we're operating in an essentially lawless market?' said Nick, exasperated.

'Unfortunately that is often the case. If your ring was being sold or displayed by a museum or state institution, we'd be able to appeal to them on moral grounds and, if needs be, threaten them with negative publicity. However, we have a private seller who is in possession of the jewel, who could argue that he has legal title...'

Fleur's heart sank. The odds against them were huge. 'How do you rate our chances? Have we already lost?' she asked.

'Not on my watch. We know from records kept that 600,000 objects were stolen by Nazis, and more than six million Jews died at their hands, so it's my life's work to restore something of what was lost. As for the Lebensborn programme, many children who didn't have the "correct" attributes were sterilised or killed, or the ones who *did* have the right looks were kidnapped from their parents in front of their eyes, as in your great-aunt's case. Someone has to pay and I'm ready for the fight. Although I have to tell you that, of the hundreds of thousands of treasures on the Art Loss Register, only a small percentage are recovered and matched each year.

'The law may argue otherwise, but the Washington Principles established in 1998 state that treasures looted by Nazis should be restored regardless of gaps and ambiguities in provenance, and the principles are largely agreed to by most jurisdictions, though they're not legally binding. The consensus is that, even if people sold willingly during the Second World War, it was because they were being forced away from their homes, jobs and countries. I would technically classify the Emerald Lake as a forced sale, even more so as the "sale" was made in return for a child's life.'

'Surely that fact alone is enough to demand that Wolfgang Fischer doesn't benefit from its sale?' said Fleur.

'In this case, that fact is the only recourse we have. The good news is, we do have an institution with a reputation at stake – Bullinger's Auctioneers – which gives us three advantages. Firstly, they won't want to be seen to be involved in the sale of a piece connected to Nazi looting. Secondly, it's in the seller's interest to sell through auction as they're likely to secure a higher price. Thirdly, the blessing of a reputable auction house gives buyers confidence. Customers get jittery if they think their name will be attached to a piece of Nazi loot, or that a lawsuit may be coming down the line.'

'I can attest to that,' said Nick. 'Particularly with a private sale – the whole point is that the buyers are below the radar.'

Joelle nodded, made a note on her iPad, then continued.

'I suggest that we buy ourselves some time by writing a letter to Bullinger's, explaining the evidence as we understand it. I'll start by politely asking them to withdraw the Emerald Lake from sale pending discussions with the seller.'

Nick held his hands over his ears. 'Obviously I haven't heard any of this when the letter drops into the inbox.'

'Absolutely,' Joelle replied. 'We need to keep the advantage of surprise. They don't know what information we have, so hopefully we'll get them on the back foot. Next, we'll be dependent on negotiations with Wolfgang Fischer himself. What we find in most cases is that some kind of settlement is agreed between the seller and the heirs. I think that's the best we can hope for. Complete restoration is unlikely.'

Fleur was resolute. No compromises. It was down to her to now.

'Maybe, but it's what I want to fight for. It's not about the money. It's about putting a wrong right, about my family's connection with the Emerald Lake. That ring belongs to Odette. It's little recompense for losing her family, but it's hers. If it turns out that I'm the sole heir, I'll never sell it. Even better, if it leads us to Odette, or to any of her heirs, we'll have struck true gold. Whatever happens, it's about publicly acknowledging the grief my family suffered at the hands of the Nazis with the return of what's rightfully ours.'

'I understand,' said Joelle gently. 'Leave it with me. First stop, Bullinger's. In the meantime, I need you to gather all the evidence you have stating that the Emerald Lake legally belongs to Odette. After that, we'll contact the seller and arrange a meeting to appeal to his better instincts.'

Something inside Fleur soared. This Wolfgang must have met Odette, be able to describe what she was like, whether she was happy, whether she ever spoke about her lost family...

'I'm not sure I can stand the wait,' she said.

'I have to manage your expectations, I'm afraid. These

conversations aren't always amicable, and I know of cases that are still raging on after twenty years of negotiations. Send me through that evidence, and I'll keep you updated,' said Joelle.

The three of them shook hands, and Nick and Fleur stepped back out onto the busy street, Fleur's family ghosts spilling out behind them. It was lunchtime, and workers were grabbing sandwiches, checking their phones and gossiping about office politics while shoppers bustled and met for coffee. It was just an ordinary day, but Fleur was lost in a green lake, swimming around in its waters, desperately searching for someone she knew was there. *We're close, Nina and Odette, I know we are.*

'Are you all right?' said Nick.

'Yes, it's just that hope almost hurts more than defeat. I can't bear it if this is another dead-end.'

'It never will be, with two little ones on the way. Keep the faith and it'll all come together. Let's get back to the flat and we'll collate all the evidence together so we can get it off to Joelle this afternoon.'

Nick's apartment was warm and sunny, books lining every wall, with more piled onto the kitchen table next to a jumble of notebooks, geological magazines and half-drunk cups of espresso. The abstract pictures on the walls, in a variety of frames and styles brought together artistically, showed he had an eye for colour, and the whole place had an intelligent, friendly, lived-in look that made Fleur feel at home immediately.

Nick cleared a space for her at the kitchen table and they worked through everything they had so far. The ordered, digitised files from the Chanel archives were invaluable, and Fleur wished that Nina could have seen this. She'd worked with a mess of fragile, torn letters and dog-eared photographs, none of it cross-referenced, much of it painstakingly gathered through decades; a drip-feed of hope and sadness that must have coloured her whole life. She would be amazed at how easily it could all be ordered now, how new connections could be made, a case put together.

Despite a mind that loved to race around in unexpected directions, Nick was laser-focused on helping to categorise everything, and quickly found the links they needed to tell the story and create a coherent paper trail.

'Years of collecting and cataloguing rocks.' He laughed ruefully.

Fleur lingered on the one photograph they had of Camille, Nina and Odette's maman, Fleur's great-grandmother. She was tiny, elfin, with a bright smile, draped in a fashionable bias-cut dress with a fur stole slung across her shoulders. Two identical little tousle-haired girls in sailor suits flanked her. Which was which? One was scowling mischievously, the other laughing. Camille's arms were wrapped protectively round both and she looked so proud and happy. *My God.* Fleur almost wished she didn't know what was going to happen to this joyful little trio.

'A moonstone for your thoughts?' said Nick.

Fleur showed him the image on her laptop. He blinked in sympathy.

'You have the same million-dollar smile.'

He held her gaze but Fleur looked away.

'She looks so complete with those two little ones,' she said.

'That'll be you, in a few months, just as proud and beautiful.'

They left the rest unsaid, buried themselves back in their work, and within a few hours they had agreed on the narrative and paperwork that should constitute watertight evidence to support their case that Odette was the true owner of the Emerald Lake.

The two most pivotal pieces of evidence had been uncovered by Nick.

First, there was Gustav Raschmann's letter bequeathing the

Emerald Lake back to the frightened little girl, his acknowledgement of the child's position in relation to fellow SS officer Dieter Fischer. Second was the original bill of sale from the auction in Paris back in 1944.

The Chanel archives had provided them with a bonus, too. Photographs of Coco Chanel wearing the ring while accompanying her aristocratic lover, Boy Capel, in 1918. She was young and smiling, chic in a black tunic and pearls, her lover carefree and laughing, blissfully unaware that another world war would darken their lives in twenty years' time.

There was a note from Coco, recently discovered, documenting the loss of the Emerald Lake to an SS officer in an attempt to save Nina by bargaining with her twin, Odette, knowing that the Emerald Lake would always somehow leave a trail.

Then there was the newspaper article picturing the Emerald Lake in a display case, and Odette/Odelia alongside the museum curator Johan Abel, at the Littenstrasse Museum in East Berlin. Even the way Odette smiled was an exact replica of the photographs Fleur had seen of Nina at around the same age. Odette wouldn't have known that her mother was already dead by then, worn down by all the fruitless searches for her lost daughter.

Nick collated all the information about the stone itself, its identifying heart-shaped inclusion, and its cut, shape, weight and saturation. He also documented its journey through time since it was first liberated from its Colombian underground birthplace. The myths surrounding it, the hands it was reputed to have passed through, until its gifting to Coco Chanel, who then in turn sent it off with Odette in the hope that such a famous gem couldn't be buried forever.

It worked, thought Fleur. *Here we are, still chasing it, but so close, eight decades later.*

Finally, they added pictures from down the decades of Nina wearing the replica like a talisman.

They pressed send on the email, and Fleur sent a prayer with it.

She sat back and looked out across the lake. It was already eight o'clock, still light, the evening rays creating shadows on the mountains beyond.

'Dinner? You three must be starving,' said Nick.

'No, I should be going, I can grab room service at the hotel. It's been a big day.'

'I'll drive you then.'

Fleur had been half hoping that Nick would insist that she stay, but things were different between them now, just friends.

'No need. You've done so much already. I'll get a cab.'

Nick looked disappointed. 'Okay, just me and my fossil collection tonight then.'

'Nerd.'

'Killjoy.'

Fleur's phone buzzed.

'The Uber's outside.'

Nick leaned in for a hug while Fleur began a misplaced air-kiss. They giggled awkwardly and Fleur grabbed her stuff to leave in a fluster. Nick watched her down the stairs and at the bottom Fleur turned round.

'Thank you.'

He smiled and saluted. 'Professional interest.'

At the hotel, Fleur went straight to her room, propped herself up on the bed, browsed the room-service menu and listlessly ordered a salad. She wasn't hungry, but she had to eat.

Outside a full moon was rising, throwing a silver trail across the lake. Fleur idly wondered if Nick had noticed it too, then berated herself for acting like a lovesick teenager.

Pregnant women aren't girlfriend material. Not even for an eccentric Antibois *who cares about every gem that ever crystallised in the crucible of the Earth.*

Room service arrived, extravagantly served from a trolley by a bellboy with gold buttons. He showily lifted a silver dome to reveal a limp salad, then loitered while she scrabbled to find some coins in her handbag in the wardrobe.

She balanced the salad on her lap and made herself eat, then got ready for bed. She was exhausted but, every time she closed her eyes, something unfinished and unsaid between her and Nick made her head spin.

Instead of reaching for a book or the TV remote control, Fleur opened Nick's box of gems and read and reread all the labels from their week together. There was a reason he had come into her life, and it was more than just a boy-meets-girl coincidence. That was not to be, but he'd helped her get closer than ever to the Emerald Lake, and perhaps, to Odette and the story of what happened to her, and that was enough. The thought calmed her, and she put the box back on her bedside table next to the photo of her mother holding her. With the two objects next to her at this late hour, she had the idea that two sentinels were there to protect her, and she drifted off.

The next morning, Fleur woke late. She drowsily looked at her watch: 10 a.m. She rolled over to say good morning to her mother's photo, but it wasn't there. She sat up and switched on the bedside light. It was on the left-hand bedside table, not the right. Nick's box of gems was next to it, but she was almost positive she'd placed them both on the other side of the bed before she went to sleep the previous night so they'd be the first thing she saw on waking.

She opened the box and the world kind of shifted. The gems were all out of order. Was she still dreaming? She sat up and checked Nick's diagram. No, she wasn't, they didn't match.

She looked around. Nothing else was changed. Her laptop and wallet were on the dressing table untouched, the blackout curtains were closed, her clothes were exactly where she'd left them on the chair.

Maybe somehow she hadn't put the gems back in the right place?

A thought struck her – the bellboy who'd delivered room service had looked shifty when she'd emerged from rummaging at the back of the wardrobe for her handbag to tip him. He was putting something in his pocket when she came back. Fleur looked for the room key. Not there.

She called down to reception. No, they said, no one had delivered room service to room 55 unless the records were faulty, which did happen, and in that case she was lucky because her dinner would be free of charge. No, the hotel didn't use silver domes, not to their knowledge anyway. Food was usually delivered on a tray with plastic covers for hygiene. They'd find another key for her right away. Not to worry, customers lost them all the time. Housekeeping generally handed them in if they were dropped. The receptionist would make enquiries.

Fleur perched on the edge of her bed and ran through her evening. She scanned the room. Nothing was stolen, she was fine. She had been in a kind of agitated state last night, so she might have got the stones out of order without realising. She decided not to give herself any more problems than she already had, so she got dressed, and checked her phone.

There was an email from Joelle. Bullinger's had agreed to withhold the Emerald Lake from the auction pending discussions between herself and Wolfgang. They'd await the outcome.

Hands shaking, Fleur called Nick immediately.

'I know!' he said delightedly, forgetting to say hello. 'She's done it! Let's hope this Wolfgang character understands what he's up against. We should also remember it's possible that all this information was withheld from him, so he may well be sympathetic.'

'Let's see,' said Fleur. 'In some ways, I feel sorry if he never knew about his father's past. On the other hand, his father took Odette that day, so, if his son suffers, it's his fault, not ours. There's one thing that's bothering me though. If he didn't know anything, why would he wait all this time to sell the ring?'

'It's certainly a smoking gun. Even so, we have to hope he has a heart to match the Emerald Lake. We should remember what Joelle said – that we can't really rely on the law.'

'We can't have got this far only for it to come to a crashing halt.'

Nick missed a beat. That statement could apply to them, too.

'What are you up to today?' he asked.

'Not much. A fondue, some yodelling, a boat around the lake. Tourist things, unless you have any better suggestions?'

'I'm glad you've got plans,' said Nick distractedly. 'I was worried about you being on your own. I've got to work today, so let's keep in touch if there are any more developments.'

'Of course,' said Fleur, more formally than she wanted to.

'You will call me if you need anything at all?'

'I'll be fine,' lied Fleur.

A dull day of waiting, without Nick, lay ahead. Fleur had better get used to it. She found a café by the lake and, wanting a familiar voice from home, called her best friend Jude and told her the latest.

'That bastard Wolfgang had better cough up. How could anyone profit from that ring after all your family went through? And as for Nick, he's still in love with you,' she said firmly.

'The reality is, we hardly know each other, and the twin thing is a bit much, even for one of the nice ones.'

'Understatement of the year.' Jude snorted. 'Seriously, what the hell are you going to do?'

'Just keep going forward,' said Fleur.

'Nina's grandchild through and through,' said Jude proudly. 'Listen, you're the only one left to carry the baton, my little orphan girl. Focus on that and keep going. She's out there somewhere, in spirit if not in body, and you have got to find her.'

A notification came through. Nick.

Have you seen? We've struck gold. Wolfgang will talk! I'm not invited, but he's in Geneva and he wants to meet you and Joelle later today to settle things – he's determined that the Bullinger's sale will be reinstated. Where are you?!

CHAPTER 32

ATONEMENT

Fleur

'Ready?' said Joelle.

'What if he doesn't agree?'

Joelle tapped the file of evidence she'd put in a buff folder for the occasion.

'He'd be a monster to ignore all of this.'

'That's what I'm afraid of.'

Fleur's clothes were getting too tight for her. She'd thought endlessly of what to wear to this meeting. In the end, she'd plumped for smart-casual – capri pants that she could no longer do up, a black top, and her favourite Issey Miyake cross-body bag, and, at the last minute, a slash of Nina's red lipstick for good measure. What the hell she was trying to portray, she had no idea, but it felt right for the occasion.

Now here she was in her restrictive clothes, feeling very small at Joelle's enormous conference-room table, Lake Geneva rendered flat and dull by the wall of smoked glass.

'I'm ready,' she said.

Joelle nodded and buzzed the receptionist to show Wolfgang Fischer in.

He was an old man with thin grey hair and rheumy eyes, but immaculately dressed in chinos, a T-shirt, Suisse Rugby SFR baseball cap and a neat zip jacket, with a stern, straight aspect to his gait, like a soldier's.

Meeting him was the strangest thing. He regarded her with a mixture of recognition and surprise.

'You have to be Fleur,' he said. 'Those haunting eyes.'

Her heart lurched. He knew Odette.

'Tell me about her,' she whispered.

He dismissed her with a wave of his hand. 'I met her at the orphanage. My parents dragged me there to see her every now and then, but she was always angry and unfriendly to me, I was very young... sorry.'

'What on earth was she doing in an orphanage? I thought she was adopted by your parents?'

'I have no idea, I'm afraid. I think my parents took pity on her and tried to help, though she didn't seem very open to it.'

So he has no idea of the real story, thought Fleur.

Wolfgang addressed Joelle. 'We haven't been introduced. I assume you're Madame Dechaine?'

'I am.' They shook hands. 'Pleased to meet you, please take a seat,' Joelle said tersely.

'When you saw her, how was she? Did she have friends, was she happy?'

He shrugged. 'I was young, and I only met her very briefly. There's nothing I can tell you.'

Fleur studied him. Was he lying, or did he have no idea who his father truly was?

'Perhaps we'll start with the matter at hand. If there's time afterwards, I know that Mademoiselle Lefevre would appreciate it if you would be so kind as to answer any questions she has relating to her great-aunt,' said Joelle.

'Please, I was close to my father and I miss him, it's difficult for me to recall those times,' said Wolfgang. His words were sad, but said entirely without emotion.

'Any memories you have, however vague, would be wonderful. My grandma and great-grandma spent a lifetime searching for her. I didn't even know she was in an orphanage.'

'But you do know that the Emerald Lake is worth millions, and now you want to petition me for money?' said Wolfgang drily.

Fleur recoiled.

'No! I mean yes, I mean that a terrible wrong was done to my family and it has to be put right.'

Wolfgang sat back in his chair and folded his arms. 'I'm prepared to make a settlement if you'll sign a non-disclosure agreement and put this matter to bed. I don't want to, but, according to your bulldog here, I have no choice if I don't want to scare off potential buyers – of whom there are several.'

Fleur was ready to fly at him, but Joelle shot her a glance.

'This is no way to begin a negotiation—' she said smoothly.

'Isn't it?' Wolfgang cut in. 'My position is very clear. Now, I want to hear how on earth this gold-digger here has a claim on my possessions.'

Please God Odette didn't have to endure too many visits from this odious man and his father.

'We do have some very compelling evidence that you are not the true owner of the Emerald Lake, enough for Bullinger's to take the jewel off sale until further notice. My client here is prepared to negotiate, but I do need you to remain open until you have all the evidence in front of you. I should also prepare you for some unpleasant information about your father that you may have been unaware of.'

Wolfgang narrowed his eyes at her.

'Let's get this over with.'

Joelle put the letter from Gustav Raschmann bequeathing the jewel to Odette in front of the old man.

He didn't move a muscle while he read it. When he was done, he pushed it back across the table to Joelle.

'How do I know this letter isn't forged?'

'We have the docket from Bullinger's in Paris documenting the sale from your father, a high-ranking SS officer, to Gustav Raschmann. We also have contemporaneous written testimony from Coco Chanel of the moment your father took Odette Lefevre and the jewel from her mother. We have a travelling replica that was kept by Odette's family, all authenticated by trusted authorities. I'm afraid your father committed a terrible crime. He stole a child for profit and tore Fleur's family apart. Even if this means nothing to you, I'm sure potential buyers will see it differently, and we would have no hesitation in putting all this information out into the public domain. We have some members of the press who are very interested in the story.'

'I understand,' said Wolfgang, smiling. 'This isn't a negotiation, it's a fait accompli.'

Joelle met his gaze. 'If you want to put it that way.'

Hope coiled through Fleur like a spring. She tried to ignore it. Eight decades had thrown up so many false leads.

'Perhaps there is some movement in my position,' said Wolfgang. 'But I want to negotiate direct with Miss Lefevre. Would you leave us?'

'My client isn't in a position to negotiate without my counsel,' said Joelle.

'It's all right,' said Fleur. 'I'll talk to him.'

She needed to play his game, that was clear – he had something up his sleeve, she just knew it.

Joelle got up to leave. 'I'll be just outside if you need me.'

When she was gone, Fleur turned to face Wolfgang.

'That was a sweet little gift your boyfriend gave you. Who

knew that rocks could hold such meaning?' Wolfgang said, almost baring his teeth.

Shit, someone *had* been in her room. Him. Could it have been him in the speedboat when they had a narrow escape; him on the Corniche des Crêtes? *Just deal with the facts*, she told herself. It was her against him now, just the two of them in the room, and this was her only shot. Fleur was spooked, but she was damned if she was going to give him the satisfaction. It took everything she had to keep her features composed.

'You learned your dirty tricks from your Stasi father, didn't you? A bit different from his previous MO. By all accounts, the Nazi way was more of a blunt instrument – daylight child-snatching was a forté of his.'

'Just a harmless warning. By the way, how are your twins coming along? Are you hoping for more girls?'

She kept dead still. Nick and Jude were the only people she'd told about being pregnant. She leaned forward.

'Don't you dare threaten me or my children. Don't you think your family have caused enough misery? What do you want?'

'I just want to be left alone to conduct my business as I please. I have something you want more than the Emerald Lake.'

They stared at each other, his eyes ice cold.

'Odette,' she whispered.

His eyes flickered in contempt. 'She's living under another name, but she's still alive, and she lives in Switzerland.'

'Where?! Are you in touch?'

He laughed drily. 'Certainly not in touch. Let's just say I've kept tabs on her. Burn your evidence, sign the NDA and we can talk.'

'I don't trust you.'

'You have no option.'

The idea that this man would benefit from the atrocities of

the past was horrific, but it was a deal she was prepared to make. The real treasure was always going to be Odette. What would Camille have done, or Nina? No question. They'd have swapped the jewel for Odette any day.

'Where is she?' said Fleur.

'Sign, and call your bulldog back in to countersign.'

Wolfgang pushed the contract over the table to her. Fleur speed-read it. Odette's whereabouts would be revealed in return for Fleur's silence. She signed and went to find Joelle, followed by the joyful ghosts of Camille and Nina.

Eight decades of searching were over. The Emerald Lake had finally done its job.

'This is for you.' Wolfgang dropped a folded piece of paper onto the table and left.

Fleur picked it up. It was the phone number, email and postal address of Odette. *I've found her, Nina.*

CHAPTER 33

A MILLION DIFFERENT BLUES

Fleur

Fleur texted Nick immediately. She couldn't contact Odette without him by her side – he'd been with her all this way. He made his excuses at work and dashed straight over to the lawyer's office.

When he arrived, Fleur was still sitting in the exact same place at the conference table. She didn't dare even move in case she jinxed anything.

She held up the paper to show Nick the details.

'She's still alive?'

'Yes! I don't know why I'm so nervous. I hardly dare call in case it all goes wrong.'

'It won't. It's like a rare gem – a glorious coming together of all the right elements to create something incredible. Call the number.'

Fleur found the digits on her keypad. Straight to answerphone. No personal words, just the standard phone company message.

Next, she emailed.

I'm Fleur Lefevre, great-granddaughter of Camille. My grandma Nina brought me up and she's been looking for you her whole life…

She didn't explain how she'd got to this point, or about Wolfgang, or anything else. A simple message was enough.

She pressed send, and received an immediate 'undeliverable' bounce-back message.

'That lying, evil bastard,' she hissed, slamming her laptop shut.

'Hold your horses,' said Joelle. 'For whatever reason, Odette has wanted to remain untraceable. It's easy to cover your digital tracks, regularly change your mobile number and email address, not so easy to move house. Maybe you should just go. It's not far from here and I can't imagine that she wouldn't want to hear from you.'

'I'll drive you, it's less than an hour away,' said Nick.

The route skirted the lake, made up of every blue from lapis to sapphire to aquamarine. The snow-capped mountains were picture-postcard cut-outs against a pristine, optimistic sky. It was the perfect backdrop for a longed-for family reunion.

Nick checked the satnav. 'Left here,' he said, and turned. 'Wow.' Nick whistled, winding down his window.

A private road led them to high iron gates, beyond which was a belle-epoque style mansion with gardens running down to the shores of the sparkling Lake Geneva.

Fleur gasped. 'The orphan did all right for herself.'

'Good for her,' Nick replied. 'Go on, try the buzzer.'

'What the hell do I say?'

'You'll find the words.'

Fleur got out of the car and pressed the intercom.

'Can I help?'

'I'm looking for my great-aunt. We've never met...'

The intercom crackled. She pressed on.

'It's a long story, but her email bounced and we didn't have the correct phone number, and I'm pretty sure she'd want to hear from me. She lost her parents and her twin during the war, and...'

'Wait there.'

A woman came to the gate, accompanied by a security guard. She was maybe in her forties or fifties, in cut-off jeans and a T-shirt. The guard was in full security uniform, with a holster and revolver on his belt.

'The owner is away,' said the woman. 'I'm her housekeeper, can I leave a message?'

'Have you any idea when she'll be back, it's urgent...'

'She likes to come and go as she pleases, I'm sorry, she never tells us when.'

'Will you say I was looking for her? It's a long story, and I'm not sure I should be telling it to strangers, or even if we have the right person. How old is the owner – can you see a family resemblance to me? I'm very like my grandma, and her twin is identical.'

'You'll understand I can't disclose any information about my boss without her go-ahead. However, I can agree to passing on any information when she's next in touch.'

'When will that be?'

'Like I say, she always surprises us.'

Fleur found a notebook and pen in her handbag and scribbled a note with her details, Camille and Nina's name, and the fact that her family had been looking for her forever.

'There's an auction tomorrow and I'd very much like to speak to her before then.'

'I'm afraid that's unlikely. She prefers us to wait to contact her.'

'But it's really urgent.'

'Are you sure you have the right person? She's never mentioned any of this before.'

Fleur thought about Wolfgang, the bounced email and telephone number. Clever. If she couldn't verify who lived here in time, the auction would go ahead and the gem would disappear as a deal between private buyers. In the meantime, no one could accuse him of not giving the correct details.

There was one glimmer of hope, though. She'd seen that housekeeper's look in the Souliers' eyes when she met them for the first time at Nina's house in Sanary-sur-Mer, and in Wolfgang's when he first saw her; a kind of haunted recognition. Wishful thinking? Who knew?

She left the note with all her details, got the housekeeper to promise to tell her as soon as she heard anything, and got back in the car. The sun was still shining, the mountains still glorious, the lake still a million different blues, but it might as well all have been made of ashes.

Nick gave her a sympathetic squeeze.

'Don't worry, we'll find her. We're so close. Would it cheer you up if I said I can get you into the auction rooms tomorrow to see the Emerald Lake before it's sold? My colleagues tell me it's stunning.'

'I'd love that,' said Fleur.

CHAPTER 34

LOT FIVE

Fleur

Fleur hardly slept that night, between obsessively checking her phone for some word from Odette and raging that Wolfgang Fischer would still benefit from the sale. She'd contacted Joelle to see if there was any legal recourse, but, having signed the non-disclosure agreement, she'd have to prove that Odette didn't live at the address she was given, and there wasn't enough time before the auction.

Knowing that she'd see the Emerald Lake tomorrow gave her some comfort, and there was still every chance that she'd find Odette. Surely Wolfgang Fischer wouldn't risk giving her the wrong details when there was so much at stake?

The next morning, she met Nick at the auction venue. It was at the Four Seasons, a grand hotel overlooking Lake Geneva, mountains in the distance, the Jet d'Eau fountain thrusting high into the sky.

Nick flashed his Bullinger's lanyard at reception, and they

were ushered through marble corridors, past opulent dining rooms and bars filled with the low murmur of the well-heeled, the thick blue and gold carpet muffling their footsteps.

The auction room was a ballroom hung with crystal chandeliers, a big screen displaying the anonymous international bidders, and a stage for the auctioneer. Nick gained access to a side room, where a makeshift film studio was set up to project images of the gem to potential buyers and there was a viewing window onto the auction room so they could watch proceedings.

A security guard holding an attaché case shook Nick's hand.

'They giving you the top job today?' he asked.

'Yep, apparently I'm the one who's bothered to research the provenance, so I get to set it up for the cameras. Fleur here's my photographer, she's going to record the gem for our files. Crack it open, will you?'

The security guard looked at his watch. 'Better be quick, the auction starts in ten.'

He opened the case, and there it was, familiar, yet new. An exact facsimile of the ring she'd known all her life. Her replica was a good one, but the Emerald Lake itself had a velvety quality, a deeper aspect, like something you could dive into. She could see why it was called what it was. She looked for the inclusion in the shape of a heart. There it was, and she imagined it beating furiously, like the ones she saw on her scan picture. To think that little Odette must have clung to this, hoped that it would connect her back to her mother and sister, only for it to slip away from her like the rest of her family.

'Fleur?'

Nick and the security guard were grinning at each other.

'She's uninitiated, I'm afraid. Literally spellbound by the first multimillion-franc gem she's seen.'

The security guard laughed. 'Happens to us all the first time.'

'Can I put it on?' Fleur asked.

'No chance,' said the security guard.

'I'll vouch for her. Just for a second,' said Nick.

'One second then, that's it.'

The security guard turned a blind eye as Fleur picked it out and turned it over, prickles crawling up the back of her neck. There, etched into the thick gold band, were two stars made out of four simple lines, each star drawn side by side, almost touching. It was the same etching as on Nina's ring.

Did Odette do this? It was like going back through time to the exact instant when this was etched by a desperate little girl onto the ring. A sliding-doors moment, when three people's lives were wrenched apart, a nightmare moment Fleur could still feel eighty years later, scratched into time like a glitch that should never had happened, echoing down the decades.

She slipped it on, felt the weight of the gold, expected to feel some kind of energy from the gem, but she felt nothing but anger and frustration. Just a cold piece of rock without a heart – the inclusion just a fluke of nature, and still no Odette. She could smash it into a thousand pieces right now, and then Wolfgang would get nothing.

Nick's hand was on her arm. 'Time to put it back,' he said gently.

Fleur didn't want to let it go, but she had to. *Come home, Odette, we're still waiting.*

A voice cut through to the studio over the computer. *Two minutes to live screen. Everything ready?*

'As we'll ever be,' Nick replied. He placed it on its mount, trained the lights to bring out the saturation and quality of the piece to its best advantage. A thing of absolute beauty and charm, and as inaccessible to Fleur as ever.

The Emerald Lake was lot 5 – Coco Chanel's lucky number, Fleur remembered as she and Nick and Fleur pressed against the viewing window to watch proceedings.

An auctioneer addressed the crowd.

'Now to the sale of the year, the much-anticipated Emerald Lake solitaire emerald ring, set in twenty-four-carat gold. The famous Emerald Lake emerald is a 500-year-old twenty-carat gem from the celebrated Muzo mine in Colombia, a rare masterpiece from nature, rumoured to have been owned down the ages by exceptional women, including Coco Chanel herself. Entirely flawless apart from a tiny heart inclusion, which in this case only increases its value. Ancient Colombian lore attributes this gem with the power of bringing together people who are meant to meet...'

The auction started at five million Swiss francs, quickly rose to double that, and the bidders gradually fell away. Only two anonymous telephone bidders remained, raising the stakes in 200,000-franc increments. Who were they?

The bidding slowed when it reached twelve million, and Fleur felt sick to her stomach. Wolfgang Fischer had waited decades for this.

'Twelve million Swiss francs. Tom, what do you have for me on the phone? We've got all the time in the world, this is a once-in-a-lifetime opportunity,' intoned the auctioneer smoothly.

The room fell silent. Fleur looked down into the crowd as an old lady with a shock of red hair stood up and waved her bidding number: 555.

'Twelve million, five hundred thousand,' she said firmly in a German accent.

The auction room clapped and cheered. Fleur jumped up and grabbed Nick in absolute shock.

'That's her, it's Odette! I'd recognise her anywhere. She's even dressed like Nina! I've got to go and warn her who's selling!'

Nick put a restraining arm on Fleur's shoulder.

'Leave her. The Emerald Lake belongs to her. If she doesn't buy it now, it could disappear forever. She's here, so she must know everything, and, judging by her house, she can easily afford it. Don't worry, I can trace her through her bidder number and you can make contact afterwards.'

They waited. The second telephone bidder shook his head, no more bids. Fleur watched, heart thumping, as Odette stood tall, holding up her number.

'Sold to bidder number 555 for twelve million, five hundred thousand, *douze million cinq-cent mille francs.*'

The gavel came down, the room erupted, and Fleur's phone pinged.

I've been waiting all my life for this moment. Come and find me in my suite, room 505. And don't worry, Wolfgang Fischer won't get away with this. Yours in love, triumph and wonder, Odette Lefevre

CHAPTER 35

GOLDEN THREADS

Odette, aged eighty-five

She's a slip of a thing. Gamine crop, strawberry blonde, a softer look in her eye than mine, but it's her, me, Nina, fresh and new: a replica, an atom from the past or the real thing. It doesn't matter because her name is Fleur and she's here, and I'm looking in the mirror fifty years ago. The jolt of recognition and love is like alchemy, a new birth, and my carefully guarded heart melts to a pulp.

'Nina...?' I ask.

She shakes her head. It's a hammer blow.

'She died two months ago, but she never stopped looking for you, and neither did your mother.'

I see everything I've lost reflected in Fleur's eyes, and Nina's last words to me punch a hole through time. *We are one. They can't split us up.* I take a tentative step towards my sister's beautiful grandchild, my arms outstretched. She doesn't hesitate and we cling to each other. My flesh and blood. We both sob.

Time is elastic, you realise, as you grow old, and, after all these years of searching, it's like I've lost Nina all over again.

'I miss her too,' Fleur says, with a haunted look in her eye. 'She was everything to me.'

Death is final. Until then, everything is possible. All the conversations I'd imagined we'd have, and, as the years went by, the heightened moments we'd need to make up for lost time, to put things right. The pain of knowing I'll never meet her is devastating, and it's even worse that I missed her by a matter of weeks.

We sit in silence for a moment, holding hands, looking at each other in wonder and sadness.

I've watched families all my life, envied them for their easy familiarity, the little careless resemblances that glue them together – a way of standing, duplicate eyes in different faces, a smile that passes down the generations – I'm always on the outside, looking in. Now here is this vision, right here in the room, and I recognise her pigeon-toes, her startling blue eyes, the way she says *really* when she doesn't mean it, a golden thread in the tapestry of our family, and she's like an angel standing in front of me, if I believed in angels.

There's a young man with her. Floppy hair, distracted manner, scruffy in a charming kind of way, intelligent eyes. He'll have to prove himself if he thinks he'll take my Fleur.

'Incredible,' he says triumphantly. 'The emerald did its job. The two of you are so alike.'

'As are these,' says Fleur.

She digs around in her bag for something, opens a ring box, and there it is, the replica Nina and I used to play with. Two crude stars, made up of four lines each, are etched on to it and it's like magic. I should be shocked, but I'm not. I know that

Nina drew them, we were always one. Fleur tells me that Nina wore her replica every day of her life.

I tell them about my life at the museum, how the real Emerald Lake was the only home I felt I had. Fleur finds two things on her phone that set my nerve ends crackling. The first is Nina's photos from the Berlin Wall, including a photo of me in the Mondrian headscarf I thought was so chic, dangling from the windowsill on Bernauer Strasse. We were there at the same time and I don't know whether to laugh or cry! I do the latter, and Fleur hugs me again. The second thing is a Red Cross poster from 1945. Nina, holding a sign, hair in plaits, the same sailor dress I was wearing the day I was taken.

Who knows me? Who can tell me where I'm from?

'There were so many times, you were so alike. I have boxes and boxes of photographs,' says Fleur gently.

I pick up the Emerald Lake, dive into its deep green, find the tiny heart inclusion where I buried my own. I own it now, Nina. I've waited for this moment for so long, and now you're gone.

Somewhere deep inside, I already knew. I hope you're reunited with Maman, that somehow you know that I've found you again in this young woman. She's beautiful, she's mine, ours, nobody's. It's everything to me that you tried to find me. That part of me, the volcano, the raging, hurt little girl who never got over losing you and Maman, can grow up at last and join the rest of me. I'm not even sure what the rest of me is. I suppose it's the woman who used that angry little me to make it my life's mission to buy back what was rightfully ours – this gem imbued with so much hope.

In some ways, I feel lucky. My purpose in life was so clear to me from the moment we were parted. Now, it's repaid me a thousand times, and that hot rage can finally cool to a peaceful green.

There's only the two of us left in the world, but there's something else.

We talk and talk, and I slide so easily into the auntie role. God knows, I know how it feels to need a maman. From the moment I set eyes on her, I knew she needed me. And when she finally confides that she is pregnant with twins, I promise her I'll be by her side. I haven't felt such unalloyed, light, airy joy since before I was torn away from you.

To have lived to this moment, to find this facsimile of you, of us, is more than I could ever have hoped for in my darkest times. I can live for the present now, and, finally, for the future, for the twins who are yet to be. I pray that world they're born into will be better than mine ever was.

I'm old, and so much time has passed, but now is all that matters, and I intend to celebrate and nurture this golden thread I've found, which joins us all together again, with all my might, with all the time I have left. Love is what matters. and I've finally found it. The glitch in time that opened when I was taken has been righted, and our story has come full circle.

Was it the Emerald Lake that brought us together? Or your determination to find me, the belief you had in the stone that Coco planted in us all, the idea that it would be possible if we kept it close?

It's a question I don't need to answer any more. My life's mission has been fulfilled, which is more than most can say. I have a family – a young woman so like you and me, Nina. Deep inside her are new beginnings, two flawless emerald twins who I'll do anything to protect, and, when the time comes, imbue with my own heart inclusion so that they will always feel loved.

EPILOGUE

Fleur staggered under the weight of the tray as she carried it to the table under the orange tree in her garden in Sanary-sur-Mer.

It was New Year's Eve, her twins' first birthday, and an unusually warm day for the time of year. The orange tree was in full bloom, and Odette was pulling faces at the two tousle-haired babies propped in high chairs either side of her.

She hesitated a moment to take in the scene. Her babies, Nina and Odette – affectionately called Nini and Etta – were giggling delightedly, their soft strawberry-blonde curls catching the winter sunlight like spun gold.

Nick spotted her standing there and smiled.

'Need any help?' he shouted.

'No, I'm nearly there.'

The heady scent of orange blossom filled the air as she set the tray down, and a breeze caught the swing hanging off the sturdiest branch.

Is that you, Nina?

Fleur still missed her, but she hoped that, somewhere, Nina knew how life had come full circle.

Nick and Fleur had made this place their home. He'd adopted Etta and Nini, loved, nurtured and treasured them like his own two precious little emeralds, with their own wildly beating heart inclusions and fierce determination to grow and flourish in this happy place. Fleur had her own perfect found family, thanks to Nina sending her here and setting Fleur on the trail she herself had never been able to complete.

'Look, it's your birthday and Maman's bought you a cake, even though you have no clue what day it is!' declared Odette.

Etta clapped her hands. 'Jewel!' she said.

Nini joined in. 'Dress!'

'Just like we were,' said Odette proudly. 'Little Etta will be a jeweller, like me, and Nini will love fashion like her great-grandma.'

Fleur laughed. 'How many hours have you spent teaching them those words, Odette?'

'Entirely their own choices,' declared Odette. 'It's extraordinary – a miracle.'

'I don't know how she does it,' said Nick with a laugh. 'It doesn't matter how many times I say "sphene", neither of them has even made an attempt. I give up.'

'Kindred spirits,' said Odette. 'We understand each other, don't we?'

Nini and Etta banged their tumblers on their trays and squealed. Fleur took them out of their high chairs and hugged them both, luxuriating in their warmth as they cuddled into her, their hair impossibly soft on her cheek.

'Make the most of every minute, it's such a special time,' said Odette, getting up to pour the tea.

'You sit down, I'll do it,' said Nick.

'I'm not dead yet,' said Odette, deadpan.

But her hand shook as she picked up the big teapot, and she

was frailer than when Fleur had first seen her, standing tall in the auction house, buying the ring that belonged to the family for a fortune amassed over a lifetime for just that purpose.

Sometimes Fleur wondered if that was what had kept her alive all this time – just sheer willpower.

True to her word, Wolfgang Fischer hadn't got away with it. He might have been watching her for years, waiting for his moment to sell, but Odette had returned the compliment. A private detective had kept tabs on him for Odette, and she'd learned that, in addition to the Emerald Lake, Wolfgang inherited hundreds more pieces of looted art and jewellery from his father. He'd sold some pieces over the years on the black market, stuffed his pockets with cash to evade being caught. He'd lived his whole lonely life in a nondescript tower block in East Berlin, guarding his treasures.

Odette had long suspected that the Emerald Lake would emerge at auction after the statute of limitations was up, and she'd been right. The reason she hadn't immediately responded to Fleur's messages was exactly as Nick had thought. She didn't want to do anything to risk the Emerald Lake disappearing again. After the auction, Odette had tipped off the Berlin police as to the treasures stashed at Wolfgang's apartment. They'd raided him, and confiscated an unimaginable collection of loot.

This lonely old man had spent a lifetime guarding Picassos, Monets, Renoirs, priceless jewellery and artefacts, stolen from Jewish families, hidden behind old chests of drawers, in newspaper-stuffed wall recesses. His walls were lined with hollowed-out books that he used to hide the cash that he'd collected on regular journeys to Switzerland, each time bringing back just below the permitted €10,000, crammed into his pockets.

He'd led a strange half-existence, his only company the carefully guarded treasures that his parents had instructed him to keep, or sell where he could.

Joelle was on the case, working with the Art Loss Register to try to reunite the other stolen possessions with their heirs, the work of another two decades, Fleur imagined.

Nick worked with Joelle and the Art Loss Register now, their jewellery and gems expert, tracing provenance and trails with enthusiasm and sensitivity. Each case was a story of tragedy, loss and, if they were lucky, reparation.

The house in Sanary-sur-Mer had a new addition: Nick's workshop, crammed with treasures thrown up from the depths of the Earth, catalogued and loved, throwing prisms on sunny days, part of their new family.

A new collection was in the making, of memories from each of the girls' milestones – turquoise for a December birth; citrine, the sunbeam stone for their first smile, aquamarine for their first words… all arranged around Nina's replica Emerald Lake to represent the miracle of finding each other.

Wolfgang Fischer was jailed for fraud, fencing and smuggling, and because of his convictions he never received the proceeds for the Emerald Lake from Odette. He didn't last more than a week in his cell. The authorities said it was old age, but it was almost like selling the Emerald Lake had closed a circle for him, too. If you were superstitious, you might almost imagine that the Emerald Lake kept him alive for the auction, to complete its mission of reuniting Nina's family. But only if you were superstitious, which of course Fleur wasn't.

As for the Emerald Lake itself, it was the beating heart of their home, kept in a safe but taken out and loved nearly every day. Odette donated the auction refund to the Red Cross, to support their work reuniting families torn apart by war.

Fleur gave Etta and Nini to Nick to hold, lit the birthday cake candles and took a photo.

'Smile!'

Nini and Etta only had eyes for the candles and each other. Nick struggled to keep them apart and persuade them to look at the camera, giving Fleur a lopsided smile as they giggled at the chaos, and Odette looked over Fleur's shoulder, as if someone else was there that only she could see.

Despite their delight at finding each other, there would always be so many missing. Fleur had managed to trace her mother Stella's birth to the convent at Aubazine that Coco Chanel had grown up in – and subsequently, she found, where Nina had given her away for adoption.

At Aubazine, in these secular times, there remained only a small cohort of older nuns who kept the place in order, visited mainly by fashionistas making the pilgrimage to Coco Chanel's childhood home. However, Fleur had found one nun who'd been a novice when Nina had given birth to Stella, and who was subsequently a midwife when Stella returned to give birth to Fleur.

Fleur begged her for details, and she relented when she heard the whole story of the Emerald Lake. *It seems there have been enough secrets in your family*, she'd said.

Stella had grown up locally, and she'd been happy with her adopted family. She'd come to the convent pregnant with twins when she was thirty-five. No one ever knew who the father was, and she didn't want to say. She died in childbirth – post-partum pre-eclampsia, a complication sometimes suffered by women carrying twins, which in this case Stella was. When she knew that she might not live, Stella had begged the nun to find her birth mother, and for her to be told about her surviving twin daughter, who she named Fleur.

Nina had always secretly kept in touch with the nuns at Aubazine to check on Stella's progress from afar. When she learned what had happened, racked with guilt about Stella, Nina adopted Fleur and brought her to grow up with her in England.

The nun told her that Nina had always wanted to shelter Fleur from her beginnings, and from her own tragedy. There'd already been too much suffering, and she couldn't bear the thought of Fleur knowing she'd lost a twin.

Fleur had been floored. She'd grown up knowing that her mother had died, but shouldn't she have *felt* that she had a twin, that there was always something missing? But she never had, and that was thanks to Nina. Fleur had had the carefree childhood that Nina never had, and she had her to thank for that.

Was Nina wrong to have kept all this from Fleur? She must have wanted her to find out eventually with the box she'd left in the open attic of Nina's Sanary-sur-Mer house, but she left a lot to chance – or perhaps to fate. Even though Nina had done what she thought was right, Fleur decided it would end with her. No more family secrets.

The children would know who their birth father was. Jake had agreed to keep her up to date with his whereabouts, his circumstances, to be there if the children themselves decided to find him when they grew up. In return, Fleur would be open about him with the twins. Jake was still adamant that he wanted nothing to do with their upbringing, no ties, no baggage, as he called it. She couldn't forgive him, but she could live with it. She had Nick. They were both relatively young to be parents, but wasn't it the way that children who lost their parents young generally wanted to create their own families? And that was what they'd done, forged their little family out of the dramatic clash of war and loss like a diamond in the pressure and heat of a volcano. And their family was just as indestructible and beautiful, if a little unconventional.

They stayed all afternoon under the orange tree, took it in turns to hold the girls on the rope swing and see their delight as the fresh breeze caught their hair and mixed with the scent of winter orange blossom and the salty sea beyond.

When the sun began to set and the girls were fighting sleep, Fleur suggested they take the party inside.

'Not yet,' said Odette. 'Didn't Nina and my maman spend

most of their time here on the beach? Let's light a fire and watch the sun set over the sea just for the hell of it.'

Having ruled her life with an iron rod in order to survive, Odette was determined to live every moment for the simple pleasure of it for as long as she had left, now that she'd found her family again.

Nick and Fleur were only too happy to indulge her every whim, treasuring every moment they had with her.

They settled Nini and Etta side by in their buggy and wrapped them up warm, and they drifted off to sleep on the walk down the sandy path to the sea, pale with sleep, cheeks rosy and clear as pink sapphires.

Nick arranged chairs, and a blanket for Odette, and built a magnificent bonfire as Fleur poured hot chocolate from a flask, made to Nina's special recipe.

'We were drinking this when I was taken,' said Odette, staring into the fire. 'Those Nazi bastards drank our share, and I shouted at them, outraged that they'd taken mine and Nina's hot chocolate. I think it was because of that I was chosen. The fearless one,' she added wryly.

Fleur watched as an ember flew up, glowed against the vivid sunset sky, then burned itself out.

'It's funny, isn't it, how the tiniest thing can have the most far-reaching consequences. If it wasn't for that fearlessness, I don't think we'd be sitting here now.'

Odette looked out across the sea, dark and endless, the sun almost gone, casting a final pink glow on the white horses.

'I wonder how many times Nina and Maman sat here, wondering where I was, if I was still out there. I felt like I already knew this place this first time you brought me here last summer. Now I can almost see them, sitting here on the beach, collecting shells together, having picnics like these. So many times I wished for a real family. You know I used to dream of a chi-chi apartment in Paris, Nina and me playing tricks on admirers, a kind of glamour between us that only beautiful twins could have? We'd meet Maman for lunch on Sundays and go shopping and take trips down the Seine on sunny days and live the kind of life I read about in glossy magazines. Not real life, but it's easy to imagine an idealised one when you don't have any other versions. I would have taken anything over the family I had, or the orphanage.'

Fleur put her hand on Odette's. Despite the fire, she was freezing.

'Don't feel sorry for me. You and Nick and the twins have made up for a lifetime of longing. Time has a way of bending and losing its potency when you're old. You learn to appreciate the here and now in vivid colours, all the more so for knowing you won't have it forever.'

'Don't say that,' said Fleur.

'Nothing is forever,' said Odette.

Etta gave the cutest baby snore, and Nini followed suit. Nick, Fleur and Odette giggled as quietly as they could.

'They're so blissfully happy, those two little things. I lived a lifetime clinging to the first four years of my life and no one can take that away from me. Make the most of this time with them.'

'I've never been more happy in my life, if a little exhausted,' said Fleur.

Nick grabbed her hand. 'And I can't believe my luck. They say good things come in threes, and we wouldn't be together if it hadn't been for you and Nina.'

'Then my work here is done,' said Odette as a crescent moon cut the sky, trailed by Venus, bright as a diamond. 'Let's get those little ones back up to the house. They need their beauty sleep, and I have my own looks to preserve. You don't get a face like this by burning the candle at both ends, and I'm so tired I'm sure I can see a double star.'

Nick and Fleur sat side by side on the veranda to see in the new year, the twins tucked up in bed, Odette propped up reading in the room next to the babies, surrounded by all the photographs of Nina and the family that Fleur had found. She'd framed every single one and covered the walls for Odette for when she came to stay, which was often.

The sea breathed in the distance, mixing its ozone with the savoury scents of the maquis, their fingertips touching as the village church bells struck midnight.

'Hard to believe that it's not even a year ago that I was standing at Nina's funeral, feeling like I was trapped in the wrong life,' whispered Fleur.

'Now do you believe in the power of stones?'

The sky was marcasite scattered on velvet, the winter orange blossom pearlescent in the moonlight, and she couldn't wait to fold herself into Nick's arms on this beautiful night.

'Yes,' said Fleur. 'Maybe now I do.'

The twins woke early the next day, at 5 a.m. sharp. Nick fed them, then got them up and changed, while Fleur took a coffee in to Odette, also an early riser. She loved the mornings with her, sitting on the bed, chatting about Nina, and hearing about Odette's adventures in Berlin as a society jeweller, her run-ins with the Stasi, tales of her saviour and mentor, Johan Abel.

Fleur knocked, coffee in hand. No reply. She opened the door gently, peeped round, waiting for the bright smile, for the familiar pale eyes to light up. But the minute she saw her, she knew.

Camille and Nina and Odette were all in this room, but gone, too. Time is elastic, but a part of them lived on in Fleur, in Nini and Etta.

Fleur held Odette's frozen hand.

'You stayed until the twins were a year old, but they were waiting for you on the beach when you saw that double star, weren't they?' Fleur whispered. 'You'll always be here. Goodbye, my sweet, brave Odette.' Fleur touched her heart and left the room to call for Nick.

Nina's ashes would be buried here, with Odette under the orange tree, and her girls would grow up side-by-side, happy and adored in this breezy, sunny house by the sea, filled with double love, twin heart-shaped inclusions etched on this place forever.

A LETTER FROM HELEN

Dear reader,

I hope you enjoyed reading Odette, Nina and Fleur's stories, their encounters with some of the most difficult and joyful moments of our recent history, and their quest to find each other through time and imagination. If you did enjoy it, and want to keep up to date with all my latest releases, just sign up at the following link. Your email address will never be shared and you can unsubscribe at any time.

www.bookouture.com/helen-fripp

I have always been fascinated by twins, and their seeming psychic connections, the threads that run through families, the familiarities and coincidences that exist despite years spent apart. There is a theory that there is a 'genetic memory' in all of us, that some children inherit the emotional and psychological burdens of their parents or ancestors when they have experienced extreme trauma such as war.

Before I started writing this book, I didn't know much about the Nazi Lebensborn programme, where SS officers were paired off with Aryan-looking women for selective breeding, in an attempt to create a race of 'super babies' and children who would continue the work of the Third Reich.

In 2025 it's hard to believe that anyone thought this was really possible. Trained Nazi race assessors made crude assessments. Everything from hair colour to lips, from teeth to hips were measured against official lists, and children arbitrarily divided into categories. Of course, however careful they were, children were born in all the 'wrong' shapes, sizes and colours.

According to the Jewish Virtual Library, it is estimated that more than 250,000 children were kidnapped and sent by force to Germany, mainly from eastern territories. Only 25,000 were found and reunited with their families after the war.

These themes were the starting point for my book, and from that came the idea of twins separated, and a constant – the Emerald Lake jewel – that would eventually help bring them back together.

Then came the characters of Nina and Odette, each shaped separately by their unique experiences, but similar in many ways. As they grow, they have a connection they can't explain, they battle with the trauma they experienced, in turn fighting it, fleeing it and embracing it to fuel their ambition, reaching out across the ether to the other half of themselves, never complete without the other.

Central to their quest to find each other is the Emerald Lake. Is the gem itself a mysterious crystal with special powers to reunite? Many civilisations have believed in the powers of crystals and gems. Or do we as humans imbue them with our own hopes and fears? We certainly use jewels to mark major events in our lives, to show affection and love, pass them down through families to remember each other by. I loved researching gemmology, finding out about the science of how gems are formed, the refractive qualities, the colours and variety, as well as talking to jewellers about their craft and inspirations. What struck me was the sheer beauty of these things, created over millennia and retrieved from deep within the Earth, each unique, with their own meaning to each of us.

So many works of art and precious family heirlooms were looted by Nazis in the Second World War. These possessions represent people's lives, their successes, their hopes and fears. They belong to them and their heirs, and to this day there are many organisations that are still working to reunite victims or their heirs with their possessions.

The separation of the twins is characterised by the real physical barrier of the Berlin Wall. Many said that their war wasn't over until the wall came down in 1989. Isolated from her real family and the rest of the world, Odette spent a lifetime both fleeing from and searching for her past, but eventually the past and the future come together in the shape of her great-niece, Fleur. In her, we find our ending, and hope for the future. As Odette always said, time is elastic, life is circular, we are all connected to our families, past, present and future whether we have been lucky enough to know them or not.

I hope you loved reading *The Emerald Twins* as much as I enjoyed writing it, and, if you did, I would be very grateful if you could write a review. I'd love to hear what you think, and it makes such a difference helping new readers to discover one of my books for the first time.

Please get in touch! I love hearing from my readers – you can get in touch through social media or my website.

Thank you for reading,

Helen x

KEEP IN TOUCH WITH HELEN

www.helenfrippauthor.co.uk

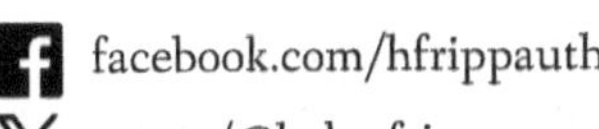

facebook.com/hfrippauthor

x.com/@helenfripp

instagram.com/helenfrippauthor

ACKNOWLEDGEMENTS

Thanks as always to my brilliant editor, Ellen Gleeson, whose analytical eye and structural input is invaluable, not to mention her encouragement when words just won't come! Thanks also to my agent, Kiran Kataria, for all the advice and support she continues to give and for always being on my side. No book published, or unpublished, has been possible without my constant first reader, Katja Willemsen, who gives her time so generously. Tina Engell provided the original spark for this story, as well as encouragement and her jeweller's knowledge on our many tramps through the countryside. Camilla Catania at the Art Loss Register shed light on the dark corners of Nazi-looted art and its attempted recovery, providing authenticity and inspiration to the journey of the Emerald Lake. Marcus McCallum, gem dealer and mineralogist, provided me with brilliant anecdotes and enthusiasm for the chemical wonder, rarity and beauty of precious stones. To all the people who have published their personal stories of their attempts to recover Nazi loot, or their experiences as Lebensborn children, thank you. Without your stories, we all risk repeating mistakes of the past.

I couldn't have written this book without my husband Nick's support, and I'm lucky to have such wonderful family and friends. Thanks to Tara, Charlie, Polly, Laurie, Niall, Niamh, Milo, Anne, John, Laura, Gerry, Nick, Fran, Rosalie, Terry, Michael, Barbara, Margaret, Serena, Guy, Edith, Arthur,

Frederick-Francis and Jemima, who all make up my own tangle of golden threads.

PUBLISHING TEAM

Turning a manuscript into a book requires the efforts of many people. The publishing team at Bookouture would like to acknowledge everyone who contributed to this publication.

Commercial
Lauren Morrissette
Hannah Richmond
Imogen Allport

Contracts
Peta Nightingale

Cover design
Debbie Clement

Data and analysis
Mark Alder
Mohamed Bussuri

Editorial
Ellen Gleeson
Nadia Michael

Copyeditor
Jacqui Lewis

Proofreader
Anne O'Brien

Marketing
Alex Crow
Melanie Price
Occy Carr
Cíara Rosney
Martyna Młynarska

Operations and distribution
Marina Valles
Stephanie Straub
Joe Morris

Production
Hannah Snetsinger
Mandy Kullar
Ria Clare
Nadia Michael

Publicity
Kim Nash
Noelle Holten
Jess Readett
Sarah Hardy